WRECKED

THE VIGILANTES, BOOK FOUR

STONI ALEXANDER

SILVERSTONE PUBLISHING

This book is a work of fiction. All names, characters, locations, brands, media and incidents are either products of the author's imagination, or have been used fictitiously. Any resemblance to actual persons living or dead, locales, or events is entirely coincidental. The author acknowledges the trademarked status and trademark owners of various products referenced in this work of fiction, which have been used without permission. The publication/use of these trademarks is not authorized, associated with, or sponsored by the trademark owners.

Copyright © 2023 Stoni Alexander LLC
Cover Design by Better Together

All rights reserved.

In accordance with the U.S. Copyright Act of 1976, the scanning, uploading, and electronic sharing of any part of this book without the permission of the publisher is unlawful piracy and theft of the author's intellectual property. Without limiting the rights under copyright reserved above, no part of this publication may be reproduced, stored in or reproduced into a retrieval system, or transmitted, in any form, or by any means (electronic, mechanical, photocopying, recording or otherwise) without the prior written permission of the above copyright owner of this book.

Criminal copyright infringement, including infringement without monetary gain, is investigated by the FBI and is punishable by up to five years in federal prison and a fine of $250,000.

Published in the U.S. by SilverStone Publishing, 2022
ISBN 978-1-946534-24-8 (Print Paperback)
ISBN 978-1-946534-25-5 (Kindle eBook)

Respect the author's work. Don't steal it.

ABOUT WRECKED

FROM BESTSELLING AUTHOR STONI ALEXANDER

SOMETHING WICKED THIS WAY COMES

I'm a wrecked man with a tortured soul.

I hide my pain and anger behind an easygoing smile and my willingness to do whatever close friends and family need. Day or night, I'm their go-to guy.

But hey, baby, I'm no bleeding heart. I'm an assassin, first and foremost. I locate, isolate, and annihilate. It's not personal, it's my job. And I do it damn well.

Speaking of doing it well... the ladies love me. And I let 'em, every chance I get. They come and they go, but there's one woman who's been a constant for a long time. She's cool under fire, a total badass, and someone I trust with my life. Sure, she's strikingly beautiful and super smart, but we're just friends, babe.

Just. Friends.

When someone close to me confides he's got a past with her, I go a little crazy. To prove a point, she crosses a line. Now, I got a whole different set of problems.

Then, her life goes sideways and she's assigned a protector.

Me.

We're together all the damn time, and she's got a wild streak that just won't quit.

Lucky me.

Until our luck runs out and we come face-to-face with the grim reaper. A long time ago, we made a pact to face death *together*. Either we come out of this alive or we die in an effin' blaze of glory.

Turns out, she's my destiny.
She's also my salvation.

1

THE RESCUE

The floor creaked as they rounded the corner in the three-story building. Nicholas Hawk held up his fist, and the five ALPHA Operatives behind him stopped. Their night-vision goggles gave the pitch-black hallway a grainy-greenish look, but without them, they'd have zero visibility.

He counted to five, but heard nothing beyond his steady breathing. Each precious second mattered, so he directed two Operatives to stay on the first floor, two to the second, and he and Danielle Fox would head up to the third.

Dressed in SWAT gear, the teams sprinted into action. Their primary goal? Find and rescue the lone prisoner. Their secondary? Get out of there alive.

They hoofed it up the stairs, the second-floor search team splitting off as he and Danielle continued climbing. She opened the fire door, he stepped into the quiet hallway.

"Clear," he whispered, their comms also equipped with micro mics.

She joined him.

"Take the rooms on the right," he commanded.

With a nod, she took off while he headed toward the first room on the left.

He turned the handle, opened the door. A body lay on the floor beneath a tattered blanket. With weapon in hand, he did a quick one-eighty, insuring he was alone, then approached the target and pulled back the blanket. It was a decoy, a mannequin, its face partially blown out, leaving a gaping hole.

He hurried on to the next room. No prisoner.

"Check in," Hawk whispered.

"Nothing," Danielle replied.

The Operatives on the first and second floors hadn't found the hostage either.

Hawk pushed on.

In the third room, a woman was tied to a chair. Her face was covered in purplish bruises, her long, dark hair pulled into a mussed ponytail, hanging askew on her head. The gag in her mouth prevented her from speaking. Her shirt sleeves were shredded, her jeans ripped and torn. She was barefoot.

His blood ran cold in his veins.

Large eyes stared in his direction, but because the room was void of light, she couldn't see him. She was trapped and hurt. But, he'd found her, and he'd get her out of there alive.

"Prisoner located," Hawk whispered as he did another sweep of the room confirming they were alone.

He knelt in front of her, set down his weapon.

"I got you," he said as he untied her gag.

He couldn't miss the slight upturn of her lips. "About time," she whispered.

"Are you hurt?" he asked.

"No," she replied.

"Can you walk?"

"I need help."

Using his switchblade, he sliced the ties binding her wrists and ankles, then helped her stand. As he was about to lift her over his shoulder, four men—dressed in black, their faces concealed behind ski masks—stormed the room.

Hawk grabbed his weapon and fired—*POP! POP! POP! POP!*—hitting all four in the chest. They dropped to the floor.

"We're outta here," he said to the prisoner.

He put her in a fireman's carry, bolted down the hallway, rushed down the two flights, and out the building, where his team waited.

When Hawk joined them, he set down the victim.

"Hostage rescued," he said. "Mission complete."

"Excellent," said the voice through the hidden speakers in the courtyard. "Please remove your night goggles."

The ALPHA Operatives pulled off their helmets. The night was warm, the building was not air conditioned, and perspiration dotted their tired faces.

"The drill is over," said the female voice. "Lights in three, two…"

Despite the low-level lighting flooding the courtyard, everyone squinted. Even in the dim light, it took a few seconds for their eyes to adjust.

Addison smiled at Hawk. "You saved me." Batting her eyelashes at him, she said, "My hero."

A female Operative snickered. "You feed his ego, there won't be room for the rest of us in this courtyard."

The team laughed.

"It was luck," Hawk replied. "Any of you would have saved her, if you'd found her."

"How many enemies?" asked Danielle.

"Four," Hawk answered.

"He got 'em all," Addison said.

The four Operatives who'd played the role of the bad guys, walked into the courtyard, paintball spatter covering their chests.

"Nice shot," one of them said to Hawk as he extended his hand.

Hawk pulled his coworker in for a hand-clasp hug. "Love these drills."

"So do I," Danielle agreed. "Addison, have you ever played victim before?"

"Never," Addison said. "I gotta say, it was a little creepy waiting in the dark all tied up. I couldn't see jack and I couldn't hear anything until Hawk walked in. Nothing like facing your demons. At one point, I wondered if you guys had taken a break."

The group laughed as Cooper Grant, co-lead of ALPHA, joined them. "Great work, team. You were two minutes faster than yesterday, but a minute slower than the day before. What worked? What didn't?"

Over the next several minutes, they debriefed. When Cooper addressed Hawk directly, he answered questions, provided a summary of what happened, his assessment, and the outcome, but he was on autopilot. Hawk couldn't shake the chill from seeing Addison tied to that chair, covered in fake bruises, her clothing shredded. Drill or no drill, he never wanted to see her like that again.

"Everyone did a solid job," Cooper continued. "The rest of the teams are finishing up. I reserved the back room of The Tiki Lounge for dinner. First round's on me. ALPHA's picking up the dinner tab."

"Time to party!" Addison said.

Hawk raked his hand through his hair. "I could use a drink and a few hours of chill."

As they made their way toward the hotel and conference center, Hawk and Addison fell in line.

Once a year, the Operatives spent five days in training. The goal? To hone their skills, learn about the newest high-tech gadgets, and hear from industry experts on the latest scams and crimes, how criminals were getting away with them, and what law enforcement could do to stop them.

The secure compound was located in an undisclosed area on the Eastern Shore of Maryland, twenty miles from the beach. The center, along with the training facility, was used by various law enforcement agencies throughout the area. The grounds were managed and run by retired government workers with top-secret clearance. The staff lived at the compound and ran it on an ongoing basis.

It wasn't fancy, wasn't a shithole either. The cafeteria food was edible, the hotel was simple and clean. They were there to train, not get pampered, so no spa, no bar. The training compound consisted of a bunch of buildings that were used for various hostage and crime-related exercises.

Though he liked the intense training and the nonstop drills, Hawk could've used a massage right about now. His muscles were burning from the get-your-ass-outta-bed at five a.m., the formation runs, the weight lifting, the rope climbing, and all the additional work he had to do as a helicopter pilot.

This week, he'd gotten four hours of sleep each night. He couldn't wait to crash in bed.

"You wanna drive back tonight or tomorrow morning?" Hawk asked.

"Tomorrow," Addison replied as she opened the hotel door for him.

He took it from her, gestured for her to enter.

"Why don't you just walk through it?" She rested her ass against the door before pulling out her ponytail tie and raking her hand through her long, dark hair.

"Seriously?" he raised his eyebrows at her. "Are we gonna fight over this too?"

"Fight? We're not fighting. I opened the door for you." She fisted her hand on her hip. "You're stubborn and won't walk through it."

Two Ops made their way toward them. "Hey, Addison, Hawk," one of the men said. "How'd you do?"

"I freed the hostage," Hawk replied, flicking his gaze to Addison. "My bad."

She laughed, then elbowed him in the ribs. "How'd you guys do?"

"We didn't get ours out in time today," the second Operative replied. "He died."

"Ouch," Hawk said. "What happened?"

"We fucked up," said the first as the men breezed inside.

Addison tipped her head toward the lobby. "Go, already. My ass is getting tired."

He walked inside and Addison caught up with him. "Are you driving to the restaurant?"

"You need a ride?"

"Well, you drove us out here, so yeah."

"Then, no, I'm not driving." Hawk loved giving Addison a hard time. She'd furrow her brows or growl at him.

"Idiot," she replied. "I'll swing by your room in thirty."

As she punched the elevator button, a new Operative hurried over. Her shirt and pants were covered in paint spatter. "Hey, Addison."

"Hey, Karen, how'd you do?" Addison asked her.

The newbie pointed to the paint. "I got shot."

Every new ALPHA hire was considered a trainee for the first ninety days. They were all assigned a mentor, and Addison was hers.

"You want me to—" Addison began.

"Hawk, I'm so glad I caught you," the woman said, cutting Addison off. "I'd love to ask you a few questions about being a helo pilot."

"Now?" Hawk's stomach had been growling for the past twenty.

"Now would be *awesome*." She smiled up at him.

2

THE MISSION

Hawk was pissed. He'd been hanging with his guys after a balls-to-the-wall week of grueling training. The last thing he wanted to do was work.

Turned out, he didn't have a choice.

"What?" Addison asked. "What problem?"

"Head back to the compound," Cooper said. "I'll let Danielle know I'm leaving and I'll meet you in the mission room." Cooper took off toward his fiancée, leaving Hawk and Addison alone.

"I can't fucking believe this," Hawk spat out. "You done eating?"

"Yeah," she replied. "Can you tell me something? Anything?"

"I've been tasked with a mission," Hawk murmured. "And I need your help."

"Who else is coming with us?"

"No one."

Cooper walked over to them. "What the hell are you still doing here? I thought you'd be out the door already. We gotta go."

line with his guys. Hawk, Cooper, Stryker, and Jericho were like brothers.

Slash leaned close. "You got a loose cannon with the new hire."

Addison nodded. "She wants to work with Hawk, so I think she's frustrated she's got me as her mentor. They've got the pilot thing in common."

Addison loved hanging with these women. They were smart Operatives who had each other's backs. She was all about girl power, so she was disappointed when Karen had resisted her guidance.

The conversation continued through dinner. At nine o'clock, Addison said her goodbyes.

"Are you going home?" Danielle asked.

"No, to a beach party," Addison replied.

"Costumes?" Slash asked.

"Absolutely," Addison replied with a smile. "I'm ready to go a little crazy. I love retreat week, but this year was super intense."

"I thought so, too," Emerson added.

She needed to grab her backpack out of Hawk's car so she could change in the bathroom. But Hawk wasn't sitting at his table. She swept the room. He and Cooper were huddled together by the door.

As she made her way over, both men turned in her direction.

"Hey," she said. "Sorry to interrupt. I need your car keys so I can grab my backpack."

"We've got a problem," Cooper said.

"And I need your help," Hawk replied.

Shame flashed in Karen's eyes. "You don't need to embarrass me."

Addison wanted to laugh. Karen had done that all on her own. "Let's take it outside."

"No," Karen whispered. "I get it. It won't happen again."

Karen walked away, leaving Addison standing there alone. Across the room, Hawk caught Addison's eye and winked.

After tossing him an acknowledgment nod, she swigged the beer, the ice-cold beverage cooling her throat. Across the room, his penetrating gaze stayed anchored to hers. She couldn't look away, didn't want to either. It was like an invisible force was always pulling them together. The only thing better than staring at him from across the room would be standing by his side.

I can think of something even better...

"We're a competitive group," Cooper continued, and Addison shifted her attention from Hawk to their boss.

"Every year, the drills get harder, the saves are more intense. We're role playing, but it doesn't feel like that when one of our own is tied up and left in a dark room. I want to thank Hawk for his helo drills. Roping out of the chopper was great, but I gotta give a shout out to Addison for climbing *up* the rope."

He paused while the team broke into applause.

She smiled, her gaze sweeping the room. Sliding down the rope was easy. Climbing back up was hard as hell.

"Great job, Addison," Cooper said. "I'm officially closing out our week. Some of you are leaving tonight. Most of you are taking off in the morning. Have a fun night. You deserve it."

As Cooper stepped down, more hoots and hollers filled the room as the line for the buffet formed on both sides.

Addison got in line behind Emerson, then Danielle and Slash stepped in behind them.

After getting their food, they sat together at one of the long tables. She glanced around for Hawk, who stood in the buffet

After the bartender set down their drinks, Hawk handed him cash. "Keep the change."

He grabbed their beers as she lifted her shot. They made their way through the crowded, noisy bar, past the restaurant, toward the private room in the back.

As soon as they entered, the delicious aroma of fried food wafted in their direction. The room was filled with long picnic-like tables. Along the left wall was a buffet. Addison's mouth watered.

Rather than taking off, she turned to Hawk. "Here's to a great week. We kicked butt, got our asses kicked, and got to hang with our peeps." She raised her shot glass, he raised his beer bottle. They clinked and drank.

"Whoo, that burns," Addison said after tossing back the bourbon.

She took her beer bottle from him and sipped. "Save me a seat."

He tossed her a nod as Stryker walked over. She took off into the crowded room in search of Emerson Easton and Danielle Fox.

Cooper stood on a chair. "Hey, team," he shouted over the chatter.

When the group of thirty quieted down, Cooper raised his glass. "Congratulations on a great week. Everyone pushed hard, did their personal best, and got the job done. To you."

"Whooo-hoo! Go ALPHA!" Karen shouted.

Silence.

All eyes turned in her direction.

Addison squeezed through the throng of Operatives until she got to her mentee. Karen's cheeks flamed red as she scanned the group.

Addison tossed Cooper a nod. "I got this." Addison wrapped her arm around Karen, pulled her into the corner. "ALPHA doesn't exist. You can't say that name in public."

"I hated seeing you tied up and injured like that."

She squeezed his shoulder. "But you saved me and my bruises washed off in the shower."

She punched up a playlist, turned up the volume, and sang along. Within seconds, Hawk was belting out the words. Despite Hawk's somewhat off-key rendition, she loved when they sang together. Everything felt right when they were flying down the road, the music blaring, the warm summer air flowing through her hair.

For the past three years, he'd been one of her closest friends in the world. She adored him from the depths of her soul.

Twenty minutes later, he pulled into the parking lot of The Tiki Lounge. Together, they walked inside, stopping at the crowded bar. Hawk squeezed in and tried getting the bartender's attention. Two attempts later, he pulled Addison flush against him.

"Smile," he murmured in her ear. "Shoot him a wave."

She loved how their bodies were pressed together. As the bartender moved closer, she leaned forward a little, caught his eye, and smiled.

"Be right with you," he said.

She fixed her attention on Hawk. Dreamy turquoise eyes peered into hers. "He'll be right with me." She offered a smarmy grin. "What are you drinking?"

"A Bud," Hawk replied.

"No shot?"

"I'm heading back tonight. If you change your mind about the party, I'll drive you home."

She caught a flash of—disappointment? Frustration? She thought she knew him, but something had his panties in a wad.

"What can I getcha?" the bartender asked.

Addison dragged her gaze from Hawk. "A shot of Wild Turkey and two bottles of Bud."

She pulled a credit card from her phone case.

The doors opened, and he waited for he to enter. On the short ride down, he said, "She wants me to be her mentor."

Addison bit back a smile. "Don't you mean lover?"

"Aren't you insulted?"

She shook her head. "I don't care what she thinks of me or that she's crushing on you. Doesn't get any more kick ass then me." She flashed a smile.

He draped his arm around her shoulder. "That's what I love about you, baby. You're a badass and you know it."

The elevator doors slid open and they walked past the registration desk. "See ya," Hawk said to the employee.

Once outside, Hawk's keyless remote unlocked his Mercedes convertible. Before getting in, she murmured, "You got yourself a nice ass, Nicholas Hawk."

He flashed her a killer smile before he slid inside. She tossed her backpack on the backseat, then dropped in beside him. He fired up the engine, retracted the roof, and shot out of the parking lot.

"What's with the backpack?" he asked on the way to the restaurant.

"I'm going to a party, later."

"Nice. Where're we going?"

"*We* aren't going anywhere." She peered over at him. "It's a cosplay party."

He stopped at the light, regarded her with a cool gaze. "Alone?"

"No, a friend got me on the list."

He narrowed his gaze. "You packin' heat?"

She barked out a laugh. "Why should I?"

The light turned green, he tapped the gas, and the sports car roared through the intersection. "Uh, how 'bout protection?"

"I'm not worried. My body is a lethal weapon." She was done talking about the party. "You did a good job rescuing me."

The only thing better than Hawk's bare ass was a pissed-off Hawk. Sometimes she'd say something just to irritate him. His eyebrows would slash down, his stare would turn intense, his jaw would tick behind his chiseled cheeks.

She dropped her backpack on the bed and walked over to him. Then, she unfastened his second button.

"I like the way you think, baby." He tipped her chin toward his. "You've never done this before."

"Easy." She tapped his button with her fingernail. "You buttoned your shirt wrong."

He glanced down. "What would I do without you?"

She kept her attention glued to the shirt as she unbuttoned, then re-buttoned it, but she could feel his heated gaze drilling into her.

When she finished, her eyes met his. *Zing!* That familiar—and very frustrating—jolt of adrenaline charged through her.

Ignoring it as best she could, she patted his shoulder. "You ready? I'm starving. I worked through lunch."

"I gotta dry my hair."

As she ran her fingers through it, a low, rumbly growl ripped out of him. Again, their eyes locked. She mussed the top, then smoothed down the sides and back. "Done. Let's go. Pleeeeease."

His lips curved. "Hangry, huh?"

"I'm dying over here."

But not for food.

On the way to the door, she grabbed her backpack. Out the door and down the hall they walked.

As they waited for the elevator, Addison asked, "So, are you gonna?"

"Gonna what?" Hawk asked.

"Teach her how to fly."

"Hell, no," he replied.

His face was even better than his body.
The Hawk Effect.
"I'll just meet you there," she said.
He scowled at her. "Get your ass in here." He retreated into his room.

She could grab a ride with anyone, but truth was, she liked him the best. From the minute she had joined ALPHA, they'd had this instant connection. Simply put, they just got each other.

She walked in and her brain skidded to a halt. Hawk was pulling on black boxer briefs, his tight, muscular, white ass on full display. She'd seen him in a bathing suit dozens of times, but never naked. If he turned, and she got an eyeful of Mr. Johnson, she might never recover. If his ass was that beautiful, the good stuff might just push her over the edge.

"Sorry," he muttered as he turned toward her. "Shut my door."

As she did, she swallowed, hard. "What took you so long?"

"Your mentee cornered me." He pulled on long, black shorts.

Addison leaned against the wall because she was *not* sitting on his bed. "And?"

Hawk went through his suitcase in search of a clean shirt. Addison eyed his open closet door, walked over and sifted through them. She pulled a white one. "Wear this."

She held it out for him and he shrugged into it.

"Did you know she's a pilot?" he asked.

"Uh-huh."

"She wants me to teach her how to fly helos," Hawk said while buttoning his shirt.

When he finished, Addison laughed.

"What's so funny?" His signature scowl made her pulse kick up a notch.

So handsome.

Her stomach dropped. Was he with her mentee, Karen? He'd never hooked up with an Operative before. Had he changed his mind?

I hope not.

She didn't care who he screwed, but he was one of the most respected Operatives in the entire organization. Sleeping with a new employee would be a bonehead move.

Although her mentee had potential, Karen got starry eyed every time she saw Hawk. Addison understood the Hawk Effect. Women went a little berserk around him. He was wicked handsome with tousled dark brown hair, bright turquoise eyes, a killer smile, and a body made of chiseled granite.

Not only was he super laid back, he was a kick-ass pilot, and he was *always* up for anything. He was a rock-solid friend, a loving son, and a very attentive grandson. Somehow, the man even made smoking look sexy. Women were drawn to him like nothing she'd ever seen.

Sure, he was flat-out gorgeous, but Addison didn't mix biz with pleasure... ever. She had her ALPHA friends and she had her cosplay friends. She kept her worlds separate and she liked it like that.

"Hawk, you in there?"

Knock-knock-knock.

On a huff, she headed toward the elevator. She'd have to wait in the lobby and bum a ride from someone else.

A door opened.

"Hey, babe, I was in the shower," Hawk called out.

She turned back. He stood there, a towel wrapped around his waist. Water dripped from his hair onto his shoulders and slid down his pecs.

So hot.

While she didn't want to stop staring at his half-naked body, she couldn't stand there gawking, so she flipped her gaze to his eyes.

Hawk pushed out of the chair. "I gotta get ready. We'll talk next week."

Karen didn't budge. "Before you take off, I've got one quick question about helo training."

Addison Skye was ready to put the retreat behind her. While she loved hanging with her fellow ALPHA Ops, she'd been balls to the wall for five days straight. Time to toss back a shot of Wild Turkey, fill her growling stomach, and chill.

After showering, she dressed in the only pretty outfit she'd packed. A white V-neck shirt that tied at the waist and matching bell bottoms. She dried her hair, leaving it to trail down her back. As she was lining her eyes, her phone buzzed with an incoming text.

"Hey, the party is a go. You in?"

Addison smiled. *That's the kind of relaxing I'm talking about.* Her cosplay friend was in-the-know when it came to costumed parties at the beach.

"Can you pick me up?" she texted him.

"Sure thing. Party starts at nine. Where you gonna be?"

"The Tiki Lounge."

He sent a laugh emoji. "What the hell are you doing there??? I'll pick you up at nine fifteen."

She sent him a heart emoji before pulling out the only costume she'd packed. She'd never gone to the beach and *not* attended a cosplay party, so she'd come prepared. After transferring her Cleopatra costume and black wig to her backpack, she finished getting ready.

With her bag slung over her shoulder, she left her hotel room, walked down the hall, and stopped at Hawk's room.

Knock-knock.

No answer. She rapped on the door again. Nothing.

Stryker Truman and Jericho Savage walked into the hotel, spotted Hawk, and beelined over. Stryker was covered in paint splotches. Jericho's clothes were paint free.

Hawk tossed them a nod. "Yo, baby, how'd you guys do?"

"Cooper finally let me play the bad guy," Jericho began. "I killed every Operative on our team."

Laughing, Stryker gestured to his clothing. "He annihilated us. It was brutal."

Jericho grinned. "It was a blast." He flicked his gaze to the new hire. "Jericho Savage."

"Yeah, I know who you guys are," Karen replied. "You're ALPHA legends."

"What's your name?" Stryker asked.

"I'm Karen. I started last month. Came over from Fairfax County PD."

"Welcome to the real world," Jericho replied.

"You two going to dinner?" Hawk asked.

Jericho said. "We gotta. I'm headin' out after. Miss my woman."

"When's she due?" Stryker asked.

"Beginning of August."

"That's just a few weeks away," Hawk said.

Stryker slapped him on the back. "Papa Savage."

"I can't wait to be a dad."

"Still not telling us what you're having?" Hawk asked.

"Nope. You'll find out when you show up at the hospital." Jericho flicked his gaze to Karen. "Is this crazy man your mentor?"

Karen gazed at Hawk. "I wish. Addison is."

"Doesn't get any better than Addison," Hawk replied. "Stick with her."

"See you at the restaurant," Stryker said, and he and Jericho took off toward the elevator.

The elevator doors slid open and Addison stepped inside. "Sure," he replied. "Addison, I'll—"

The doors started to close and he shoved his foot inside.

"Just when I thought I was free and clear," she muttered.

He shot her a smile. "Thirty." He removed his foot.

She flipped him the finger as the doors closed.

"Whatcha need?" he asked the trainee.

"Maybe we can talk at dinner." She tucked her strawberry blonde hair behind her ear.

"No can do. We can't discuss anything work-related in public."

"Cooper said we're in a private room." She unbuttoned her paint-soaked shirt, revealing a white tank underneath.

As she slipped the shirt off, he did *not* glance at her chest. He'd never dated an Operative, hadn't slept with one either. Wasn't about to fuck that up now.

"We'll talk next week," he said.

Ignoring him, she moseyed over to the sitting room, sank in a chair at one of the small, round tables, and waved him over. "Five minutes."

Rather than sit beside her, Hawk sat across the table. She leaned forward, shoved her boobs together. Again, he didn't look, but his peripheral vision gave him an eyeful.

"I've got my private pilot's license," she began. "Addison mentioned that you're the only Operative who's also a pilot."

"Yup."

"I love flying, so I thought it would make sense if I learned to fly helos." Leaning back, she cocked her head to the side. "Can you train me?"

Hawk bit back a laugh. She could take legit flying lessons at any regional airport in the Washington-Baltimore region. "No can do. Kathy, right?"

Her smile fell away. "It's Karen."

"I'm not qualified to teach, plus my schedule's packed."

The three of them hurried out as the last glimmers of day inched below the horizon.

Cooper jumped in his SUV. Hawk and Addison slid into the Mercedes. Hawk pulled out of the parking lot while Addison got busy on her phone.

"I just canceled my party plans," she said. "Did you pull me for this because you didn't want me going to that cosplay party?"

After jumping on Route 50, Hawk hit the gas. "You gotta be kidding me. When have I ever been up in your business? You own a cosplay club, for chrissakes."

"Right, sorry." She sighed. "What's the job?"

"Cooper got word that the Festival Shooter is in Ocean City."

"Isn't this a job for Jericho? Don't we need a sniper?"

"Sniper shot from a helicopter above a huge crowd is too risky. Coop needs the perp taken out in his hotel room."

"I've been drinking."

"How much?"

"A shot and a beer."

"We've all been drinking," he replied.

As he glanced over at her, a car cut him off. Hawk slammed on the brakes, swerved into the other lane. The other car's brake lights went on, the vehicle's driver waited for Hawk to pull alongside him.

"We don't need this," Hawk bit out.

He and Addison glanced over. Despite the darkness, the driver was screaming at Hawk and pointing his finger at him.

"I'm gonna take this exit and—"

"He's got a gun," Addison said. "And I'm not armed."

"Neither am I."

Hawk jumped onto the exit ramp, pulled onto the shoulder, and hit the brakes. Addison glanced out the back as he tapped the button while the convertible top rose up over them, blanketing them in darkness.

"He's gone," Addison said. "That was insane."

On a growl, Hawk called Cooper.

"Yeah," Cooper answered.

"We ran into a little road rage prob," Hawk said.

"You okay?"

"We're fine," Hawk replied. "We had to pull off Route 50. Addison's checking for an alternate route. Be there shortly." He hung up.

Addison turned on her nav app. "Since the compound isn't on any map, I put in the gas station that's near it."

Hawk pulled onto the road and drove to the compound by back roads. Once behind the gates, he parked at the mission building beside Cooper's truck. The one-story building was dark.

"We've been drinking within the twelve-hour window of a mission," Hawk said. "How do you wanna play this?"

While that shot of Wild Turkey wouldn't have fazed him, she coulda been buzzing from it.

"I can do it," she replied. "What did you have?"

"Just the one beer."

They exited the sports car. "So, you're good?" he asked.

"I'm good," she replied as they sailed inside.

Cooper was seated at the head of the conference room table, his attention glued to the six monitors affixed to the wall. Surveillance cameras had captured images of Ocean City, the buildings, the outdoor music venue, and the beach. The eeriness of the jet-black ocean was a formidable sight.

Hawk and Addison sat beside each other, facing the wall of monitors.

"Alright, let's get started," Cooper said. "The shooter books two different rooms in the same hotel. One on the top floor, where he does the shooting, and the second on the first floor. If there's no balcony, he cuts out a portion of the window. After the shooting, he switches out his disguise, heads downstairs to his first-floor hotel room. He stays there until everyone's evacuated. Once outside, he escapes unnoticed."

Cooper tapped the keyboard. Photos of six men appeared on the screens. "His MO is simple, yet it's worked every time." The first photo was of a clean-shaven man wearing a straw hat. His long, light brown hair flowed down his shoulders. He wore a flowered shirt and a big smile.

"He blends into the crowd," Hawk added.

"He wants to be invisible," Cooper said.

The second photo was a businessman wearing a suit. His blond hair was short and neat. He wore black-framed glasses, his eyes a bright green. No facial hair.

"Nice disguise," Addison said. "I wouldn't have pegged him for the same man."

Cooper pointed a red-light laser at two different pictures. "He used these two disguises at the Austin music fest." Cooper redirected the laser to two different photos. "He looked like this at the Portland concert."

"He's a master of disguise," Addison murmured. "Does he always change up his looks?"

"No," Cooper replied. "He's used the long brown wig at an Albuquerque festival and again at a Miami one."

"How the hell are we gonna find him if we don't have a damn visual?" Hawk checked the time. It was nine thirty.

"What does he look like without the disguises?" Addison asked.

"We don't know," Cooper replied. "That's why this has been such a challenge."

"If we locate him, shouldn't the FBI arrest him?" Hawk asked.

"It's an ALPHA kill-on-contact job," Cooper explained.

"According to hotel records, he hasn't checked in, but my CI tells me he's there, so we gotta find him before he opens fire."

"No pressure there," Addison muttered as she and Hawk exchanged glances.

"What time does he strike?" Hawk asked.

"Between eleven and eleven thirty," Cooper replied.

Cooper tapped on the keyboard. One of the screens displayed an aerial map of the beach. "You'll land on the Pamplona." Using a pointer, he flashed the laser light on the building, located in a sea of concrete structures that spanned the popular ocean avenue. "It's fifteen stories high. Take the elevator to the first floor, cross the street, and walk the half block to the Harbor House Hotel." Again, using the laser, Cooper directed their attention to the second hotel. "This hotel faces the music venue, which is right on the beach."

"If he's there, we'll find him," Hawk said.

"Once we land—" Cooper began.

"Wait," Addison interrupted. "You're coming with us?"

"I'm heading into the crowd," Cooper explained. "I'm hoping to spot him on his balcony."

Hawk shook his head. "That's too dangerous."

"I got this." Cooper studied them. "We've all been drinking within the twelve-hour window."

"I'm okay," Addison said.

"I'm sober," Hawk replied.

"The stakes are high," Cooper pressed. "You up for this?"

Addison nodded. "Affirmative."

"Absolutely," Hawk added.

"If the shooter succeeds, this will be his fifth attack," Cooper explained. "We've gotta stop him *before* he opens fire on that crowd."

"Understood," Hawk said. "If I can hack into the hotel's surveillance system, I'll try to find him that way."

Cooper handed them comms. They grew silent while they

slipped them into their ears. Next, he opened the door to the supply closet and pulled out three Kevlar vests. "Hide these under your shirts."

Addison glanced down at her clothes. "I gotta change."

"We'll stop at the hotel on the way to the chopper," Hawk said as he grabbed the body armor.

"Who needs a weapon?" Cooper asked.

"I'll use mine," Addison said.

"I have my Glock, but I need a second." Again, Hawk checked the time. Nine-forty.

Cooper pulled a Glock and shoulder holster for Hawk. After Addison collected the Kevlar vest, they bolted. First stop, the hotel.

In the parking lot, Hawk handed Addison his hotel keycard. "Grab my Glock, a black shirt, and my laptop."

"You'll need that sport coat in your closet," she said.

Cooper pulled to a stop. "What's going on?"

"I need to start the preflight check," Hawk said. "Can you light up the chopper for me?"

"I got you," Cooper replied.

"Key's in the ignition," Hawk said to Addison.

"I'll meet you at the helipad," she called out before jumping into Hawk's car and taking off toward their lodging.

Hawk and Cooper hopped in Cooper's truck. Two minutes later, they parked near the helipad. As Hawk made his way toward the Bell 407 helicopter—stationed at the facility for training purposes—Cooper turned on the stadium lights, illuminating the giant bird.

Hawk ran through the checklist. Didn't matter that he'd taken the bird out yesterday. He'd run through the inspection again. Unlike some jets, the helicopter had no ejection seats. If the chopper had a malfunction, he and his crew were going down.

Not on my watch.

Halfway through his inspection, Addison drove into the parking lot, cut the engine, and got out. Pausing, he checked her out. Truth was, he could stare at her all the damn day. She was all of five feet four, muscular, yet small boned. Strong, but delicate at the same time. Long dark hair, translucent blue eyes, thin lips, big smile that lit up her beautiful face.

She'd changed into black fatigues, a black T-Shirt, and a floor-length black duster. She'd pulled her dark brown hair into two braided pigtails that trailed down her chest, a knit cap on her head, black combat boots on her feet. While her outfit was extreme for a night at the beach, Addison could pull it off. That woman looked hot in every damn thing she wore.

Beneath that long, flowing jacket she was packing heat. Most likely, multiple weapons. She had one job. To assassinate the Festival Shooter, and he had no doubt she'd get the job done.

Over her shoulder hung his backpack. His jacket and shirt were draped over her arm, his Glock in her right hand.

He wasn't just attracted to her physically. She was super smart, very energetic, and completely fearless.

"Hey." She set his clothes and weapon on the passenger seat, laid his backpack on a back seat. "Need my help?"

"I got this," he replied as he checked the rear propeller.

Cooper, phone to his ear, jogged over. He finished up the call, but grew silent while Hawk ensured the bird was flight-worthy.

"Chopper's ready," Hawk said yanking off his white shirt. "What's the word?"

"According to my source, the shooter might have checked in under a new alias, but we don't have confirmation," Cooper explained. "He spotted someone wearing the long-haired wig and a baseball cap. My CI lost him, which means he changed his disguise."

Hawk tugged on the black shirt, then flicked his gaze to Addison. "Button me up, boss."

She hesitated for a split second, then a ghost of a smile lifted the corners of her lips. Despite the stressful situation, Hawk would do what he could to diffuse it. They needed to be totally relaxed to pull this off.

She buttoned him up, then held out the holster. He slipped it over his right shoulder, inserted the secondary weapon. Next, she held out his jacket. Once that was on, he tucked his Glock behind his waist, beneath the sport coat.

Cooper chuckled. "Do you normally dress him?"

"He's challenged when he does it himself," Addison replied. Then, the playfulness in her eyes fell away. "We gotta head out."

"Get in," Hawk said. "We can't stop him from here."

Cooper jumped in the back, pulled the door shut. Like earlier, Addison rode shotgun. Hawk settled into the pilot's seat. They strapped in, pulled on headsets. Hawk fired up the bird.

"Coop," Hawk said through the mic, "tell me you contacted ATC about my landing on the rooftop."

"I made a call," Cooper replied. "It shouldn't be an issue."

"We're about to find out," Hawk replied. "Tower, this is Bravo King Whiskey Alpha Alpha. Alpha Alpha requests clearance for lift off."

"Alpha Alpha, you're cleared for lift-off," said the controller.

"Alpha Alpha requests touching down on the Pamplona Hotel rooftop in Ocean City," Hawk said.

"Run that by me again," said the controller.

"Alpha Alpha requests touching down on the Pamplona Hotel rooftop in Ocean City," Hawk repeated.

"Right, Alpha Alpha cleared for rooftop landing."

"Here we go, babe," Hawk said, as the helo lifted off the ground.

Hawk loved flying. Even with the high stakes of an ALPHA

mission, flying relaxed him. As he headed east, toward the ocean, he kept his eye on his instruments, listened to the drone of the propellers. He was one with whatever craft he flew because, by doing that, he could feel if something was off.

Ten minutes later, as the twinkling lights of the bustling beach city zoomed into view, Hawk glanced at the tablet, strapped to his thigh, which provided an aerial view of the town. "I'm setting her down on the Pamplona."

"Confirmed," Cooper said through the headset.

While Hawk wasn't going to say anything, he was concerned. This was the first time they had no visual on their target.

How do we take out a domestic terrorist if we don't know what the hell he looks like?

And what about the thousands of civilians in the crowd? How would they find the shooter before he launched his attack, if they were flying blind?

As Hawk approached the hotel, he glanced around. Mid-July and the beach town was packed. Sidewalks were crowded with tourists, and the lights from the dozens of buildings made night feel like day. Add in the weekend-long concert. It was mayhem. Hawk touched down on the rooftop, killed the engine, and unbuckled.

"Coop, grab my backpack," Hawk instructed as he unstrapped the tablet from his leg.

They exited—the slowing blades a reminder to keep their heads down—and strode toward the rooftop fire door. Cooper tugged, but the heavy metal door didn't budge. He made a call. "We're here."

"This is insane," Addison said. "How are we going to find him?"

She stood so close to Hawk, her arm brushed against his. A thrill raced through him. He turned toward her, inhaled her scent. The aroma so familiar, he hardly noticed it. Except that he *always* noticed her.

"I've got a plan," Hawk said. "I'll fire up the laptop from the lobby and hack into their surveillance system. Cooper'll be on the beach. Addison—"

The heavy rooftop door creaked open. A man Hawk didn't know held it open from the inside.

Cooper tossed him a nod before flying down the stairs. Hawk gestured to Addison. She shook her head, then flicked her gaze to the stranger. "You go. I'll take the rear."

The stranger went next.

"Don't trust him?" Hawk murmured.

"Do you?" Addison whispered.

"If Coop does, I have to."

"I trust no one." She gestured with a flick of her chin. "Go."

Hawk took the stairs, the tap-tap of Addison's boots echoing off the walls as they made their way down.

At the next set of doors, the stranger swiped a keycard. The light turned green. He opened it and paused. "Good luck."

Cooper took the door from him, and the man vanished down the hallway. Hawk, Addison, and Cooper hurried to the elevator. They rode down to the lobby with a family of four. The teenaged girl gave Addison's outfit a double take.

"You look soooo cool," said the girl. "Mom, that's what I want to wear."

The mom smiled at Addison. "Aren't you hot in all that black?"

"Surprisingly not," Addison replied.

The elevator doors opened on the seventh floor, another group stepped in, and the crowded cab continued down. It stopped three more times, but no one else got on.

This is taking for-fucking-ever.

On the first floor, the doors opened, and everyone hurried

out. They strode out of the hotel, crossed at the light, then continued the half block to the Harbor House Hotel.

Cooper pulled to a stop in the hotel's circular driveway, handed Hawk the backpack. "Keep me posted."

"We'll be in constant contact," Addison said. "Please be careful. You don't have backup. Why didn't you bring Danielle?"

"He thinks it's too dangerous," Hawk answered for him. "Nothing's gonna happen to you," he said to Cooper. "I won't let it."

Cooper flashed a smile. "I know that." He regarded Addison. "Get it done." He hurried toward the boardwalk.

"I've got an idea," Hawk murmured to Addison. "You ready to hear it?"

"Been ready," she replied.

They entered the Harbor House, the hotel lobby swarming with activity. Guests spoke with clerks at the front desk, while a short line waited for assistance. There were people milling around, some in groups. Others stood alone, their attention directed at their phones. Most of the sofas were taken, but Hawk found an empty chair.

He sat, flipped open his laptop, and got to work.

Addison walked around the lobby, her focus sweeping from person to person to person. While the shooter worked alone, she wasn't going to rule out an accomplice. She was looking for a man in a disguise, a man who blended in, a man who didn't want to draw attention to himself.

She made a slow pass around the lobby, but no one caught her eye. She returned to Hawk.

"I'm in," he said.

"Nice," she replied. "Now, I need a keycard."

"You're Jane Calley, room 404," he said. "You lost your keycard. As soon as you get a replacement, I can recode it."

"Got it." She stood in line.

A short moment later, one of the clerks motioned for her. "I can help you."

"Hi, I'm in room 404 and I lost my keycard."

The clerk started typing. "What's your name?"

"Jane Calley."

"Can I see your ID?"

Busted.

"It's in the room." Addison smiled, but not too big.

The clerk stopped typing. "I'm sorry, but I can't give you a keycard without ID. We've had some issues with break-ins."

Hawk was by her side. "What's wrong, babe?"

The clerk's gaze stilled on Hawk.

Here we go. Addison bit back a smile. He was about to charm the clerk into giving him a keycard.

"My IDs in our room," Addison said to him.

"Damn," Hawk replied, "So's mine." He flashed the clerk a smile. "How 'bout I wait down here while my wife runs upstairs and grabs her ID?"

"I'm not supposed to," whispered the clerk.

"Help us out," Hawk said.

"I've got to run to the Ladies' room," Addison said. "Be right back." She beelined toward the end of the counter where someone had just dropped off a card. She snatched it up, shoved it into her duster pocket, and returned to find the clerk giggling.

The clerk handed Hawk a keycard. "You're so funny, Mr. Calley."

"I'll mention you in my review," Hawk said. "Thanks for your help."

They stepped away from the reception counter and walked around the corner.

"Smart move leaving," Hawk said.

Addison held up a keycard. "Someone dropped this off at the counter. That's why I left."

"What's going on?" Cooper asked through their comms.

"I've got to program the keycards." Hawk returned to the lobby, sat in a different chair on the other side of the room, and got busy.

Every second felt like a damn eternity. Addison studied the guests. No one looked like the shooter in *any* of his expected disguises.

"I've got something," Cooper said.

"Go," Addison replied.

"There're twelve beach-facing hotel rooms on the top floor," Cooper explained. "All, but three, are lit up. Facing the hotel from the beach, the first room. The next, two doors after that. The third is the eleventh room, all the way down the hall."

"Got it," Addison said.

"I'm programming the keycard to give us access to any beachfront room on the top floor," Hawk said.

A lone man with red hair wearing a straw hat walked into the lobby and caught Addison's attention. "I got eyes on someone." She took off after him, rounding the corner as he approached the elevator bank.

One of the cab doors slid opened, and a crowd entered.

"He's getting on an elevator," Addison said. "Straw hat, red hair that touches his collar. He's wearing a flowered shirt and white pants."

She hurried over. As the doors shut, she glimpsed the man. Well, not the man, but his hat. "Target verified."

"Are you sure?" Cooper asked.

"Affirmative," she replied. "He's wearing the straw hat. The one with the three black stars sewn onto the front."

"I'm watching to see if any of the hotel rooms light up," Cooper said.

Hawk appeared at her side, pushed the up button as guests gathered at the elevator bank.

Addison loved these missions, but they rarely included a situation where thousands of innocent people were involved. She had one goal, but there were so many things that could go wrong. Rather than think about those, she focused on finding the shooter and eliminating him.

The elevator doors opened. She and Hawk entered, along with several other guests. They rode in silence, while the cab stopped on multiple floors. Finally, they were alone in the elevator.

"I've got your back," Hawk murmured.

She turned, their eyes met. "You better." Then she smiled. "And I've got yours."

"Same three rooms are still dark," Cooper said.

"Copy," Hawk replied.

The doors slid open. They exited, walked to the room closest to the elevators.

Addison held the keycard against the reader. The light turned green. She shoved the card into her pocket, grabbed her Glock. After a quick glance at Hawk, she opened the door.

A middle-aged couple was making out on the bed.

"Sorry," Addison said. "Wrong room." She shut the door, shoved her Glock behind her waist.

"Negative on room one," Hawk said.

"Copy," Cooper replied.

They hurried to the second room. Again, Addison pulled out the card, held it against the black box. The light turned green. She opened the door. The room was dark.

"Who is that?" called out a woman.

A light flicked on, the guest bolted upright in bed.

"Sorry!" Addison called out. "Wrong room."

She and Hawk hurried out, pulling the door shut behind

them. The woman yanked open the door. "How did you get in here?"

Addison held up her keycard. "Sorry. Have a good night."

"You didn't answer my question," the hotel guest hollered.

"We'll check with the front desk as soon as we get into our room," Hawk said.

"I've got movement on the balcony of the eleventh room," Cooper said into their ears. "The balcony door opened. The room is dark. No none came outside."

"That's gotta be him." Hawk took off toward the end of the hallway, Addison had to run to catch up.

She swiped, dropped the card, grabbed her weapon. They threw open the door, rushed inside.

A man stood there in the dark, the lights from the venue bathing him in shadowed light. The straw hat and wig were gone. In his arms, he cradled an automatic assault rifle. He raised the weapon.

POP! POP! POP! POP! POP! POP!

Both Addison and Hawk opened fire on him, the shots muffled by their silencers. The shooter staggered back, then dropped.

"Target hit," Hawk said. "Man down."

"Confirm," Cooper said.

Addison knelt next to the body, felt his carotid. "Confirmed." Then, she bolted toward the small table by the window, the glow of a laptop catching her eye. "Oh, no. This is bad."

"Ah, fuck, no," Hawk bit out as he stared down at the computer screen.

3

THE PACT

Hawk shut the door to the hotel room, cleared the bathroom, then shoved his Glock in the back of his pants.

"What'd you find?" Cooper asked.

"Laptop with a split screen. He's got two surveillance cams aimed at two backpacks." Hawk sat at the small table, his fingers flying over the keyboard. "C'mon, baby, talk to me."

"Like, abandoned backpacks?" Cooper bit out.

"Yeah," Addison murmured.

"Fuck. *Fuck*," Cooper muttered. "He upped his game."

"Cooper, I'm coming outside," Addison said. "We gotta find those backpacks before they detonate."

"Give me another minute," Hawk said. "I might be able to defuse them from here."

"If the shooter learned how to build and detonate a bomb, our *only* chance of saving everyone is to find the bags and get them the hell outta there," Addison said.

"Fly them out?" Hawk asked.

"And drop 'em over the ocean," Addison replied.

"I found it," Hawk blurted.

Addison stared at the screen, but she couldn't read code.

After a few seconds, Hawk growled. "Addison's right. One is set to detonate in twelve minutes, the second fifteen seconds after that."

"He's pure evil," Addison bit out. "If we push hard, we can find those bags in time."

Hawk and Addison ran out of the room, toward the exit sign. They flew down the stairs and out the front door. On the sidewalk, Hawk pulled Addison to a stop.

"You got this," he said.

"*We* got this," she replied before she bolted toward the beach.

The sidewalks were crowded with vacationers. The streets were clogged with traffic. Hawk hurried around families, couples, groups of partiers as he dodged strollers, even leashed dogs.

Down the street he ran until he got to the intersection. Not bothering to wait for the light to change, he jogged across the busy street. The traffic was moving so slowly, he made it across in seconds, then bolted inside the Pamplona, through the busy lobby, and over to the stairs.

Beads of sweat trickled down his temples, his back was soaked with perspiration. He wiped his forehead, yanked open the door, and almost crashed into a couple making out in the stairwell.

He jumped around them and climbed the stairs two at a time. By the time he got to the top floor, his thighs burned. Pain only fueled him to go faster. He jogged to the maintenance-only door and turned the handle. Locked.

Dammit.

Since Hawk didn't have his lock pick set with him, he pulled out his Glock, aimed at the door and fired—*POP!*—just as a family with two young children loomed into view.

Fuck.

He yanked open the door, ran the stairs, and hurried onto the roof. After jumping into his helo, he flipped on switches, the engine roared to life. Seconds later, he lifted off the ground. He'd already used up six precious minutes.

If Addison and Coop didn't find those bags in the next five —he shoved that thought out as he flew the helo toward the music venue.

Time wasn't on their side, but Hawk had every confidence they'd find those backpacks.

Addison ran onto the beach. "Cooper, where are you?"

"I just got off the phone with my contact at the Bureau," Cooper replied. "I'm near the stage, but I haven't found anything."

"I'm heading into the crowd," she said.

"Look for a light pole," Hawk said through the comm. "The backpacks are black, but they were lit up."

"Where are you?" Cooper asked.

"Look up," Hawk replied as he zoomed over the crowd.

Even though the beach was thick with concertgoers, the wind gusts from the propellers sprayed sand in every direction.

"Fly out over the water," Addison said. "You're kicking up sand."

"Spotlight's not helping?" Hawk asked.

"Not if I can't open my eyes," she replied.

Hawk flew out over the water and shone the light onto the crowd. Addison hurried through the throngs of people as the music came to an abrupt halt.

"Hey, everyone," said the band leader. "We gotta lay low for a little. Why don't you all go play some mini-golf, or hang at a bar for a few. We gotta clear the beach."

"Oh, no," bleated Addison. "I hope no one panics."

"I found a bag." Cooper said. "Safe to pick up?"

"Don't jostle it," Hawk said. "It shouldn't explode, but I wouldn't test it."

As Addison moved around the people, her boots sunk into the soft sand, which made it harder to hustle. "I see a bunch of food trucks lined up on the sand. I'm heading over there."

"Three minutes," Hawk said. "Find that bag."

Addison pushed on, her focus sweeping left and right. She passed a group of guys in line by one of the food trucks. "Hey, beautiful. You wanna wait with us?"

Ignoring them, she continued on. As she ran behind one of the food trucks, she saw a lone black backpack. "I think I found it."

"Where you goin'?" asked one of the guys from the group.

"Ah, crap," Addison said. "I don't have time for this. Hawk, I'm next to the Mexican food truck. It's called—"

"Tacos and More," Hawk said. "Whatcha need, babe?"

"Sand in a douchebag's face."

The roar of the helicopter, along with the bright light, grew closer. Everyone turned away from the spray of sand. Addison grabbed the backpack.

"I've got the second bag," she said. "Hawk, we need a pick up."

"I'm gonna touch down," Hawk said.

"On my way," Cooper said.

People scattered as Hawk lowered the chopper. Keeping her head down, Addison trudged over, opened the sliding door, and climbed into the back seat.

"A minute and a half," Hawk said. "Coop, where are you?"

"Twenty seconds out."

Hawk shifted toward her. The second their eyes met, a calmness filled her soul. They'd been in plenty of pressure-cooker situations before. This wasn't their first rodeo—or their first one together. She pulled the comm from her ear.

"I'm not letting Cooper in," she said as she buckled up.

His gaze never strayed from hers. He nodded, once. No point in speaking. They both knew what could happen, what they were facing.

They'd stared death in the eyes before and they'd managed to escape its grip.

Cooper ran over. Breathing hard, beads of perspiration covered his face. Like them, his hair was soaked. "Move over," he said.

She shoved the comm into her ear. "Give me the backpack."

After he handed it to her, she said, "Step away from the helo."

"What the hell are you—" Cooper blurted.

"Thirty seconds, Coop," Hawk said. "We gotta fly."

"Fuck," Cooper yelled. "You can't—"

"Hawk and I have a pact," Addison said. "We face death *together*. Three's a crowd for this party." She shoved Cooper back. "Go!" she yelled to Hawk.

As the craft lifted off the ground, she pulled on the headset.

"Twenty seconds." Hawk flew away from land, full throttle.

The bird sailed over the black ocean, gaining altitude as the beach lights faded and darkness surrounded them. The wind whipped through the cockpit, making Addison's eyes water. She lifted the backpack, set it on her lap.

"Fifteen seconds," Hawk said. "It's go-time, baby."

Repositioning, she held the sack outside and let it go. Then, she picked up the second bag, held it outside the craft, and dropped it. "Backpacks released."

"Hold on." Hawk continued flying straight ahead at full capacity.

Addison leaned forward, gripped Hawk's shoulder. Of one thing she was absolutely certain. She would rather die with him than live without him. That's how much his friendship meant to her.

KABOOM!!!!!!!!!!!

Their bodies shook and the helicopter wobbled from the shock of the blast as the ocean erupted, spraying in all directions. Seconds passed while Hawk struggled with the cyclic stick before regaining control.

"One down," she said.

"That woulda done a lot of damage," Hawk said.

"We saw the explosion from the beach," Cooper said through the comm. "How are you both doing?"

KABOOM!!!!!!!!!!!

The second explosion reverberated through the helo as Hawk continued flying on full power.

"Talk to me!" Cooper yelled through their earpieces. "Are you okay?"

"Hawk?" Addison craned forward. "Talk to me."

Glancing over his shoulder, he gave her a thumbs-up. "Confirmed," he said. "We're good."

She unplugged the headset and unbuckled, then climbed through the space, carefully maneuvering into the co-pilot's seat. After plugging in the headset, she murmured, "That was intense."

"Jesus, Addison," Hawk said. "This isn't a car for fuck's sake."

After buckling herself in, she held out her hand. He threaded his fingers through hers.

"We got it done, baby," he said.

She smiled at him, released his hand. "We always do. But... that definitely felt like we cheated death."

"Nah, we had this." Hawk turned the helicopter toward the beach. "Coop, need a ride back?"

Cooper chuckled. "I'll be the one waiting on the rooftop."

"See you in ten," Hawk replied as he headed toward the shore.

They flew in a comfortable silence, but Addison couldn't

help but think... what if? What if they hadn't found the second backpack? What if the bomb had detonated *before* hitting the water? What if one of them hadn't made it out alive?

Hawk was her closest guy friend in the world. She glanced over at his handsome profile. Headful of mussed dark brown hair, razor-straight nose, chiseled jawline and perfectly sculpted lips. A sigh escaped as she soaked up all that male beauty.

He glanced over. "You okay?"

"Yeah. You?"

"Never better, baby."

As her heart rate returned to normal, her mind wandered.

Sure, they'd kissed. A peck here or there, but that was it. Over the years, she'd thought about being with him. It would be fun, but it would ruin their friendship. He was a wild man when it came to women. A one-and-done kinda guy.

But, she was just as wild. Sex was a no-strings thing that Addison did in costume.

As the lights of the town town loomed large, Hawk said, "I like our pact."

"Fight to the death together," she replied.

He chuckled. "I thought it was, 'live together, die together.'"

"Same thing."

"I think we should get married." Hawk slowed the bird as he flew over a building.

"*What*? You're kidding, right?"

"If neither of us is married by the time I'm forty, we get hitched."

"I'm not getting married," she replied matter-of-factly. "You know that."

"Ah, c'mon, you don't mean that, do ya?"

"Why wouldn't I?"

"You're perfect wife material."

She huffed. "I'm not sure if I'm flattered or insulted."

"It's a compliment. You're a total hottie, a badass, you're smart, hardworking. You like adventure and you're fearless. Here's a proposition for you. If we're not married when I'm forty and you're thirty-seven, we marry each other."

"Like seconds?" She glared at him. "I'd rather be someone else's first choice than your last. Hard pass for me."

He touched down on the rooftop, but he didn't cut the engine. "Coop, we're here."

"Give me a few," Cooper replied. "I'm talking to the FBI."

"I think we should stay at the compound tonight and take off first thing tomorrow," Hawk said.

"I'm gonna grab a ride from someone else," she replied.

"Whaaaa? You're not mad at me, are you?"

Crossing her arms, she eyed him. "If I *were* to get married, I would do it because sharing my life with someone meant something. I love you, Hawk, I do, but I wouldn't marry you just because I couldn't find my person."

He pulled off his headset, carefully removed hers. Then, he cradled her hand in his. "Forget I said anything. This was an intense week. Then, instead of celebrating, we got thrown a mission." He smiled, sending a fresh hit of adrenaline careening through her.

She nodded, squeezed his hand, and let go. "I'm bummed I didn't get to blow off steam at my party, but I'm so tired from the retreat, it's probably better I crash. I'll ride home with you tomorrow."

"I'm taking off at seven."

"Why so early?"

He stared at her, eyes wide as saucers.

She raised her eyebrows. "Now, what?"

"My sister's wedding is tomorrow. I'm in it. You're coming with me."

"Ohgod, I completely forgot. It's at one, right?"

"At the farmhouse."

The metal door to the rooftop flew open. Cooper jogged over, climbed in the back and pulled the door shut. "Excellent work, you two. Congratulations. You're being hailed as heroes, except no one knows that it was you."

"Fine by me," Hawk replied before they pulled on their headsets and he lifted off.

Cooper stuck his head between their seats. "Addison, you okay?"

"Long week, longer day," she replied.

Cooper flashed a smile. "Great work tonight."

After Cooper buckled in, Addison glanced over at Hawk.

She'd never marry him. He loved women too much to settle down with one. Plus, she loved her roleplaying with strangers too much to abandon it.

For the first time since they'd become friends, her heart ached for something she'd never wanted, but now realized she couldn't have. She and Hawk were too much alike—but also too different—to ever turn their friendship into a romance.

4

HAWK'S FAMILY EVENT

The following afternoon, Hawk drove up the long, gravely driveway to his grandparents' farm.

They called it a farm. *He* called it their property. Yes, they had chickens and they used to have dairy cows. Nowadays, most of the land sat unused while area developers salivated over the hundred-plus acres, hungry to snatch it up.

He regarded his passenger. Addison looked beautiful in a sleeveless, cinch waisted, halter dress and stilettos. She'd pulled her hair into a twist, leaving her neck exposed. If there was anything that caught his attention, it was a sexy woman with an exposed neck. He couldn't stop himself from thinking about moving in close behind her and kissing her neck until she purred with pleasure.

His cock twitched.

"So, what color would you call that?" he asked, redirecting his thoughts.

Addison peered his way. "Call what?"

"Your dress."

"The tag said dusty pink. I call it desert rose."

"You clean up well."

She barked out a laugh. "Bummer I can't say the same about you."

"What's wrong with my suit?"

"Meh." She bit back a smile. "You're in a white shirt and dark pants. So, what?"

"Wait 'til you see me strutting down the aisle."

"Cocky. Arrogant. Egomaniac."

He shot her a smile. "That's me, baby. What I want to know is who gets married outside in July?" Hawk pulled into the oversized driveway and parked. "Let's go find the fam."

Together, they walked the cracked cobblestone path and up the old, wooden steps to the double-wide front doors. He pushed one open and waited for her to walk through. When she did, her vanilla scent wafted in his direction.

Damn, she smells good.

Hawk's grandfather ambled out of the kitchen toward them. When he saw Hawk, he broke into a grin. "There he is, and Addison too!" Grandad extended his long arms and she gave him a hug.

Tall and sturdy, Grandad had the physique of a man who'd spent his life working outside. He was healthy, fit, and always wore a big smile.

Then, Granddad pulled Hawk in for a bear hug. "How's my number one?"

Hawk patted his grandfather's back. "I'm good. How you doing?"

"The farmhouse is *the* place to be. Family's in the kitchen. The wedding party is upstairs. You should check in with Kerri. She's been asking for you."

"You wanna come up with me?" Hawk asked Addison.

"No, you go," she replied. "I'll hang with the Grands."

Granddad laughed. "Come in and say hello before you go up."

As they followed Grandad toward the kitchen, Addison murmured, "It's like you're a celebrity or something."

Hawk glanced over and winked. The closer they got, the louder the chatter.

"Look who wandered in," Grandad exclaimed as they entered the spacious country kitchen.

Heads turned. Conversations slowed, then stopped. Hawk's gaze swept across the room, then darted back to two people sitting at the kitchen table. His mom and his brother.

His dad, standing nearby, broke into a smile. "You made it!"

"Of course, we did," Hawk replied before hugging it out with his dad.

The next few minutes was a sea of hellos and hugs with Grandmom, his aunts, an uncle, a few cousins, and Lamar's mom and dad.

Hawk's sister, Kerri, had been dating Lamar for a few years. He, too, came from a large, close-knit family.

"So," Lamar's dad began, "are you and Addison next?"

"Next?" Addison asked.

"You know, tying the knot," Lamar's dad continued. "Gettin' hitched." He chuckled. "Or are you more the life-partner kinda couple?"

"Honey," Lamar's mom scolded.

"We're just friends," Addison replied.

"That's good, too," Lamar's mom said.

"I think 'just friends' is terrible," Hawk's dad blurted. "We love Addison."

"You'd have some beautiful babies," Hawk's aunt added.

Hawk flicked his gaze to his mom, then his brother. "No kids for me," Hawk blurted.

Silence.

Ugly, awkward silence.

Fuck. I shouldn'ta said that. He hated when he went on auto-pilot.

Lamar sauntered into the room, beaming. "It's my big day!"

Hawk pulled his future brother-in-law in for a hug. "Looking good, babe."

Lamar did a slow turn, showing off his tailored wedding suit.

"So handsome." Lamar's mom dabbed the corner of her eye with a tissue.

"Let's go, fam! I gotta get me married." Lamar led the way toward the front door.

"Mom and I will wait here for the bride," Hawk's dad said.

"I'll go up and check on things." Hawk's mom hurried out of the room.

As everyone sauntered toward the front door, Hawk's cousin made his way over. After a hand-clasp hug, Tommy said, "You look good, Nicky. How you been?"

"Good to see ya, cuz," Hawk replied. "It's been a while."

As kids, they played together whenever their families got together. Tommy was thirty-three to Hawk's thirty-two. He was five ten to Hawk's six one. His straight brown hair had gotten longer, now brushing against his shoulders. He had friendly brown eyes and a muscular physique. He was a Maryland cop who'd gone undercover, his most recent job taking him to Philly for six months.

"You back for good or heading out on another gig?" Hawk asked as they made their way through the house and down the front porch steps.

"I'm back and living in an apartment in Falls Church."

"We'll catch up," Hawk said as they headed toward the giant tent on the side lawn.

"Absolutely." Tommy leaned forward, caught Addison's eye. "How are you?"

"Sorry," Hawk said. "Addison, my cousin Tommy."

"Hi," she replied.

"We'll talk at the reception." Tommy hurried to catch up with a relative.

As Hawk and Addison made their way toward the oversized tent, Hawk's brother pulled up alongside Addison.

"Hey," Prescott Armstrong said.

Hawk and Prescott weren't just brothers, they were best friends. Their mom had been married to Prescott's dad, but he had died when Prescott was a baby. When Hawk's mom remarried, Hawk's dad loved two-year-old Prescott like he was his own, legally adopting him a few years later. Even so, their mom had never changed Prescott's last name... for a reason.

Towering at six three, Prescott had wavy brown, sun-streaked hair. Like their Granddad, he spent a lot of time outside. His current passion was water skiing. If he wasn't working, he was on the water.

Addison looped one arm through Hawk's, the other through Prescott's. "My two favorite Ops," she whispered. "How was it, Prescott?"

Prescott's recent ALPHA assignment that had taken him out of town, so he'd missed the annual training camp.

"Intense." Prescott had lowered his voice. "Brutal." Then he cracked a smile. "It's damn good to see you two. I heard some shit went down last night."

"It was crazy," Addison murmured. "We cut it pretty close."

"We got it done." Hawk cracked a smile. "I missed you, bro."

"I missed Addison," Prescott deadpanned.

On a chuckle, Hawk made like he was gonna sucker-punch his brother.

They walked inside the large party tent and pulled to a stop. Rows and rows of white folding chairs lined both sides of the aisle, a beautiful flowered wreath draped the back of every chair. Guests were moseying toward the seats while a quartet played in the back corner.

"I'll walk you to your seat," Hawk said to Addison.

"I got this," she replied. "You guys should find the wedding party."

"They're right outside the tent." Prescott tossed a nod in that direction.

"Go," Addison said, before eyeing Prescott. "We'll catch up later."

Hawk slipped into his suit jacket. "Button me up."

Addison stared into his bedroom eyes before fastening his jacket. Then, she straightened his tie. "See ya, boys."

"Let's get our baby sis married," Hawk said to his brother.

After both men took off, Addison needed a second to get herself together. She hadn't seen Tommy in months, hadn't thought about him either. If she'd known he was Hawk's cousin, she would never have hooked up with him.

But she didn't know, so she had. More than once.

Months ago, she met him at a private cosplay party. They saw each other at another party not long after. The hookups were no big deal... until he asked her to meet him for coffee. Out of costume, as herself. She wasn't interested, so she declined.

While she wasn't trying to keep her identity a secret, she played in character and stayed in character, so she never told him her name.

As she made her way toward the rows of guest seating, Tommy pulled up beside her.

"It's great to see you again," he said. "Now, I've got a name to go with your beautiful face."

"Hey, Tommy." She didn't care that they'd gotten together. What she *did* care about was whether he'd want to pick up where they left off.

Not interested then. Not interested now either.

"I'm sitting with family," he said. "We've got room. Come and join us."

"I'm good, thanks."

He shrugged a shoulder. "You shouldn't be alone at a wedding. I'll hang with you."

She was stuck with him.

They found an aisle seat on the bride's side a few rows behind the family.

"How have you been?" he asked.

"Good." She didn't want to chat, but ignoring him wasn't gonna fly. "You?"

"I was in Philly, for work, but I'm back." He paused. "Not gonna lie, I thought about you while I was gone."

She should have been flattered, but she wasn't. Yes, he was good looking, but she wasn't feeling the vibe. She'd turned down his invitation for coffee months ago and she wasn't changing her mind.

"What's your story with Nicky?" he asked. "You guys talking. Together?"

"I'm a...we're close..." she trailed off.

Close what? Friends. More like, each other's sloppy leftovers if no one else wants us.

"I get it," Tommy replied. "Relationships are complicated. He's a lucky guy." He leaned close. "I was gonna make a few calls, see if I could find out anything about you. I really wanted to see you again."

What the hell?

The processional music began. Everyone turned as the wedding party made their way down the aisle.

"That's Lamar's brother," Tommy whispered as the first couple proceeded by. "That's Lamar's cousin and his wife," he added after the second couple passed them.

Turning toward him, she offered a polite nod.

Prescott was escorting one of the bridesmaids. Addison

craned to see Hawk, a pretty woman by his side.

A twinge of pain shot through her. Funny how she stayed cool during a mission, yet seeing Hawk with another woman wound her up pretty good. He offered the bridesmaid his arm, and she latched on to his bulging bicep, her cheeks flushing.

Hawk's body was dope, no question about that. His broad shoulders dwarfed Addison, but it was his granite pecs that always stole her attention. A bare-chested Hawk was sexy as hell. If that wasn't enough, he had a granite eight-pack, a nice tight ass, and strong striated thighs.

Down the aisle they strolled. His gaze swept the crowd, until it locked on hers. This time, a surge of adrenaline powered through her. The intensity in his bright eyes scorched her like she was staring straight into the sun.

Hawk's gaze jumped to his cousin. His left eyebrow twitched, his jaw ticked. Everyone had tells. What did those nonverbals mean? She had absolutely no idea.

The quartet's piece reached a crescendo. Kerri waited at the beginning of the aisle, flanked by her mom and dad. Everyone stood.

Slowly, they began the trek to the altar. All that separated Hawk's sister from the end of an era as a single woman was forty feet. Once she got there, she was committing her life to one man, and he to one woman. Together, they'd build a life. Share joys, triumphs, sadness and defeats. She'd have his back and he'd have hers.

Could their love sustain them for decades?

Kerri's white gown trailed behind her. Her light brown hair had been swept into a stunning style, but it was her radiant smile that said it all. The second she and her parents started down the rose-strewn path, her attention jumped to the man at the end of the aisle. When she locked gazes with Lamar, the love in her eyes shone brightly.

Lamar beamed as his bride made her way to him. Kerri

kissed her mom and her dad, then took that final step to her forever man.

Addison held her breath as they gazed into each other's eyes. Lamar leaned forward, whispered something to her, then took her hand and faced the clergy.

The ceremony was beautiful. The bride and groom asked some of their friends to speak about them, their relationship, and their path to this moment.

"I've known Lamar since we were ten," said one friend. "He was all about football. We watched it on TV together, played it in the leagues, all the way up to high school. That was Lamar's love until biology, then his focus turned to research. He was passionate about his work—still is. I remember the day he told me about Kerri. We met for a game of racquetball and he said, "I met my future wife yesterday. When Lamar makes up his mind about anything, he's all in. You two make a great team. I appreciate you and I love you both."

To Addison's surprise, Hawk took the mic. "I'm Nicholas Hawk, Kerri's brother, and this is our older brother, Prescott." Hawk redirected his attention to his sister.

"Kerri, you followed Prescott and me *everywhere*. We'd build a fort, you'd crawl inside, park yourself in the middle, and *not* leave. We'd go outside to play. Five minutes later, we'd see you running across the lawn after us. We'd be having a pillow fight and you'd surprise us with *our* nerf guns and annihilate us. Every time we'd tell Mom we didn't want you tagging along, she'd say, "She's your sister and she loves you. Your job is to love her back and to protect her. Go, go on, and do your jobs."

He paused to smile at his sister. "If a day goes by and I haven't gotten a text or a call, I check in with you. I do it because it's my job, babe. You and Lamar are good together. Make a great life for yourselves. You deserve it, sis." Hawk handed the mic to Prescott.

"Mom," Prescott began, "Nicky and I want to thank you for

teaching us how to love. You made us look out for Kerri. Forced us to be nice to her, though we did try to bury her in the snow that one time. As you can see, she survived." He paused while the guests laughed. "We watch out for each other because you told us to. Thanks for teaching us a life lesson we live every single day. We love you."

Addison wiped the tears that had streaked down her cheeks. She glanced around. She wasn't alone.

That was beautiful.

When the ceremony ended, everyone headed toward a second large tent set up in the expansive backyard.

"It was good catching up," Addison said to Tommy.

Tommy chuckled. "Well, since we're all going in the same direction, I'll walk over with you." As they filed out, he said, "Tell me about you. Where do you work?"

"I'm a financial consultant," she lied.

"With an accounting firm?"

"I have my own small business," she said as they left the air-conditioned tent. The bright midday sun had her fishing out her shades from her small bag and sliding them on. After popping on his sunglasses, Tommy removed his suit jacket.

Once inside the reception tent, Addison glanced around. The band was set up near the entrance which included a large area for dancing. Round tables took up the majority of the space, with the head table at the far end.

A server appeared with a tray of flutes. "These have champagne," he explained, "and these are sparkling water." They both chose champagne.

When the server left, Tommy raised his glass. "To you."

She clinked glasses, sipped the chilled drink. "I'm sorry I'm not—"

"Don't sweat it," he said. "Are you still going to those cosplay parties?"

"No," she replied. "I don't have time." She could have told

him about the cosplay club she owned with her cousin, Liv Savage, but she didn't want to lead him on. Instead, she opted to change the subject. "What kind of work are you doing now?"

"More undercover stuff, only I get to stay in the area for a while. It'll be good to be home. I missed my friends and this crazy family."

Since neither could talk about their jobs, and she didn't want to seem overly interested, she grew silent.

The smooth jazz tune coming from the band picked up tempo. Addison glanced around. The wedding party was lining up by the entryway.

"Good afternoon, ladies and gentleman," announced the band's front man. "It's my great pleasure to introduce the bridal party."

Two at a time, the bridesmaids and groomsmen danced their way into the large, tented space as guests formed a horseshoe around them.

Hawk entered with the same bridesmaid, but he wasn't touching her as he strutted into the space. She caught up to him, slipped her hand in his, then spun him around, then around again.

While Addison had downplayed how he looked, he was scorching hot in the tailored dark suit, bright white dress shirt, and colorful tie. Form-fitting clothing that clung just right to show off his striking physique. No matter what he wore, Nicholas Hawk was flat-out gorgeous.

The introductions continued, then the band leader said, "Put your hands together and let's give a warm welcome to the newlyweds, Kerri and Lamar!"

To the applause and shouts of joy, the bride and groom entered the tent holding hands. Lamar pulled Kerri close, kissed her gently, then spun her and dipped her.

Once the bridal party began mingling, Addison needed to

move on. "It was good catching up with you," she said to Tommy.

Before she could escape, Hawk loomed into view. As he sauntered toward her, a shadow darkened his gaze. There was something about him that calmed her *and* riled her at the same time. Their gazes stayed anchored on each other's. Everything in her world was better when he was in it.

"Moving in on my woman?" Hawk asked Tommy.

Tommy stepped back. "Of course not."

Hawk squeezed his cousin's shoulder. "I'm just messing with you. Addison and I are chill. Best buds, huh?" He wrapped his arm around her, pulled her close, and kissed the top of her head.

Busted.

Tommy's expression brightened, his attention jumping to Addison. "Best buds, huh? I love that."

A reception line was forming. Addison wanted to wish Kerri and Lamar well, plus she needed to get away from Tommy, so she excused herself.

As she took her place in line, she glanced back. Hawk and Tommy were still chatting it up. No way would Addison tell Hawk she'd gotten together with his cousin. They never talked about their hookups and she wasn't about to start now.

A server swung by with flutes of champagne and sparkling water. After Hawk grabbed a champagne, he took a long sip.

"You still hanging at Jericho Road?" Tommy asked.

"I stop by when I can. I've been spending more time at Addison's cosplay club in Alexandria."

His cousin's eyes widened. "Dude, are you for real? She owns a cosplay club?"

"Lost Souls." Hawk sipped the champagne. "You into playing dress up?"

"I've got a friend who is. He brought me to a few private parties. It was a good time. Cool costumes, pretty women. Sometimes things got a little wild." Tommy grinned. "It worked for me." Pausing, he sipped the bubbly. "Do you play there?"

"I installed the security system, so I help Addison out with tech upgrades. I'm her IT guy. You want me to add you to the list?"

"Sure," Tommy replied. "That'd be great."

The band leader announced it was time for lunch to be served and asked everyone to make their way to their assigned tables.

As the guests started moving toward the tables, Tommy glanced around. "So, you and Addison are friends."

"Yeah, why?"

Tommy nibbled the inside of his cheek. "Bro, I don't usually... er... kiss and tell, but Addison and I, we got together a coupla times at these private parties."

What the hell?

Normally chill, heat blasted Hawk's chest. He wasn't expecting that, and he didn't much like hearing it either.

"Look, Nicky, I'm still interested in her," Tommy added.

Hawk wanted to tell him to go for it, but the words got stuck in his throat. "You mean, you slept with her?"

Tommy raked his fingers through his hair, tucked a chunk behind his ear. "Shit happens, you know? If you guys were together, I wouldn't have said anything, but—" he smiled— "you're just friends."

The bridesmaid Hawk escorted down the aisle hurried over. "Hi, Hawk." She curled her fingers around his bicep and smiled up at him. "Can I get another escort?"

Hawk's smile made her flush. "This is my cousin, Tommy," Hawk said.

"How's it going?" Tommy asked.

"Hey! Aren't you having the best time?" The bridesmaid slid her gaze back to Hawk. "I think we have to sit together."

A surge of testosterone had him wanting to find Addison. "I'm not sitting at the head table."

"Dang. Save me a dance." The bridesmaid scooted into the crowd.

Tommy's smile grew bigger. "I can hang with Addison if you want to spend time with—"

"No." The biting edge in Hawk's tone was too intense.

Take it down a few.

He swept the room. Addison stood alone on the other side of the tent.

"I'll talk to you, babe." Without waiting for Tommy's response, Hawk took off toward his date.

Frustration coursed through him. He and Addison were work partners who'd become close friends. Never one to get jealous, he hated knowing that his cousin had been intimate with her.

Fucking hated it.

It wasn't his business. He shouldn't care... but he did.

After pulling the pack of cigarettes from his pocket, he tapped one out, and lit up. One long draw didn't take the damn edge off. As he made his way over, he checked her out.

She's rocking that dress.

Pulling to a stop inches away, he peered into her eyes. "Hey."

Addison regarded him for an extra beat. "What's wrong?"

She knows me well.

"All good," he bit out. "We're at table two."

He took another drag, then a few steps. He glanced over. No Addison. She hadn't moved, her hands hitched on her hips, her eyebrows jutting into her forehead.

On a growl, he walked back over. "What?"

"What is up with you?"

"I told my cousin, Tommy, I'd get him on the list for Lost Souls."

"Okay," she replied. "So?"

"I told him you owned the club."

"Whatever," she deadpanned.

He couldn't read her. Was she annoyed with him? Did she care that Tommy was coming to her club? Did she want to see him again? He didn't have a fucking clue.

They meandered through the maze of tables in a stilted silence, the frustration morphing into agitation. He knew she'd been with his cousin. Should he come clean or forget it?

Based on her chill reaction, she wasn't gonna tell him. And for reasons he couldn't understand, he hated that even more.

5

THE KISS

Prescott, Grandmom, and Granddad were chatting away at table two. After stomping out the cigarette, Hawk pulled out Addison's chair, unable to shake the image of her with his cousin. What costume had she worn? The renaissance bar wench? What about her slutty cheerleader costume? Or maybe the dominatrix outfit? He'd seen her in several at the club. What he hadn't seen was her *out* of them.

His chest tightened.

After she sat, his Granddad's thick cough snagged his attention. Granddad was sweating pretty good too. Neither of them had any water. "Granddad, take off your suit jacket. It's hot as hell in here." Rather than wait, he helped him out of his jacket.

"Thank you, Nicky."

"I'll get us water." Hawk went in search of a wait person and found two talking nearby.

"Can I get chilled waters for table two?"

"Sure," said one of the catering staff. "Be right over."

Hawk returned to the table.

Grandmom smiled. "You take good care of us, Nicky."

The server walked over with a single glass of water.

Ah, for fuck's sake.

"Who needs this?" asked the server.

Tommy pulled out the empty chair next to Prescott and eased down.

Hawk's rumbling growl had Addison craning to look at him. "I need six waters," Hawk bit out. "*Six.*"

"No problem." The attendant started to leave, but Hawk stepped in front of him, dwarfing him in stature. "I'll take that one."

Hawk set the water goblet in front of his grandfather.

Granddad drank half, then slid the glass to Grandmom. "For you, lovey."

As she drained the glass, Hawk locked eyes with Addison. His grandparents shared everything, they looked out for each other. They were each other's entire world. That was the kind of relationship he wanted, but would never have.

Addison's lips curved upward, before she turned toward Grandmom. "How'd your vegetable garden turn out?"

"Oh, I'm so glad you reminded me," Grandmom replied. "I have two big basketfuls of tomatoes. After the reception, you can help me pass them out."

Addison smiled. "I'd love to, but I'm going to save a few for myself."

"You better," Grandmom said and patted Addison's hand.

The server returned with a tray of waters. After he set each of them down, Hawk pushed out of his chair, slipped a folded bill into the guy's hand. "Thanks for taking good care of us."

The man smiled. "I appreciate it. I'll keep those waters coming."

Though irritated, Hawk nodded. He shouldn't have to tip a guy to do his damn job. "I'll take a champagne." He eyed the group. "Champagne?"

"Granddad and I will share a glass," Grandmom replied.

Everyone else wanted bubbly too.

The server nodded. "Be right back."

Conversations resumed, and Hawk forced himself to calm the hell down. So what if Addison had hooked up with his cousin? She hadn't known it *was* his cousin and it was none of his business anyway. He shouldn't care who she slept with.

Only he did. And he didn't like that it had been with Tommy.

After lunch was served, the band leader called the newlyweds up for their first dance.

"So romantic," Addison murmured.

Hawk slid his gaze to her as she watched his sister and Lamar share their first dance as husband and wife. Truth was, he'd always been attracted to Addison, but they worked together. He had one rule. No sex with anyone at ALPHA or at his company.

She returned his gaze, and the intensity in her eyes had him wanting more.

When the song ended, the band invited the wedding party to join them.

Hawk pressed his mouth to Addison's ear. "Dance with me."

He loved her scent. A mix of shampoo and vanilla... and Addison.

She hitched a brow. "Do I have to?"

"Smart ass."

On the way to the dance floor, he clasped her hand. Her fingers were small and silky smooth, her nails long. Once there, he pulled her into his arms. Rather than thread hers around his neck, she rested her fingers on his shoulders. Too much damn space separated them.

"What's up with you?" Addison whispered. "Why are you angry?"

"Tommy is interested in you."

Up went her eyebrows. "How do you know that?"

"He told me."

Muscles running down her back tightened. It was subtle, but he felt them go taut. Rather than respond, she started humming along to the familiar tune.

"Are you gonna make me ask?" Annoyance punctuated his words.

"Ask what?" she quipped.

"Are you going out with him?"

Her right eyebrow arched. "No."

More silence.

"Good," he murmured.

Slowly, she lifted her chin. The second her gaze met his, their connection was immediate and powerful.

The song ended. The guests started applauding while Hawk and Addison stood there staring into each other's eyes, the energy whizzing around them.

She shook her head, let him go, and marched back toward their table.

Ah, fuck.

In a few strides, he caught up with her, wrapped his hand around her arm and guided her over to the side, away from the tables. "You can do better than him."

"Seriously?" she asked.

"Yeah, I'm not joking."

A growl shot out of her and she narrowed her gaze. "Stay out of my business," she warned.

Addison loved hanging with Hawk's family. They were so many of them and they were a lot of fun. They were nothing like her own small, fragmented family.

At the moment, though, she was not happy with Hawk.

Why should he care if she went out with his cousin? It's not like *they* were going out.

She'd agreed to go to the wedding because she and Hawk had the best time together. They were always laughing and joking. On a mission, they had each other's back. The relationship they'd built outside of work only strengthened their bond at work. But his territorial behavior was pissing her the hell off. She owed him nothing when it came to his cousin and she couldn't understand why he'd even care.

She returned to their table and struck up a convo with Prescott, who'd been gone for weeks. She had a zillion questions about his mission, but she couldn't talk shop. So, they chatted about the weather and current events. Anything and everything that she could think of because she just wanted neutral.

Hawk was eyeing her like she needed a bodyguard and Tommy was leering at her like he could pounce at any moment.

Lunch was served. She'd pre-selected the fish. Hawk had gotten the chicken.

"Addison," he said.

She acknowledged him, but she did not smile.

"Try this." He held out his fork. "It's got a little heat, just the way you like it."

She eyed the utensil.

He shot her an encouraging smile. "Go on."

She opened her mouth, he slid the fork in. She pulled off the morsel and chewed. He was right. It was prepared exactly how she liked it. "It's good."

"You want half?"

They shared their entrees when they went out to eat.

"Salmon?" she asked.

"Bring it."

She forked off the flaky meat and fed him. His gaze never

left hers while he pulled it off the fork. After swallowing, he said, "Nice."

They each sliced off a portion of their protein and moved it to the other's plate. When he placed his hand on her upper back and offered a gentle caress, relief coursed through her.

Back on track, she smiled. Now, he was acting normal.

After lunch, and more dancing, the newlyweds cut the cake and fed each other. Lamar threatened to smear frosting all over Kerri's mouth. Instead, he gave her a small bite, followed by a tender kiss.

Addison was the first to admit she was a romance junkie. She felt eyes on her and turned. Hawk was studying her intently.

"They're cute, aren't they?" he murmured.

"He's so romantic," she whispered. "I love that."

The cake was sliced and delivered, along with piping hot cups of coffee.

Hawk must've slipped a hefty bill to their server because Addison had never been so hydrated in her life. Water goblets always filled and enough coffee to keep them charged through the weekend.

Despite the cold air being blown into the tent, the sweltering July heat and humidity had managed to work its way inside. The hot coffee had to be abandoned for icy-cold water, the condensation running down the slippery glass.

At just after six, the band announced the newlyweds were heading out. Bridesmaids flitted from table to table handing out satchels of dried flowers. As guests began forming a line that stretched from inside the tent toward the farmhouse, Hawk asked his grandparents if they needed an assist.

"We're slow," Grandmom said exiting her chair, "but we'll get there."

"What can we do to help you?" Hawk asked.

Addison loved how attentive he was toward them.

"There is one thing," Granddad replied. "With everything going on here with the wedding, I forgot to collect the eggs the past couple of days."

Hawk regarded Addison. "Come with me."

Though she'd never let on, she loved his bossy side. "To the henhouse," she said, pushing out of her chair.

Hawk rose. "You still got cartons in there?"

"Of course," Grandmom replied. "Bring the eggs into the kitchen and we'll give them away."

"And the tomatoes," Addison reminded her.

"Yes!" Granddad shouted. "There are dozens of 'em."

Hawk regarded Prescott and Tommy. "You guys going back to the house?"

Prescott pushed out of the chair. "I'm taking off in a few. I'll talk to you tomorrow." The brothers hugged it out.

"You're a sweaty mess," Prescott said.

"No shit. Who the hell gets married outside in July?"

Prescott tossed a nod at Addison. "Wanna catch up this week?"

She nodded. "I'll text you."

Tommy stood. "Good seeing you, cuz." He offered his fist and Hawk fist-bumped him back. Then, he slid his gaze to her. "Bye, Addison."

"See ya." After grabbing her small handbag, she and Hawk made their way toward the exit.

At six-fifteen, the intense heat of the day had inched its way into a more tolerable range, but when Hawk placed his hand on the small of her back, the heat from his palm sent her temperature soaring. His hand was large and warm, but it was the gentle way he touched her that made her heart skip a beat.

"You left the bag of dried flowers," he said.

"Yeah, I'd rather go see the chickens."

"How come?"

"The wedding was beautiful," she said. "The reception was

fun. Hot, but fun. Food was good and I love hanging with your grandparents. I'm just not into throwing things at people."

He laughed. "What about the dancing? You didn't mention that."

"Who'd I dance with again?"

He draped his arm over her shoulder. "I'm sure that bridesmaid wouldn't have forgotten me."

"Probably not, but come tomorrow, you would have forgotten all about her."

He stopped in front of the henhouse, flicked his gaze in her direction. "You're right. I would have."

After opening the door, waited for her to step inside. Once she did, he followed. The blast of chilly air was a welcomed reprieve.

The chickens, startled by their late-day arrival, started clucking and squawking.

"Relax, chicks," Hawk said before turning to Addison. "This is how cold the reception shoulda been."

"Ah, c'mon, women love seeing men dripping with animal magnetism. On the right guy, it's super sexy."

"Seriously?"

Addison picked up a basket. "Yes, but it's hard to look sexy soaking wet at a wedding."

"Did I ruin my reputation?" He collected a basket and moved to the other end of the henhouse.

"Depends on how many women you've slept with."

"In general, or today?"

"Today, Hawk."

"Well, all of 'em."

She laughed. "Then your playboy reputation is still intact." Moving slowly, so as not to frighten the first chicken, she reached in and collected the first of four eggs.

"Hello, pretty, can I have that?" She placed the egg in the basket, then scooped the other three, one at a time.

The next chicken wouldn't budge, so she nudged it a little and it moved away. She collected those eggs, pausing to stare at one of them. "This one is covered in freckles. This one is super light, and these are darker. All these shells are just a little different, like people, yet they're all the same on the inside. Maybe my life would have been easier if I'd been a farmer instead of an assassin."

"Farmers work their asses off."

"I wouldn't have minded. It definitely would have been a less-violent life."

"Not if you had to kill an animal."

"Well, I'd be killing it to put it out of its misery or to eat it," she replied as she walked to the next coop. When she reached inside, the chicken pecked at her hand. "Hey! You need to learn some manners, missy!" She stared at her finger.

In an instant, Hawk was by her side. "Babe, you know Henrietta is aggressive."

"I didn't notice it was her. I was focused on the eggs."

He took her hand, examined her fingertip. "I'm sorry, Ms. Skye, but we need to amputate your hand with a meat cleaver."

"Idiot." When she went to tug her hand away, he pressed her finger to his lips, dropped a soft kiss on it.

Then, everything went into slow motion. Her gaze jumped to his mouth. His lips were full and soft, his entire being focused on the small red mark on her finger. His tanned face, flawless skin, and eyes the color of a tropical ocean were even more breathtaking up close.

"Better?" he murmured, those beautiful turquoise pools drilling into hers.

"No, it's throbbing a little."

She wasn't talking about her finger.

He kissed her digit again, only this time, his gaze stayed locked on hers. Then, he ran the tip of his tongue over her skin.

A coo floated out of her, hovering in the air between them. She hoped he hadn't heard.

One more tender kiss to her injury before he placed her hand against his cheek. Heat burned its way up her arm. A groan threatened to escape, but she swallowed hard.

His expanding pupils, black as midnight, had blanketed his light eyes. Her breath hitched.

Then, his mouth found hers. Her eyes fluttered closed on a groan, which had him deepening the embrace. Her body roared to life, the intensity of his tongue on hers jump-starting her insides, her body yearning for his.

He nibbled her lip, then slid his tongue back inside her welcoming mouth. Rather than increase his speed, he took his time, teasing her tongue with his. His other hand slithered around her waist and he pulled her close. Unable to control the need coursing through her, she thrust her tongue hard against his. The kiss turned brutal. Biting, pawing, grinding bodies unable or unwilling to stop. The noises coming out of them were foreign to her ears.

Her gritty growl had him devouring her while she pressed herself flush against him. His long, thick hardness pushed against her abs.

His breathing had shifted. It was subtle, but she heard it, felt his warm breath coming faster on her cheeks.

She was spiraling, losing control, her body thrumming with lust. Then, reality smacked her hard and she ended the kiss. But she couldn't break away. Her hand was no longer on his cheek. She'd buried it in his beautiful, thick head of hair. His palm was now glued to her ass.

"Ohmygod, what the hell was that?" she whispered between gasps.

She inhaled a deep breath, but it didn't help. She was on fire, her body burning with unrelenting desire. That kiss—*his kiss*—had slayed her.

She did *not* want to separate from him. Being in his arms felt phenomenal. With little more effort, he could shatter her into a million pieces.

When he kissed her, he owned her. Fully and completely. The only thing that mattered was the sinfully beautiful man in her arms. She was melting from the intensity of their embrace. He was a ravenous lion, and she... his willing prey.

Normally in total control, her heart was pounding away in her chest. Her pulse hadn't risen above eighty during the entire ALPHA retreat. Right now, it was hammering away like a hummingbird.

"Just a kiss." His gravelly voice shot straight to the wet space between her legs.

Not 'just a kiss'. He kissed me because he knows.

His cousin had blabbed. That idiot couldn't stay quiet and keep their hookups to himself.

That was *not* Hawk's business, but he was making it his by jumping into the mix with his machismo crap and alpha tendencies. Why else would he kiss her?

Frustration trumped lust. She wasn't going to discuss Tommy with him and she didn't care that he knew. Exhaling a harrumph, she glared at him. Though she couldn't deny he was a fantastic kisser, she wasn't going to throw away an amazing friendship because he was jealous over nothing. His imagination had probably gone off the rails about something she hadn't even thought twice about.

This is why I'm not in a relationship.

She pushed away from him, steeled her spine, and forced herself to get it together. "Let's finish collecting the eggs."

As he held her gaze, a growl shot out of him.

Breaking their connection, she eyed Henrietta with determination. After a little coaxing, the hen moved away and Addison transferred her eggs to the basket.

Once all the eggs had been collected, she lined up cartons

and started filling them. She could have been ambivalent about their kiss, but she wasn't. She could have been curious, too.

Instead, she was seething.

Who the hell does he think he is? We have the best relationship. Why screw it up by kissing me?

After filling the first egg carton, movement caught her eye. Hawk had opened the henhouse door and was leaning against the doorframe smoking.

"Put that out and help me," she hissed.

With the lit cigarette dangling from his luscious lower lip, he sauntered over. The tension rolling off him only further pissed her her. In all the time they'd been friends, they'd never had any problems. Not a single one.

One kiss later, and they weren't even speaking to each other.

They filled the cartons in a biting silence and left. The chip on his shoulder hovering like an angry storm cloud.

She owed him no explanation. *He* never discussed *his* hookups. Over the years, she'd introduced him to a couple of her friends or acquaintances. She didn't know if he screwed them, and she didn't much care either.

Later that evening, he'd probably meet some random woman. A stranger would fuck the fury out of him and he'd be satisfied. Sadness settled into her soul. She didn't want that person taking that from him. She wanted to do that for him... and with him. She wanted to be the one who riled him to orgasm, then snuggled him to sleep.

Stop it.

Shaking away the thought, she pulled him to a stop at the foot of the farmhouse porch steps. "Hey, are we okay?"

"You tell me," he growled.

She waited, hoping he'd confirm her suspicions. Instead of clearing the air, he said nothing. Wild blue-green eyes pinned her in a heated gaze.

On a huff, she charged up the steps, opened the front door.

Before going inside, she turned back. He hadn't moved, the cigarette smoke obscuring him in thick fog.

If they couldn't get past this, their friendship would suffer. While that would wreck her, it wouldn't break her. She'd been abandoned before and it had only made her stronger.

But losing Hawk would hurt. It would hurt a lot.

6

LOST SOULS

An hour later, Hawk pulled into the driveway of Addison's Arlington home. The ride had been as frosty as the reception *should* have been. She'd pulled up a playlist and the music had filled the silence. He'd lowered the roof of his Mercedes. She'd pulled her hair into a ponytail. Actions that were familiar to them. Only the cold silence was new.

She got out, shut the door. "Thanks for bringing me to Kerri's wedding. I had fun."

"Don't forget your tomatoes," he said. "And take the eggs."

Instead of grabbing the bag and the carton, she just glared at him.

Her fuming gaze was having the opposite effect. An angry Addison was hot as hell.

"The next time Henrietta pecks my finger, don't kiss me." With an attitude that screamed "fuck off", she strode up her walkway, stood in front of the scanner, then vanished inside.

Sex with Addison Skye was a bad, bad idea. But, after that scorching kiss, it was the *only* thing he wanted.

Hawk drove home, went inside. After showering, he dressed in tattered jeans and a black T-shirt, ran his fingers through his damp hair, and was out the door. Twenty minutes later, he pulled into the parking lot, found a spot out back. He collected two bags of tomatoes, strode to the front door of Lost Souls, bypassing the long line that wrapped the side of the building.

No fucking way am I standing in that.

"Heyo, my man," called out a clubber. "You gotta wait in line like everyone else."

Ignoring him, Hawk continued toward the front door, until a different dude stepped out of line, blocking him from passing. "Where you going?"

"I'll give you three guesses." Hawk was not in the mood.

The guy cracked his knuckles. "Don't make me hit you."

Hawk laughed. This man had no idea what he was capable of.

"Are you fucking laughing at me? Get in line, bitch." The guy's tone had turned gruff.

"No."

The guy's arm flew back. As it launched forward, Hawk blocked it, then kicked him in the solar plexus, all without dropping the tomatoes. The guy gasped for breath as the bouncer jogged over.

"What's going on, Hawk?" the bouncer asked.

"Hey, Tony, I've got a meeting with Liv. Dude told me to wait in line. He tried to hit me, so I stopped him."

The bouncer bit back a smile before eyeing the member. "You okay, man?"

The man had gotten his breath back, but he was glaring at Hawk. "I'm gonna sue you."

Hawk got up in his face, stared down at him. "Enjoy your evening. Don't bother coming back. You just lost your membership."

"Who the fuck are you?" the guy yelled.

"The new owner." Hawk flicked his gaze to the bouncer.

"Handle this." He walked to the front door, yanked it open, and went inside.

Lost Souls was *the* place to be for cosplay in the DMV—the District, Maryland, Virginia. At the hostess stand, he held his phone under the scanner. The light turned green, but the hostess asked to see what was in the bags.

"Tomatoes." He showed her.

With a smile, she waved him through, and he set off into the crowd, thick with costumed people.

Good for biz.

He swung by the bar, caught the bartender's attention. She was an attractive woman—taller than average—with dark hair, dark eyes, and a warm smile. Addison and Liv had hired her a few months back, when their head bartender had quit. So far, so good.

"Hey, Hawk," she said. "What can I get you?"

"A bottle of champagne."

She rattled off two brands. Neither were top shelf, but it didn't matter. He selected one, along with a small bottle of sparkling water.

"Four glasses," he added.

She smiled. "Someone's celebrating. I'll have one of the servers bring them over to you."

As he bulled his way through the throng of clubbers, he heard, "Yo, Hawk!" Jericho waved him over. He and Liv were sitting at a four-top tucked in the corner.

After setting the bags on the table, he eased down. "From the farm."

Liv peeked into one of them. "I'll take a bag."

"Is Addison meeting us?" Hawk asked.

"That's the plan," Liv replied. "Is this one for her?"

"Yup," Hawk bit out. "She here?"

"Not yet." Liv studied him. "You okay?"

"Never fuckin' better," Hawk replied.

"What crawled up *your* ass and died?" Jericho asked.

A server appeared with the champagne, a small bottle of sparkling water, and four flutes. "Do you want me to open these?"

"We got it, babe," Hawk replied. After the server left, he eyed Liv's expanding tummy. "Can't fit in a booth, can ya?"

Jericho and Liv laughed. "No, I can't," she replied.

"How's 'lil Savage doing?" Hawk asked.

While Jericho and Liv knew the gender of their baby, they were keeping it a secret.

"Baby's great, but my body has been taken over by an alien."

A familiar emptiness churned through him. Ignoring it, Hawk pushed on. "You're, what, seven months?"

Liv beamed. "Eight."

"You feel good?" he asked.

"I feel *fantastic*," Jericho replied.

Hawk and Liv laughed.

"I'm doing great," she said. "A little tired, but only because I'm so busy. Speaking of busy, I'm gonna print the bill of sale."

As Liv pushed herself up, Jericho stood, and moved the chair out of her way. She leaned up and kissed his cheek. "See you boys soon." She vanished down the hallway toward the office she shared with Addison.

Jericho sat, shifted his sights to Hawk. "How was Kerri's wedding?"

"Nice. Hot as hell. The AC units in the tent weren't getting the job done."

Jericho drained the beer from his glass. "You didn't answer my question. What'd goin' on with you?"

"Nothing."

"I hate when you lie to me."

"Nothing worth mentioning."

"It's me you're talking to."

"I got pissed at Addison, so I kissed her."

Jericho chuckled. "That's one way to handle it. And?"

"It's complicated."

"You two are damn good together," Jericho said.

"No shit," Hawk replied. "I gotta make it right."

"Why?"

"Now she's madder than hell at me for kissing her."

Addison parked in her spot at Lost Souls. As she exited her car, her phone rang with a call from Ronald Jenning.

She answered. "Hey, Ronald, what a surprise."

"How's my favorite CIA case officer?" he asked.

She laughed. "It's good to hear from you. How are you?"

"Life is crazy, but good. We just moved, so the new house is all about finding our way around the boxes. Becky's doing great. Kids are getting big. They really want a dog, but we're holding out on that one."

"Congrats on the move," Addison said.

"I'm flying to DC this week for a bunch of meetings. You got time for lunch on Tuesday?"

"I'd love that," she replied. "It'll be fun to catch up."

"Looking forward to it." Ronald ended the call.

Ronald Jenning was the Navy SEAL who took out Abdel Haqazzii, the terrorist she'd been hunting down during the two years she lived in the middle east. She and the DEVGRU triggerman started working together once her team was confident they'd located Haqazzii's compound. From the beginning, they both had the same objective... eliminate one of the most wanted terrorists in the world.

After that mission had ended, she returned to the US. Transitioning back to her life in the states had been harder than she'd anticipated. Ronald and his wife, Becky, had invited her over for dinner on several occasions. They helped with that transition, and she'd always been grateful to them for that. When Ronald moved on to Naval intelligence, he stayed in the DMV. His most recent assignment had taken him and his family out of the area. She'd never forgotten their kindness toward her.

She slid her phone into her bag, said "hey" to Tony the bouncer, and stepped into the fun world of make-believe. The techno-beat swept her away, the low-lit lighting created a sexy vibe, and the array of creative costumes kept her entertained for hours.

This was her playground, and she loved it.

What she didn't love was that she hadn't had a moment to play in it. Not once, since she and Liv had opened the club, had she invited anyone upstairs into one of the private suites. She'd received Invitations to Escape, but she'd declined all of them. One of the guys had creeped her out. She had her suspicions another was married. A few invitations had been from women. She was into men, so she'd passed on those, too.

She loved owning and running the club, but she wouldn't mind taking an hour or two and escaping into her own naughty imagination... with a playmate.

Hawk and that searing kiss popped into her thoughts. That should *never* have happened. His mouth on hers, his arms around her, his hardness pressing against her had sent her pulse into the stratosphere. That one kiss had reminded her that all work and no play made her grumpy as hell.

As she headed toward the bar, several members said "hello" or shot her a friendly wave. She stepped behind the bar to check in with her head bartender.

"Hey, Liliana, how's it going?" Addison asked.

Liliana shot her a warm smile. "Welcome back. How was your business trip?"

Liliana Moore had been working there for three months, one month as head bartender. She was reliable, friendly, and quick at slinging drinks. She never dressed in costume, but always wore a crisp shirt—either white or black—and black pants.

"Lots of boring meetings," Addison lied. "What's been happening here?"

"Smooth sailing, except we haven't signed up many new members." Liliana replied. "I don't have the gift of gab like you."

"I'll focus on that after my meeting."

Liliana glanced at her outfit. She'd worn a peasant blouse, shorts, and four-inch stilettos.

"No costume?" Liliana asked.

"Not tonight."

With a nod, Liliana waited on a customer.

After pouring herself a half glass of red wine, Addison made her way around the dance floor—filled with costumed clubbers—and down the hall toward her office. She stood in front of the scanner, the light flicked to green, and she entered the cozy space.

Liv was typing away on the keyboard, her very large baby bump catching Addison's full attention.

"Hey!" Liv pushed herself out of the chair.

"Hey, mama!" Addison hurried around the desk and hugged her cousin. "You got so much bigger in just one week."

"I know. My body has been invaded by 'lil Savage. I missed you. How are you? I heard the week was crazy intense."

Addison raised the wine glass. "Hopefully this takes the edge off."

Liv laughed as she got comfortable on their second-hand sofa. "Come sit with me."

After Addison joined her, Liv ran her hand over her large belly. "The baby's kicking." She took Addison's hand and placed it on her abdomen.

Addison smiled. Ever since Liv and Jericho had

announced their baby news, she'd loved seeing how their life was changing, and how their love for each other continued to grow.

"That baby is definitely ready to come out," Addison said. "Wow, that's one strong leg."

Liv was beaming, and Addison delighted in seeing her cousin this happy.

Addison sipped the wine. "I thought Jericho would be here with you."

"He's hanging out there."

"How are you doing?" Addison asked.

"I'm good. Work's keeping me busy. The nursery is all done, in both houses. One more month until the big day, then, I'm *really* gonna be busy." She looked around, then started to get up.

"What do you need?" Addison asked.

"My phone. It's on the desk."

After Addison handed it to her, Liv sent a quick text. "I can't believe I haven't asked you this, but Jericho and I would love for you to be the baby's godmother."

"I'd love that," Addison said with a smile. "Thank you. Who's the Godfather?"

"Jericho hates having to pick one friend over the other, but he finally made up his mind." Liv's smile fell away. "I have one more thing to tell you. I've been putting this off because I wish I didn't have to say this."

She studied Liv's face. "Are you okay?"

"Totally fine, just a little sad. Do you remember when I told you I was thinking of selling my half of the club?"

Addison heart dropped. She loved co-running Lost Souls with her cousin. It had been *their* baby from the beginning. "You sold your half."

"I have a buyer, but I want you to feel totally comfortable before I accept the offer. I was concerned about selling to a stranger or to someone who would want to change things up. Anyway, I want you to—"

Knock-knock-knock.

Addison rose and opened the door. Her heart jumped into her throat. Hawk stood there, his wicked-hot gaze drilling into her. He'd changed into a black T-shirt that stretched against his taut muscles and tattered jeans that hugged his massive thighs. Jericho stood beside him.

She flicked her gaze from one to the other.

"Come on in," Liv called from the sofa.

Addison's brain kicked back on as Hawk squeezed by. His just-showered scent surrounded her and she breathed him in.

He cleans up so good.

With a tray in hand, Jericho walked in, shut the door behind him. On it was a small bottle of sparkling water and four flutes.

Hawk set a bottle of champagne on the desk, held out a brown paper bag. With a gleam in his eyes, he said to Addison, "You forgot your tomatoes."

Somehow, he made that sound deliciously dirty.

She flicked her gaze to the champagne. "What are we celebrating?"

The second she uttered those words, she knew.

No, no freaking way.

Hawk was Liv's potential buyer. When she slid her gaze to him, he was waiting. Before today, she would have jumped up and down with excitement. Now, her feet were firmly planted on the floor.

"I heard you kicked some serious ass during the mission," Jericho said.

"Mission?" Addison mumbled, her gaze cemented on Hawk.

This cannot—cannot—be happening.

If he couldn't handle her hookups with his cousin—which

happened months ago—their friendship would never survive any Invitations to Escape.

"Yeah," Jericho replied. "You, Hawk, the chopper, the beach."

"Right," Addison said. "Yeah, good. Good mission."

Jericho and Liv exchanged glances.

"Addison," Liv began, "Jericho mentioned to the guys that I was thinking of selling."

"Uh-huh," Addison bleated.

"Hawk said he was interested in partnering with you," Jericho said. "His off-tune singing aside, he'd make a great business partner."

As Liv chatted away, she held up a what looked like a contract, then continued talking. When she finished, Hawk popped the champagne cork. She hadn't heard a word Liv had said. Not one single word.

"You drinking?" Hawk asked Jericho.

"Hell, yeah," Addison blurted.

"You driving, babe?" Jericho asked Liv.

Liv nodded.

Jericho raised the flute. "Fill her up."

Hawk filled three flutes with bubbly while Jericho poured sparkling water for Liv.

Hawk held out a flute. As she took it, he said, "I want to buy Liv's half. You wanna talk about it or are you good with it?"

Addison couldn't decide if she wanted to chug the champagne from the bottle or throw up the few sips of wine she'd already drunk.

Silence.

Liv pushed off the sofa. "We'll give you two a minute. I'm taking my sexy husband onto the dance floor and having some pregnant fun with him."

Jericho clasped his wife's hand. "Come on, 'lil Savage, let's dance with mama."

They shut the door behind them.

Alone with Hawk.

Normally, that would be cool. She'd been alone with him dozens and dozens of times. Her gaze met his. Warmth travelled from her chest, up her neck to her cheeks. She took a mouthful of champagne. Down the hatch it went.

"If today hadn't happened," she began, "I would have already signed the contract, but we got derailed... over nothing. We gotta clear the air if we're gonna own a business together."

Hawk sat on the sofa. She sat beside him, leaned back, crossed her legs. He glanced at her thighs, then jumped his gaze back into her eyes.

"You go first," she said, hoping he'd come clean about her hookup with Tommy.

"That kiss should never have happened," he said.

Strangely, her heart broke. While she should have rejoiced with a fist pump and a hug, then thanked him for coming to his senses, her throat tightened, the emotion burbling to the surface.

"What kiss?" She forced a laugh, but it felt fake. "Is that it?" She hated that he was withholding something from her, but she was doing the same damn thing to him.

Except that her sexual history was none of his business. Furthermore, she didn't care about the hookup. Ancient history.

But he did, or he wouldn't have cornered her in the henhouse.

Maybe he no longer cared that she'd been with his cousin, but it had triggered a chain of events that had brought them to this tense moment.

"What else is there?" he pushed back.

She repositioned on the sofa, sipped the champagne, hoping he'd come clean. She was met with more silence.

Now, *she* had a reason to be angry. He was lying to her. How was that going to help this partnership? Worse… this could hurt them in ALPHA. They trusted each other. How could she trust him knowing he wasn't being honest with her?

Pushing off the sofa, she scanned the contract. It was a straightforward document, already signed by Liv, transferring ownership to Hawk. She pulled a pen off the desk and started signing. When finished, she handed him the pen.

He countersigned.

This should have been a moment of celebration. They were taking their friendship to the next level. Going forward, they were business partners. Sadly, her heart felt empty. She was more disconnected from him than ever before.

So much for full disclosure.

When he finished signing, he left the contract on the desk. "Well, partner, how do you want to kick off our first night together?"

Addison could think of a few ways. They had nothing to do with business and everything to do with the private suites upstairs.

If she thought the name of the club—Lost Souls—was apropos before, it most definitely was now.

7

PROVING HER POINT

Hawk would have pulled Addison into his arms and hugged her, but their stilted conversation had him thrusting out his hand.

"Looking forward to partnering with you, babe," he said.

"Welcome to Lost Souls." She hadn't smiled. Not even once.

In truth, he hadn't regretted kissing her, but he wanted to push past it and get them back on solid footing.

"What do you normally do when you're here?" he asked.

"Anything and everything," she replied. "Interview a prospective new hire, order supplies or alcohol. Spot-check the suites to make sure they're clean. Mostly, I try to sign up new members. Liv and I took out pretty substantial loans, so the faster I can turn the bottom line from red to black, the happier I'll be."

I could wipe out her debt with one quick payment.

But he wasn't going to offer that. Addison was an independent business owner who could manage her own finances.

"When do you kick back? Relax? Dance?" He finished his glass of champagne.

That actually made her lips curve. "Ever since opening the

club, I've done nothing but work. I'm not complaining, it's just that I thought I'd have more down time." She held his gaze for an extra beat.

"What about the... what are you calling them?"

"Invitations to Escape." She sipped the champagne. "I've gotten a few invitations, but I wasn't interested." She finished the glass, then held up what was left in the bottle.

He declined, so she set it down.

"I'd offer to give you a tour, but you've probably already seen the suites."

He shook his head. "Never been upstairs."

She furrowed her brow. "Sure, you have."

"No."

This time, she didn't hide her surprise, her eyebrows jutting into her forehead. "What do you do when you come here?"

"Upgrades for the security and surveillance systems I installed for you. If my boys are here, I'm out there talking to them."

"I'll take you on a tour when we close."

He nodded, once. "What are we doing now?"

"Signing up new members."

"We'll do it together," he said, fully aware of how that sounded.

The air turned electric.

The desire to pull her close and kiss her again had him scraping his fingers down his whiskered face. Breaking eye contact, she turned and left the room.

After telling Liv and Jericho they'd be running the club together, they walked them out.

"I've been meaning to ask if you'd be the baby's godfather," Jericho said in the parking lot.

Hawk stilled. All eyes on him while they waited for him to say yes. He wanted to, but he couldn't get the word out. Instead, his chest tightened, the ache so familiar and raw all these years later.

"You don't have to do it," Jericho said.

Hawk forced a smile. "Of course, I will. You know I never say no to my guys."

Jericho pulled him in for a bro-hug. "That's great."

"I'm honored."

"And the best part," Liv added, "is that Addison is the baby's godmother."

When she shifted toward him, he couldn't look away. This should have been another celebration, but the fire in her eyes had him convinced she was still fuming over their kiss.

After saying their goodbyes, Jericho and Liv left.

When he regarded Addison, she was waiting. "You know, you don't have to do God stuff with the baby."

"I don't have an issue with doing God stuff," he replied.

"Well, you looked like you didn't want to do it. Don't you like babies?"

He loved babies, loved kids. He threw his arm over her shoulder. "It's all good. Let's go sign up those members."

Back in their office, he reprogrammed the security system he'd installed, giving himself access to everything. She collected a tablet and they left, shutting the door behind him.

After spending over an hour chatting with prospective members and signing up a few, Hawk needed a damn break. This was starting to feel like work. He worked his ass off at his company *and* at ALPHA. Enough was enough.

The song pounding through the speakers ended, and a slow one started.

"Time to chill," he said.

"Now?" she replied.

"Right now." He threaded his fingers through hers and led her onto the dance floor, slipped his arms around her waist, pulled her close, and waited.

Same as the wedding, she placed her hands on his shoulders, as if she were going to push him away.

Not gonna cut it, not this time.

"I won't bite you."

"No, but you might kiss me."

"Relax, woman, that's not happening." He hugged her close. "We're just celebrating our new partnership."

She wrapped her arms around his neck as they started swaying and moving to the sensual beat. The vibe was chill. As he held her in his arms, he thought about their sexy kiss. Then, his imagination jumped to their naked bodies moving as one, his on hers, while they *really* got to know each other.

"Yo, there's the motherfucker who knocked the wind outta me," the guy from earlier glared over at Hawk.

Ah, fuck.

"What's he talking about?" Addison asked as the man pushed his way toward them.

Hawk's instinct was to stand in front of Addison, to block her in case the guy was gonna swing another punch. But that would be a bonehead move on his part. Addison could defend herself.

"We got into a thing outside," Hawk murmured.

Addison broke from Hawk, addressed the guy. "I'm Addison. What's your name?"

"Motherfucker."

"This is my club and I've never had a fight here," she said. "Don't ruin my streak. Can we talk outside?"

The guy glared at Hawk. "He said he owns the club."

"He's my business partner," Addison said. "I don't want to ask you to leave, so can we play nice?"

"Lemme deck him and we'll call it even," the guy replied.

Liliana had lowered the music, and a crowd had formed around them. If a fight broke out, mayhem would ensue. Someone would get hurt. The police would get called.

Hawk wanted to shut this shit down, but he wasn't gonna jump in. Addison was handling it.

She fisted her hands on her hips. "My patience is running out. Either you walk away and enjoy your evening in *my* club or I haul your ass out."

The guy laughed as he gave her the once-over. "You? Haul my ass out? You're a tiny thing, honey."

She pointed toward the front door. "You gotta go."

When the patron wouldn't move, she grabbed his arm. He yanked it away.

Hawk flicked his gaze to Addison. "Ready?"

She nodded once.

They each grabbed one of his arms and strode toward the door. He freed himself from Addison, but couldn't escape Hawk's vice grip. When the clubber went to swing at her, she blocked his punch, then swept her leg under his feet, forcing him to the floor.

Together, they picked him up and escorted him out.

"Don't come back," Addison said in the parking lot. "You aren't welcome."

"Go to hell," the guy hollered.

Back inside, Addison jumped on the bar. "Most of you have met me by now. I'm Addison and this is my club. I've got a new biz partner. That's Hawk."

He flashed a wave.

"Everyone having a good time?" she asked.

There was a mix of applause, a few hoots, but the rest just stood there, staring up at her.

"I will *not* tolerate bullshit, bullying, or anything else that's less than respectful. If you're nice and you're friendly, you're welcome here. If you aren't, get the hell out." She waited a few seconds, before she smiled at the group. "Liliana, turn that song back up! Let's party!"

She hopped down, walked over to Hawk, and said, "Dance with me."

As they resumed dancing, several members and guests swung by to let her knew they appreciated that she didn't put up with that customer's crap.

Hawk pulled her close, lowered his head, and murmured, "Nicely handled."

"We make a good team," she whispered. "Let's not fuck this up."

Addison was ready to make a point and she knew *exactly* how she was going to do it. She loved being friends with Hawk, but they'd derailed when Tommy had told him about their hook ups.

She needed to get them back on track. While her idea was out there, she had to do something.

When the last customer left, and the staff was busy cleaning up, the bouncer locked the front door. "Addison, you ready to check the suites?"

"I'll do it with her," Hawk offered.

"Hey, man, good to have you on board," Tony said. "I'm gonna take off."

Addison followed him to the front door, locking it behind him.

"You guys signed up a lot of people," Liliana said as she wiped down the bar, "after everyone settled back down."

"Yeah, that was crazy." Addison slid onto a bar stool. "What set that guy off?"

"I didn't wait in line," Hawk replied. "And I might have gotten into a thing with him."

Addison spun toward him. "You hit him?"

"Only to stop him from hitting me."

On a chuckle, Liliana finished cleaning up, then slung her bag over her shoulder. "See you Wednesday."

This time, Hawk followed her out, locking the door behind her. When he returned, he sat beside Addison at the bar. "What's her name?"

"Who?"

"The head bartender."

"Liliana Moore."

Hawk nodded. "Got it."

"Did I tell you she has the same name as my mom?"

"For real?"

"Yeah, my mom's name is Liliana and her maiden name was Moore."

"You never talk about your mom."

"Would you, if yours ran off with a cult leader?"

He gave her shoulder a gentle squeeze. "No."

"Liliana and I have a bunch of stuff in common. It's pretty cool. We both have birthdays in August. I went to GW. She's going there for grad school. And we both have older sisters who are artists."

"That's a lot."

"I know." She smiled. "We bonded, plus she's so reliable. One less thing I have to think about." She pushed off the barstool. "Ready to clear the rooms?"

"Lead the way, babe."

She stood in front of the scanner, but the light didn't change until he stepped in front. Then, it flashed green. Hawk opened the door and waited while she breezed through.

On the second floor, she stood there, staring down the hallway. "We're not alone."

He listened, but heard nothing.

"The last door on the right is closed. There are probably people in there. We'll check that one first."

Hawk reached for his Glock, but he'd left it at home.

She cracked a smile. "We're gonna ask them to leave, not shoot them."

"Habit."

As they walked past the open doors on either side of the hallway, they both glanced inside. The rooms were low-lit with different colored bulbs. She stopped in front of the closed door.

Knock-knock-knock.

"It's management," Addison said with a commanding tone. "We're closing up for the night."

No response. She knocked again. Still, nothing.

"We're coming in." She stood in front of the scanner, the light flashed green, and she opened the door.

A costumed woman was going down on a man, her sultry sounds hijacking Addison's attention. The man was sitting in the corner chair, clothed in a shirt and a cape, his pants on the floor. His eyes were closed.

"Fuck, that feels good," the guy ground out.

The live sex show was turning grumpy Addison into lust-filled Addison. As desire ripped through her, she peered over at Hawk. He slid his gaze to her. Her insides roared to life, the thought of taking him into her mouth and sucking him off had her biting back a moan.

Stop! Get it together.

Pushing out those thoughts, she refocused her attention on the couple across the room. "Hey, guys."

The man's eyes flew open. "Shit, shit."

The woman pulled off him, turned. "Did we run over again?"

Addison nodded. "Yeah."

"Can I get a minute?" the man asked. "You know, to finish?"

"You've had an extra thirty," Hawk replied. "Pull your pants on. You gotta go."

"Damn."

He rose, tugged on his pants.

"Sorry," said the woman as the couple grabbed their plastic swords and shields before brushing past them.

With Hawk by her side, Addison followed them downstairs. The clubbers left without incident and they locked the front door behind them.

"We've still gotta clear the rooms," she said before they traipsed back upstairs.

One by one, they checked the suites and their private bathrooms. In the room where the couple had been playing, the smell of sex still hovered in the air.

After clearing the bathroom, she found him staring at the wall of kink toys.

"You like using these?" he asked.

"Depends."

He lifted the nipple clamps. "What about this?"

She eyed the small metal clamps with the rubber tips. "Are you sure we should be talking about this?" Even in the dimly-lit room, she couldn't miss the hunger in his eyes.

"This is our business."

His gritty rasp captured her full attention, while another hit of adrenaline jetted through her. "It's our job to run a club, not share what turns us on, what doesn't, or any fetishes—"

"I'll go first," he said cutting her off. "I don't like blowjobs."

Her mouth dropped open. "You're kidding, right?"

"No, it's a hard pass for me."

"Well, you haven't gotten one from me," she murmured.

A growl shot out of him.

The air turned turbulent while heat shot through her.

She sashayed close and took the nipple clamps out of his hand. "I tried these, once. The pain reminded me not to get too comfortable with the pleasure. Pleasure is fleeting, but pain... pain sticks around."

She pinched the end of her finger with one of the clamps.

The discomfort was mild when compared to the sting on her tender nipple.

She flicked her gaze to his. "Hold out your finger."

When he did, she loosened the pressure, clamped it on the tip of his finger. "How's the pain?"

"None."

"Ever used these?" she prodded.

"No." His rumbling growl landed between her legs.

She removed both clamps from their fingers. "Wanna try it?"

"Are you daring me?" His voice had dropped, the grittiness making her clit throb.

"Take off your shirt," she said.

Wasn't the first time she'd dared him to do something, but it *was* the first time she'd dared him to do something sexual.

He yanked off his T-shirt, stood there bare chested. She broke eye contact to fiddle with the clamps. "I'm adjusting the pressure."

"Are you telling me I can't handle the pain?"

"Nice and easy is more my style." She dropped her gaze to his chest, then his nipples. Slowly, she ran her fingertip over his nubs. Her delicate touch ignited his need and he released another growl.

"I want your nipple wet."

Ah, fuck.

He should have put the brakes on this, but after that kiss, there was no way he was stopping her.

Leaning close, she licked his nipple, then flicked her tongue back and forth over his sensitive skin. The tease was sensational, and he hardened in his pants.

"So sexy," she whispered.

On a whisper-soft moan, she licked the other one. He loved how she took her time, running her warm tongue over his heated skin.

When she stopped, he wanted to tell her to keep going. He needed her to unleash her anger on him, to take out her frustration and passion on him. He was confident he could handle whatever she threw his way.

Slowly, she raised her head. Desire sprang from her half-hooded eyes. Her breathing had shifted. This was an Addison he had never seen before.

And she was sexy as hell.

"I'm going to clamp this on your nipple. If it's too painful, I'll remove it. Okay?"

"Yeah," his voice was raspy, the need traversing through him, his trapped cock pulsing inside his pants.

She closed the clamp over his right nipple. The pressure was light, but unrelenting.

"You okay?"

"Yes." He was mesmerized by her every movement. Everything was magnified. Her breathing roared in his ears like thunder.

She placed the second one on his left nipple. He flinched. This clamp was tighter.

"Too much?" she asked, a devilish twinkle in her eyes.

"Kiss me," he said. "I'm not asking. I'm telling."

She stood tall, pressed her lips to his and kissed him, sending waves of pleasure careening through his sex-starved body. She fastened her arms around his neck, he deepened the kiss. Her moans shot through him, and he grabbed her ass and squeezed.

The kiss went feral in seconds, the discomfort of the clamps replaced with a pent-up need that had him stroking her ass with one hand and snaking his arm around her with the other. When she bumped against the clamps, he grunted.

She broke away, removed the clamps, then unzipped his jeans. His erection turned to granite in the already tight space.

"Whoa," he bit out.

"Take off your pants."

"What—"

"I'm gonna suck you."

He should have pushed back, should have argued, but he was on fire, the lust coursing through him so hard, his balls hurt.

"You don't like blow jobs." With a confident gleam in her eyes, she said, "I'm about to change that."

He wanted her. He wanted to pleasure her, make her scream his name while she shattered into a million boneless pieces.

"*Addison.*"

She stilled from the sternness in his voice.

"You don't know what you're doing," he said.

"Yes, I do," she replied. "Do you want this or don't you?"

On another growl, he took her face in his hands and kissed her. Slow and sensual while he teased her with his tongue on her lips, then he pressed inside. She welcomed him into her mouth while she stroked his cock through his pants.

"I want *you*," he ground out. "So fucking badly."

Her breathing was erratic, and he loved the effect he was having on her. He was never one to relinquish control, but as he stared into her eyes—eyes that were so familiar to him—he wanted her to take the lead.

"Suck me," he ground out.

She helped him out of his pants and his boxer briefs, then she led him to the chair—the same chair where the guy was getting blown twenty minutes ago. She nudged him back. He sat. Mr. Johnson, stiff as steel, jutted skyward.

"Are you sure?" he asked. "Sex changes a friendship."

"Not ours. Lean back and relax, 'cause I'm gonna take real good care of you."

She tucked her long tendrils behind her ears, placed her hands on his thighs and started caressing them. The build was slow, her touch exhilarating. He studied her face as she stayed focused on his legs. Slow, gentle caresses over his aching muscles. Back and forth, up and down.

Then, she slipped her hand under his balls. His eyes drifted closed, the pleasure streaming through him. But he forced them open. This was something he did not want to miss.

"You got cooties down here?"

He smiled. "I'm clean."

She caressed his shaft, ran her fingertips across the head before leaning over and tasting him. When she placed him into her mouth, he growled, low and deep, and long.

"Mmm," she said.

Anticipation oozed out and she took him in deeper. His shaft thickened as she licked him like a lollypop, then devoured him into her mouth. He was a big boy, but she did a good job taking in most of him. Her hair had fallen over her cheek and he tucked it behind her ear.

Her eyes were closed, but when he groaned, they fluttered open. Her gaze found his. Seeing her mouth around his cock was intense. As if she sensed they were crossing a line for which there was no going back, her lips lifted at the corners, before her eyes closed.

She continued sucking and licking, the streams of euphoria pumping through him in rapid-fire succession. The overload of pleasure sent him flying high, the thrumming of his cock hijacking his senses.

He inhaled, blew out another groan. Her scent filled his soul. His empty, angry soul. She started sucking harder, her every moan sent hits of adrenaline powering through him.

When she raked her teeth over his shaft, he blurted, "Jesus, Addison, you feel so fucking good."

His raspy voice sounded foreign to him, like she'd unleashed a part of him he didn't know existed.

Her moans were coming faster, she was massaging his balls with more pressure, then, she deep throated him, taking all of him so that he pressed against the back of her throat.

"Here I go, baby," he said through gritted teeth. "Fuuu-uuuuuck."

The ecstasy shot out of him so hard, the orgasm ripped through his chest. Euphoria so intense, he ground out her name. He was breathing hard, wracked with so much pleasure, he couldn't speak. He just sat there in absolute rapture.

She slowed, lightened her touch. Then, she pulled off him, vanished into the bathroom.

What the fuck just happened?

Kneeling at his feet, she caressed his thighs. "Was that good?" Her minty breath wafted in his direction.

He opened his eyes. Her half-hooded lids were sexy as hell. He wanted her. Wanted to root himself inside her. Wanted to bring her *all* the pleasure, all night long, until she lay in his arms, fully sated and completely boneless.

"I'm not sure if you wrecked me forever or I've been reborn." He sat up. "I can't wait to watch you come. Lie on the bed."

"No."

"What do you mean *no*?"

She pushed up onto her knees, leaned close. "That was me making a point," she murmured.

He stared at her for an extra beat trying to make sense of her words. "What the hell are you talking about?"

"This was no big deal, just like my hookups with Tommy."

Reality crash-landed in the middle of his post-sex high. "Ah, for fuck's sake, Addison."

"Hookups are two people finding physical pleasure with each other. That's it. You have 'em and I don't get all weird on you."

"I don't have 'em with your relatives."

Her gaze narrowed. "I didn't know he was your cousin, but who cares if I did? You kissed me in the henhouse because you got all territorial. This hookup was no different. Just a fun time. No strings. Doesn't mean a damn thing."

He glared at her, the tension gripping the muscles running along his shoulders. "That's bullshit. We aren't two strangers spending a couple of hours together. We're close. We've partnered on missions. Our relationship is built on trust and respect."

She pushed off him, stood there glaring down at him, her hands anchored to her hips.

As he started to rise, she didn't budge. They were inches away staring into each other's eyes.

"Excuse me," he ground out.

She wouldn't budge, so he stepped around her. On a huff, he pulled on his underwear and jeans, tugged his shirt over his head. "That blowjob changes everything. Abso-fucking-lutely everything."

"It changes *nothing*," she quipped.

"You can tell yourself that if it makes you feel better," he said.

She stormed past him and into the hallway. They walked down to the first floor in a seething silence. After grabbing her handbag from the office, they left.

He walked her to her car, parked nearby. She opened the door, turned back.

"All this could have been avoided if you had told me why you'd gotten angry at the wedding. We could have talked it out, and you would have learned that hookups don't mean any more to me than they do to you."

She got in her car, slammed the door, and started the engine.

"Lower your window," he said.

She did.

Staring into her eyes, he regarded her with a cool gaze. "But if I had said something, I wouldn't have gotten the best blow job I've ever had."

Turning on his heel, he sauntered to his car.

She drove over. "Go fuck yourself Nicholas Hawk."

He grinned. "I'd much rather you do it."

On a growl, she drove out of the parking lot.

"No going back now, babe," he said as he lit up a cigarette and sucked down a satisfying drag.

TUESDAY, MID-MORNING, Hawk pulled into ALPHA's parking lot. After the intense retreat last week—and the mission immediately after—he shouldn't have been called in at all. But here he was, driving around back of the nondescript warehouse-looking structure in Tysons.

He exited his convertible, walked to the scanner. The heat of the sun was beating down on him. The July day was gonna be a scorcher, but he loved it. The hotter the better.

What *wasn't* better was his relationship with Addison. They hadn't spoken since his life-changing blow job two days ago. Not a text, no phone calls. Nada.

He hated that the sex had driven a wedge between them. She mattered to him... a lot. But he had to play this cool, so he was gonna chill.

The scanner light turned green and he sailed inside, popping his shades on his head. Down the hall to the break room for a cuppa joe. Next stop? Cooper's office.

The door was open. Cooper was on his computer, so Hawk moseyed in. "Hey."

Cooper, shot him a smile. "Thanks for coming in."

Hawk sank into the guest chair. "I figured we'd covered everything last week. Is there fallout from the Festival Shooter mission?"

"No," Cooper replied. "I've got a new hire and I think you'd make a great mentor."

More shit he didn't have time for. But Hawk never said no to family or close friends. Ever. It was a promise he made to himself years ago. Life was short—too damn short. When they needed him, he was there for them. No questions asked.

Hawk sipped the black coffee.

"You up for it?" Cooper asked.

"When have I ever said no to you?"

"Never," Cooper replied.

Knock-knock.

Providence Luck, co-lead of ALPHA, stood in the doorway. "Hey, Hawk."

He tossed her a nod. "How's it goin'?"

"Never a dull moment." She walked in, shut the door. "I'm sorry to interrupt."

"I can step out," Hawk said.

"No, you're fine." She shifted her attention to Cooper. "I just found out an Operative has been seeing someone on our Internet team. They never documented their relationship with HR. Normally, I'd let it slide, but one of them is married."

"Dammit," Cooper bit out.

"You wanna follow the rule book or let this slide?" she asked.

"We gotta follow protocol," Cooper answered.

"Is that code for the firing squad?" Hawk asked, and they both laughed.

"The married one is willing to end things, but the single one isn't," Providence continued.

"That's a problem. The single one can blackmail the

married one, for starters," Cooper explained. "This puts the entire organization at risk."

Providence tucked her short hair behind an ear. "We'll have to let one of them go."

"Agreed." Cooper sipped his coffee.

"I'm heading into a meeting, so I'll circle back with you after lunch and we'll figure it out," Providence said.

"We can recommend one or both to a different agency," Cooper suggested.

Providence nodded before casting her attention on Hawk. "Nice job with the Festival Shooter." She left, closing the door behind her.

Hawk shifted in his chair. "Did you and Danielle document your relationship with HR?"

"Not right away. We needed to figure us out first."

Hawk got that. Right now, he and Addison were in some bizarre state of limbo. One sexy kiss, one amazing blowjob, and they weren't even speaking.

Cooper's desk phone buzzed and he put the call on speaker. "You ready for us?"

"Your new hire is waiting in the conference room," replied the employee.

He and Cooper headed to the conference room. When they entered the man at the table looked up, slid his gaze from Cooper to Hawk. Surprise flashed in his eyes, then a smile split his face.

"No way." Hawk's cousin pushed out of his seat and extended his hand. "I'll be damned."

Hawk's brain stuttered to a stop as he shook Tommy's hand.

"I can't believe this," Tommy said. "Wow, I had no idea."

"I'm just as surprised," Hawk replied.

The men sat around the table.

"How's your first day been so far?" Cooper asked Tommy.

"Great. I still can't believe this organization exists, and I'm a part of it." Then he regarded Hawk. "Does the family know you work for ALPHA?"

"Nobody, babe," Hawk replied. "You can't talk about this *with anyone.*"

Tommy nodded emphatically. "Gotcha."

"Tommy has had a successful career in local law enforcement," Cooper began. "After his last gig, he was ready for a change. We got word and here he is."

"ALPHA Meat Packing." Tommy chuckled. "My boss told me I had to go. We thought it was a joke."

"No joke," Cooper said.

"So, cuz, what do you do here?" Tommy asked.

"I'm an Operative and a pilot."

"Our *best* pilot," Cooper added. "There's pretty much nothing he can't fly."

"If it's got wings, I can get it airborne," Hawk said.

"Every new employee goes through a ninety-day training period," Cooper explained. "We know you're seasoned, but it's SOP."

"Sure," Tommy replied.

Cooper leaned back, crossed his ankle over his thigh. "We also assign a mentor. Based on your relationship with Hawk, he's yours. Neither of you are obligated and either can request out if it's not the right fit. Hawk will bring you on any missions he's scheduled to do, unless I override that."

"It'll be an honor to work with you," Tommy said to Hawk. "I'm looking forward to spending extra time with you. We've got a lot of catching up to do."

Hawk's thoughts jumped to Tommy with Addison. Did she blow him too? The thought of them together sent frustration coursing through him.

"Hawk," Cooper said.

How many times did they hook up?

"*Hawk*," Cooper repeated.

What kind of role play did they do? Dammit, stop!

"Yo, Nicky," Tommy chimed in.

Hawk blinked several times. Both Cooper and Tommy were staring at him.

"Where'd you go, man?" Tommy asked.

"I'm right here," Hawk mumbled.

Cooper studied his face. "You okay?"

He forced a smile, hoping it was more relaxed that his churning guts. "All good."

He hated—fucking hated—that Tommy had been with her. Normally never jealous, he needed to work this out or he couldn't be his cousin's mentor. Tommy hadn't done anything wrong and it had nothing—*nothing*—to do with him.

Then, why the fuck did he have a stick up his ass over this, and what the hell was he gonna do about it?

I know exactly what I'm gonna do and it goes against every fucking ALPHA protocol there is.

Cooper rose. "Tommy needs a work alibi. He can always use Providence's shell marketing company, Luck Marketing. I'm here if you need me." He extended his hand to Tommy. "Welcome to ALPHA."

Tommy stood and shook it. "It's good to be here."

"I'll talk to you," Cooper said to Hawk before shutting the door behind him.

"Seriously, dude," Tommy said. "I can't wrap my brain around this. So, you run Hawk Security *and* you're in ALPHA?"

"Right. I'm not here full time. There are a handful of us who take care of the most violent criminals."

"Take care of?" Tommy asked, emphasizing his question with air quotes.

"We take 'em out."

Tommy's eyes widened. "You're a trained killer?"

"Specialty agent."

"And pilot," Tommy said. "You gotta be the busiest person I know."

Hawk's phone buzzed with a text from Prescott. "Need your help."

"In five," he replied before shifting his attention back to Tommy.

"You're gonna be at ALPHA full time, but you still need a cover," Hawk explained. "Tell people you work for Luck Marketing."

Tommy chuckled. "No one's gonna buy that. I've been in law enforcement since college. I don't know jack about marketing. What about a consultant at your company? I've been brought on board to talk about the latest trends in criminal behavior, so you can expand your product line."

"Nice. That'll work."

"Do I need business cards or something to look legit?"

"No cards," Hawk replied. "Just mention Hawk Security and change the subject. The less you say, the better. Are you going to target practice regularly?"

"I haven't been in a while."

"Schedule it weekly. We'll go together sometime." Hawk pushed out of the chair. "Let's find you an office and get you set up with a computer."

"The HR manager mentioned a tracker on my phone," Tommy said. "What's that about?"

The day was slipping by and Hawk had a shit-ton of work to do. "Let's talk and walk."

As they headed down the hall, Hawk asked, "Can I see your phone?"

Tommy handed it over.

"I'm adding a tracking app," Hawk explained. "If you're taken, we gotta be able to save your ass."

Every ALPHA Operative had a tracker chip in their necks. All other employees, including the trainees, had the phone app.

After Hawk downloaded the app, he went in search of an empty office, but found none, so he headed into the cubicle area.

"This is where the Internet team works," Hawk explained. "They track down the criminals."

Donetta popped over. "Hey, Hawk." She smiled warmly at Tommy.

"Hey, babe," Hawk said. "Donetta manages our Internet team. Tommy's an Op-in-training. Can he camp out here until an office opens up?"

"Sure thing," Donetta replied. "We just hired several new Ops, so space is pretty tight. Danielle's going to move into Emerson's office. Once that happens, Tommy can move in there."

Hawk glanced at the time.

"If you need to take off, I can help Tommy get settled in," Donetta said.

"You sure?" Hawk asked.

"Totally."

"How 'bout I grab you guys Vietnamese take-out?"

"Bro, you don't have to," Tommy said.

Donetta grinned. "The one around the corner?"

Hawk pulled up the menu on his phone. "Look this over and I'll get you whatever you want."

Two minutes later, Hawk had placed their order.

"Donetta, can you get Tommy set up for scanner entry?" Hawk asked.

"No worries," Donetta replied. "I'll take him over to IT. I do this all the time for my team."

En route to pick up the food, Hawk called his brother back.

"What took you so long?" Prescott answered.

"Easy, baby," Hawk replied. "I got reeled into being someone's mentor."

Prescott laughed. "What a time suck."

"No shit. Guess who?"

"Seriously, Nicky, how am I even gonna—"

"It's Tommy," Hawk said, cutting him off.

"Our cousin? How'd he get into ALPHA?"

"He must be good. Anyway, now, I gotta deal with him."

"What's the problem? You've always liked him."

"I'm short on time. Where are we meeting?"

"I'm working at the black site," Prescott replied.

"Be there in thirty. I'll bring you something from the Vietnamese restaurant."

Hawk hung up, fished out his cigarette pack, tapped one out, and lit up. That first puff filled his lungs and he held it an extra second before blowing it out. He'd started smoking ten years ago and, while he'd cut back, he hadn't quit.

He pulled in to the restaurant, went inside, and added two more meals to the take-out order.

While waiting, his phone buzzed with a text from Addison. Relief powered through him. This was the longest they'd ever gone without any kind of communication.

"We have racquetball tonight," Addison texted. "You in?"

"Why wouldn't I be?"

She sent an angry-faced emoji. "Yes or no."

He chuffed out a laugh. "Yeah, baby," he texted.

"Target practice after?"

"Y," he texted back.

Being chill and laying low had worked. She was still pissed, but he could work with that. Truth was, he'd missed her like crazy and he was determined to get them back on track.

Back on track *his* way. He and Addison were about to get crazy, Nicholas Hawk style.

8

BLACK OPS

Addison had been fuming for the past two days. Sex with Hawk to prove a point had backfired something wicked. Seeing him like that, taking care of him in that way, had unleashed her inner beast.

Shaking off that deliciously naughty thought, she entered the busy Tysons restaurant. Addison couldn't wait to see her friend Ronald Jenning. To her surprise, he wasn't waiting at the table. He wasn't just punctual, he was ten minutes early, without fail.

After being seated, the server swung by to fill her water. "Are you dining alone?"

"No, I'm meeting someone." Addison checked her watch. "He'll be here shortly."

After ordering a sparkling water with lemon, she sent Ronald a text. "I'm in Ziti's at a table."

No dots appeared. That didn't surprise her. Ronald was a stickler for *not* texting while driving.

After reading the menu, she decided what she wanted. The server returned with her water and asked if she wanted an appetizer. Not wanting to start without her friend, she declined.

While waiting, she re-read Hawk's texts. She'd worked her ass off to get into ALPHA and she didn't want to screw that up with an office fling.

The biggest problem about hooking up with him? He'd been right. Not all hookups were the same. Cosplay hookups and a Hawk hookup were two *completely* different things.

Since then, she hadn't stopped thinking about him. Rather than thinking about going to target practice together, going for a run, or strategizing about an upcoming mission, all her thoughts had turned sexual.

She wanted to kiss him, she wanted *him* to go down on *her*. And she wanted to take him inside her. She could *not* stop fantasizing about them naked in her bed. His large, rock-hard body on hers while they moved as one beneath the sheets.

The server returned, chasing away her very sexy fantasy.

"Ready for that appetizer?" he asked.

She checked the time. Ronald was twenty-minutes late. She had a meeting she had to get to, so she placed a to-go order and tapped out another text.

"Ronald, did you get held up in meetings? I'm still at the restaurant. I hope you're on your way!" She included thumbs up and smiley emojis before sending it.

Ten minutes later, the server returned with her to-go bag. Still no Ronald, so she paid the check and left, bummed that she hadn't been able to connect with him while he was in town.

By the time she arrived at the black site, she was famished. She drove around back, tapped the remote in her ALPHA-owned SUV, and drove into the large hangar-like garage that housed a fleet of identical vehicles.

Feeling like a pack mule with her handbag, computer bag, and take-out bag, she made her way toward the scanner. It flashed green, permitting her entry. The door slid open, she sailed inside and hurried down the hall toward the conference room.

"I'm starving," she announced after entering.

Hawk, Prescott, Sinclair Develin, and Dakota Luck were watching a brutal video of a terrorist group murdering several innocent civilians. Her stomach dropped, her voracious appetite killed.

"Oh, no." She flicked her gaze from the large monitor on the wall to the four men seated around the table.

The screen went dark.

With a smile, Dakota stood. "Good to see you, Addison."

Sin and Dakota were identical twins. Fortunately, they wore their hair differently, which made it easy to tell them apart. Sin styled his back, whereas Dakota had perfected a bed-head look, his mussed, brown hair going in every direction.

"Hey, boss." She shook Dakota's extended hand, before regarding the other three men. "Is this a brothers-only meeting? I don't have a brother, but my sister would have passed out at the sight of that."

"It wasn't pretty," Sin said. "Congrats on the Festival Shooter mission. How've you been?"

Her attention jumped to Hawk, a whisper of a smile dancing on his sexy mouth. She hitched her eyebrow at him.

"Fine," she bit out. "Just fine."

"Have a seat." Dakota sat back down.

After setting her bags on the table, she eased into a chair. "What's going on?"

"I stepped away from ALPHA to handle some issues with my real estate company," Dakota began.

"I remember," she replied.

"My business partner returned, but instead of jumping back in to co-run ALPHA, I've been leading a top-secret specialty group."

"The *true* gem of ALPHA," Sin added.

"BLACK OPS," Dakota explained.

What the hell?

"I'm listening," she said.

After Dakota provided a high-level overview, he finished with, "BLACK OPS assassins eliminate on sight."

"We think you'd be a solid addition to the team," Sin added.

Excitement coursed through her at the same time dread pounded her guts. These missions would be crazy dangerous. "I'm not sure this would be the right fit for me."

"Why?" Dakota asked.

"If some of the missions are in the Middle East, I can't do those."

"Then, you won't," Dakota explained.

"So, I have a choice?"

Leaning back in the leather chair, Dakota offered a reassuring smile. "Always."

"Would I live here or abroad?"

"Here," Dakota replied. "Home base is right here."

"This black site?" she asked.

"It's secure and it's near ALPHA HQ," Dakota replied.

"Who else is in?" she asked.

"Just us four," Prescott replied.

She regarded each man, her gaze stilling on Hawk. Her heart was racing in her chest. The five years she'd spent with the CIA had been intense, especially the two overseas. Intense and sometimes downright terrifying. She wasn't sure she could handle that again. She didn't want to be wishy-washy, but she wasn't about to knee jerk either.

"I need to think about this," she said.

"I don't need an answer now," Dakota said. "The mission isn't for several months, but training would start in the fall. If you join us, you'd be splitting your time between ALPHA missions and BLACK OPS."

"Got it," she said. "I can head out if you need to—"

Dakota's phone rang. "If you're even considering the opportunity, stay, so I can bring everyone up to speed at the same time." He glanced at his phone. "It's Providence." He answered. "Hey, honey, I'm in a meeting."

"Hi, Daddy." The toddler's voice blasted through his speaker.

"Hey, Gray-Gray," Sin said, "It's Uncle Lalla."

"Mommy, I can't know," the tyke said. "Lalla talks to me."

"Babe?" Providence asked.

"You're on speaker," Dakota said. "I'm in a meeting, and Sin's with me."

"Hi, Sin," Providence said.

"Hey, sister-in-law," Sin replied.

"We just got home from the doctor and Graham insisted on calling you," Providence said.

"Put him back on."

"Daddy?"

"I'm right here, Graham," Dakota said. "How are you feeling?"

"I have ear boo-boo," his toddler explained. "Ear fucktion."

Everyone in the room smiled.

"That's a new one," Sin said, and the team cracked up.

"Now we know why your ear was hurting, huh, bud?" Dakota said to his young son.

"Uh-huh. Mommy says I have medthin for my ear." He giggled. "Mommy funny. Bye, Daddy."

A second later, the child said, "Bye, Lalla."

"Love you, babe," Providence said before the line went dead.

Addison couldn't help but smile. It was the mental break she needed. Her head was swimming from the day.

First, Ronald didn't show, which wasn't a big deal. People stand each other up all the time, but not Ronald. If she could count on anything, it was him showing up, or calling to let her know he couldn't.

"Addison, you want me to heat your chicken parm?" Hawk asked.

"How'd you know I brought food?" she asked.

"We have noses, babe," Hawk replied.

"And ears," Sin added.

Hawk picked up the carry-out bag. "You walked in and told us you're starving."

She pushed out of her chair. "I'll go with you. I need some water."

"I got you," he said, but she followed him out anyway.

"You okay?" he asked as they made their way down the quiet corridor toward the break room.

The black site was a maze of corridors and closed doors. There were sleeping accommodations in one wing that included a family room, and a newly remodeled kitchen with cupboards stocked with non-perishables.

The building also housed a surgery center, a recovery room, and a break room. Another hallway housed offices. Each work space had nothing but a desk and a couple of chairs. If Dakota was setting up his home base there, she was confident there would be no pictures of his wife or their two children. Nothing to put him or his family at risk if the location was breached.

As she and Hawk made their way down the hall, she peered over at him.

"Doing okay, babe?" he repeated.

"Uh-huh."

They entered the break room. She should have been totally pumped. Being hand-selected for BLACK OPS was an honor. Three years ago, when she returned to the US, she'd told herself she'd never take a job or an assignment oversees that would put her in that kind of danger again. But, here she was, facing that very decision.

Hawk held out a bottle of water.

She twisted off the lid, chugged down several gulps, letting the cold water rinse away the tension. Then, while her lunch heated in the microwave, he draped his arms over her shoulders and stared into her eyes.

"I don't want my being here to be the reason you don't take this job," he murmured.

She opened her mouth, but he placed his index finger over her lips. Tingles flitted through her.

"I'm sorry I acted like an ass," he continued. "I'm sorry our friendship was put to the test. I would love—*fucking love*—if you joined BLACK OPS. We've had each other's backs for years. There's no one I trust with my life more than you."

She threw her arms around him and hugged him. "I'm sorry," she whispered. "Our friendship means *everything* to me. You were right." He wrapped his arms around her and held her flush against him.

Every tense muscle in her back released, the pounding in her head vanished. Being with Hawk had crazy healing powers. She couldn't explain it, but it had been that way from the beginning.

She wanted to explore something more with him, but not if that meant losing their friendship. Her heart ached, but it was the smarter choice.

She broke from him, drank down more water. "Working with you is one of my favorite things in the world. I don't want to mess this up again. I'm sorry I was trying to prove a damn point. There's hookups... and then—"

"There's us," he said finishing her sentence.

Hawk was fucked. So fucked. He knew *exactly* how she felt. He wasn't going to say anything now... maybe never. Even if she didn't take this gig, he wanted her head in the game. Sex was a great distraction, unless it got in the way of two people being able to do their jobs.

While their hookup had rocked him good, he needed to put her first. The offer had rattled her. He didn't think Dakota had picked up on her signals, but no one in that room knew her like he did.

He'd take the fucking high road and be her friend. That's what *she* needed. Didn't matter that he hadn't been able to stop thinking about her. He'd gotten a taste of something he liked... and he liked it a lot.

But he'd give it up, for her.

He offered what he hoped was an encouraging smile before he pulled her lunch from the microwave, set it on the small table, then grabbed some utensils from the drawer. "Come on. Eat it before I do."

With a grateful smile, she sat and took a mouthful. Her eyes lit up and she sighed. "This is the best."

"What were you doing at Ziti's?"

After swallowing down the pasta, she said, "I was meeting my friend Ronald."

He waited, unsure who that was.

"Ronald Jenning, the SEAL with DEVGRU, who took out terrorist Abdel Haqazzii when I was with the CIA. He and his wife Becky were so supportive when I returned stateside." She forked another mouthful.

Hearing the name Abdel Haqazzii sent a rush of fury pounding through him. "I didn't know you were involved in that."

"I was the CIA case agent in charge of finding Haqazzii," she replied before taking a bite of breaded chicken. "Ronald's in DC for work. He wanted to have lunch, but never showed."

"Maybe he got stuck in meetings."

"He didn't text me or call."

"I'm sure he will," Hawk said as Prescott entered the break room.

"What happened?" Prescott asked.

Hawk stared at him for a second. "Sorry, we've been talking."

His brother shook his head. "You two get into some kind of mind-meld when you're together. Reality goes poof." Pausing, he regarded Addison. "You okay?"

After pushing out of the chair, she collected the container of food. "Totally. Let's get back in there and hear Dakota out. I won't be able to make up my mind if I don't know what I'm dealing with."

Three hours later, their top-secret meeting ended. Hawk was all in, but Addison had said very little all afternoon.

"Thanks for your time," Dakota said. "This is a lot to digest. The missions will be dangerous, so strength training, combat training, and weapons training are all a priority. I'm available twenty-four seven for any concerns or questions. This goes without saying, but you cannot discuss this with anyone, even within ALPHA."

They all verbalized their commitment to secrecy.

"Addison, lemme know." Dakota shot her a smile. "I'll be in my office, down the hall, if you want to talk to me before you head out."

"I'm going to need a few days," she replied. "Maybe longer."

Addison collected her things, but waited for Hawk in the hallway. They made their way into the hanger. At Addison's vehicle, he asked if she was heading back to ALPHA.

"Hell, no," she replied. "I need to go for a run."

"You want a running buddy?" he asked.

"Only if you don't slow me down."

He laughed. "I'll do my best to keep up. Where do you want to run?"

"Your neighborhood. I love running along the river. Do you

mind if I shower at your place, then we can go to target practice?"

"What about racquetball?" Hawk asked.

"Maybe," she said. "I need to be outside, not inside. I'll swing by my place, grab some clothes."

"I'll follow you, then we'll drive over together." Hawk had driven his ALPHA SUV.

She jumped in hers, he got in his, and they drove out of the garage, both stopping to make sure the oversized door closed before they drove around to the front of the building and onto the dirt road.

He hated that they'd put the brakes on something before it had even started, but he was relieved they were back on track. He followed her to her house, street parked, and got out. She was standing in her driveway, staring at her house.

"What's going on?" he asked, following her gaze.

"The surveillance camera on the side of the house is missing and the front door camera has been shot out."

He wrapped his fingers around her arm and pulled her away from the house. "Let's sit in my car."

As soon as they got into his vehicle, he opened his laptop, hopped onto Hawk Security, and went in search of her account.

"The camera on the side of the house went down last night," he said. "Didn't you get an email about that?"

"I didn't check."

Rather than lecture her, he pulled up the front camera. It was working until four in the morning when it suddenly went dark.

"I'll assume you didn't hear the gunshot," he said.

"If I had, don't you think I would have done something about it?"

"I can install new cameras, but I'm not sure it's safe for you to stay here alone."

"Hmm," she replied.

"What?" he asked.

"My house alarm never went off, so they didn't break in."

Hawk checked the camera mounted on the other side and the one in back. "The other two weren't messed with."

"Could've been kids," she said. "It's summer break. Maybe they're bored. Let's clear the house together."

He wanted to push back, but didn't. Better to assess the situation before he expressed his concern about her staying there alone.

After he pulled his Glock from the locked glovebox, they exited his truck. It was just before five, so the neighborhood was busy with people returning from work. As they made their way up the walkway to her front door, Addison said hello to a neighbor passing by with her dog.

She stood in front of the scanner. The light flashed yellow, indicating it knew she wasn't alone. Hawk stepped up. The light turned green and Addison turned the handle.

"Do you have your weapon?" he asked.

"In my bedroom safe."

"First, we'll get your weapon, then we clear."

Once inside, she hurried through her clutter-free living room and down the hall.

In all the years he'd known her, he'd never ventured beyond the living room and kitchen. He stood in her bedroom while she unlocked her safe. This room hadn't been ransacked either. Like the living room, it was neat, but it wasn't clutter-free. There were at least ten freakin' brightly-colored throw pillows covering her bed.

While she pulled her weapon, he cleared the room, then hurried into her bathroom. Also, clear.

With her Glock in hand, they checked the hall bathroom, the kitchen, and the basement.

Back on the first floor, Hawk stood in front of a closed door across from the hall bath. "You skipped this room. We gotta clear it."

"It's locked," she protested. "No one was in here."

"They could be hiding in there." He frowned at her. "Don't make me break this door down."

"You're being unreasonable."

"Are you staying here tonight?" he asked.

"Of course, I am."

He growled. "Then, open this fucking door so I know you're safe, for fuck's sake."

She was on him, her mouth pressed against his, her arms around him, while her fingers sunk into his hair. The kiss was brutal and wild and so fucking perfect. On a groan, he thrust his tongue into her mouth. Her moan landed between his legs and he started to firm in his pants.

Like two feral animals being freed from their cages after days of imprisonment, the kiss intensified. He pinned her against the wall and she wrapped a leg around him, reached around and grabbed his ass.

The need to bury himself inside her had him grinding against her. Her groans turned to gasps and she broke away to kiss his jawline, bite his earlobe.

If he didn't stop this runaway train, they'd be naked in seconds, and screwing seconds after that. He needed her, and he couldn't think clearly, the desire muddling his thoughts.

Her phone rang. The caustic interruption had him slowing the kiss until he dropped a tender one on her lips, then on her forehead.

On an agitated grunt, he moved away, shoved his hand down his pants, and rearranged his stiff junk.

"Hello?" Addison answered, gasping for breath. "Hey, Liliana. What's up?"

Addison's cheeks were flushed, her lips swollen, her eyelids hooded, her pupils fully dilated. She looked how he felt. Like she wanted more. The kissing was fun, but it wasn't enough. Not nearly enough. He wanted to sink inside her, run his hands over every supple inch of her, fuck her so good, she would beg him for more.

And he would give her exactly what she needed, over and over again.

No. Not happening.

He backed away. He was good at one-time hookups, but being with someone more than once meant he cared. He couldn't let his emotions take over. If he did, he'd admit how he felt about her... and they'd be back to not speaking all over again.

"No problem," she said snagging his attention. "Wait, today's not Wednesday. It's *Tuesday*." More listening. "Okay. Gotcha. See you tomorrow." She hung up.

Her gaze connected with his. The second it locked into place, emotion took over. He fucking hated that, and needed to shut that shit down.

He took another step back. Had to or he'd maul her. Her tempting vanilla scent, those intense, sexy-as-hell eyes, and her hot little body were all pulling him back to her.

"Liliana, our bartender, thought it was Wednesday and she was running late," Addison said. "Our club isn't open on Tuesdays... or Sundays and Mondays either. Just Wednesdays through Saturdays." She sucked down a breath. "Sorry. I'm rambling."

"What the hell is happening with us?" he bit out. "This is insane. I can't stop thinking about you and that amazing blowjob."

A moan escaped her. She crossed her arms as if trying to shield herself from him. "Maybe, now, you'll be more open to receiving them."

He chuffed out a laugh. "From *you*." He flicked his gaze to the door. "Open this so we can clear the room, then we gotta get the hell out of here before I toss every one of those throw pillows off your bed, rip off your clothes, and fuck you for days."

"Ohgod, ohgod." She stepped close, ran her soft fingertips over his chiseled cheekbone and across his whiskered skin. "I can't breathe around you."

"Take a breath and open that door or I'll shoot out the goddamn lock."

Using a key, she unlocked the door and stepped inside. He followed, glanced around, and his jaw dropped.

"What the hell," he uttered.

Addison shouldn't have crossed the line with the blowjob, but he'd started it with the kiss. Now, as his gaze floated around the room, she knew she'd have to take their relationship to the next level. Her insides were on fire, the pent-up energy threatening to explode out of her.

She had to have him and she'd didn't care at what cost.

In the corner of the room stood a simple desk, her laptop the only item on it. There were three monitors on the wall. Those were dark.

This room was her work-at-home command center. She could access anything and everything she needed. Because the security system Hawk had installed was ALPHA-approved, she'd been given permission to work from home when it made sense.

But that wasn't what had hijacked his attention. Addison had taken her painting hobby in a different direction. What had started out as a beginner art class with Hawk had turned into an obsession. She loved painting men and women in intimate poses. While the pictures were somewhat abstract, there was no denying she'd painted men with broad shoulders, washboard abs, and a nice tight ass.

There were four pieces hanging on the walls, and several leaning against the closet. He walked over to one and stared at it for the longest time.

"This guy looks like me."

"Hmm, you think?" Despite her nonchalant answer, she was so busted.

The man in the paintings was tall, broad shouldered, with blue-green eyes, and a mop of dark brown hair parted on the side. In truth, Nicholas Hawk was her type, or he became that when she met him. Hard not to like a man who looked like that.

In one of the pictures titled, "The Aftermath," the man was propped against a pillow in bed, a naked woman lying across his lap. He was smoking.

Now, Hawk knew her *real* secret. Not that she'd been painting, but that she'd been painting *them*.

"You're so talented," he said.

"You think?"

He cupped her chin, tipped her face to his. "Yeah, baby, I do. These are beautiful."

She melted from his encouraging words.

The air cracked with electricity while they stared into each other's eyes.

He tucked her hair behind her ear. "You wanna get outta here?"

Hawk seduced like the devil, and she wanted to let go and get lost in him... all of him, all night long.

Sex with you would check a lot of boxes.

She hated what she was about to do. But, she had to put the brakes on them before they took this too far and ruined everything.

"Okay, so things have gotten a little crazy with us," she murmured. "The kiss, the BJ, more kissing. We gotta get ourselves together. I'm struggling enough with whether or not I should join BLACK OPS, but I won't if we're looking for alcoves for a quick make-out session before we snuff some bad guy."

He laughed. "I'd be fired up, for sure." He paused while his gaze searched her face. "Grab some clothes and we'll go to my place."

"It's been a long day," she said. "I'm gonna pass on hanging with you tonight."

A shadow darkened his eyes. "Dammit, Addison."

"We gotta take a step back." Her heart tightened as she made her way toward her front door.

Seconds later, he was by her side. "I've got a few surveillance cams in the SUV. I'll install them before I take off."

"Thank you," she replied.

Despite the tension rolling off him, he still put her first.

Women throw themselves at him, and I'm pushing him away. I gotta be the biggest idiot on the planet.

She went outside while he mounted the new cameras. Minutes later, he was finished.

"If those kids come back, call me." He hesitated for a second, then he was gone, taking her heart with him.

I just let the best man I've ever known walk away. It's okay... I did the right thing.

If she had, then why did she feel so empty?

9

SHOCKING NEWS

After a restless night, Addison got ready, downed a quick breakfast, and headed out to CIA headquarters in Langley, Virginia.

At seven that morning, her former boss's assistant had called. She was being summoned to an on-site meeting. Twice, after she'd left the Agency, they needed her assistance with specific terror cells, which she'd been happy to provide.

After slogging through rush hour traffic, she drove to the compound, stopping at the guard's gate. She flashed her FBI badge, one of several given to her when she became an Operative. Since ALPHA was a covert organization, every Operative had badges for several agencies, which included the State Department, Homeland Security, ATF, DEA, and FBI. The badges gave them the freedom to do their jobs without revealing that ALPHA actually existed.

"I'm here to see Henry Bufford," Addison told the guard.

After a brief phone call, the guard opened the gate. "Know where you're going?"

"I do." She drove in, followed the road around to the monster building, shaped like an H. After parking in a visitor spot, she pulled her weapon from her handbag, locked it in her glovebox, and made her way toward the front door.

Once inside, she checked-in at the large reception desk. A few minutes later, a man walked into the lobby and over to her.

"Hello, Ms. Skye. How've you been?"

"Good, thanks. You?"

As he escorted her to her former boss's office, she passed two case officers. One was on his phone, but the other offered a friendly wave.

Henry's office door was open. Rather than walk in, the assistant stopped in the doorway. "Ms. Skye, sir."

Henry pushed out of his chair. With a welcoming smile, he said, "C'mon in, Addison."

They shook hands. He gestured to a guest chair, before sitting behind his desk. The assistant closed the door behind him.

"Thanks for coming in," Henry said. "How are you?"

"Good, sir. You?" She sat.

"I became a grandpa." He held up a picture of an adorable baby.

"Congratulations."

Addison had rarely shared anything about her personal life while at the Agency. She wasn't about to start now.

"Are you still with…" Henry trailed off.

She flashed her FBI badge. He nodded.

"Addison, you remember Ronald Jenning?"

"Of course. I just talked to him last week."

Henry's eyebrows went up. "About what?"

"He was coming to the area and we were supposed to catch up over lunch." Dread crept down her spine. "But he didn't show."

"Unfortunately, he was killed," Henry said.

Her stomach dropped, her mouth went bone dry.

"You knew I'd been in touch with him, didn't you?"

Henry nodded. "We got his cell phone password from his wife—"

"Ohgod, Becky. The kids." Addison steeled her spine. "What happened?"

"His rental car exploded Tuesday. I called you in because we're concerned it was a retaliation strike."

"For what?" she asked.

"Abdel Haqazzii," he replied.

A shiver skirted through her. "DEVGRU took him out *three* years ago. Wouldn't a strike have happened back then?"

"After Haqazzii's death, the terror cell scattered," Henry explained. "It could have taken them years to regroup, or form a different cell under new leadership. We're looking into all possible options."

"And you think I might be in danger?" Addison confirmed.

"You're the one who found Haqazzii's compound hidden away in that town," Henry reminded her. "You were adamant we'd find Haqazzii and his team living there, despite confirmation that the compound was vacant. So, yes. We think you should keep a low profile."

"That's a little extreme, don't you think?"

"We didn't want Ronald to go public with his story, but he was offered a lot of money for that book deal."

"I wasn't named in his book though," Addison pushed back.

"No, you weren't," Henry agreed, "but Haqazzii was the most wanted terrorist in the world. If a new terror cell has formed, we're concerned they're going after everyone involved."

"Sir, I'd like to reach out to Jenning's wife. What does she know?"

"That he was fatally wounded in a car explosion."

Knock-knock.

"Come in," Henry said.

His assistant opened the door and stepped aside. "Ms. Robinson is here, sir."

Associate Director Anita Robinson sat in the guest chair next to Addison and offered a warm smile. "Good to see you, Addison."

"You, as well," Addison replied.

"We can relocate to a conference room, Anita," Henry said.

"This is fine." Anita regarded Addison. "I'm sure Henry has advised you to lay low until we get some answers."

"He has," Addison replied.

Addison wasn't going to push back, not with the Assistant Director, but she didn't work there anymore. She was an ALPHA Operative, with an option to go BLACK OPS. Go into hiding? She wanted to laugh. Only a coward did that, and she was no coward.

If anything, she'd find the son of a bitch who did this to Ronald. *That* would give her peace of mind.

Anita held her gaze. "But you won't, will you?"

"I'm not going into hiding, unless told to do so by my current employer."

"Understood," Anita said.

"Will there be someone from the Agency tailing me?" Addison asked.

"I'm not at liberty to discuss that," Anita replied. "We just want you safe."

"Thank you, ma'am." She flicked her gaze to Henry, then back to Anita. "I'm going to call Becky—Ronald's wife—and offer my condolences."

"Of course," Anita said.

"What about my going to the funeral?" Addison asked.

"If you go, please let Henry know," Anita answered. "I would consider bringing someone with you. Always good to have an extra pair of eyes and ears." She offered a warm smile. "I heard your career is going well."

Addison nodded. "I like what I'm doing."

Anita rose. "From what I learned, you're very good at it."

She walked to the door, glanced back at Henry. "I'll catch up with you later."

Anita left, shutting the door behind her.

"When I was in the Middle East, I had several assets," Addison said. One, in particular—a woman we helped relocate to the US—was the reason I found Haqazzii. Will she be notified?"

"No," Henry replied. "We don't get involved with former assets." He pushed out of his chair. "Thanks for coming in. I hope you'll reconsider our advice based on the seriousness of the situation."

"Thanks for letting me know about Ronald."

Henry walked her to his assistant's desk, told her he'd be in touch, and returned to his office.

Addison was escorted to the lobby.

On the way to her car, she thought of Ronald, Becky, and their children. Emotion clogged her throat, but crying wouldn't bring her friend back. Hunting down his killer wouldn't either, but it might bring closure for his family. If anyone could find out who was behind the car explosion, it would be her.

With phone to ear, she made the first of two calls.

"Cooper Grant," he answered. "Where are you?"

"You should know. I've got a chip in my—"

"I'm not online," he interrupted. "I talked to Anita Robinson earlier. Where are you?"

"Langley. I was told to go into hiding."

"Yeah, she recommended the same thing to me," Cooper said. "Work at the black site this afternoon."

"I don't want this to turn into a thing," she pushed back.

"If Jenning's death is connected to the Haqazzii terror cell, you'll need to drop below the radar."

"Jenning went on dozens of missions. The car explosion could have been related to any one of them."

"But he went *public* about the Haqazzii strike," Cooper said.

"But I wasn't named in his book."

"CIs and assets can be turned. You found Haqazzii. Someone could have spent the last three years hunting for the people who took him out. Who else was killed during that raid?"

"Four additional adults," Addison said. "I can't discuss details, not even with you."

"I want you to lay low until we hear back from them."

It could take months for the CIA to find out who killed Ronald.

"Got it," she replied, not wanting to get into it with her boss. Cooper ended the call.

Though she doubted someone was tailing her, she'd watch her back. That was nothing new.

She opened her car door, let the heat of the day rush out. Before this morning, she'd never thought twice about starting her vehicle. She eased into the driver's seat, inserted the key, turned the ignition. Her vehicle started.

Relax. No one is hunting you down. Jenning went public. I didn't.

She lowered the windows, letting the stifling heat escape, cranked up the air, then made the second call.

"Yes," answered the familiar voice.

"I need to talk to you."

"I thought you might. I was headed to a meeting, but I changed my plans."

"Should I come to your office?"

"No. Meet me at our spot."

"Be there in twenty," she said.

"Park at the circle and tell the guard you're meeting me."

Addison glanced around the parking lot, packed wall-to-wall with cars. "The last time I did that, I got towed."

He chuckled. "That won't happen again. You can't park in an underground garage. Too easy for someone to put a package under your car."

"I'm not going to get blown up!"

"Addison, no emotion. What happens when we let emotion take over?"

"We become vulnerable." She inhaled, counted to four, released the breath.

"And then, what?"

"The enemy strikes," she replied.

"Very good. See you in twenty." The line went dead.

She sat in her car another moment, focusing on her breathing. Inhale, hold, exhale, hold. The tension slipped away, her heart rate slowing back down. She wasn't afraid, but she wasn't stupid either. If someone associated with Haqazzii got to Ronald, they could get to her too.

There was no need to panic. Panicking only made things worse.

I got this.

Addison left Langley, en route for the National Gallery of Art in Washington, DC.

Twenty minutes later, she pulled up to the circle. The guard moseyed over. "Can I help you?"

"I'm here to see Z," she said.

"Hold on." Using his two-way radio, the guard contacted someone. Seconds later, he said, "Park in front of the red car, right over there." He pointed to the other side of the circular driveway. "Put this on your dash." He handed her a pre-printed sign that allowed her to park there the entire day.

Now, we're getting somewhere.

Addison parked, but before getting out, she pulled her Glock from the glovebox, tucked it beneath her suit jacket against her back.

As she made her way inside, she let the hot July sun warm her. She loved the heat, the clammy air clinging to her skin. The only thing better than being outside in the summer was going for a good run in the heat and humidity.

As she walked around the building toward the museum's front entrance, she did a slow three-sixty.

The sidewalks were peppered with tourists, workers, runners. It was the Nation's Capital in the middle of the summer. It was impossible to know if someone was tailing her. No one seemed to be paying her any attention, but they could be watching her from a block away.

She entered the museum, opened her small handbag so the guard could check for a weapon. Not the best method, since hers was on her person.

As soon as she strolled into the first exhibit room, she spotted him admiring a painting. Seeing him made her smile. She sidled over, slid her arm through the crook of his elbow and rested her head on his shoulder.

"Hi, Daddy."

He kissed the top of her head. "Hello, dear. How are you doing?"

"I'm sad that Ronald was killed."

"Let's walk."

Her father, Phillip Skye, was one of the most powerful men in the world. Known only as Z, he worked at FBI headquarters in Washington, DC. Rather than take his earned corner office on the executive floor, he worked in a windowless shithole in the basement. On more than one occasion, she'd pulled out her service weapon as she made her way to his office. That's how creeped out she'd been in that part of the building.

Today, however, they were meeting at their favorite place. The art museum. It was their go-to, father-daughter spot. After her mom had left them, she, her older sister, and their dad, had been lost. Nobody knew how to cook, their dad didn't know about their after-school activities, what they were learning in school, or what subjects they were struggling with. While Addison and her sister were close, their dad was like a stranger to them. He worked long hours and they didn't see him much.

When he was home, he was kind to them, but he wasn't super interested in their lives.

Somehow, they figured out a way to survive. They each learned to cook a few meals. He worked fewer hours, he helped them with their homework, watched Addison play team sports. Every month, he'd take them to a museum. DC offered so much in the way of arts, so they'd spend a day moseying around and learning.

Over time, this museum became their favorite. The art was beautiful, the museum tended to be quieter than some, and there were always new exhibits coming through. All three of them came to appreciate the works that lined these walls.

Addison's sister became an artist, but Addison wanted to have a relationship with her dad that extended beyond high school. So, when he encouraged her to double major in International Relations plus Government and Politics, then take a job with the CIA, she did.

It was only after she'd been recruited into ALPHA, three years ago, that she learned about his *real* job. He'd told his daughters he was a government worker who spent his days in meetings. They'd accepted that. They had no reason not to.

But her dad controlled a lot of what happened in law enforcement. And most of it wasn't pretty. While her dad was slight and less than average height, he more than made up for it in power.

"Are we being tailed here?" she asked as they paused to study a painting of two small children.

"I have protection on me—on us—so yes, we're being followed."

She didn't bother glancing around.

"I was told to go into hiding," she said.

"Cooper will come up with a plan."

"Or he'll do whatever you tell him."

"Cooper Grant doesn't know I exist," her dad said.

With her arm still looped through his, they meandered on to the next painting.

"Well, Sinclair Develin does, and he'll relay the message." She peered over at him. "Same thing." She caught his eye. "This isn't my first rodeo with you, Dad."

His sheepish smile made her chuckle. Her father rarely admitted to *anything*.

"I've been recruited for BLACK OPS," she murmured, "but I'm thinking of turning it down."

He pivoted from the landscape painting to her. "Why would you do that?"

"Some of the missions will be international."

"You enter a country, you take care of business, you leave."

"Unless I don't make it out. I wouldn't want to get caught on foreign soil."

"There's no room for error on these missions, Addison."

"Well, we *are* human, you know. Sometimes things *don't* go according to plan. People make mistakes, missions go sideways."

"You have time to consider this."

In the course of her life, her dad had given her great career advice. She stayed silent while they finished studying a painting in one of the many side salons. When finished there, they moved to a larger room, her gaze resting on a huge painting hanging in the center of the wall.

A war scene, a bloody battle where there were no victors. She studied the faces of the fallen.

"Do you think I should take the assignment?" she asked.

"The four men you'd be working with are smart—*very smart*—excellent at their jobs, and ruthless. You can hold your own, of course." Pausing, he glanced in her direction. "But it's good to know these men would have your back… and you'd have theirs. I'd like for them to find another woman for the group, but they haven't yet."

"I don't want to go into hiding. I want to track down Ronald's killer."

"Don't do that," was all he said.

He grew silent as they moved from piece to piece. They left one salon, moved across the hall to the next one.

"Are you armed?" he asked.

"Of course, I am."

"Good."

More silence.

Her dad stopped to admire a painting that had been there for years. "You know," he began. "I've never noticed the look of love in the man's eyes."

The painting was of a couple from centuries earlier. A woman, in the portrait's foreground, cradled a swaddled baby in her arms while a man sat in the background, his attention on the woman and the infant.

"This painting always reminded me of us. Mom holding you or your sister, while I sat clueless in the background, too consumed with my own career to pay attention."

She regarded him.

"But this man has a soft side," he said. "I always hated seeing him just sitting there, but maybe he's got their backs. There's a kindness in his eyes I never noticed until today."

He stepped closer, studied the famous painting for another moment. When he turned back, she thought she saw tears in his eyes.

What is happening?

Her dad never cried. Ever. Not even when her mom had abandoned them.

He cleared his throat, put his arm around her, and they continued on.

"Do you have any reason to think you're in danger?" he murmured.

Her thoughts jumped to the surveillance cameras on her

house. He might insist she move out, might put an armed guard outside her front door, or worse, assign someone to tail her. While she hadn't told him she owned a nightclub, she had every confidence he knew.

"I had a little thing with a couple of my security cameras out front."

He flicked his gaze her way.

"One was stolen, the other was vandalized, but Hawk already replaced them, so it's no big deal. Probably neighborhood kids. You know, they were bored during summer break, you know, just out having some fun. We call it vandalism, they call it excitement, entertainment, whatever."

"You're rambling, Addison. That's one of your tells. You're trying to convince me so I won't worry."

Busted.

"When?" he asked.

"Yesterday."

Her dad grew quiet as they stopped in front of another painting. He tilted his head. Perhaps he was experiencing it from a different perspective. He could have been thinking about the vandalism to her cameras. Sometimes, he was hard to read.

"If I tell you you need a bodyguard, that means I don't think you can protect yourself. If I say you're capable of protecting yourself, and you're ambushed by multiple assailants, and you can't manage them alone—I would never forgive myself. And I would never get over losing you."

In silence, they left the salon and followed the signs for the temporary exhibit. This was always the best part of their outing. New pieces of art that were on loan from another museum for a limited time.

They entered that section of the gallery. More people had flocked to see these paintings and their forward momentum was slowed by the sheer number of art aficionados.

"What do *you* think, Addison?"

Her dad never asked for her opinion. He barked orders, people jumped to execute them. Like the paintings before them, this was something new.

"Well, I'm *not* going into hiding. You didn't raise a coward."

That made him smile.

They paused to admire an abstract piece of art.

"Your art is so much better than this," he murmured.

She put her arm around him and gave him a little squeeze. "Thanks, Daddy." After another second, she said, "I'm going to watch my six and live my life."

"Sounds like a plan."

They continued through the new exhibit, mostly in silence, until one of them commented on a painting.

Her dad had a tell, too. He'd pulled his phone from his pocket and was holding it in his hand. Phone in hand told her he was itching to make a call.

"Daddy, I'm going to the restroom."

"I'll wait in this salon for you," he replied.

Addison left, then circled back. She peeked around the corner, her gaze sweeping the busy room until she found her target.

Philip Skye was a man of action and he was going to ensure nothing happened to her. While she appreciated his concern, she didn't want someone reporting back to him on every move she made.

As she suspected, he was on his phone, his hand cupped over his mouth so no one could hear him or read his lips. Her father was paranoid, but for good reason. On more than one occasion, someone had tried to take him out.

He finished the call, slipped the phone back into his pocket.

There were some things her dad did *not* need to know. Giving ALPHA Operative Nicholas Hawk a blowjob was at the top of that list.

10

INVITATION TO ESCAPE

Late Wednesday afternoon, Hawk shifted his attention from the monitor on the wall to the four ALPHA Operatives—Emerson, Slash, Barry, and his cousin Tommy—sitting around the conference table at ALPHA HQ.

"The mission is Sunday, 4 a.m.," Hawk said. "Meet here at midnight for prep, then we'll fly to the Eastern Shore. Like every mission, we go in together and we leave together." He glanced around the table. "Tommy is a seasoned pro, but we gotta look out for him."

"I got you," Slash said to him.

"Same," Barry replied.

"Cooper, Danielle, and I are headed to target practice after this," Emerson said. "You guys are welcome."

Slash and Barry declined.

"I'm in," Tommy replied.

"Hit me with your questions," Hawk said to his team.

There were none. Everyone filed out, except Tommy.

"How's your first week going?" Hawk asked.

"I love working here. Donetta's been super helpful explaining different aspects of the organization to me."

Hawk logged out of ALPHA's secure website, shut his laptop.

"I was planning on swinging by Lost Souls tonight," Tommy said. "Were you able to get me on the list?"

"Bro, I forgot." Hawk pulled up the app on his phone and added Tommy as his guest. "Done."

"How do I become a member?"

"I'll sign you up later."

Tommy pushed out of his chair. "Do you have to sponsor me?"

"No, but I'm one of the owners."

Tommy's eyes widened. "No shit. Why didn't you say anything? Did Addison sell out?"

"Addison's business partner sold me her half. I couldn't say anything until we did the deed." A very sexy Addison, going down on him, flashed in his mind.

He loved women, he loved showing them a good time, but he never thought about 'em after. With Addison, it was the exact opposite. He couldn't *stop* thinking about her.

The only thing he couldn't get past was how he *hadn't* taken care of her. That was about to change, first chance he got.

"Are you swinging by the club?" Tommy asked, plucking him from his sexy thoughts.

"Not 'til later. I'm headed to the farmhouse. Granddad's been looking to hire someone, but he hasn't found anyone. I've been swinging by a coupla times a week to help them out. Can you meet me there?"

"Where's Prescott?" Tommy asked.

"He'll be there."

"Yeah, so I'm gonna pass. The farmhouse has never really been my jam, but I'll catch you tonight." After pushing out of his chair, Tommy left the room.

In the parking lot, Hawk mounted his motorcycle as

Cooper, Danielle, Tommy, and two other Operatives exited the building.

"Wow, you bought it," Danielle said. "That is sick. I'd love to borrow it sometime."

"Anytime, babe," Hawk replied.

"Nice bike," Tommy said. "What is it?"

"Harley Davidson Low Rider ST," Hawk replied.

"Whad'ya do with El Diablo?" Cooper asked.

"Sold it," Hawk replied.

"I don't remember you owning a motorcycle," Tommy said.

"My friend, Sin, got me into riding."

Tommy's eyes widened. "As in Sinclair Develin? You know the Fixer?"

"I know the Fixer, babe." Hawk pulled on the helmet, flashed a peace sign. "I'm out."

He started the bike and its distinctive low rumble vibrated through him. He dropped it into gear, gunned the engine while letting out the clutch, and roared out of the parking lot.

Not long after, he arrived at his grandparents' farmhouse, parked out front, and went inside.

The house was quiet and dark, so he flipped on lights as he made his way toward the kitchen. It was only ten after six in the evening, but he expected to see them eating dinner.

He spotted them on the back-porch swing. Granddad had his arm around Grandmom and he was singing to her. It was soft enough that Hawk couldn't hear the lyrics, but he could see how happy Grandmom was. Emotion tightened his throat. It was unusual to see them having a quiet moment together. The song ended and they kissed.

The front door opened and Prescott walked in. "Nice bike. You ended up getting the Low Rider in black."

Hawk tipped his chin toward the porch. "He was singing to her."

Prescott glanced over. "Looks like he's doing a lot more than singing to her now."

Their grandparents were kissing each other pretty good.

"Well, I'm *not* interrupting *that*," Hawk said, and Prescott laughed. "I'm going into the barn to see what's going on."

Hawk and Prescott each grabbed a giant door and pulled it open, then stood there staring inside. There were dozens of wooden crates strewn about the space, along with numerous farm implements. Several power tools lay on the floor.

"How the hell did it get this way?" Prescott asked.

"When Granddad's farmhand quit," Hawk replied.

Two hours later, the barn had been cleaned and organized. The brothers were sweaty, hungry, and thirsty.

They found their grandparents sipping wine on the back porch.

"Hey, what a great surprise," Granddad said. "It's Scotty and Nicky!"

"What are you two doing here?" Grandmom asked.

"We've been cleaning out the barn for the past two hours," Hawk replied.

"I was just out there last week," Granddad said. "It didn't look so bad."

Hawk and Prescott exchanged glances.

Grandmom rose. "Let's get you boys something to eat."

They retreated into the kitchen where Grandmom pulled out leftovers and fixed them each a plate.

While they wolfed it down, Grandmom asked about their day.

Since neither could discuss ALPHA or BLACK OPS, Hawk said, "I bought a nightclub."

"Good for you," Granddad said. "You didn't sell Hawk Security, did you? That's what made you wealthy, Nicky."

"Still got the security biz," Hawk answered after swallowing down the chicken. "I'm half owner of the club. Addison owns the other half."

"How you gonna work that into your schedule?" Prescott asked.

"Who the hell knows," Hawk replied.

"How's *your* empire, Scotty?" Granddad asked.

"In effin' shambles," Prescott replied.

"Still doing battle with your uncle?" Grandmom asked.

"Every chance I get," Prescott replied and Hawk chuffed out a laugh.

The guys finished eating, dropped their empty plates in the sink. "Thanks for dinner," Hawk said. "Always love your chicken, Grandmom."

She beamed at them. "You boys were always such good eaters."

"They still are," Granddad added.

"You ready to get outta here?" Hawk asked his grandparents.

Granddad and Grandmom exchanged glances. "Are you taking us to your nightclub?" Granddad asked.

"Move," Prescott clarified. "Are you ready to downsize? This is a lot to handle on your own."

"Where would we go, Scotty?" Grandmom asked. "We've been here forever."

Wasn't the first time they'd dismissed the time-to-move conversation. Rather than push it, Hawk hugged them both.

"Thanks for helping us out," Granddad said. "We love you."

"We love you too," Prescott replied before they left.

In the driveway, Prescott said, "I'll talk to Mom. The farm is too much for them and we're both too busy to maintain it."

"Let me know what she says." Hawk mounted his bike.

"You're as busy as I am, but you find the time to run a nightclub. I gotta make some changes. All I do is work."

"You gotta play. Come to my club."

"What's it called?"

"Lost Souls."

"The new cosplay club in Alexandria?"

"That's the one. Been there?"

"No, but I've heard it's *the* place if you're into costumes and kink." After a pause, Prescott broke into a grin. "Wait. You're not into dressing up. Are you finally making your move on Addison?"

"Don't go there."

"Nicky, you could be missing out on something great. I know you don't want to get hurt again but you—"

"I wasn't hurt. I was *wrecked*."

"You can't spend your life alone, not when you've got someone who really cares about you... and you care about her. I see the way you two look at each other. You gotta take a chance, put yourself out there with her."

Hawk wasn't about to get into it, so he pulled on his helmet, started the bike, and flipped up the visor. "Love you, brother."

He rode out as the sun dipped below the horizon. Once he hit the main road, he accelerated at full throttle, but no matter how fast he rode, he couldn't outrun the pain of the past.

Addison had been serving drinks behind the bar with Liliana all evening. Most nights, she'd dress up, but not tonight. Her heart was heavy from Ronald's death.

"You okay?" Liliana asked, plucking her from her thoughts. "You're pretty quiet and you haven't even tried to sign up a new member."

Addison poured a draft beer, set it on a napkin in front of a customer. After he took it, she peered at Liliana. "A friend of mine died."

"I'm so sorry," Liliana said. "Were they sick?"

"Car accident." Addison wasn't going to tell her that Ronald was killed when his car exploded.

"That's tough." Liliana waited on a customer, then got busy making a cocktail. After she served it, she turned back to Addison. "Are you going to the funeral?"

"I'm not sure. He lived out of town."

They grew quiet while they served drinks.

During a lull, Liliana moseyed back over. "Death is hard. I've lost people I cared about. I wish I could say something to help, but grief is real and everyone works through it differently."

"He left behind a wife and young children."

"Hopefully, he's in a better place," Liliana said. "It's the family that has to go on without him. That's hard because they feel lost... until they find their way. Maybe they'll figure out a way to honor him so they can keep his memory alive."

Addison offered a rueful smile. "Thanks for saying that."

She needed to call Becky. Normally good with words, she knew there was nothing she could say to make this better for her or her children.

She'd been a mess when her mom had abandoned them. This was different. Her mom had chosen to leave. Ronald had been taken from his family. A jolt of pain stabbed her chest. She couldn't begin to imagine their shock and grief.

"I've got to make a call." Addison glanced around. "Can you handle—"

"Absolutely," Liliana replied. "Take your time."

Alone in her office, Addison called Becky Jenning. She had no idea what she would say, but it didn't matter. Nothing could bring Ronald back. Her heart was breaking for his family.

"Hello?" answered a woman.

"Becky?"

"No, this is her mom. Who's calling?"

"Addison Skye."

"Can you hold on?"

Addison paced in her small office. A moment later, "Addison, it's Becky."

"Becky, I'm so sorry."

"Thanks for calling. I was told he died in a car explosion. Do you know anything more?"

The pit in Addison's stomach grew larger. "I don't. I was told the same thing."

"Is it related to a job? Was it random? Were others killed? I need answers. I've got to have some kind of closure." Becky choked back a sob.

Addison couldn't share what Henry and Anita had told her. "I don't work at the CIA anymore, but I'll see what I can find out. They'll have answers once they complete their investigation."

"That could take months."

"I know. When's the funeral?"

"I don't have his body," Becky said. "I'm not even sure there is a body. We're doing something small with family. Ohgod, Addison, this is killing me." She started crying.

The anger Addison kept in check jumped to the forefront. She felt helpless. If anything, her call had made things worse.

"Hello, this is Becky's mom. Becky had to step away."

"I'm so sorry," Addison said. "Tell her I'll get her some answers." Addison hung up. She just stood there, staring at nothing, wondering how she'd get information from an organization that kept everything under lock and key.

Knock-knock.

"Addison, it's Liliana."

Addison swung open the door. "What's up?"

"There's a customer waiting at the bar for you." Liliana smiled. "He's super cute. I've gotta get back." Her head bartender left.

She grabbed a tablet, pulled the door closed. As she made

her way through the crowded club, she spotted Tommy sitting at the bar in a Star Wars costume. Frustration slithered down her spine. He had every right to be there. Maybe he wasn't even there to see her. She *had* met him at a kink party, after all.

The night they'd met, he'd been dressed in that same warrior costume. He'd caught her eye, they talked, but not about anything personal. Dumb stuff, but he was chill. She liked his vibe, so they spent a little time acting out a scene, then things had turned kinky.

Addison walked behind the bar. "Hey, you found my club."

"Nicky got me on the list."

You're not helping me, Hawk.

Liliana sidled over, set down a beer, then shot Tommy a smile. "On the house."

Addison flicked her gaze from her to Tommy.

"Appreciate it." He lifted the glass, swigged. "Liliana talked me into joining. Club's got a great vibe."

"Thanks." Her frustration stood down and she smiled. He wasn't interested in her. He was here to make new connections.

After signing him up, she brought him over to the photo station. "Pick a backdrop," she instructed.

"Help me."

They stood side by side while she scrolled through. They found a cosmos one, so he mounted his phone and stepped into the pic. She snapped it, then he uploaded it to his profile.

The song changed to "Gimme Shelter" by The Rolling Stones.

"You gotta dance with me," he said.

"I don't—"

"Relax," he said. "It's just a dance." He started moving his hips in place.

A woman dressed as an action hero danced her way over and joined them. Addison started to leave, but the woman pulled her back.

"Stay, Addison. It's cool. Like you say, everyone's welcome." The clubber offered a friendly smile as she moved closer to Tommy.

Addison needed a moment, so she let the rhythmic beat sweep her away. The three of them moved farther into the crowded dance floor. Tommy twirled the other woman, then he did the same to her. The beat built to a crescendo and she inhaled a calming breath. She'd watch her six, limit her activity, and get some answers for Becky.

For all she knew, the explosion could have been related to any of his SEAL missions over the years. Or maybe it wasn't related to them at all.

Hawk parked his bike in the vacant owner's spot, near the front door, and braced for more pushback from club members. After dismounting, he locked his helmet.

"Nice bike," a guy said.

Hawk tossed him an acknowledgment nod.

Tony the bouncer was standing by the front door and shot him a wave. "How's it going boss man?"

"It's going, babe," Hawk replied. "How you doing?"

"I'm hanging loose. Go on in."

Hawk walked in, the Stones tune catching his ear. He stopped at the hostess stand, but she waved him on. "Hey, Hawk, you don't have to stop anymore."

When he smiled, color flooded her cheeks. "Thanks, baby."

Expecting to see Addison behind the bar, he spotted Liliana alone. He pulled up to the side of the bar where servers picked up their drink orders. "Yo, Liliana, you seen Addison?"

Liliana sauntered over. "She's dancing with a total hottie."

What the hell? He craned to see, but the crowd was too

dense. As he pushed toward the dance floor, he passed a group of women.

"Hi, aren't you the new owner?" asked one of them.

"I am," he replied over the music. "Whatcha need?"

"You," another answered. "I need you."

"It's unanimous," said the third woman. "We each want a turn."

Hawk slid his gaze from one to the other. He didn't care that they were attractive. None of them were Addison.

"I sent you an Invitation to Escape," said the fourth, "but you haven't responded." She struck a pose. "Maybe now you'll reply."

"Wish I could, but I'm all booked up."

The song ended. He glanced around and caught sight of Addison, Tommy, and some woman on the dance floor.

Hairs on the back of his neck went up. *No fucking way.*

"Enjoy your evening, ladies."

He took off toward Addison as a slow song started. As he moved into view, her gaze met his and he caught a flash of excitement in her eyes.

He walked over, directed his full attention on her. "Dance with me."

Not asking.

After taking her hand, he winked at his cousin, and moved away. He had no idea if she was into threesomes, didn't want to know. He wanted her for himself and he did *not* share.

When he'd reached the other end of the dance floor, he turned to face her. In that second, he had his answer. She reached up, rested her arms on his shoulders, and caressed the back of his neck with the tips of her fingernails, sending a thrill down his spine.

"What took you so long?" she murmured.

"I'm here now."

He slid his arms around her, pulled her close, and stared

into her eyes. Nowhere else he'd rather be. She was with him, and he was good.

When the song ended, she rose up and whispered, "I need to talk to you." This time, she clasped his hand, took him into their office. He thought she was going to say something about her dancing with his cousin. He didn't give a fuck about that. Leaning his ass against the back of the desk, he waited.

She stood close, but not close enough to pull her into his arms and hold her. *That*, he didn't like.

"My friend, Ronald—I was supposed to have lunch with him at Ziti's," she began. "His car exploded and he was killed." Tears pricked her eyes.

He definitely wasn't expecting this.

"I'm sorry, baby. Are you in danger?"

"No, but I was told to lay low, just in case."

"By whom?"

"The CIA and Cooper," she murmured.

"Was the hit targeted? Random?"

"As far as I know, no terror group has come forward, and the investigation could take months."

"Hmm."

"What?"

"I was at HQ today," he murmured. "Coop didn't say anything."

She furrowed her brow. "Why would he? It doesn't involve you."

He stared at her in disbelief. "We're partners. Cooper should have told me you might be in danger."

"Sorry, my brain is scrambled."

"You gotta be at the top of your game, Addison."

She fisted her hand on her hip. "I'm not in danger!" she whispered, frustration tinging her tone.

Ah, shit, here we go.

"I'm *not* scared and I'm *not* going into hiding. The only

reason I told you is because I'm sad. That's it. A good man died leaving behind a broken family. I called his wife. She wants answers. I don't know anything. My stupid words of condolence are bullshit. They have two young children. I can't make this better for her, for her family." Addison choked back a sob.

Hawk pulled her into his arms, slowly caressing her back. He sucked at these moments. Didn't matter what anyone said or did. The pain of grief was real. Physical pain, mental pain, emotional turmoil. He knew that firsthand.

After a moment, she disappeared into their private bathroom, returning with a long trail of toilet paper. She blew her nose, wiped her tears.

Her phone buzzed. She pulled it off the desk. "Ugh. Tommy sent me an Invitation to Escape." She flicked her gaze to Hawk. "He's persistent."

"Well, you were dancing with him."

Daggers shot from her eyes. "Are you telling me I was leading him on? It was a dance. I thought he got the message. I told him no. Plus, that other woman joined us."

"You danced, he saw a green light. Most guys are just looking for that next green light."

She bit back a smile. "Are all men that simple?"

He shrugged. "I don't like complicated, especially when it comes to women. You know that about me." He scraped his fingers down his whiskered cheeks and she tracked their movement. "He figured if you danced with him, maybe you'd go upstairs with him. He's into you, so he had to try."

She tapped the app. "I declined."

He moved her hair off her cheek, tucked it behind her ear. "I know *exactly* what you need."

"Ohgod," she whispered. "What do I need Nicholas Hawk?"

He kissed her forehead. "I got you. Trust me on this."

Hawk pulled out his phone, opened the Lost Souls app, but all the rooms were booked. He sat behind their desk, logged into the computer. After rearranging a few things, he rounded the desk, clasped her hand. "We're going upstairs."

"I'm not—"

"No, we're not, but I promise you'll like it."

They left their office, returned to the main room. If possible, it was even more crowded. While that was great for business, Hawk didn't give a fuck. All that mattered was helping Addison through her loss in some small way.

"I've gotta let Liliana know," she said.

Tommy was parked on a barstool, chatting up the bartender. Hawk hung back while Addison went behind the bar and spoke with her. Liliana glanced over at him, then finished her conversation with Addison.

Tommy waved him over.

Hawk squeezed in beside him at the bar. "Nice costume."

"I don't see you for months. Now, I see you all the time. Can I buy you a beer?"

"Later." Hawk slapped his cousin on the back. "I gotta take care of something."

Addison made her way over.

"I sent you an Invitation to Escape." Tommy pointed to his costume. "We had so much fun—"

"Yeah, I declined," Addison said, cutting him off. "Like I said, it's not gonna happen for us."

Tommy shifted toward Hawk. "No problem. I get it."

From behind the bar, Liliana moseyed over. "What are you still doing here? I thought you were taking a break."

"You're leaving?" Tommy asked.

"They're going upstairs," Liliana replied.

"Damn," Tommy muttered under his breath. "You're not even wearing costumes."

"No costumes needed," Hawk replied before ushering Addison away.

11

PUTTING ADDISON FIRST

Hawk escorted Addison through the club and over to the metal door leading upstairs. She stood in front of the scanner, the light flashed yellow. Hawk stood next to her and the light turned green. As Hawk opened the door, a guy and a girl headed toward them.

Hawk blocked their passage. "Hey, guys, where you going?"

"Upstairs," said the guy.

Rather than get into it with them, Hawk shut the door. "Go ahead."

"Why'd you close the door, man?" asked the clubber.

"Stand in front of the scanner," Hawk demanded.

"You stand in front of it. It turned green for you."

"Are you a member?" Addison asked.

"I'm here, ain't I?" asked the guy.

"We want to join," said the girl. "We're going upstairs to check it out."

"Nice try," Hawk said. "You can check out what the rooms look like on the app."

"Have you been members for a while?" the woman asked.

"We're the owners," Addison replied.

"Dude, you gotta let us up there," the guy said to Hawk.

"I can't, brother. We'll sign you up when we come back."

"Can you give us a discount?" asked the guy.

Hawk stood in front of the scanner again. The light turned yellow. After Addison stood in front of it, the light turned yellow again. The door wouldn't open because it detected the other couple lurking behind them.

They waited until the couple moved away before standing in front of the scanner for the third time. This time, they were cleared to enter.

As they walked up the steps, Hawk said, "I don't know how Jericho deals with the public. I don't have the patience for this crap."

Strangely, Addison laughed. "It's just people acting human. Liv told me he doesn't spend his evenings at Jericho Road anymore. He likes spending time with his wife."

"What do you think of that?" he asked.

"I think it's romantic. What do *you* think of that?" she quipped.

"I don't have a wife, so I don't think anything."

She couldn't contain her smile "You're an idiot, you know that?"

His pulse kicked up. Seeing Addison happy and relaxed was his hot button. He could stare at her for hours, then stare at her for several more.

He led her into the Pink Room. An explosion of pink everywhere. Pink sofa with a pink sheet over it. A pink chair in the far corner. Pink light bulbs bathed the room in a soft flow. Pushed against the wall sat a massage table.

Once behind the closed door, he yanked his T-shirt over his head.

She sashayed over, ran her fingernails down his chest. "As tempting as you are, I can't. It's not like I don't want to. I mean, blowing you was fun, but I'm not gonna hook up without a costume."

For a woman who wasn't a big talker, sometimes she said a boatload. He tilted her face toward his, dipped down and kissed her. "As tempting as you are, and you are extremely tempting, I'm going to relax you."

"Uh-huh."

"Strip down, babe. Put on my shirt if you're uncomfortable being naked."

Wanting to give her space, he left the shirt on the massage table, then went and parked his ass in the pink chair. Never sat in a pink chair before. For a pink chair, it was pretty damn comfortable.

She pulled her shirt over her head. Her black push-up bra had him swallowing down his burgeoning desire. Never before had he done this for anyone, but she wasn't okay. If she wasn't grounded and thinking clearly, she'd be vulnerable. He had no idea what the hell was going on with the explosion, but if it was related to her in some way, he needed her to be aware of every little thing going on around her.

She wiggled out of her skin-tight pants. Addison in a black thong was enough to turn him hard, but he fought the urge best he could. Rather than turn away from him, she unhooked her bra, let it fall off her shoulders.

And that's when his Little General wasn't so little any more. His twitching cock turned into a semi, but when she slid off that thong, he was ready for action. Addison under him, over him, and in front of him. Her naked body writhing with ecstasy while he rode her to the fucking moon.

A naked Addison was pure pleasure. Small, sexy breasts with pert nipples that begged to be sucked. Even in the dimly-lit glow of pink lights, he couldn't miss her hairless pussy.

"What scene are we doing?" she asked, plucking him from his arousing thoughts.

"Hop on that massage table," he said. "I'm going to relax you."

She laughed.

Addison's joyous expression touched the deepest part of his broken soul. Pulled by an invisible force, he went to her. "Lie facedown on the table."

She furrowed her brows at him. "Wait, you're serious? You're going to massage me? With your magic wand, right?"

He chuffed out a laugh. "No, baby, my hands. Just my hands, Addison."

She handed him back his shirt before lying on the table. He covered her with the sheet and retrieved massage oil.

"You comfortable?" he asked.

She turned toward him. "Is this a joke?"

"No."

He hadn't given anyone a massage in a long, long time, but he had to do this for her. Something special, just for her. He drizzled oil into his palm, rubbed his hands together, then placed them on her shoulders. Her skin was warm and soft.

Only forward.

They fell into a comfortable silence while he ran his fingers across her shoulders and down her back. He hadn't paused to look at a woman in a long time. Yeah, he checked them out. And he absolutely appreciated their naked form, but that was for *his* benefit. Who was he kidding? It had been one long blur of meaningless hookups. Addison was a gorgeous woman, but her inner beauty was what drew him to her, and kept him anchored there since their friendship began.

"You're gentle *and* firm," she murmured. "Feels amazing."

When he ran his knuckles down her back, she let out a moan. "You might have a magic wand, but those fingers are your real jewels."

"It's my knuckles, babe."

"Mmm, I love it."

"I gotta tell you a work thing," he said.

"Okay."

"Cooper assigned me a mentee."

"Nice."

"Tommy."

"Ouch. Is that awkward or did you get over the hookup thing?"

"I got past it... mostly."

"You're not at work much. Why didn't you tell Cooper no?"

"Tommy's my cousin. I don't say no to family and close friends. You know that."

"Whoa, that's a lot of muscle."

He lightened the pressure. "Better?"

"Much." Her back muscles relaxed as he worked her tight knots.

"He doesn't know you're an Op," Hawk continued.

"He'd probably get down on one knee and propose if he ever found out." She laughed.

Hawk did not.

She peered around at him. "That was a joke. When did you get so territorial?"

"We're good friends. I didn't like that he's been with you."

"I told you, it meant nothing. You and I did something sexual and it was no big deal for us."

Silence.

"No big deal... right?" she repeated.

"I got a rule. No hookups with anyone from work," he said. "ALPHA or my company."

"This'll be our little secret."

"What happens if one of us wants to do it again?"

She chuckled. "If we did anything... it would be costumed role playing. That kinda doesn't count."

"What the hell does that mean?"

"It's not romance. We're not making love or anything. It's

sex in a scene where we play different characters, have some fun, and go our separate ways."

"And here I thought *I* was emotionally unavailable."

"Welcome to Addison's fucked-up world where sex is a physical release, and people are kept at arm's length so she doesn't get hurt."

He grew silent while he let those words sink in. In that regard, they were more alike than he realized.

When he finished rubbing her back, he asked, "You want your glutes massaged?"

She glanced back at him. "God, yes."

Addison needed to change the subject. Being with Hawk in this way made her feel extremely vulnerable. Not because she was naked, but because she was herself. And he was running his large, strong, and very sexy hands over every inch of her body.

"Feels great," she murmured.

It was arousing as hell, yet comforting and intimate at the same time. Letting down her emotional guard wasn't something she allowed. But she adored Hawk. As a friend, she loved him. He was one of her go-to people. And at work, he was her number-one choice on a mission. Always.

The pampering was phenomenal. She couldn't remember the last time she'd gotten a massage.

"You know, I'm gonna be wanting a massage every week now," she said as he moved on to her thighs.

He leaned down, kissed her bare shoulder. "Then, I'll do it."

She melted from his words, his actions. Every damn thing about this amazing god of a man made her wish she could halt time... for just a little while.

The past week had been unusually intense, but Hawk's behavior was in a category all its own. She wasn't sure how to process it, and she needed a clear head if she was going to try to get answers for Ronald's widow.

She released a sigh. "I'm so sad about Ronald, but I'm also sad for his widow. I can't believe he's gone. His children lost their daddy."

"I'll help you find his killer," he said.

"Thank you," she replied. "Honestly, I don't think I'll ever find out who did it. It took me years to find that one terrorist and there were several of us doing it full time. Death is so difficult, you know?"

"Yeah, babe, I do."

They fell into a comfortable silence while he worked her calves, then massaged her feet. "Okay, I'm all done."

When she rolled over, she gazed up at the most handsome man she'd ever known. But it wasn't his killer looks that made her heart pound hard, it was the selfless gesture of putting her first.

"Wow, thank you." When she sat up, the sheet pooled at her waist, revealing her breasts.

Rather than gawk, he set her clothing on the table, then placed his greasy hands on the sides of her face, tipped it toward him, and kissed her. A kiss that didn't last nearly long enough.

After putting on her bra and shirt, she got off the table, slid on her thong and pants. "Your turn."

"That was to help you get centered. You gotta watch your six and you need to be at the top of your game. I'll meet you at target practice tomorrow after work."

"What about the club?"

"We've got employees who can handle things until we get here."

She put her arms around him, leaned up and hugged him. "You're good man, Nicholas Hawk."

He shook his head. "No. No, I'm not."

They left the room.

As they made their way down the stairs, he asked, "What are you doing for the rest of the night?"

"What I do best," she replied. "Sell memberships."

Hawk chuffed out a laugh. "That, darlin' is *not* what you do best."

In the first-floor stairwell, she pulled him aside. "What *do* I do best?"

He pinned her against the wall and kissed her. Deep, long, and filled with a raw need that had her grinding into him. Her brain froze while she sucked down a jagged breath. He rested his arm on the wall over them while the embrace intensified.

Then, he slowed the kiss down and stared into her eyes. "Kissing me is what you do best. Being a badass Op is what you do best." Then, he nosed her hair away from her ear, pressed his warm lips against her hot skin, and whispered, "Sucking my cock is what you do best."

With a wickedly-sinful smile that set her insides on fire, he walked through the door and into the club, leaving her wanting more.

And more is exactly what we're gonna do.

The rest of the evening flew by because Addison was fueled from Hawk's massage. Despite his no-sex rule, she was going to live out one of her favorite fantasies with the only man who'd ever starred in it.

After the club had closed and the waitstaff had taken off, she asked Hawk to clear the rooms with the bouncer, then swing by their office. When he left, she changed into a costume, sat behind their desk and waited, her heart pounding out of her chest. Tonight, she hoped he'd give her what she *really* needed.

All of him.

A few minutes later, he walked in. "Hey, babe, whad'ya need?" She pushed out of the chair and his eyes dropped to her outfit. "Holy hell."

His heated gaze raked over every inch of her, from the little red and white nurse's hat perched on her head, to her snug nurse's uniform that barely covered her ass, down to the thigh-high boots on her legs.

"You," she replied. "I need you."

A throaty growl rumbled out of him, while steely eyes drilled into hers. He scraped his fingers down his whiskered cheeks and over that chiseled jawline.

When his gaze met hers, fire burned in his eyes.

"Fuck, Addison. You don't know what you're saying."

She hitched a brow. "Oh, yes I do."

With a gleam in her eyes, she brushed past, her swaying hips and rounded ass stealing his full attention. He could tell her no or he could follow. If they went forward with this, their relationship would never be the same.

Relax, babe. It's just sex. No big deal.

But being intimate with her *was* a big deal. He should walk away now. But no way would he put the brakes on this. He wanted her because of *her*, not because he wanted sex.

He left the office and strode down the hall as she vanished around the corner. She was waiting for him, holding open the door to the stairs, a subtle smile tugging on the corners of her sexy mouth.

A mouth he couldn't wait to kiss.

Like the evening at their retreat, he took the door from her. Rather than argue, she pushed up on her toes and whispered, "Always the gentleman."

One step at a time, they climbed. Adrenaline powered through him. Despite her sexy costume, this was different. She might be fucking for fuck's sake, but he wasn't.

When he threaded his fingers through hers, she gave his a little squeeze. In silence, they continued up the stairs.

One more door to open, then it was nothing but sweet, sweet pleasure for as long as she could last. Because he was not gonna stop once they got started.

He opened the door to the second floor. She stopped to peer into his eyes. "When we enter the Blue Room, I'm not Addison. I'm the nurse assigned to care for her patient. Okay?"

She swallowed, then steeled her spine. Her breathing was slow and steady, but there was a vulnerability in her eyes he'd never seen before.

"Understood," he replied. "You know, I'm a virgin when it comes to role playing."

Her simple smile lit his insides on fire. His semi twitched, trapped behind his snug boxer briefs.

"I'll take good care of you." She squeezed his ass before gliding through the door. In front of the Blue Room, she said, "I'll be in in a moment."

He entered, and she shut the door behind him.

Blue light bathed the space. His gaze jumped to the bed, covered in a blue, satin sheet and a few pillows, a small table, and several sex toys hanging on the wall. A basic room with space to act out a scene or get right down to the good stuff.

After yanking off his T-shirt, he removed his shorts and boxer briefs. Naked, with a raging boner, he went to the table in search of a condom. As he stood there, in the faint blue light, movement in the doorway caught his eye.

"What are you doing out of bed?" A sly smile lifted her lips.

Addison's voice was softer than usual and a little more breathy. As she sauntered over, his heart kicked up speed. She wrapped her warm fingers around his waist and guided him to the bed.

"What am I going to do with you?" she asked. "Every time I come in here, you're wandering around." After pulling back the satin sheet, she peered into his eyes. "How are you feeling today?"

Hawk had never role played in his life, but if there was anything he was good at, it was faking it until he figured it out.

"My body hurts," he said. "Can you help me?"

"I can make you feel *much* better." When she bent over at the waist to fluff the bed pillows, her dress rode up, revealing her sexy, round bottom.

He slid his hand under the dress and caressed her bare ass. "Mmm, I feel better already."

"Oh, you're a frisky one." After stepping away from the bed, she said, "In you go."

The innuendo was not lost on him. Biting back a smile, he climbed in and lay on his back, his shaft shooting to the moon.

She gazed down at him with Bambi eyes, then let her attention drift to his chest, his abs, his straining junk, and his thighs, then retraced her trail while a moan ripped from her throat.

Slowly, she rolled her tongue across her lower lip. "Are you thirsty?"

He glanced at her chest, her breasts spilling from the partly unzipped dress. "Thirsty *and* starving."

She climbed on him, straddled his thighs, but she didn't touch his throbbing cock. He couldn't wait to see what she'd do next.

Leaning forward, she planked over him. "I don't normally kiss my patients, but I'm going to make an exception for you. I think kissing will ease your pain. What do you think?"

"Everything you do will help," he ground out.

Normally, he had phenomenal breath control, but he couldn't get a handle on it. She leaned over, pressed her lips to his, and kissed him. On instinct, he wrapped his arms around her. She opened her mouth, slid her tongue into his, and released a long, deep moan.

Within seconds, their kiss turned wild. She bit his lip. He bit hers back. She yelped, then groaned.

"Fuck, I love that," she said, her throaty voice sexy as hell. "The harder, the better."

Pushing off him, she sat up. The air was charged with lust, the need to enter her had him moving beneath her. Even in the dim blue light, the lust in her eyes shone bright.

"If you're starving, I'm going to sit on your face, so you can eat me. Will that help you feel better?"

"Fuck, yeah," he uttered.

He loved how seriously she took the scene, never straying from character. She directed him to slide down on the bed. As soon as he did, she squatted over his face and slowly lowered her pussy over him.

Addison Skye was a dirty, dirty girl.

And he fucking loved it.

He slid his hands under the dress, grabbed her ass to steady her, and licked her wet folds. Soaking wet, her pussy juices dripped into his mouth. He tongued her tender, silky flesh, tasting her for the very first time.

And, fuck, she tasted so damn good. He feasted on her pussy, licked her swollen clit while she held onto the headboard, groaning and crying out.

"That feels so good," she said. "Fuck me with your mouth, patient."

Her sexy sounds had turned into gritty, husky groans. He was teasing her, running his tongue over her, then plunging it into her pussy again and again. His already hard shaft had turned to granite while her sweet, sweet juices slid down his cheeks.

Then, she started crying out and shaking over him. "Yes, yes! I'm gonna come so hard."

Her entire body shook, as she blurted out his name. "Fuuu-uuuck, Nicholas, sooooo good."

Breaking character to call out his name never sounded so damn hot, and wetness coated the head of his cock.

Addison was a take-charge lover. She'd placed her sweet pussy on his face and she let him know—without question—what she needed. She was unlike anyone he'd ever known... and he loved that about her.

She moved off him, but she didn't leave the bed in search of a towel. Instead, she lay on him and kissed him hard, her tongue thrusting against his. Then, she slowed the kiss, and stopped.

Gazing into his eyes, she whispered, "I'm going to fuck you back to health, patient."

Still sucking down breaths, Addison straddled him, and stared into his eyes, black with desire. Giving in to the lust never felt so good and she couldn't wait to take him inside her.

"I want to make you feel better." After she placed his hand on her zipper, she stroked his thick, hard shaft.

Lucky for her, he needed no instruction. Slowly, he unzipped the dress while his scorching-hot gaze drilled into hers. His attention dropped to her breasts, her hard, aching nipples, down to her abs, then back to her breasts. Reaching up, he pulled the dress off her. Now, she was completely naked, save for her little hat and thigh-high boots.

In one easy movement, he flipped her onto her back and wedged himself flush against her. "I'm thirsty, nurse. I need something to suck on."

She loved this side of him. Naughty Nicky was unexpected, and sexy as hell. Play first, then fuck. And he was a willing, eager partner.

"Suck my tits," she commanded.

Rather than latch on, he traced the areola with his finger.

When he came full circle, he pinched the erect nib. She gasped from the brief sting of pain. Then, he did the same to her other one. When he finished, he leaned over, glanced up at her, then covered her nipple with his mouth.

Pleasure erupted over her, streams of desire making her insides throb. She grabbed a pillow, shoved it behind her head, and watched as the most beautiful man she'd ever known sucked her tit. The need to touch him had her stroking his muscular back, her fingers exploring the striations in his shoulder, the bulge of his bicep.

She started moving on the bed, gyrating her hips off the satin sheet, silently begging him to enter her.

"The only way you're going to get better is if you fuck me," she said. "The harder you do it, the better you'll feel."

"If you think so," he hissed.

"I'm on the pill," she murmured. "I use a diaphragm when I play, but it's not in me." She hated that she had to pop out to tell him, but this was an important. "Wear a condom."

He kissed her. "Yes, nurse."

She couldn't help but crack a smile. She loved playing with him, loved that they weren't strangers hooking up. Revealing this side of her was freeing and sexy as hell.

He left the bed and she tracked his movement like a lioness hunting her next meal. Leaning up on her elbows, she watched with great interest as he pulled one from the drawer. "Latex, extra large."

"You're a big boy," she murmured.

He ripped the packet, rolled on the condom. Seconds later, he was crawling back in bed, the smell of sex hanging in the air.

"Nurse," he said, the rasp of his deep voice catching her ear. "Roll over and put your ass in the air."

He'd done what she'd expected. He took control. Trembling with desire, she rolled over. Now, on all fours, she craned to see him.

"You ready for hard, fast, and so damn good?"

"Please, patient," she begged.

He fisted his shaft, positioned at her opening. Quivering with anticipation, she dropped her head, closed her eyes. He inched the head inside, then his long thick shaft. Her body bowed to his while she released a long, deep moan.

"So good," he roared behind her.

He grabbed her hair, fisted it into his grip, tugged and thrust. The slide was slow, deep, and so damn good. In and out while she moved against him. She dropped down, allowing him to sink in all the way. She couldn't stop the gritty sounds coming out of her, couldn't stop trembling from the onslaught of pleasure.

Her body was primed, another orgasm rising to the surface.

Then, without warning, he stopped moving, his hardness rooted inside her. She craned to see him. The rapture on his face was beyond beautiful. He looked like a different person. The constant anger in his eyes had been replaced with arousal, his half-hooded gaze made her moan.

He withdrew and her stomach dropped. Didn't he want to finish? *Ohgod, maybe I don't do it for him.*

He sat on the middle of the bed, his erection pointing skyward. "Straddle me."

Excitement had her hurrying into position. She guided him to her opening, and sank down, the euphoria stealing her breath, her thoughts.

"Yessss," she cried out.

She opened her eyes to find him peering into hers.

Moving slowly, she couldn't stop moaning from the sheer pleasure of him inside her. Instead of closing his eyes, his gaze hovered on hers. Up and down she glided, the glorious build taking her higher and higher. When he placed his hands on her hips to control her movement, his growl made her wetter still.

In and out, faster and faster. His cock turned to lead as her orgasm started deep in her belly.

"I'm gonna come," she blurted.

"Oh, yeah, baby, come for me," he ground out.

Gliding faster, the orgasm exploded through her in wave after pounding wave of sweet, sweet ecstasy.

"Here I go." He pulled her close, kissed her hard, their bodies releasing the purest of pleasures while their kisses turned savage.

She raked her fingernails across his back, letting herself let go with him. Still breathing hard, she went limp, the relaxation spreading through her once-tense body.

He wrapped his arms around her, held her close. Their breathing fell in line, then their lips melded. Soft, tender kisses that had no business in a role play in the Blue Room of Lost Souls.

For the first time in forever, she didn't feel lost. She felt like she'd been found.

But she couldn't let on. Role playing was all about the sexy times with none of the emotional intimacy.

And that's all this was.

She told herself that, but as she stared into his eyes, she didn't believe it. All she wanted to do was kiss him, bring him home with her, and love him all night long. The pull was that strong.

"Patient," she said shoving down the emotion. "Feeling better?"

"Definitely," he replied, "but I'm thinking we should go again... for medicinal purposes."

Those eyes, that face, his body. So, so tempting. She could go another round, no prob. But if she did, she'd be doing it as herself.

Not happening.

Despite how badly she wanted him again, she pulled off, the separation making her heart ache. "We should take off."

Disappointment flashed his eyes before he pushed out of bed. In silence, they cleaned up and dressed.

Had they taken their relationship to the next level or killed the friendship they had?

12

HAWK'S INSTALL

The following morning, Addison drove to the shopping center near her house and jumped in the waiting Uber. She'd hidden her long dark hair under an auburn wig and worn large, black sunglasses that concealed half her face. After a moment of small talk, the driver went silent and Addison stared out the window.

Last night, after their roleplaying, Hawk had pulled on his clothes and waited in the office while she changed out of her nurse's costume. It was a seamless transition that could have been awkward, but wasn't. She had no regrets... and no expectations they'd do it again.

In the parking lot, he'd pulled her into his arms, dropped a soft kiss on her lips, then waited while she got in her car and drove away.

No words spoken. No words needed.

Once at home, she had trouble sleeping. Not because she was afraid the vandals would come back, but because every time she'd drift off, she'd relive Hawk's strong hands caressing her body, his ravenous kisses stealing her breath, and his talented, talented mouth bringing her endless pleasure. But it was the look in his eyes that had stolen her heart.

The driver headed over Memorial Bridge and into DC, along with an army of fellow commuters. It was impossible to know if she was being followed, but she'd always been cautious when it came to seeing Melinda.

Melinda, once called Habibi, was Addison's most reliable asset when she lived overseas. In exchange for her valiant efforts in locating Haqazzii, Habibi was offered a new identity and a new life in America. The day after DEVGRU gunned down the terrorist at his compound, the CIA team was on a plane back to the US.

A scared and excited "Melinda" was with them, carrying nothing more than an overnight bag and a passport with her new identity.

Addison had invited Melinda to live with her. At first, Melinda was afraid to leave the house. But slowly, over time, she ventured out, got a job, worked hard, and saved like crazy.

Three years later, Melinda owned her own coffee shop located in the heart of the GW campus. She loved being around college students and had taken a few classes herself. From time to time, Addison stopped by to check on her. Today, however, her visit was strictly business.

The driver dropped her a block from Melinda's coffee shop. The sidewalk was crowded, the street jammed with traffic. On foot, Addison was making better time than the moving cars next to her.

Her phone rang with a call from her boss.

"Good morning," she answered.

"Don't come in to ALPHA," Cooper said.

"I was planning on working from home," she replied.

"Work at the black site."

"I can do that," she replied.

"Hawk said you two are going to target practice later today."

"Right," she replied, grateful Cooper had brought it up. She'd forgotten all about it.

"After you finish at the range, head into The Village and practice your hand-to-hand combat, along with your sniper skills."

"We just finished an entire week of drills at retreat week from hell," she pushed back.

"Do it," he said, but she heard the smile in his voice. "And don't go easy on Hawk. He can take it."

On a chuckle, she hung up.

I'm definitely up for some hand-to-hand with Hawk.

She arrived at the coffeeshop, went inside, kept her sunglasses on. After glancing around, she spotted Melinda working the register. Addison waited in line. When it was her turn, she placed her iced coffee order.

As she paid for the drink, Addison murmured, "Ten thirty, tonight."

Melinda held her gaze for an extra second before swiping the card and handing it back to her. "Thanks for coming in."

Addison waited for the barista to make her drink, then left, walking a block in the opposite direction. One Uber ride later, she was back at the shopping center and sitting in the back seat of her ALPHA SUV.

Off came the wig and supersized sunglasses. She pulled out the hair clips, fluffed her hair, and hopped behind the wheel. She'd parked at the far end of the lot, away from any store-mounted surveillance cameras, but it was impossible to know if she'd been followed.

As she started the vehicle and took off for the black site, a shiver ran through her. She'd always been the one hunting down the criminals. Never before had she been on the receiving end.

Hawk exited the Chevy Chase estate, slid on his shades, and lit up a cigarette. He was tired as hell from a terrible night's sleep.

Addison's stunningly sexy and nude body was etched into his brain, their role play a first of many. Of that he was certain. No way was he going back to just friends when they had so much fun fooling around.

He inhaled the cigarette, the invigorating hit of nicotine powering through him. Two of his crew stepped outside and down the front steps of the elaborate home.

"Yo, boss," said one of them. "We fixed the wiring and took care of that glitch."

"Nice job," Hawk replied before sucking down another drag.

The guys moseyed over to one of three Hawk Security vans parked out front at the circle and went heads-down on their phones.

Hawk had started his company from nothing, had worked his ass off for a decade, and now owned the most successful security and surveillance business in the region. The majority of his business came from government and commercial accounts, but he had thousands of residential clients whose homes were protected by his proprietary state-of-the-art system.

In addition to his installation teams, his forepersons managed the jobs, while a staff of seasoned salespeople brought in new business. Rather than farm out the monitoring and customer service teams, he kept that in-house as well.

Nowadays, Hawk was too busy running his company to oversee the installs. That's what his forepersons did. When this new client had hired his company to install a hundred-and-fifty-thousand-dollar home security and surveillance system, they'd insisted Hawk personally oversee the job. Since the monthly services fees to monitor the estate were more than most people's rent, he'd agreed. With his personal net worth fast approaching forty mil, he was happy to burn a few hours and manage the job. Word-of-mouth was still his number one marketing strategy. Provide the best equipment along with exceptional service, and let the client sell the system for him.

One more drag before stomping the cigarette and tossing the butt into a van's ashtray.

Back inside, he sat at the massive kitchen island where his laptop had been doing a final calibration test. Earlier, his team had found a system bug, which they'd resolved. Looked like everything was good to go. Time to find the homeowners, record their voices, pair that with the system, and ensure it worked for all commands. Once that was done, he was outta there.

The client, Ken and Sabrina Stoolin, owned a prominent Chevy Chase plastic surgery center. Ken was the surgeon, and his wife, Sabrina, the practice manager. The middle-aged couple had just purchased the home and wanted it outfitted with all the bells and whistles. Security cameras everywhere, voice-activated commands to lock and unlock doors, regulate the lights, the fireplace. If Hawk Security offered it, they bought it.

They'd even canceled patient surgeries for the day so they could both be there for the install.

Ken's lit cigarette lay perched in a nearby ashtray, but the homeowner wasn't in sight. He checked the first-floor home office. Not there, so he called Ken. No answer. Then, he called Sabrina. Her ringing phone was sitting on the kitchen counter.

Where the hell are they?

Ken's phlegmy cough snagged his attention and he followed the sound up the massive staircase. At the top, he called their names. Nothing. He'd been at the residence since eight that morning and he needed to get to the office. Agitation had him chuffing out a grunt.

More nasty-sounding hacking had him walking down the hall.

As he passed bedroom after bedroom on the second floor, grunts and groans caught his ear. The door at the end of the hall was partly closed, but Ken's throaty cough had him peering around the bedroom door.

No fucking way.

A naked Sabrina was bent over the side of the king bed while his newest installer banged her from behind. If this was a porn flick, he would have laughed, but this was his multi-million-dollar business.

If Ken saw this, he'd fire him, then probably sue his ass. As Hawk stepped into the bedroom, he got an eyeful. Ken—also naked, with a lit cigarette dangling from his mouth and thick smoke hanging over him—sat in a corner chair, rubbing one out.

"What the fucking fuck," Hawk roared.

All eyes whipped in his direction. Ken let loose, his ejaculate shooting in the air. Then he started coughing so hard, Hawk thought he'd hock up a lung. With his dick in hand, Ken ran into the bathroom to address his coughing jag.

"Give it to me, baby," Sabrina cried while bucking against his employee.

"Oh, yeah," his installer shouted.

Un-fucking-believable.

Hawk's interruption had triggered their orgasms.

Ken returned to the bedroom, wearing a bathrobe, his incessant coughing temporarily subdued.

"Install's done," Hawk bit out. "You have two minutes to get downstairs." Then, he eyed his employee. "See me before you leave."

"Ohgod," Wayne muttered. "I am so fired."

As Hawk jogged back downstairs, he started laughing. Not only was that one fucked-up scene, the good doctor had been smoking while jerking off.

That was fucked up.

Ken Stoolin hid his age well with his dyed hair and tailored suits, but stripped down, the fifty-something looked like hell. His frumpy, lumpy body and protruding paunch told the true tale. And all that chain smoking wasn't doing him any favors either.

Once outside, Hawk pulled out his cigarettes. Instead of shoving one into his mouth, he stared at the pack. For the past decade, he'd been ruining his lungs and disrespecting his body. At thirty-two, the smoking hadn't slowed him down. He was still a fast runner, still a beast in the gym. But what kind of damage was he doing that he *couldn't* see? What was he doing that could hurt him down the road?

I'm done. I'm fucking done.

With the pack in hand, he approached his installers waiting on the front lawn. He held up the cigarettes. "Any takers?"

One of his guys raised his hand. "Sure."

After handing it over, Hawk said, "Sorry for the hold up. The new installer was fucking the wife while her husband got his rocks off by watching."

Several installers burst out laughing, a few looked shocked.

His senior foreperson, José said, "Yeah, Ken propositioned me. Offered me a hundred to screw his old lady while he jacked off."

"What'd you tell him?" Hawk asked.

"I love my job, I love my wife, and there's no way I'm doing yours."

"Why didn't you tell me?" Hawk asked.

"Boss man, that's not the first time I've heard crazy shit or seen stuff I didn't need to see. I do my job, go home, and tell my wife." José shrugged a shoulder. "People are messed up."

Ken, now dressed, rushed outside, another lit cigarette dangling from his lips. "We're ready for you."

Hawk nodded, then addressed José. "Let's finish the install."

As they headed up the walkway, Wayne, his installer, slunk by.

Hawk stopped. "You got another install this afternoon?"

"Sure do," Wayne replied.

"Who you riding with?"

"Me," José answered.

"Drop him back at the office," Hawk said before walking into the home.

Hawk would need to hold an all-employee meeting because of this douche bag, get HR involved, and make sure everyone knew that fucking a client was gonna get you fired.

Pain in my ass.

Back inside, José asked Ken and Sabrina to record their voices. They acted like screwing the technician was no big deal. No one said anything to Hawk about what he'd walked in on. Neither of them apologized either.

It took three times for José to record Ken's voice because of Ken's incessant coughing. They finally finished up, then got the hell out.

Hawk could have easily brought Wayne back to the office with him, but he wasn't this guy's buddy. He was the boss man. Time to put some distance between him and the idiot who decided that sex with a client was not a problem.

After sliding into his Mercedes, he checked texts. There were several, but the one from Addison caught his eye. "What time can you meet me for target practice?"

"How's five?" he texted.

She replied with a thumbs-up emoji.

He pulled up a playlist on his phone, drove back to the

office feeling pretty damn good that he'd gone cold turkey. Unfortunately, in a few hours, the nicotine craving would kick in and he'd be on the hunt for a smoke.

Not this time.

He pulled into Hawk Security and parked. Once inside, he glanced around the spacious lobby of his five-story building. Before heading to the elevator bank, he checked in with his receptionists, then rode up to the top floor.

Once in his corner office, he checked email. One hundred and two unread. He was supposed to be in an executive meeting in twenty minutes, but that would have to get pushed back.

He called his HR director.

"Hi, boss man," Silas answered.

"I've got an HR issue."

"I'm two minutes from a meeting."

"Reschedule it," Hawk said.

"Yup, be there in a minute."

Hawk hung up and cracked his neck. Didn't help. He needed to go for a run. He thought of Addison. Now that he'd gotten a taste of her, he wanted more... a lot more.

After jumping on his phone, he opened the Lost Souls app, found her profile. He cued up an Invitation to Escape for later that evening, and included a personal message.

"Ladies choice. Prisoner and Warden, Cheerleader and QB, or Prof and Student. Play with me and escape reality."

Knock-knock-knock.

Silas stood in the doorway. Hawk sent the invitation, waved his HR director in.

"What's going on?" Silas asked after shutting Hawk's door.

"I walked in on a new installer screwing a homeowner while her husband jacked off in the corner."

Silas stifled a snicker. "Inappropriate laughter."

Hawk cracked a smile. "It was like seeing bad porn by accident."

Silas laughed. "Sorry. I can't help myself."

Hawk started laughing. "It was pretty crazy. I gotta let Wayne go, then we gotta set up an online class or bring in someone to talk about why employees can't engage in sexual acts with clients."

Silas nodded. "Yeah, this is gonna cost us."

"No shit."

"I'll get on this and let you know."

"Coordinate everything with Mags," Hawk instructed.

"Does she know?" Silas asked.

"No, I'm gonna tell her after we escort Wayne out."

"Where is he?"

"José is dropping him off." Hawk called downstairs.

"Hey, boss man," answered one of the receptionists.

"Is Wayne down there?"

"Sure is."

Hawk hung up.

Silas rose. "I'll bring him up here." His HR director left, shutting the door behind him.

Hawk checked his phone. A message waited in the Lost Souls app from Addison. His heart kicked up speed.

"After the club closes, I'm all yours," she texted. "I like Prisoner Warden or Boss and Prospective Hire."

Hawk's smiled. He couldn't fucking wait.

A few moments later, Silas returned with Wayne. The men sat in the guest chairs across from Hawk. Rather than launch into anything, Hawk said nothing.

"I guess I screwed up," Wayne said.

"Why don't you tell us what happened?" Silas asked.

"I was working upstairs with my team and the homeowner called me into the hallway. He told me he'd pay me a hundred bucks to screw his wife."

"Why didn't you tell him no, then let your supervisor know?" Silas asked.

"Dude, his wife was hot. She had porn star tits. I mean, I couldn't get my hands around 'em. I haven't gotten laid in months, and it was an easy hundred. Kinda a no-brainer."

Ah, for fuck's sake.

Hawk and Silas exchanged glances.

"I got a little weirded out when the husband stayed, but I figured he wanted to make sure I didn't hurt her. Dude ended up jerkin' off. I shouldn't have done it, but I'm not gonna lie. Fucking her was great."

"Right, so this is unethical, unprofessional, and goes against company policy," Silas continued.

"Are you for real?" Wayne asked. "What policy?"

Hawk's growl got their attention. Wasn't it common knowledge *not* to screw the clients? How did this guy get hired in the first place?

"Did you have intimate relations with clients at your former job?" Silas asked.

"If someone wanted me to fuck 'em, I fucked 'em."

"That's not how things work here," Hawk said. "I gotta let you go. Silas will escort you out."

"Dude, come on. I like working here."

"If you'd been remorseful or if this had been the first time, or if the owner had coerced you to do it—" Hawk said.

"I can change my answer to one of those," Wayne interrupted. "Yeah, he coerced me. Told me he'd kill me if I didn't have sex with his wife."

Silas started to laugh, but covered with a cough. "I'm sorry, Wayne, but today's your last day with us."

Wayne stood. "That sucks. I can't believe you're letting me go over this. This is bullshit, man. You're gonna be sorry you fired me."

Hawk stood. "We'll escort you out."

The elevator ride was filled with silence that Hawk wasn't going to fill. This was all on Wayne.

In the lobby, laughter caught Hawk's ear. His cousin, Tommy, was laughing it up with two of his receptionists and his general manager, Mags.

What the hell is he doing here?

13

THE LATE-NIGHT RENDEZVOUS

After escorting Wayne out, Hawk made his way over to the energetic group.

Tommy broke into a grin. "There he is!"

"How's everyone doing?" Hawk asked his employees.

"Doing great," said one of his receptionists.

"Busy day," answered the second.

The third receptionist was on the phone, but she acknowledged him with a smile.

"Hawk, you didn't tell me you hired your cousin," Mags said.

Now what's he gone and done?

His general manager, Margaret Larson—who went by Mags —had been through a lot during her recent divorce. Over the past couple weeks, she'd been smiling more, joking more too. She'd lost her dog in the custody battle, but had recently gotten herself a rescue from the local shelter. Hawk was relieved his GM was coming back from a challenging time in her life.

While he didn't pry into her personal life, she confided that she put herself on a few dating sites. She'd been talking to a few guys, not looking for anything serious, just wanted to get back in the game.

Hawk regarded his cousin. He didn't remember Tommy not having an "off" switch, but the guy was loose with his words. Too loose. He shouldn't have stopped by and he sure as hell shouldn't be telling everyone he worked there.

"When did you hire him?" Silas asked.

"He's doing some consulting for me," Hawk lied.

Tommy held up a large fast-food bag. "I brought lunch, cuz. How 'bout a tour?"

Hawk had already pushed his morning meetings to accommodate his porn-star clients. No way could he burn through time with someone who didn't actually work there.

"I'll do it," Mags offered.

Tommy grinned. "Great. And if you haven't eaten, there's a burger in here with your name on it."

"Thanks, Mags," Hawk said. "Tommy, let's chat for a second."

Hawk moved away from reception, forcing Tommy to follow, but not before he turned to Mags and shot her a smile. "Don't move a muscle."

Far enough away from prying ears, Hawk asked, "What's going on, Tommy? Why are you even here?"

"Dude, it's my cover," Tommy murmured. "I need to see where I work, you know, in case someone asks."

"You can't be blabbing that you work here. You don't."

"I gotta ask you something. You told me you and Addison were just friends. Why'd you go upstairs with her at the club?"

Hawk gaped at him. "Bro, what is up with you?"

Shoving his hands into his pants pockets, Tommy started shuffling back and forth. "Nothing, why?"

Frustration tinged Hawk's tone. "I'm *not* talking about Addison and you gotta back off. She said no. Move on."

"When I was in Philly, I thought about her—a lot. I was hoping she would change her mind about me."

Hawk squeezed his shoulder. "If she told you no, she's not interested. I've known her for a while and she's not into playing games. She's very direct. Let this one go."

Tommy glowered at him. "Got it. Well, I joined the club, so I'm gonna get my money's worth."

"I hope you do. It's a fun place to hang out." Hawk's phone rang. It was his installation director. "I gotta take this. Don't talk to anyone about working here."

"Gotcha," Tommy replied.

"Hey," Hawk answered.

"I just heard what happened with Wayne." His director started laughing. "What a cluster."

Hawk headed toward the elevator, punched the up button. "I'm on my way upstairs." He hung up to his installation director's hysterical laughter.

I'm not gonna get a damn thing done today.

Addison had been at the firing range for ten minutes when she felt eyes on her. She turned to see Hawk staring through the observation window behind her. Her heart skipped a beat when her gaze met his.

She put down her weapon and left the room. "Hey, how long you been standing there?"

"Long enough to admire your form," he replied.

She hitched a brow. "Are you flirting with me, Nicholas Hawk?"

"I love watching you shoot." He winked. "You got a great ass."

A whisper-soft moan ripped through her. She couldn't wait for their role play when the club closed.

"The lane next to me was empty, but it's not now," she said trying to get them back on track.

His steely eyes stayed cemented on hers. "I'll share yours."

Being in that small space turned up the heat. She'd always loved shooting with him, but things were different now. They'd crossed that line and she couldn't go back. Didn't want to. She was hooked on him and she couldn't wait for more.

The Hawk Effect.

She waited while he slipped in ear plugs and pulled on goggles. Then, with his weapon in hand, they turned their attention to the target.

They stood side by side, readied their shots, and fired. They'd been shooting together for so long, it was like second nature. Normally, she'd focus on her breathing, to ensure her aim was steady, but his scent wafted in her direction and broke her concentration.

When she fired, the bullet missed the target completely.

He glanced over at her. "What's with your stance?"

She lowered her weapon, looked down at herself. "What do you mean?"

He set down his gun, walked behind her.

Ohgod, this isn't helping.

Spread your legs a little wider.

Please, stop talking.

He nudged her thigh with his knee. A thrill ran through her.

Oh, boy, now he's touching me.

Resting his hands on her shoulders, he whispered, "Why so uptight? Relax your shoulders, babe."

She sucked down a breath, then released it slowly. Didn't help.

He anchored his large, muscular hands on her hips and adjusted them so they were perpendicular to the target. Her insides heated.

"Drop your center of gravity a little more."

Warmth spread through her while his hands stayed glued to her. A few seconds passed while she got herself together before dropping down.

"Nice."

His velvety voice made her tremble with excitement. She'd have to kick him out of the galley if she couldn't focus.

He released his hands. "Ready your shot."

She homed in on the center of the target, inhaled, and pressed the trigger.

BANG!

She hit the target this time, but not the bullseye.

"Again," he said.

Though she followed his instructions, her insides were humming with desire. Her fingers trembled. Normally, she was a steady shot. Rarely missed. She imagined him stepping close, nuzzling her neck, wrapping his strong, sinewy arms around her and pulling her close while his hardness pressed against her ass.

Her thoughts had gone off the rails.

Get it together. Now.

Heaving in a breath, she found her center of gravity, bent her knees, and readied her shot. Then, she fired.

BANG!

The bullet pierced the center of the target.

"There's my girl," he said. "Welcome back."

He took his position beside her and they fired in tandem. Round after round after round. They were in complete sync, their bullets overlapping each other's every single time.

When they finished and had packed up their weapons, he asked, "You okay?"

"Yeah. Why?"

He stepped so close she could see the translucent turquoise

specs in his blue eyes. "You missed the target. You were having trouble concentrating. What's going on?"

She wanted to tell him that being around him was exhilarating, that his touch electrified her, that she couldn't wait until she could escape into his arms. That getting lost in him was the only thing she craved.

Instead she said, "Nothing's going on. Thanks for having my back. You want to go into The Village?"

"Sure," he replied.

The Village was located behind the shooting range. It was reserved for law enforcement groups to practice real-life scenarios in a pretend town. Six buildings covered the campus and it offered a more authentic place to work on technique and accuracy than the firing range.

Before entering the space, they pulled on their body armor.

It was just after six and they weren't alone. A group of cadets was working in building six with their commanding officer.

"Live rounds," Hawk said.

"Let's stick to the first two buildings," she replied.

They worked on sharp shooting. Addison was more accurate, but Hawk fired more rounds faster. Then, they worked on pop-up targets. For those, they were equally matched.

As they were returning to building one, she said, "I wish I was this relaxed during a mission."

He flicked his gaze in her direction. "You aren't?"

"Hell, no. My adrenaline is pumping. I'm laser focused, which can be bad because I might miss an ambush or a second shooter. Are *you* relaxed?"

"Yeah, I mean, it's not like flying where I'm really in the zone, but I'm pretty chill. It would take a lot to rattle me."

"How are you able to do that?"

"Ten years ago, I hit rock bottom. My life got ripped apart and I was gutted."

She stopped walking and stared at him. *Why have I never heard this before?*

"I wasn't eating, I couldn't get out of bed," he continued. "I didn't care if I lived or died."

Instead of pressing him with questions, she waited, hoping he'd say more. When he didn't, she caressed his back. "I'm so sorry."

Movement near building two caught her eye. Someone, dressed in black, peeked out from the side of the building, his face obscured by a baseball cap. He raised his arm, a weapon in his hand.

Addison plowed herself onto Hawk, pushing him over. They hit the ground as a bullet whizzed by. They jumped up and ran for cover behind building one.

With her heart pounding out of her chest, she stood with her back against the cement structure, breathing hard. "Were you hit?" she whispered between gasps.

"No. You?"

"Negative." After several seconds of silence, she regarded him. "What the hell was that?"

"Either a stray bullet from the cadet class or someone is trying to kill us."

Back to back, and with their guns drawn, they retrieved their duffle bags, then hurried back to the main building. There, they found owner Tucker Henninger working at the check-in counter.

"Hey, guys." Tucker's easygoing smile was replaced with a furrowed brow. "What's wrong?"

"We were in The Village and a stray bullet almost hit us," Addison said.

"Which building?" Tucker asked.

"Two," Hawk answered.

Tucker checked the log. "I've got three groups back there now, but someone cut a hole in my chain link fence. People have been sneaking in. I fixed it, but they might've come back." He regarded them. "You okay?"

"We're fine," Hawk bit out.

Clearly, he wasn't okay. Frustration poured from his eyes, his lips were slit in a thin line, and his muscles were ticking in his jaw.

An angry Hawk was a very, very sexy Hawk.

"I'll look into it," Tucker said. "Thanks for letting me know. Glad you had your Kevlar."

As they ventured into the parking lot, Hawk bit out, "Our body armor won't do jack if we'd been hit in the head."

He was seething with frustration, and she knew exactly what she wanted to do about that. Her body ached for his, she had to touch him. Had to feel that connection. So, she stroked his back as he walked her to her car.

"I love your touch," he murmured.

At her SUV, she opened the liftgate, set down her bag.

"I appreciate that Tucker is so chill, but for fuck's sake, if that was my business, I'd throw on the spot lights and hunt that asshole down," he growled.

Addison stepped close. "You're so angry." She leaned up. "I find that so damn sexy."

They were on each other, the incendiary kiss sending hit after hit of adrenaline flying through her. She slipped her fingers into his hair and fisted handfuls while his growls turned her wet with need.

With one hand around her waist, he palmed her ass with the other. "Fuck, you feel good. I can't wait to give you what you need."

"I need naughty Nicky," she said between kisses. "Naughty, naughty Nicky."

His lips curved as he slowed the kiss. "I'm gonna give it to you so good, babe. Make you purr like a kitten."

"Ohgod." She sucked down a breath. "I gotta go or I'm gonna be dry humping you in the parking lot."

He cradled her chin, dropped another searing kiss on her mouth. "We can do a lot better than dry humping."

Desire thrummed through her. Pausing, she stared into his eyes. "Mmm." Then, she shut the back hatch. "I'll meet you at the club."

"I'll follow you back to your place. We can drive there together."

As much as she craved his company, she needed her car, so she could sneak out and meet Melinda.

Hawk's phone rang. "Now what?" He checked. "It's my mom. I'll call her back."

"Talk to her." Addison opened the driver's side door and climbed in. "I'll see you at the club."

She shut the door, started the engine, and backed out of the spot. With a little wave, she drove away.

In a few hours, naughty Nicky's gonna be all mine... and I can't wait.

"Hey Mom," Hawk answered.

"Granddad had a little mishap. He was climbing down the ladder—"

"What the hell was he doing on a ladder?"

"And he fell. He's at the hospital, and I'm headed there now with Dad. They're running tests to see if he's got a concussion, and his hip is hurting."

"For fuck's sake," Hawk bit out.

"Nicky, what's that all about?"

"I'm stretched a little thin and I'm already spending time at the farm helping them out. I don't have time to—"

"Nicholas," his mother interjected, "you don't need to do that."

"Well, Mom, I kinda do. If I don't go, nothing gets done. They don't have a farmhand and they can't keep up with everything."

"Are you doing it alone?"

"Prescott helps, when he's in town."

"What about Tommy?"

"No."

"Grandmom is going to stay with us. Dad and I will find a farmhand or two. Why didn't you say anything to us?"

He didn't need to answer that. She, of all people, knew that if someone needed help, he helped. No questions asked.

"Nicky, it's one thing to grab eggs when you're there, but you don't have to work the farm. You can't save everyone, honey."

"What hospital is he in?"

His mom relayed the information and he hung up.

As he drove home, he thought about what his mom had said. She was right. He couldn't save everyone, but when he cared about someone, he was all in.

Changing course, he drove to the hospital.

"There's my number one," Granddad said with a grin.

His Granddad was in good spirits, surrounded by Grandmom and his parents.

"What a great surprise!" Grandmom pushed out of the chair and hugged him.

Hawk sat on the hospital bed. "I hope you're done with the circus acrobatics," he said, and everyone laughed.

"Mom and Dad are going to hire some help," Grandmom said.

His mom's phone rang. Kerri and Jamal wanted to video chat. The phone got passed around, while the newlyweds chatted about their honeymoon adventures. Hawk stayed for longer than he'd intended, but he always made time for his family.

Every. Single. Time.

It was after nine by the time he got to Lost Souls. Like every night, things were in full swing. The bar was busy, the dance floor crowded, the picture-posing corner packed with costumed clubbers. He scanned the room. No Addison.

On his way toward their office, he found his target, in the hallway, her tablet in hand, and chatting with two women.

Addison was dressed in a black latex costume that hugged her curves, sending a blast of heat through him. She wore a black eye mask and black gloves. Looking like a burglar about to go on the prowl, he couldn't take his eyes off her.

She's scorching hot.

As he approached, all three women turned in his direction.

The second he locked eyes with Addison, a jolt of energy powered through him. Her eyes were covered in smoky shadows, her lips painted black, and her enticing vanilla scent washed over him.

He ran his hand down her back, stopping shy of her ass, but his fingers twitched to cup her curvy backside.

"This is my business partner, Hawk," Addison said. "I was just signing—"

"Oh, wow," said the blonde. "I know you."

The brunette regarded her friend. "This is the guy I was telling you about, you know, the one with the bedroom eyes."

"Small world," the blonde said as she flicked her head, sending her hair flying off her shoulders. "I'm mad you never called. Why didn't you? Didn't you have fun with me?"

Rather than get into what happened months ago, Hawk stayed silent. No point poking the bear.

"I'd love to reconnect with you." The brunette gestured toward Addison. "She was just telling us about the Invitations to Escape. Do you do those?"

He slid his gaze to Addison. "I do—"

"Yes!" hissed the blonde. "I'm in. You owe me."

"—with Addison," he said, finishing his sentence.

Addison clasped his pinky, gave him a quick squeeze before letting go. He loved that about her. An understated action that let him know she liked what she heard.

Both clubbers gawked at her. "You are one lucky girl," said the blonde. "That man can fuck."

Jesus, have some class, will ya?

"I know, right?" added the brunette. "He's off the market, is there even a reason to join?"

Tony, the bouncer, strode down the hall. "We got a problem outside."

"Let us know if you want to sign up," Addison said.

As she and Hawk followed Tony out front, Addison removed her mask.

Two men were standing in the parking lot, both armed with switchblades. They were circling each other like two bulls about to charge.

"Thanks, Tony," Hawk said. "Keep everyone away."

"Absolutely," Tony replied as he corralled people back in line.

"Ready?" Hawk asked Addison.

She shot him a quick nod.

Walking side by side, they approached the men.

"Hey, guys, what's going on?" Hawk asked.

"This dude asked my girl to hook up in your fucking club!" hollered the larger man.

"If I'd known she was yours, asshole, I wouldn't have asked," replied the slender guy. "She coulda said no, but she didn't. Guess you're not enough for her."

"Fuck," Hawk grumbled. The smaller one was goading the larger one.

"Put your weapons away," Addison said, her commanding

voice catching their attention.

"Get lost, lady," said the smaller one.

"We're the owners," Hawk said. "If you don't listen to her, we call the cops. You got three seconds to put the knives away."

"Tell this motherfucker to stay away from my woman." The big one was waving his arms, the knife's blade catching the light from the parking lot lamp.

"I asked, she accepted," said the slight man, "You ain't my problem."

The bigger man lunged, his blade pointed out.

"Now," Hawk blurted.

Moving into action, Addison swept the smaller man's legs out from under him, sending him crashing to the ground.

Hawk grabbed the wrist of the large man and twisted. The knife dropped. Addison kicked it away. Hawk continued twisting his arm until it was behind his back, then he applied an arm bar to force the man to the ground, facedown.

Hawk pulled his Glock. "Do. Not. Move."

A few in the crowd screamed when they saw Hawk's gun.

The smaller man started to get up.

"No," Addison bit out. "On your stomach."

The slight man lay back down.

"Don't touch me," said the larger man.

"Stay down," Hawk bit out. "Tony, get the cops here." Hawk glanced around at the expanding crowd of spectators. "Guys, you gotta clear out."

Tony jogged over, phone to his ear. "Cops are on the way."

Hawk nodded in acknowledgment, his gun pointed toward both men.

"Move everyone away," Hawk instructed his bouncer.

The police arrived, took Hawk and Addison's statements, then hauled both men away.

As they made their way toward the front door, Hawk slid his fingers around Addison's arm, appreciating her striated muscles. A small arm that packed a lot of strength. He pulled her aside, peered down at her.

"Nice job," he said.

"You, too, partner," she replied.

He stepped closer. "You look scorching hot, baby. I can't wait peel that off you."

She pushed onto her toes. "Me, too."

Her gaze drilled into his, the blackness of her pupils bleeding into her light eyes. All he could see, all he cared about, was the woman standing inches away. Somehow, she'd broken through his guarded exterior and had curled her way around his soul.

They came together in a tender kiss. Her lips curved, her sigh floating in the air between them.

They went inside, Liliana hurried over. "What happened?"

"A fight," Hawk replied.

"Over a woman," Addison added.

Liliana slid her gaze from one to the other. "Who won?"

"Neither," Hawk replied.

"Was it a blood bath?" Liliana asked.

Addison smiled. "No."

With a gleam in her eye, Liliana said, "Those are always the most fun." She winked, then returned behind the bar.

"I'm going to find those women and sign them up," Addison said.

"You don't care that I had sex with them?" Hawk asked.

"The question you should be asking is, do *you* care that you had sex with them?"

"No, I don't," he replied.

"Then, why should I?" She gave his triceps a squeeze before launching into the crowded room.

In that moment, he knew. He told himself that he'd *never* feel this way again. But he did. Addison had claimed his heart and there was nothing he could do about it. Love makes everything better, except for Hawk, it made everything worse. Much, much worse.

Damn that woman. Damn her.

Just after ten that evening, Addison grabbed her handbag from the office and hurried down the hallway. Leaving out the club's back exit would trigger the alarm, so she was forced to use the front door.

She spotted Hawk talking to a few people at the picture-taking stand, so she kept her head down as she powered around the members and their guests. Once outside, she found Tony.

"I'll be back soon," she told him.

"No worries," her bouncer replied.

She hurried around back where she'd parked her ALPHA SUV. All vehicles in the fleet were equipped with bullet-proof glass, but it wouldn't stop her from blowing sky high if someone had attached an explosive to the underside. Yes, she was taking her chances, but she'd never been one to run from danger.

She drove over the bridge into DC, then headed for her alma mater, George Washington University. Rather than park in front of the closed coffee shop, she drove around the block, pulled down the alley and parked by Melinda's back door.

There was one other car parked nearby.

She slipped on the black eye mask, pulled her Glock from her bag, and got out. After closing the door quietly, she made her way to the back door.

Knock-knock-knock.

A second later, Melinda pushed it open, and jumped. "Oh, my goodness."

"It's Addison," she whispered.

Addison entered, pulled the door closed behind her. The room was dark, save for a small table lamp set on low.

After removing her mask, Addison hugged her. "It's good to see you."

"You, too. Let's sit."

They got comfortable at the small table where Melinda had set out a few sweet treats and a pot of tea and two mugs. "Please, help yourself." Melinda poured tea into both mugs.

Normally energetic, Melinda had bags under her eyes and she hadn't smiled once.

"How are you doing?" Addison began.

"The coffee shop keeps me busy. I've been missing my family more than usual. I know my parents are getting older and I wish I could see them again."

"I'm sorry."

Melinda smiled. "It's okay. I love my little business, love being around the college students, too."

"Are you still working long hours?" Addison asked.

"Most days," Melinda replied. "I stay open late a few nights, so the students can grab coffee or meet up with friends. How have you been?"

"Good, busy." Addison leaned forward and clasped Melinda's hand. "I wanted you to know something... something important. Do you remember the military man who took out Haqazzii?"

"Jenning, the one who wrote the book."

Addison nodded. "He was killed in a car explosion."

Melinda gasped. "Was it a terrorist bomb?"

"They don't know. I'd like to hire a bodyguard for you while it's being investigated."

"Why? I have no ties to my former life. I'm still very private. No one knows my true identity, except you. I'm not worried, but I am always cautious."

"I would feel better if you were protected. And I'd pay, so no worries about that."

This time, Melinda's smile touched her warm, brown eyes. "You've kept every promise you ever made to me."

"You're my friend and I care about you."

Melinda smiled. "Thank you for caring. I'll let you know."

The women chatted for a few minutes more, then Addison slipped on her mask and snuck out the way she'd arrived. She kept the headlights off until she'd turned onto the main road.

Her mom had taught her and her sister that ignorance was bliss. But it was her dad who taught her that knowledge was power.

Addison believed that telling Melinda had been the right choice, but as she drove back to Lost Souls, she wondered if, in this case, ignorance might have been the better option.

14

WICKED HOT

Hawk was frustrated as hell. Addison had left the damn club. Then, Liliana had some kind of medical emergency and bolted.

He didn't have a problem tending bar. Loved chatting it up with the customers. The majority of them were chill. They were there to kick back, have a beer, meet new people. The costumes were cool too.

What had him seeing red was his vanishing partner. If she had something to do, then do it. But, for fuck's sake, tell him.

He hadn't texted her, hadn't called her either. But he wasn't gonna do nothing while she was out there alone. When she hadn't returned by quarter to eleven, he pulled two waitstaff off the floor and brought them behind the bar. "Serve drinks for five minutes."

"Sure," said one.

"I can fake it, but I don't know some of the—"

"Help each other out. I'll be in my office."

He bulled his way through the thick crowd, locked himself in the office. Despite not having his ALPHA laptop with him, he logged in virtually, then located her by the chip in her neck.

While this might have overstepping, he was too pissed to care how she'd react.

She was at a Northwest DC coffee shop in the heart of the GW campus.

What the hell?

He didn't know if she was okay. Was she alone? What was she doing there when they had coffee at their own fucking club?

He slammed his fist on the table. "Dammit, Addison." After logging out and deleting the history, he returned to the bar.

"That was fast," said one of the servers. "This was fun."

"You know how to sling drinks?" he asked.

"I'm okay," she replied. "If you need help, I'll stay."

"Sure," Hawk replied.

"I'm going back on the floor," said the male employee.

The server, dressed as a princess, helped him keep the drinks flowing, but he kept his eye on the floor, so he'd catch Addison when she returned.

His cousin Tommy loomed into view, found a seat at the bar. He'd styled his hair away from his face, had on a white button down.

Hawk dropped a napkin down. "Hey, cuz, you're here late."

"Yeah, I took someone to dinner."

"Nice," Hawk replied.

"Why didn't you bring her here?"

"Thought I'd swing by on my way home, check things out." Tommy eyed the fill-in bartender. "Where's the regular crew?"

"Not here."

Tommy laughed. "Yeah, I see that."

"Whatcha drinking?"

"Whatever's on draft."

Hawk filled the glass with beer, set down the cold drink.

"Hawk security is dope," Tommy said. "I didn't realize you're in the *entire* building." He took a long swig. "You're like Superman with everything you've got going on."

"Granddad fell off the ladder," Hawk said.

"Jeez, is he okay?" Tommy asked.

"He's in the hospital."

A woman squeezed in beside Tommy and smiled at Hawk. "Hi, Hawk, can I get a climax?"

Hawk retrieved the other bartender. "Can you make a climax?"

"Sure," the fill-in bartender replied.

While she got busy making the cocktail, the woman asked Hawk how his night was going.

"Good, babe. You doin' okay?"

She moistened her lower lip. "So good."

Hawk left to wait on another customer. After the bartender had finished making the drink, she said, "You should serve it to her."

Hawk scowled at her. "What difference does it make?"

"She ordered a climax from *you*. She wants *you* to deliver on it." The princess bartender waggled her eyebrows, then moved down the bar to wait on a group of guys.

Hawk set the cocktail in front of the woman. "Can I steal you for a dance?" she asked.

"No can do, baby."

"I'll dance with you," Tommy volunteered.

The customer glanced from Hawk to Tommy. "Okay."

After shoving off the stool, Tommy winked at Hawk before following her onto the dance floor.

At eleven, Addison scurried by, glanced over at the bar, and did a double take. A zing of energy charged through him. She didn't owe him an explanation, but how could he have her back if he didn't know where the hell she was?

She vanished down the hall, returning a moment later.

"Hey," she said joining them behind the bar. "Where's Liliana?"

"Bolted," Hawk said. "She had a medical emergency."

Addison pulled off her mask. "Is she okay?"

"We didn't get into it." Then, he hitched a brow. "How's your evening going?"

"I had a thing I had to do."

"No shit," he said, glaring at her.

Addison thanked the server who'd been filling in.

"I liked working behind the bar," she said. "If you ever need a sub, let me know."

"Absolutely," Addison replied. "I'm announcing last call. Can you brighten the lights for me please?"

The server turned up the lights, leaving Hawk and Addison alone behind the bar.

"Last call," Addison said before lowering the music.

After clearing out the rush of clubbers looking for their last drink, the next thirty minutes flew by. As the guests started leaving, Tommy moseyed back over.

"Hey, Addison." Tommy parked himself on a stool.

"How's it going?" she asked.

"What happened to climax girl?" Hawk asked.

"She wanted you," Tommy replied.

Hawk could feel Addison's gaze drilling into him, but he tossed his cousin a nod. "I wouldn't sweat it."

"Plenty of other women," Tommy replied, his attention focused on Addison. "You wanna hang out and have a drink after the place clears out?"

"She can't," Hawk replied.

Addison's eyebrows jutted into her forehead.

"You got plans?" Tommy asked her.

"She does," Hawk replied.

"You got laryngitis?" Tommy asked her.

"Hawk's right," Addison replied as Hawk's gaze met hers.

The constant tug was there. He couldn't deny it, couldn't ignore it. Despite being pissed at her, he couldn't wait to get her alone.

She dragged her gaze away. "My answer hasn't changed, Tommy."

After Addison went to lock the front door, Hawk leaned forward. "Stop. Pestering. Her."

Tommy sighed, then swigged his beer. "Have you ever met someone who just blows you away?"

Biting back a growl, Hawk cleared the glasses off the bar.

"Oh, fuck, bro," Tommy blurted. "I completely forgot about Josie."

"Who's Josie?" Addison asked.

Tommy needs to shut the fuck up.

When Hawk regarded her, curious eyes peered up at him.

"She doesn't know?" Tommy asked "I thought she's your best friend."

"Know what?" Addison asked.

Hawk left the bar, walked over to his cousin, and laid his hand on his shoulder. "I'll walk you out."

Two of the servers said goodnight as they passed the bar.

Tommy lifted the half-full glass of beer. "I'm not done."

"We gotta close up," Hawk said. "Come on."

"I think I'm in trouble," Tommy said while waving goodbye to Addison.

As they headed toward the door, Tony, the bouncer, walked inside. "You want me to clear the suites?"

"I'll do it," Hawk said. "Take Tommy out with you."

"Sorry about what I said," Tommy muttered as he exited the building.

Hawk had never talked to Addison about Josie. He sure as hell wasn't about to start now.

Addison *thought* she knew Hawk. Clearly, she did not. He'd never mentioned anyone named Josie. Neither had anyone in his family, including his brother Prescott.

After locking the door, Hawk stood in the middle of the empty dance floor, one hand hitched to his hip. "Come. Here."

She couldn't miss the power in his voice, the ever-present confidence rolling off him. Her insides came alive as she flipped up the bar door and sauntered in his direction. One slow step at a time.

While she couldn't wait to be in his arms, to feel his mouth on hers, to strip down and get lost in a fantasy, she would play this chill. The last thing she wanted to do was show her hand and scare him away. Keeping things casual was the way to play this, no matter how she *really* felt about him.

His stance looked relaxed, but the intensity in his eyes was blazing hot. As she made her way over, he checked her out. Being eye-fucked by Hawk was better than the real thing with any other man.

His scorching gaze drove her wild. His constant frustration had his eyebrows slashed down, while muscles ticked in his chiseled cheeks, drawing attention to his sculpted jawline.

Tonight, the fire in his eyes turned her inside out. She was going to fuck him, get fucked by him, and have some late-night fun with the sexiest bad boy she had ever known.

She pulled up inches away, her panties damp with arousal, her breathing shallow, her pulse soaring. She loved being in control, especially during role plays. As she stared into his eyes, then at his mouth, she wasn't interested in control.

She was interested in *him*.

He hitched a brow, then flashed a wicked smile.

Rather than turn away from her, he started walking backwards toward the elevator. The searing connection binding them together pulled her forward. When he got to the wall next to the elevator, he didn't punch the button. He didn't move at all. He just stood there waiting for her to come to him.

When she pulled to a stop in front of him, he had her pinned against the wall before she realized what he'd done. He dipped down, kissed her with a wildness that had her moaning into his mouth.

Their embrace was raw and gritty. Tongues thrashing, his needy groans made her knees weak. He ground against her. She reached around, grabbed his muscular ass, and squeezed.

Panting hard, she pushed him away. When she turned to tap the up button, he pressed against her back. "I can't wait to make you scream my name."

His gravelly whisper sent a thrill through her.

Turning, she faced him. Hungry eyes drilled into hers while the back of his finger caressed her cheek.

"What are you doing to me, Nicholas Hawk?"

"Same thing you're doing to me, babe."

On the brief elevator ride, he stood behind her, wrapping his strong arms around her and nibbling the back of her neck. "You smell good," he murmured.

When the doors slid open, he clasped her hand and led her out. One by one, they cleared each suite. They were alone in the Red Room.

She had a decision to make. Role play a scene or have straight-up sex.

As if he could read her mind, he retrieved the keyless handcuffs from the hook on the wall. "What's it gonna be, Skye? Your way or mine?"

Her breath hitched. "What *is* your way?"

"Just you," he replied. "Under me, over me, until I've drained every ounce of ecstasy you have to give me."

"Ohmygod," she whispered before chugging down a breath. "What's my way?"

"You're the prisoner and I'm the evil warden."

She moaned. "Ohgod, are you going to punish me?"

He stepped close, caressed her breast, teasing her already hard nipple, trapped behind the latex suit.

"I'm going to punish you for trying to escape my prison."

"So, I'll be at your mercy," she groaned out.

He grabbed her by the arm. Firm, but not painful. This was the side of Hawk she loved when they were on a mission together. And he was about to unleash all that raw, angry energy onto her.

"The last time someone tried to escape," he began, "I put them in solitary confinement until they broke."

His voice was gruff, like sandpaper scraping across her skin.

"Role play," she whispered, her body coming alive with desire.

"We're gonna need a safe word," he said. "Because if you say no, I'll stop, and you might be playing in the scene."

"We'll use traffic colors. Yellow means ease up and red is a hard stop."

"Got it," he replied.

Then, he gripped her shoulders, forced her against a wall, and pinned her with his body. Being trapped by Hawk made her gasp with excitement.

"I hate it here," she said, letting her imagination take over. "The food sucks, the yard time is bullshit. I'd rather die than stay in this shit hole."

"Before I lock you up, I need you to feel the consequences of what you did." He leaned down, his face inches from hers. "Where'd you get these clothes?"

"Fuck you."

His sinful smile made her heart pound faster. "I can do that."

Moving slowly, he unzipped the one-piece down to her waist. The tight latex gave way, exposing her breasts.

"Let's see what kinda tits you got." His raspy voice made her quiver with anticipation. He tugged the tight outfit off her shoulders and eyed her breasts, then ran his finger over her nipple. "Nice. Very nice."

"Get your stinkin' hands off me," she hissed.

He knelt, removed her stilettos, then dropped a tender kiss on her tummy before gazing up at her. Beyond the lust, the connection was there... stronger than ever.

After a long second, he shifted his gaze to her breasts, releasing a rumbly growl before stripping the outfit off her. She was naked, save for the tiny black thong that barely covered her pussy. He slid his fingers inside, the heat from his skin made her tremble with desire. He tugged it down and helped her step out.

Now, she was totally naked and desperate to devour him.

"Mmm," he murmured. "I love pussy." He pressed his nose against her sex, and inhaled.

When he stood, he gazed into her eyes while he stroked her opening. Jolt after jolt of adrenaline charged through her. She was on fire, her insides throbbing with an unrelenting need. She wanted him inside her, but she didn't want to rush. Taking their time meant a stronger release.

"You're dripping wet," he ground out. "Lie on the bed facing me, *prisoner*."

"No," she bit out.

He grabbed her wrist, strode to the bed, and pushed her onto it. She lay on her back in the center, staring up at him. Stunning male beauty, coupled with a wild intensity stared back as shivers of excitement skirted through her.

He glared down, his gaze narrowed. "I'm gonna punish you either way," he ground out. "Might as well enjoy it."

"You're not allowed to do this to me."

"Watch me." He pulled her toward the edge of the bed before shoving a pillow under her head. "Put your arms over your head, so I can cuff you."

When she did, he stalked around the bed, snapped the soft, play cuffs into place. Then, he leaned over her, and kissed her. "You are so beautiful," he whispered.

She melted from his tender words.

He strode back around the bed, knelt in front of her pussy and inhaled. "You smell good enough to eat."

He feasted on her sex with a rawness that made her groan with pleasure. Licking, sucking, but when he nipped at her, she cried out. The snap of pain jolted her, but she loved every filthy thing he was doing.

The onslaught of pleasure had her closing her eyes and rolling her head back.

He stopped eating her. Her eyes shot open.

"No, prisoner. *Watch* me punish you."

Then, he pulled her ass off the edge of the bed. While he continued licking her clit and fingering her pussy, he ran a finger over her anus.

"That's so dirty," she ground out while the euphoria had her hurtling toward an orgasm.

So much pleasure, *everywhere*. The orgasm started deep inside her, bursting out in a series of violent convulsions while the ecstasy cascaded through her. She released a long cry as he nursed her through her orgasm.

When it ended, he gently removed his fingers, kissed the hood of her clit. Then, he leaned over her, pressed his lips to hers, and kissed her. "You did good, prisoner."

The bliss on Addison's face was addictive. A just-sexed Addison was sheer perfection. Already a stunning woman, her relaxed expression gave him hope. He couldn't explain it and he wasn't gonna analyze it. He just loved seeing her like that.

He washed his hands, but not his mouth. He wanted to

savor her sweet, sweet pussy juices a little longer. Back in the suite, he uncuffed her, then helped her sit up.

Despite his throbbing cock and aching balls, his focus stayed on Addison, ensuring *her* needs were met. In that moment, she was his entire world.

"Suck me off, prisoner."

"What will I get in return?" When her gaze met his, a smile ghosted across her face.

"Another orgasm."

"I want you to punish me," she said. "Fuck me hard and force me to come."

He wasn't expecting that, but he'd roll with it.

"Blow me and I'll punish you real good," he replied.

Sitting on the edge of the bed, she wrapped soft fingers around his shaft and licked the head. Wetness oozed out, and she ran her tongue around the sensitive rim. Once, twice, then she took him into her mouth. He pulled her hair from her face and held it in a tight ponytail, so he could watch her every move. She licked and sucked, rolling her tongue over his sensitive flesh.

"That's good, baby," he said. "Work me into your mouth."

She cradled his balls, took in more of him, then pulled him back out. She took her time, let his wetness, along with her saliva drench his cock as she pumped him slowly up and down.

On a gritty moan, she deep-throated him, raking her teeth up and down his shaft while she massaged his balls. Her talented tongue never stopped moving, neither did her hands. In and out, again and again while her raw, feral sounds had him growling through the euphoria.

"Mmm," she moaned before sucking hard.

Her intensity pushed him over the edge.

"Here I go, prisoner." Pounding ecstasy had him gritting his teeth while he climaxed into her hot, welcoming mouth. Knowing it was Addison only heightened the euphoria, as he surrendered to the ultimate pleasure... and the ultimate escape.

When he finished, she vanished into the bathroom. He lay on the bed, savoring his sex high. Seconds later, she slinked over, and crawled on top of him. He caressed her silky thighs while her wicked-hot gaze stayed locked on his. Role play or not, he was hooked.

Leaning over him, she pressed her lips to his and kissed him hard. She clawed his shoulders while he raked his fingers down her back, stroked her ass. She bit his earlobe, swiped her tongue over his lips. He flipped her onto her back and continued kissing her until he broke away to kiss her nipples. When he placed his mouth on her tender flesh and sucked, she mewled like a wild cat.

The more he sucked her hard nipple, the more he needed her. First one, then the other. He nibbled on her neck, fondled her breasts. He couldn't get enough of her, the unrelenting desire to bury himself deep inside her had turned him hard again.

Tonight, he'd come prepared with a condom of his own.

"I'm gonna fuck you now," he said, resuming the role play, "and I'm gonna fuck you hard, and fast, and so damn good."

"Yesss," she hissed.

He flipped her onto her back, pushed out of bed, and extracted the condom from his pants' pocket. After rolling it on, he planked over her. "Time to fuck, prisoner."

"If I do this, no solitary confinement."

"That depends on how good you fuck."

She wrapped her fingers around his shaft, placed it at her opening. With a gleam in her eyes, she spread her legs. "You're an evil, evil man."

He plunged inside her, the euphoria drawing wild sounds from them both. He loved being with her, wanted to take things slowly, but this wasn't an opportunity for him to be intimate with her. He was going to finish this role play and do what she needed. He was going to fuck her.

"Harder," she growled. "That feels so good. Oh, I need this."

He drove himself inside her, then withdrew. Harder and faster while she bucked against him. Again and again while the pleasure continued building to a deafening crescendo. Their raw, filthy fucking was turning him into a beast. The gritty sounds he was pulling out of her had him barreling toward another release.

"Yes," she cried out. "Fuck, fuck, I'm coming."

He released inside her, the ecstasy stealing his thoughts and quieting his demons. She clung to him while she surrendered to the sweetest of pleasures.

She could role play all she wanted, but this wasn't just another hookup for him. And based on the way she was peering into his eyes, it wasn't for her either.

As they drifted back to earth, he wasn't ready to disconnect, so he stayed rooted inside her. But he repositioned, so he wasn't crushing her with his weight. He drank in her beauty before dropping a lingering kiss on her lips.

"You did good prisoner," he said.

Her just-got-fucked smile was the best reward. "Right back atcha, warden."

He peered into her eyes for a long moment as he weighed his options. He had to come clean about tracking her, but was now the best time to tell her?

More silence.

She leaned over, kissed him. He kissed her back, then ran the back of his finger down her cheek.

Tell her now.

"I got concerned when I realized you left the club, so I used the tracker," he murmured.

"Oh, wow."

"I've never done that before."

"Thank you for telling me." She paused. "I went to see a friend of mine, a former asset. She owns a coffeehouse in DC, near GW. I wanted to tell her about Jenning's death, and I offered to hire protection for her."

"Addison, you should have brought me with you, to make sure no one followed you."

"I was careful."

"I get that you're independent and super competent," he said. "But you gotta tell me."

"Were you angry?"

"Very."

She shot him a relaxed smile. "You're sexy when you're angry."

"Not again, Addison. I mean it."

"What will you do to me if I make you angry?"

He fought the smile, but her expression was so fucking adorable, he couldn't resist. He dipped down, kissed her. "We gotta tell HR we're seeing each other."

She nudged him off her and he slid out. He hated that she'd severed their connection. She scooted toward the edge of the bed.

With her back to him, she murmured, "There's nothing to tell. We've hooked up a few times. It's no big deal. We're not in a relationship. As far as I'm concerned, we don't even have to do it again. We'll go back to being just friends."

Leaving him on the bed, she walked into the bathroom. He wanted to laugh. There was no way she was going to stop having sex with him. She liked it too much. And if it meant doing more of these fantasy role plays, he'd be more than happy to oblige her.

Sex with Addison made an already good relationship even better. As long as they didn't fall in love, he'd be good for a long, long time.

15

THE RIFT

Energized from his late-night role play with Addison, Hawk strode into work early on Friday. He had a full workload, but after yesterday's fucked-up install, then firing Wayne, his goal was to get through the day without a single glitch.

The morning got hijacked with meetings. As soon as afternoon hit, he was on the phone with his forepersons confirming that the day's installs were happening without issues.

He was thrilled to find out that his employees were doing their jobs and that his clients were behaving themselves. While his trust in humanity had *not* been restored—he was an ALPHA Operative, after all—he would take a win wherever he could get one.

His phone rang. It was Stryker. "Yo, babe," Hawk answered.

"Hey, what time is poker tonight?"

Hawk blanked.

"You're hosting," Stryker said.

So much for smooth sailing. "Yeah, babe. I'll grill."

"You sure?" Stryker asked. "You didn't remember."

"I got it. I'll send out a text. Thanks for the call."

"Don't you mean, thanks for the reminder?" On a chuckle, Stryker hung up.

Hawk pulled up the text thread with Stryker, Cooper, Jericho, and Prescott. "Yo, boys, poker at my place. I'm grilling steaks. Who's in?"

Within seconds, Prescott responded, "I got the beer."

Cooper texted, "Corn for grilling."

"Coleslaw and fries from The Road," Jericho added.

Stryker sent a watermelon emoji and everyone laughed at his text.

Hawk shot off another text. "I'll be home by six."

Then, he realized Addison would have to work the club without him. Even though Liv hadn't been there every night, he wouldn't abandon her. Rather than text, he shut his office door and called her.

"Hey, what's happening?" she answered.

"I forgot I've got the guys for poker tonight."

"That sounds fun. Do you need me to jump out of a cake or something?"

He chuckled.

"Seriously," she continued, "why are you telling me?"

"Who's going to help you at the club?"

"We've got staff. You don't have to be there every night."

"I'll swing by after. Whatcha doing?" he asked.

"I'm at the black site. Dakota's got me doing a bunch of work on two new terror cells that are gaining traction. I'm hoping this research leads me to Ronald's killer."

"You gotta leave that to the pros."

"I *am* the pros. All I'm doing is taking this assignment in a specific direction."

"*Addison.*"

"Don't Addison me," she replied. "Cooper's calling. I'll see you later." She hung up.

It was four o'clock. Time for his weekly sync-up with Mags,

his GM. With his water bottle in hand, Hawk made his way down the hall toward the break room.

His phone rang. It was Cooper.

"Hey, babe," Hawk answered.

"I gotta talk to you about Sunday's mission," Cooper said.

"I'm at work."

"You don't have to say anything," Cooper continued. "Slash's Dad died, so she's headed home. I've got you, Stryker, Barry, and Tommy, but he's in training, so we need a replacement for Slash. I asked Addison. She's in."

"Got it," Hawk replied.

"You good with that?"

"Why wouldn't I be?" Hawk asked. "We usually work together."

"Just confirming. I'll see you in a few." Cooper hung up

Hawk filled his bottle, then, as he made his way back toward his office, he called Addison.

"Hey," she answered. "Miss me already?"

"I *have* been thinking about you."

"Don't go there."

"Why the hell not?"

"I'm in the conference room and I can't talk," she whispered.

"Cooper said you're joining my crew on Sunday."

"Right."

"Did he tell you Tommy'll be there?" Hawk asked.

"I completely forgot he's even in ALPHA."

"Do you care if he knows you are too?"

"It shouldn't be an issue," she replied.

"He's obsessed with you."

"You think?"

"Yeah, I do, babe. He asks you out all the time. You tell him no, but that doesn't stop him."

"I never think about him," she replied. "I don't care what he thinks or how many times he asks me out. I won't back out of a mission because the new guy is allegedly into me."

"Not alleged, Addison."

"I love when you say my name," she murmured.

"You're gonna have to leave the club early on Saturday."

"I'm in, unless you don't think I'm the right Operative for the mission."

"I always think you're the right one."

"You charmer you."

After hanging up, Hawk drank down half the water before calling Mags. When she didn't answer, he grabbed his laptop, and went in search of his general manager.

Mags was seated at her desk, his cousin Tommy relaxing on her love seat. His arm was thrown over the back of the couch while he sipped from a lidded cup.

Not again?

"Hey, boss man," Mags said, her cheeks flooded with color. "Look who dropped by."

"Hey, cuz," Tommy said. "How's it going?"

Hawk wanted to ask his cousin why he wasn't at work. Instead, he said, "What are you doing here?"

"I'm taking Mags to dinner, then a movie."

"Or a concert," Mags added.

Tommy shot her a smile. "Whatever you want."

"We've got a meeting," Hawk said to Mags.

"Oh, I'm sorry. I completely forgot. Any chance we can move it to Monday?"

She'd never missed a meeting and he wasn't gonna bust her chops for this one. If Tommy was moving on from Addison, that was reason enough to let the meeting slide.

"Monday works."

"Thanks for being so flexible," Mags said with a smile.

"You guys have a good weekend," Hawk said.

"See ya," Tommy replied.

That was Hawk's last meeting of the day. Time for him to cut out early himself. After shutting down his computers, he pulled his office door shut, and took off toward the elevator. As he passed Mags's office, he glanced in as Tommy tucked Mags's short hair behind her ear and kissed her.

Hallelujah. He's moved on.

On the way home, he stopped at the liquor store, then hit the local butcher for steaks.

"Someone's having a dinner party," said the butcher.

"Poker night."

"Dang, we eat chips at my poker nights. You're doing it up right, Hawk."

"Gotta feed my boys before I take their money." He winked, grabbed the wrapped meat, and left.

After a long run, he stopped at the gym for weights, then back home.

At six fifteen, the guys started showing up. First, Stryker and Cooper, then Prescott. Not long after, Jericho arrived.

Hawk had lined up the bottles on his kitchen counter. Whiskey, tequila, rum, and vodka. Hanging with his boys was the easiest thing Hawk did. While grilling the steak and corn on his balcony, Prescott joined him.

"I stopped by the hospital to see Granddad," Prescott said.

"Any improvement?"

"Slow. Mom and Dad are trying to convince them to sell the farm."

"That can't be going well."

"No, but Grandmom is staying with them, and she likes it."

"Good," Hawk replied as he started flipping the meat. He lifted the lowball glass, sipped the top-shelf whiskey. "I gotta talk to you about a woman."

Prescott's eyebrows hiked up. "Really? That's good."

"No, it's not."

"She pregnant?"

"No, I've got it bad for her, but I'm struggling."

"Josie?"

"Yup, but there's more," Hawk said.

Jericho opened the French doors, stepped outside. "Heyo, boys." He glanced from one to the other. "You two look damn serious. What's going on?"

"Family drama," Hawk replied. "Granddad fell off the ladder."

No way in hell was he discussing Addison.

The steaks were done. Hawk placed them on a platter, retreated inside, and left them on the kitchen island. Stryker and Cooper were hanging in his living room.

"Smells great," Cooper said.

As Hawk was headed back out, Jericho and Prescott came in, the charred corns piled high on a tray.

The guys each grabbed a steak, two corns, along with fries and coleslaw from Jericho's restaurant. Like usual, they pulled up chairs at the kitchen table and dug in.

"You ready to be a dad?" Stryker asked.

"Hell, yeah," Jericho replied. "Less than a month."

Hawk wondered how he'd feel when his friends started having families. While he was excited for them, it was hard to hear. Prescott caught his eye and offered a supportive smile.

His brother tossed a nod toward Stryker. "What about this guy? He's getting married next weekend."

Stryker smiled. "I'm a lucky man. Emerson's the best."

The conversation continued, but Hawk's thoughts had drifted to Addison. He was ready to take the next step with her. Nothing major, just more than the club hookups.

"What do you think, Hawk?" Cooper asked.

Hawk flicked his gaze from one man to the other. "About what?"

"Addison going into BLACK OPS," Cooper replied. "I think she's gonna do great, but you've done more missions with her than anyone."

"Yeah, she'll be good, but—" He stopped.

Silence.

"But what?" Jericho asked.

Hawk drained his water glass. "Nothing."

"Is she having second thoughts?" Cooper asked. "I know she's concerned about leaving the country. Is that it?"

"I'm not her mouthpiece," Hawk replied. "Talk to her."

"She hasn't said anything to me," Cooper said. "I think she's concerned I'll sideline her because Jenning's dead."

Hawk grew silent. If he started talking about her, he might not stop. Better to say nothing.

They cleaned up, started playing cards. He loved hanging with these men. No shop talk, just spending time together.

It was after ten when they played their last game. After everyone settled up, the guys headed out. Everyone, except Prescott.

With a nightcap in hand, his brother moved to the sofa. Hawk lowered the music, sat on the chair across the room and dropped his head into his hands. After a moment, he sat up straight and leaned back.

"Out with it, Nicky."

"Not a word, to anyone," Hawk said.

"Now, you're just insulting me, brother."

"Addison and I have been hooking up."

Prescott leaned back, crossed his ankle over his thigh. "You're smart not to have said anything in front of Cooper. I love him, but he would haul your asses in to HR."

Both men laughed. Hawk appreciated that his brother always knew how to lighten the mood.

"I love her company, always have," Hawk said. "I'd pick her over anyone to go on a mission with me."

"Sounds good so far."

"I don't do relationships."

"So, enjoy her company."

"It's complicated."

"You've come a long way. Don't be so tough on yourself. You've always pushed yourself to do better, do more, be there for everyone. She's your friend. You've added sex. If that works for both of you, then it's enough."

"I gotta tell her why I can't give her more," Hawk said. "She deserves that."

"Do you want more?"

When Hawk stared out the window, his reflection stared back. "Yeah, I do, but I don't think she does."

"Maybe if you tell her where you're coming from, it'll help."

"Thanks for talking. How's things been since you've been back?"

Prescott shrugged. "Who the hell knows anymore?"

"What does that mean?"

"I'm here physically, but somewhere else mentally."

"PTSD?" Hawk asked.

"No, but I'm feeling restless."

"How's AE?"

Armstrong Enterprises was Prescott's conglomerate of companies that had been in his family for generations.

Prescott rose. "Talk about fucked-up family dynamics. It makes our family seem like the most normal group on the planet."

Hawk opened the front door to his townhome. Prescott trotted down the steps and Hawk stepped outside.

"Granddad was asking for his number one," Prescott said. "You should swing by the hospital tomorrow and visit him."

Hawk huffed. "I wish he wouldn't say that out loud."

"He sees what I see. You're good to all of us and he appreciates that about you."

"Thanks for being so cool about it," Hawk said.

"I love you, Nicky. We've never been competitive or jealous of each other. Mom would have killed us both."

They laughed.

Prescott got into his car and Hawk retreated inside for his car keys. Then, he slipped into his Mercedes and headed to Lost Souls.

Prescott was right. He needed to talk to Addison. It would be easy to continue having no-strings sex with her, but he needed to tell her the truth. Their relationship was too damn important to keep this from her. She deserved that... at the very least.

Addison couldn't wait to see Hawk. While he'd been playing poker, she sent him an Invitation to Escape with a message. "Boss and prospective hire. Wear a suit so I can strip you out of it."

Not only was ready for more, he'd wrecked her for any other man.

Now I know why these women throw themselves at him.

Tonight, she dressed in a pair of straight-leg dress pants, a lacy black camisole, a clingy suit jacket, and stiletto sandals. She loved role playing, but being with Hawk took it to a whole nother level.

From the moment she'd arrived at Lost Souls, she'd been handling one thing after another. Her chef had called out sick, so she and the cook had to pare down the menu. Then, she had to update the servers and bartenders.

Friday night meant the club was hopping from the moment the doors opened, which was great for business... until a health inspector popped in for a surprise visit. So, she followed the inspector around to ensure she answered all her questions.

Then, just as the health inspector was leaving, her sister called to catch up. When Addison told her she'd have to call her back, her sister burst into tears. An hour later, Addison was back on the club floor, mingling with members.

Two minutes after that, her second bartender flagged her down. "We're getting slammed," he said. "And I've gotta use the restroom."

Addison hurried behind the bar and started chatting it up with customers while she served drinks as fast as possible. Even after the bartender returned, she stayed behind the bar to help out.

When they finally cleared out the crowd, Addison asked both bartenders if they needed a break.

"Can I talk to you in private?" Liliana asked.

Ah, crap, she's quitting.

Addison loved owning the nightclub, but the turnover was way more time consuming than she'd anticipated. Once in Addison's office, she asked if Liliana was okay.

"I'm so sorry about last night," Liliana said.

Addison blanked. "Last night?"

"I had to leave."

"No worries. Hawk covered for you."

"I got my period early," Liliana volunteered. "And I didn't have my cup with me. Then, I got cramps so bad, I curled up in a ball."

Addison had been there. "I appreciate your telling me, but you didn't have to. Things come up."

"You're a cool boss," Liliana said. "Thanks for understanding."

Relieved, Addison smiled. "That's it?"

"You seem like you're doing better, you know, after you lost your friend," Liliana said.

"I'm still sad, but I have to push on."

"I totally get that," Liliana said.

"Who did *you* lose?" Addison asked.

Liliana paused. "Someone I loved very much." She headed toward Addison's closed office door. "Thanks for being so understanding. I gotta get back to the bar." Liliana left the office.

When Addison stepped into the hallway, Hawk loomed into view wearing a T-shirt that stretched against his bulging biceps and wide chest, and tattered black jeans that accentuated his massive thighs. Every cell in her body came alive while blood whooshed through her veins.

Even in the dim light, hunger radiated from his piercing eyes. Part man, part beast, he stalked his way toward her. She held her breath in anticipation of what he would do.

Kiss me.

He wrapped his arm around her waist, pulled her into the office, and shut the door. Then, he backed her against the door and peered into her eyes. The energy in the room turned electric. She wanted to jump in his arms and kiss him, then mount him. Her entire body craved his. His penetrating stare stripped her naked, but his gaze hadn't strayed from her eyes. She couldn't regulate her breath, couldn't stop the need coursing through her either.

"Miss me?" he murmured.

"Oh, you weren't here?" she quipped. "I didn't notice."

He dipped down to kiss her, only he didn't. Sexy bedroom eyes drilled into hers. The energy turned frenetic, the desire to kiss him made her knees weak.

She waited to see what he'd do next. Instead of devouring her, he dropped a soft, romantic kiss on her lips, then one on her cheek. She melted from the tenderness. Then, he pulled her into his arms and held her.

"I missed you like crazy," he murmured. "Like fucking crazy."

Ohgod, yes. Wait... no! Don't tell me this.

His words slayed her.

Forcing down the mounting emotion, she whispered, "We're fuck buddies, Hawk. Friends with benefits."

He didn't back away, the hunger in his eyes didn't go away either. He dipped down and kissed her again, this time deepening the embrace. She groaned into him, threw her arms around his neck, and jumped into his arms.

He wrapped her tightly and held her while the kiss turned passionate. Kissing Hawk was one of her favorite things to do. It was easy and effortless, and so damn perfect.

When he slowed the embrace, he didn't put her down, didn't stop staring into her eyes. "You look hot."

That's when her brain caught up to her eyes. He was wearing casual clothes. "What happened to your suit for our role play?" She unwrapped herself from him and he set her down. "Did you see my invitation?"

"Yeah, I did."

"I haven't had a second all evening. Did you reply?"

"No. We gotta talk about that."

Her heart dipped. Leading with emotion had left her vulnerable with him. She needed to put some distance between them, so she stepped away.

"No problem." Steeling her spine, she stood tall. "It's been crazy, tonight."

He furrowed his brows. "What's been going on?"

She hated the weird vibe he was putting out. Rather than get into it with him, she pushed on.

It's just easier this way.

"The chef called out sick," she said. "I had to work with the cook to change up the menu, then the health inspector stopped by."

"How'd we do?"

"She wouldn't say. She completes her report in a week or two. Then, my sister called from Denver. Her boyfriend dumped her and she was a mess. I was on the phone with her for an hour."

Up went his eyebrows. "An hour?"

"That's why I don't have a boyfriend. I can't stomach all that emotional drama."

He chuffed out a laugh, but the joy didn't reach his eyes. Why tell her he missed her, kiss her crazy good, yet not agree to another hookup?

"I've gotta get back out there," she said.

For as revved as they'd been three minutes ago, the sexual tension had been replaced with a stilted awkwardness. He hadn't worn the business suit because he didn't want to play with her.

Pushing out the melancholy, she opened the door, and headed down the hall. She wanted him to stop her and tell her what was bothering him.

But he let her go.

One of the members waved her over. There was a problem with the green-screen backdrop at the photo station. As she got busy working on it, she glanced around for Hawk and saw him chatting it up with a group of women.

Her heart broke. She wasn't enough for him. He was used to variety. Maybe role playing wasn't his jam. She might not have been submissive enough for him. She didn't know, but she was gonna do what she did best.

Push him out of her thoughts and power on.

Last call came and went. When the club had emptied out for the night, Tony moseyed inside. "Hey, guys, I'm taking off, unless you need me for something."

"Can you check the rooms with me?" Addison asked.

She wasn't gonna end up like her sister, a sobbing emotional wreck because she'd gotten dumped.

"I'll do it with you, babe," Hawk said.

"I got this," she replied. "Tony, you don't mind, do you?"

"Of course not," Tony replied.

They cleared the rooms in record time. Easy to do when the attraction isn't there. When they came back downstairs, Hawk was sitting alone at the bar, nursing a sparkling water. The staff had cleared out. She locked the door behind Tony and walked back into the room.

For a split second, she felt directionless and lost. *Should I sit beside him? Should I go behind the bar? Should I not even mention the role play?*

"Come sit with me," he said.

She pulled up a stool. He'd poured her a sparkling water. "What's this for?"

"We're going on a mission in twenty-four, so I'm not drinking."

"The rule is twelve hours," she replied.

"I'm flying the chopper, so it's a minimum of twenty-four for me."

She sipped the water, then took another sip before setting the glass down.

"I don't want to go upstairs," he said.

Like she hadn't figured that out for herself. "No problem," she said, breaking eye contact to stare at the never-ending stream of bubbles in her glass.

"Come home with me," he said. "I'll throw on a suit and we can play out your scene."

She stilled.

He waited.

She had to say something. "But we're here and we've got a bunch of empty suites."

"I'm just gonna say it, straight out," he said. "I'm all about the no-strings hookups, but it's different with you. We're friends—close friends. We work together. We go on intense missions where we have each other's backs." He chugged half the water. "Fuck, I'm not good with this."

"Then, stop talking, take me upstairs, and fuck me."

"Come home with me."

This can't be happening. "Why?"

"It's more intimate. You can stay."

"*What*? All night?"

"We can go for a run in the morning. I'll make you breakfast."

Her head was spinning. She didn't do overnights. No way was she gonna stay at his place, then spend the day with him. "I... I can't."

"I'm not asking for anything, except to hang with you," he continued. "I've made you food plenty of times. What's the big deal?"

"Seriously? Where would I sleep? Would we have sex again?"

A sadness ghosted over his face. She'd insulted him. Didn't mean to do that, but she was kind of freaking out here. She didn't do sleepovers. She did hookups and role plays. That's it.

"Is that my only choice?" she asked.

"Or your place," he replied. "We can go there."

The walls were closing in, her hands turned clammy. Her heart was pounding so fast, she thought she'd pass out. Where was this coming from? Everything had been great between them... for years. She should never have given him that blowjob. She'd wanted to prove a point, but it had backfired in the absolute worst way.

"My Granddad's still in the hospital," he continued. "I'm swinging by tomorrow. I'm sure he and Grandmom would love to see you."

He can't be for real.

"I can't do this. I thought hooking up with you would easy. You don't do relationships. Neither do I." She pushed off the stool. "I gotta go. I'll see you at HQ."

"Yo, babe, Tommy's gonna be there."

"I don't give a fuck about Tommy and, at the moment, I don't give a fuck about you either."

16

PREPPING FOR THE MISSION

Saturday night, eleven thirty.

Hawk was the first to arrive at ALPHA. He drove around back, parked the SUV near the door, and made his way inside. The place was quiet. He dropped his computer bag on the conference table and paired his laptop so he could project the images on the drop-down screen. Then, he pulled up the blueprint of the building, along with photos of the men they were taking out.

He walked into the supply room, pulled six comms from the shelf and made his way back to the conference room. Normally chill, he was on edge. Not about the mission. About Addison. He hadn't been able to shake her from his thoughts all day.

Despite the run, the weight lifting, and the attempt to do a mindful meditation, he fucking hated that she'd stormed out on him. He was concerned the tension would prevent them from working as a team. If anyone detected the friction between them, it might affect the outcome. He'd never been in this situation before, but he had to move past it... for now.

He turned his attention to the screen and studied the faces

of the criminals. There was added pressure when he was leading a team *and* flying the helo. Plus, he had to keep an eye out for Tommy.

Earlier in the day, Addison had texted him. "Liv and Jericho are managing the club for us tonight."

"Thanks for taking care of that," he'd replied. "I'm getting to HQ early."

She never responded to that text.

The mission, as far as missions went, was straightforward. Fly to the location, surprise the fugitives, eliminate them, fly back.

Addison walked in. The divot between her eyebrows was deeper than usual.

"Hey, babe," he said. "How you doing?"

"I'm okay." She set her computer bag on the table.

Like he expected, she'd worn a black shirt, black pants, and her long, black duster. She hadn't pulled her hair out of the way and she didn't have on any camouflage paint yet. He'd left his team enough time to get mission-ready.

The old Addison would have asked him about his day. She would have told him something about hers. Not tonight, though. She dropped into a chair, turned her attention toward the images he'd projected on the screen.

"I want to go back to being friends," she murmured.

A stabbing pain shot through him. He fucking hated that she wouldn't even look at him. "You sure?"

"Yup. I made a mistake." Her ice-cold tone sliced through him.

He wanted to push back, but not here, not now.

The tension rolling off her was brutal. When she turned her gaze on him, daggers shot from her eyes. He needed their heads in the game, so he'd play this chill. If he incited her, he'd have to pull her from the mission and possibly stand down himself. Scrubbing a mission because two Operatives can't manage through their conflict would never fly. Operatives were expected to bring their A-game.

No A-game? No mission. No exceptions.

"I'll do whatever you want," he lied.

"Thank you," she said as Barry strolled into the room.

"Hi, Hawk," Barry said. "How's it going, Addison?"

"Yo, babe," Hawk said. "You ready to get this done?"

Barry smiled. "I've been chasing some of these scumbags from my days with the Bureau, so I'm pumped for this mission."

Barry had been with ALPHA for six months. Before that, he'd worked at the FBI's Tucson field office in Arizona. Hawk didn't know him well, but the few times he'd run into him at HQ, they'd talked shop. This was their second mission together.

Stryker and Emerson rolled in next. "How's everyone doing?" Stryker asked before pulling out a chair.

Emerson sat next to Addison. "Hey," Emerson said. "It's great to see you."

"You guys, too," Addison replied.

"Skye, you riding shotgun, or am I?" Stryker asked Addison.

"You can," she replied.

"Addison is with me," Hawk said. "You two are partners on this one."

Emerson and Stryker exchanged glances. "I got your back," Stryker said to his fiancé.

"You better," Emerson replied with a smile.

Tommy strolled in, sat next to Barry.

"We're all here," Hawk said. "Let's get started. Has everyone met our newest Op, Tommy?"

Stryker hadn't.

"Whoa, dude," Tommy blurted. "What's Addison doing here?"

"She's an Operative," Hawk replied.

"Oh, wow." Tommy shot Addison a smile. "How come I've never seen you here before?"

"I work special assignments," she replied.

Hawk had a time frame to manage, a team to ready, and a group of ruthless fugitives to eliminate. This wasn't the time or the place for Tommy's puppy-dog eyes and flushed cheeks. No doubt, his cousin had it bad for Addison.

"Alright, team," Hawk began. "Let's run through the specs. Over the past four years, there have been prison breaks at three max-security correctional facilities in Colorado, Texas, and New York. These guys staged riots, killed multiple guards and civilians, and all vanished once they escaped.

"They made their way to a lake house in Mississippi," Hawk continued. "A few got jobs under assumed names, but most of them were selling drugs or breaking into homes and stealing laptops, TV's, and jewelry. The FBI sent in a SWAT team, but the fugitives has been tipped off. They ambushed the agents, wounding all of them and killing two.

"The criminals fled, the trail went cold, until last week," Hawk added. "A woman from North Carolina hadn't heard from her aunt and uncle in a few months. They live in a remote location on Maryland's Eastern shore where the homes are spread out and hidden by trees." Hawk dimmed the lights, then sat back down.

He projected the picture of the property on the screen.

"When the woman's relatives didn't return her texts or calls, she drove up to check on them. She found cars parked out front and on the gravel driveway. Two men were talking outside. She didn't recognize them or the vehicles. Since she was afraid to get out of her car, she didn't stop. Instead, she called the FBI."

Hawk projected aerial shots of the home. "These FBI drone shots confirmed this is their hideout." Pausing, he glanced at the team. "Hit me with your questions."

There were none, so he tapped the laptop and mugshots of

the men appeared on screen. "Our mission is to eliminate the twelve men pictured here. The FBI was holding out hope that the aunt and uncle are still alive." Hawk flashed a different picture on the screen. "These mounds in the woods behind the house look like freshly dug graves. We have reason to think the homeowners are buried there."

"These men are ruthless," Stryker said.

"Yeah," Hawk continued. "Which is why we're taking 'em out."

"Any women or children there?" Barry asked.

"Unconfirmed," Hawk replied. "None were visible from the drone pics." He flashed the pictures of the fugitives on the screen again. "We only take out these men."

The next portion of the meeting covered any challenges they could encounter. It was more like a brainstorming session where all possibilities were discussed. Everyone was encouraged to participate, and Hawk was relieved when Addison started offering ideas. The tightness around her eyes disappeared as she moved into mission mode.

They studied the layout of the home from pictures the niece had provided the FBI.

"As of Friday, the property was occupied, but it might be vacant, with explosives set to detonate if someone enters the building," Hawk explained.

"Gotcha," Stryker said.

"Stryker and Emerson, you'll take the lower level," Hawk said.

"Copy," Emerson said.

"I'll work with Addison," Tommy said.

Addison slid her gaze to Hawk. "I partner with Hawk," Addison said.

Good sign.

"I'm putting you with Barry, Tommy," Hawk explained.

"That'll work," Barry replied.

"Nothing like baptism by fire, Tommy," Stryker commented.

"Tommy and I went to the shooting range," Barry added. "He's gonna do great."

"Barry and Tommy, you'll take the first floor," Hawk said. "Addison and I will handle the top floor."

"Got it," Addison said.

"If someone gets out, let 'em go," Hawk said. "Do not separate from the team and go after them in the woods. Is that clear?"

They each acknowledged that it was.

"I've got camouflage face paint if anyone wants it," Hawk said. "Tommy, where's your go-bag?"

"At my desk," Tommy replied.

"No wallets, no phones, no jewelry," Hawk explained to his cousin. "Stryker and I will have burners." He regarded each of them. "If you aren't up for this, stay behind and talk to me." On a nod, he said, "let's get this done."

He passed out the comms. After they did a sound check, everyone filed out, except Addison.

He did *not* want her backing out, but he didn't want their personal relationship to get in her head space and take her off her game.

"You sure you're okay working with me?" she asked.

He shut the door, but he didn't touch her, didn't step into her personal space either. "We've had each other's backs for years. That hasn't changed for me, especially not in the last twenty-four hours." He studied her face. "You good with me—I mean, working with me?"

"We make a great team."

The tension that had been gripping his shoulders released a little. "You need my face paint?"

She nodded. "Of course, I do."

He pulled the face paint stick from his duffle and handed it to her. When she took it, her fingers brushed against his, and that familiar zing of energy traveled through him.

She held his gaze for a beat.

"Thanks," she said before leaving him alone in the conference room.

This cannot be happening with her.

Rather than get mired in his feelings, he stashed his laptop, shouldered his bags, and made his way through ALPHA to the men's locker room. There, he left his phone and watch, pulled a burner. He turned it on, but it was dead.

"Fuck."

He grabbed another. It had more charge, but not enough, so he plugged it in.

Stryker, who was pulling his hair into a man-bun, glanced over. "You okay?"

"I'm low on juice," Hawk replied.

"I got you," Stryker said before tossing him a burner.

"Thanks, bro."

Stryker walked over. "What's going on?"

"Nothing."

Stryker furrowed his brow. "You seem a little off."

"All good," Hawk replied, but Stryker had to know he was full of shit.

That man didn't miss a damn thing.

"I'm here if you wanna talk before we head out," Stryker said.

Hawk had come dressed in black. He pulled on his black knit cap, sat on the bench, and swapped his running shoes for black combat boots. On went his Kevlar vest, his shoulder harness. He tucked one Glock into that, slid the second behind his back.

Snatching his helmet, he went to check on Tommy and Barry. Barry was ready to go. Tommy was sitting on the bench, phone in hand, texting.

"Everyone good?" Hawk asked.

"I can't find my face paint," Barry said.

"Addison's got mine," Hawk replied. "Meet me out there. We'll use it when she's done."

"I'll walk out with you," Barry said.

"You coming?" Hawk asked Tommy.

He glanced up from his phone. "Be there in a minute."

While Hawk and Barry waited outside the ladies' locker room, Barry said, "I'm not usually one to say anything, but Tommy was video chatting with his girlfriend."

What girlfriend? Is he talking about Mags?

"Anyway, I told him to hang up when she asked where he was," Barry continued.

Frustration had him clenching his teeth. "What'd he tell her?"

"He said he had a thing to do, but he'd call her tomorrow."

Hawk growled. "He cannot fucking keep his mouth shut. Thanks for telling me."

"Be discreet," Barry murmured.

The door to the ladies' locker room opened. Addison and Emerson sailed out, their faces concealed with camouflage paint. They were both wearing black knit caps. Two braided pig tails for Addison. Emerson's long hair was hidden inside the cap. Emerson wore a short leather jacket, but Addison still had on her long black duster.

Addison acknowledged the men before holding out the stick to Hawk. "It's low, so I'll order more."

Taking it from her, he and Barry headed back into the locker room.

Addison needed a second alone. She was full-blown lying to Hawk, something she'd never done before. Her emotions were out of control. She should pull herself from the mission, but that would leave Hawk without a partner. She'd never do that to him, but she needed to leave her feelings at HQ if she was going to be good to anyone, herself included.

"I'll be outside." Addison made her way down the hall.

Tommy caught up with her and her stomach roiled. "This is pretty crazy. Did you know I'd joined ALPHA?"

"Hawk mentioned it," she replied.

"Why didn't you say anything to me?" Tommy asked as they stepped outside.

"Where? At the club?" She shook her head. "We don't talk about ALPHA in public."

"Yeah, right. I just figured you would since we're in the same top-secret group. You know, like a fraternity."

He really doesn't get it.

Rather than continue their pointless conversation, she grew quiet. Time to move into mission mode. The sooner she could get centered, the more focused she'd be. Having Hawk as her partner was a good thing, except now, it was a distraction. She was lying. He had to know. Her brain was scrambled eggs. Never before had a man gotten to her like he had.

It's the Hawk Effect.

Strangely, that had her biting back a smile. She used to laugh when it happened to other women, but the same damn thing had happened to her. *And it's all my fault.*

The rest of the team filed outside.

Hawk in all black with his knit cap and his camouflage paint always gave her a jolt of energy. He had it going on all the time, but a mission-ready Hawk was a total badass.

If he noticed her checking him out, he ignored it.

Addison! Focus! This isn't a role play... but it would make for a phenomenal one.

Breaking eye contact, she started her box-breathing as Hawk led them over to the far end of the parking lot where both ALPHA helicopters waited. A Bell 407, like the one at the training facility, and a Bell UH-1Y Venom.

Stryker fired up the lights so Hawk could start his pre-flight inspection.

"I'm flying the Venom," he said.

The Venom was a larger, Marine helicopter that had been modified for ALPHA. Behind the cockpit sat the body of the bird, equipped with two rows of four seats that faced each other. That freed up the center section for cargo or to transport additional Operatives. The last time he'd flown this helo was when he'd been part of a mission to rescue Cooper's niece.

They waited while Hawk did his pre-flight inspection.

Addison stood apart from the group to focus on clearing out any emotional baggage that could get in the way of her doing her job. A few minutes passed before she realized Tommy had *not* stopped running his mouth.

"Life as an undercover cop was so different," Tommy said. "I was immersed in their gang. They trusted me with their lives." He chuckled. "I had them fooled so bad."

"Yo, Tommy," Stryker said. "It's quiet time."

"Seriously?" Tommy asked. "What for? We're just going to a house and taking out some dudes."

Addison flicked her gaze to Emerson who shook her head. Each of them knew the gravity of what they were about to do. They might be walking into an ambush. They could all die, or get shot up so badly, they'd never walk again.

There wasn't a rule preventing Operatives from talking on the way to a job, but they just didn't. Maybe they'd learned it from one another. Maybe it had been passed down from the beginning. Addison didn't know, but she appreciated the silence.

When no one responded to Tommy, he finally shut up.

A cell phone started ringing and Tommy pulled his from his pocket. "I'm gonna take this real quick."

Stryker grabbed the phone, killed the call, then shut it off. "You're gonna get us all killed."

"Sorry, I'll put it on silent," Tommy said.

Hawk jogged over. "What the hell is going on?"

Stryker held up Tommy's phone. "Tommy brought this with him and it was on."

Hawk shook his head. "Let's take a walk."

"Can I have my phone?" Tommy asked.

"No. It stays here. Didn't you fucking hear Hawk's instructions?" On a growl, Stryker strode toward the building.

Hawk dropped an arm over Tommy's shoulder and led him away from the group.

Tommy jerked away. "You got something to say to me, say it."

"No personal phones on a mission," Hawk said. "I said that for *your* damn benefit in the conference room. No phones, no IDs, no jewelry. We got two burners for emergency purposes. If something goes down, these guys cannot know who we are."

Stryker jogged back to the team.

"Sorry, I must've missed that," Tommy explained.

Hawk and Stryker exchanged glances.

"You been drinking?" Stryker asked Tommy.

"Not tonight."

"What about earlier?" Stryker asked.

"I had a few beers at lunch," Tommy replied.

"I gotta pull you from the mission," Hawk bit out.

"What? For drinking at noon? C'mon, this is a slam-dunk job. I can do this."

"I gotta finish the inspection." Hawk strode back toward the Venom.

Addison could stand there and do nothing or she could get involved. She approached the group. Stryker's eyebrows were pinched together. He was pissed.

"Tommy, why don't we go talk?" Addison suggested.

"You're not gonna bite my head off, too, are you?" Tommy asked.

As they moved away from the team, she said, "ALPHA only hires the best. You wouldn't be here if multiple people didn't think you could do this."

"I *can* do this."

"I don't know what your life was like when you were undercover, but I'm sure there were some intense moments."

He nodded. "Of course."

"The person leading the mission is responsible for the mission as a whole. If you fail, it falls on Hawk. If someone gets killed, Hawk's going to shoulder that loss. If anything goes wrong, Hawk will accept responsibility, whether it's his fault or not. We have got to watch our sixes, but also make sure we succeed as a team."

"Understood," Tommy said.

"I need you to be completely honest with me. How much did you drink?"

"I had a few beers at lunch."

She studied his face. "Do you understand the seriousness of this mission?"

"I do. I'm sorry if it doesn't come across that way, but I love working at ALPHA. I'm stoked to be here with you now."

As she regarded him, he smiled. "I think you know I had it bad for you." He held up a hand. "I moved on. I'm seeing someone and she's cool. I think it's great that we're doing this together. I can do this job, no problem."

"Do you want to partner with Hawk?"

"You said you normally work with him."

"I do, but he's your mentor."

"I'm good with Barry."

She extended her hand. "Okay, let's get this done."

He shook it. "Thanks for being so chill about this... about everything. I've never met anyone like you."

In silence, they made their way back to the bird. "I'm gonna talk to Hawk," she said.

She waited until Hawk finished the inspection, then she approached him. "Hey, Tommy can do this."

"Thanks for talking to him."

Addison stepped close. "I'm sorry I said anything about us. Are we good?"

"We're good," he replied before waving over the rest of the team. "We're ten minutes behind schedule. Everyone ready to do this?"

They were.

The sliding door to the body of the craft was open.

"Let's fly," Hawk said.

After Stryker, Emerson, Tommy, and Barry climbed in, he slid the door shut, then he shifted his sights to Addison. "Ready, partner?"

"Ready."

She climbed into the cockpit, pulled the door shut. One of her favorite things was flying with Hawk. If she was addicted to anything, it was him in a cockpit controlling a multi-million-dollar machine like it was an extension of himself. He was confident, in control, and completely at ease.

He had it all. He was the most amazing, impressive man she'd ever known. And she'd just ended things before they'd even got started.

If it's for the best, then why does my heart hurt so damn bad?

17

MAN DOWN

As Hawk walked around the craft, he patted the side of the metal bird. "Okay, baby, do us right."

He jumped in, bucked up, and started the helicopter. Pausing, he listened to the propellers, ensuring nothing sounded unusual. Then, he pulled on his headset.

ALPHA should have pre-cleared him to fly within the FRZ —Flight-Restricted Zone—but he'd run into problems before.

"Tower, this is Bravo King Whiskey Alpha Alpha," Hawk said. "Alpha Alpha requests clearance for lift off."

"Go ahead, Alpha Alpha," replied the air traffic controller.

"Alpha Alpha landing in an open field on the Eastern Shore." He gave the GPS coordinates.

"We have your request. One second."

Silence.

"Alpha Alpha, confirm you're not crossing into DC," said the controller.

"Confirmed. Alpha Alpha is flying around DC airspace," Hawk confirmed.

"Alpha Alpha, you're cleared for lift-off."

"Alpha Alpha cleared for lift-off," Hawk parroted back.

"Here we go, babe," Hawk said, before the helo lifted off the ground.

He needed to fly wide of DC. If he crossed into the prohibited area—even by accident—he'd have two F-18 Hornets on his ass in seconds. They'd either escort him out or shoot him down. No thanks to either option.

Hawk loved flying. It was like oxygen to him. When he learned to fly, during college, he'd double up on lessons during exam week. It calmed him down that much. He felt like one with whatever craft he was in. Piloting came easily to him. Always had. But he felt the pressure when he had passengers. He accepted the risks that came with flying, but his passengers trusted him. That meant a lot to him.

As he flew south, he stared out at the lights below dotting the landscape. Despite the late hour, people were awake.

He appreciated that Addison had talked to Tommy, who had finally quieted down. He wasn't sure if Tommy had first-mission jitters or if the man didn't have an off switch.

He glanced over at Addison. She returned his gaze, the whites of her eyes framed in green, brown and beige face paint. They shared a smile. Simple and brief, but it spoke volumes. He wasn't gonna let her go, but he couldn't force her to stay either. Maybe she was right. They had some sexy fun, but they were better at being *just* friends.

Like hell we are.

The attraction was there, always had been. So was their connection.

We're better together... in every possible way.

He continued south until he was past restricted airspace, then veered east. They were behind schedule, but he could make up time in the air. The weather was perfect. No wind, no rain, great visibility. He felt confident they'd complete the mission successfully and fly home as the sun was cresting the horizon.

Forty-minutes later, he touched down in a deserted field two miles from the wooded homesite, and cut the engine. He removed his headset, slid the comm into his ear.

"Blades are still moving," he said. "Attach your silencer before you exit. Tommy, the mic in the comm is strong enough to pick up a whisper."

"Copy," Tommy replied.

"Stryker and Emersion will enter through the back door. Everyone else, through the front," Hawk said. "Ready?"

They each answered to the affirmative.

After exiting the bird, they strapped on their helmets, lowered the night-vision goggles, and made their way north. Hawk set the pace. He didn't want to push them hard, but this wasn't a stroll in the park either. His pulse was slow and steady, as was his breathing. He lived for these missions, but he knew that things could go sideways fast. While he rarely got rattled, not every Operative had his calm demeanor.

When leading a mission, he wasn't just aware of his own surroundings, he always tried to stay cognizant of his team's as well. That would pose a challenge because his team was heading to different floors.

They entered the woods in their two-person formation. He and Addison, Tommy and Barry, Stryker and Emerson.

On occasion, someone stepped on a stick, the crack of wood piercing his ears. As they made their way toward the rear of the home, he slowed his pace.

It was five 'til four. The foliage thinned out the closer they got to the house. Two lights shone from two different rooms upstairs. The basement was dark. Hawk stopped, motioned for Stryker and Emerson to approach the back door.

"Wait for my command before you breach," he murmured.

"Copy," Stryker replied.

He and the remaining three took off toward the front. The house was dark. He stood with his back against the side of the home and peered around the corner. The front porch light was off.

"We have to move fast, once we're on the porch," he murmured. "Try the back door."

"Unlocked," Emerson murmured.

"On three," Hawk said before glancing back at his team. "One, two—"

He rushed up the steps to the front door and tried the handle. It, too, was unlocked. He burst in, Addison close on his heels.

Leaving Tommy and Barry to clear the first floor, he and Addison strode toward the staircase. Hawk took the steps two at a time. At the top of the stairs, he eyed the hallway. All the doors were closed. "First room on the right," he murmured. "We doing left-right?"

"Copy," she whispered.

He flung open the door. Two men were sleeping in the double bed. One rolled over. Even in the dark, he confirmed they were two of the fugitives.

POP! POP! POP! POP!

Per their usual plan of attack, Hawk took out the man on the left while Addison shot the man on the right.

Addison checked the closet. "Clear."

They hurried out, crossed the hall. Addison entered first. One in the bed, two sleeping on the floor, to the left of the bed.

Addison readied her shot on the lone man in bed. *POP! POP!*

Hawk took out both fugitives on the floor. *POP! POP! POP! POP!*

A door down the hall slammed shut.

"Things just got interesting," Hawk whispered.

She pointed to the light spilling from the bottom of the closed door. They flipped up their goggles, burst into the next room. A man, lying in bed raised his arm, a gun in his hand, and started firing.

BANG! BANG!

A bullet whizzed by Hawk's shoulder, another hit him in the chest, the armor taking the hit. Both he and Addison opened fire.

POP! POP! POP! POP!

He flipped off the bedroom light, they lowered their goggles, and cleared the closet. As they strode to the room at the end of the hall, the door opened. They backed against the wall, waiting.

Nothing.

Despite the surrounding darkness, they couldn't step in. They'd get sprayed with gunfire or they'd get overpowered. There could be multiple thugs waiting to ambush them.

Then, Addison touched him. Hand signals for them to return to the room they'd just vacated. She vanished into the room. He followed.

"I think this might be a shared bathroom," she whispered. "I'll surprise them from here, then you enter from the hallway."

He left, waited outside the bedroom. He could hear whispers, but couldn't tell how many were in there.

"On three," she murmured. "One, two—"

He burst in as she charged from the bathroom. There were three men. None of them had on night goggles. Didn't matter, they raised their guns and started firing.

BANG! BANG! BANG! BANG! BANG! BANG!
POP! POP! POP! POP!
POP! POP! POP! POP!

All three dropped. He and Addison shot them in the chest and in the head. It was a fucking bloodbath.

"You okay?" he murmured.

"Kevlar hit," she whispered.

"Where?"

"Dead center."

A first for her.

"Can you walk?"

"Yeah. I'm more shaken than injured."

Her ribs were gonna be sore. She'd definitely be black and blue.

"Multiple down," Stryker whispered through the comm.

As Hawk opened the closet door, someone hiding in the corner caught his eye. He was one of the fugitives. The criminal raised his gun.

BANG!

The guy shot him in the chest.

Hawk opened fire. *POP! POP! POP!* Two in the head, one in the chest.

Addison opened fire on the second man he *hadn't* seen, crouching behind clothes on the other side of the closet.

POP! POP! POP!

Breathing hard, they stood there, staring at each other. That was his second hit to the chest. Now, his blood was whooshing through his veins, his senses on high alert for the smallest sound, any movement.

"Hall closet," he murmured.

"Hawk," Stryker said through the comm, "First floor office, near the front door."

"On our way," Hawk whispered.

They left the bedroom. Addison pulled open the closet, using the door as a shield. He stood, gun at the ready. Empty.

"Clear," he murmured.

They hurried down to the first floor. The front door was open. Blinding light coming from the room, so they flipped up their goggles.

Tommy was performing CPR on Barry. Hawk crouched down. Barry had been shot between the eyes at close range.

"God, no," Hawk bit out. "What happened?"

Tommy continued performing CPR while Stryker pulled Hawk away.

"Tommy said someone came out of nowhere and opened fire, then ran out of the house," Stryker explained. "Tommy wanted to go after him, but he didn't want to disobey your orders. He said he'd been in the kitchen, Barry was in here. He didn't realize Barry had been shot until he saw him on the floor."

"I heard nothing from him through the comm."

"He told me the comm fell out," Stryker said.

"What a cluster," Hawk bit out. "What happened next?"

"He said he started administering CPR," Stryker continued. "I found him when Emerson and I came upstairs."

Hawk hurried back to Barry. Despite the discomfort from taking the bullets to his body armor, he said to Tommy, "I'll take over."

"I'm not getting anything," Tommy said. "C'mon, Barry, breathe. You gotta breathe."

Hawk knelt beside Barry. "Let me try."

Tommy moved away and Hawk began compressing his chest, then pausing to breathe into him. Again and again, but Barry's condition didn't change.

"C'mon, Barry," Hawk said. "Come back to me. Breathe."

As Hawk continued trying to resuscitate his teammate, he knew it was futile. Barry was gone, and Hawk's heart broke.

After another ten, Hawk called it. "He's gone."

"Are you sure?" Tommy asked kneeling beside Barry.

"We've gotta bring his body back," Addison whispered.

Hawk had fucked up. He'd failed. A man had gotten killed on one of his missions. This had never happened before, but he could have prevented it if he'd partnered with his cousin. He would never have split from Tommy. They would have worked as a team.

"How many in the basement?" Hawk asked.

"Two," Emerson replied. "They never woke. You?"

"Eleven," Hawk replied. "Most of 'em were active."

"Fourteen, total," Stryker said. "Counting the one who escaped."

"You want me to call Cooper while you fly us back?" Emerson asked.

"I fucked up," Hawk replied. "He's gotta hear it from me."

"How'd *you* fuck up?" Stryker asked.

"I should've kept Tommy with me. I'm his mentor."

"There's risk with every mission," Stryker said.

Hawk shook his head. "This is on me."

"We've got to go," Addison said.

"No, I can save him." Tommy stared administering CPR again. "Five more minutes."

"Make the call," Stryker said. "I got this."

"There's a fugitive on the loose," Hawk said. "We've got to go *now*." The urgency in his voice grabbed their attention.

"Stryker and Tommy, carry Barry out," Hawk said. "Addison, Emerson, and I will cover you."

Once at the chopper, Hawk made the call.

"How'd it go?" Cooper answered, his voice groggy.

"Thirteen taken out, one escaped," Hawk said. "Barry got ambushed."

"Are you taking him to the black site?" Cooper asked.

"He's gone," Hawk replied, his voice barely above a whisper.

"Jesus, no. What happened?"

Hawk relayed what Tommy had reported.

"Where were you?" Cooper asked.

"Addison and I covered the upper level. Stryker and Emerson the lower one. Barry and Tommy stayed on the first floor."

"I'll have a vehicle waiting to take Barry's body for autopsy," Cooper explained.

"I'm sorry. It's my fault. I fucked up."

"Don't go there," Cooper said. "Just get back here safely."

Hawk was not okay. Death messes with everyone, but he took responsibility for his team. They all went in and they all got out. He never once believed someone wouldn't make it out alive.

Addison hurt. Her chest ached from where the Kevlar vest had stopped the bullet. But that was nothing compared to how broken she was over Barry's death. Was it her fault? She'd talked to Tommy. Maybe he hadn't been up to the mission. Maybe he should have been paired with Hawk.

They flew home in a heavy silence. Barry's body lay beneath a blanket in the center of the craft. Hawk didn't utter a word the entire flight back, save for clearing their flight with ATC.

When they arrived back at HQ, Cooper was waiting in the parking lot. The men transported Barry's covered body to a waiting van. Everyone traipsed inside to remove their SWAT gear and collect their things.

In the locker room, tears filled in Addison's eyes. Who would Cooper give Barry's belongings to? She had only chatted with Barry a few times. Didn't know anything about him personally. Did he have someone special in his life? Who did he leave behind? Besides his ALPHA family, who would mourn the loss?

Emerson swung by, her face still covered in camouflage paint. "Stryker and I are taking off. If you want to talk, I'm a call away."

The two women hugged.

"Thanks," Addison said. "Same."

As Addison scrubbed the paint off her face, she rinsed away the tears, but the levee had been opened and more slid down her cheeks. She dried her face, pulled the scrunchies from her braided hair. She looked like she'd been up for a full twenty-four hours, but she didn't care. She felt gutted. First, Ronald Jenning, now Barry.

On her way out, she saw Hawk in Cooper's office. She kept going, then stopped and retraced her steps. In Cooper's doorway, she knocked.

He waved her in.

"I'm sorry to interrupt," she said. "It wasn't Hawk's fault, no matter what he tells you."

"I know that," Cooper replied. "How are you doing?"

Addison shrugged, then sighed.

"She got hit in the chest," Hawk said.

"You want to see the team doc?" Cooper asked.

"I'm fine," Addison replied. "Just broken over Barry."

"If you need to talk, I'm here," Cooper said. "If you need to speak to a professional—"

"I have Liv," Addison said, cutting him off. "But thank you." Then, she pinned her gaze on Hawk. "Thanks for having my back."

"Thanks for having mine, babe," Hawk replied.

"You both shouldered almost the entire mission," Cooper said. "That's a lot for two people."

"And one of us *still* got killed," Hawk bit out.

When Cooper dismissed her, she locked eyes with Hawk one more time before leaving.

It was after nine Sunday morning.

She felt numb as she drove home. She wasn't hungry, wasn't thirsty. Despite what they'd accomplished, the mission felt like a monumental failure. She parked out front, went inside her house.

She dropped her handbag on the sofa, then walked around her home, staring at nothing. She stood at the front window. She sat at the piano, but couldn't play. She thought about calling her dad, but decided against it. What could he do? Yes, he wielded a lot of power, but even he couldn't bring Barry back.

An hour passed.

Her chest hurt from the bullet, but her heart ached for their loss and for the grief that Barry's family would endure.

She thought about painting, but that wouldn't bring her any relief. She wanted to be with Hawk. Maybe he'd come over, sit with her for a little while. They would find a way to manage through this, together.

She fished her phone from her bag as it started ringing from a blocked caller.

She wanted to answer, "Hey, Daddy," but she would never be that foolish.

"Hello," she answered.

"Addison, it's Sin. Close your blinds in your front room."

"What?"

"Do it now."

She closed her front blinds. "What's going on?"

"I need you to pack clothes for a few days. Include disguises with wigs and glasses. You have those, right?"

"I do. Are you going to tell me—"

"You have ten minutes—"

"You gotta help me out here. What am I packing for? Am I leaving the country?"

"Pack things you'd wear to work. Include work-out clothes, lounge items, night clothes. And whatever you wear to your club."

"Got it."

"When you're finished, call me back. Don't make any other calls, not even to Z." The line went dead.

What the hell?!

Was BLACK OPS sending her on a mission?

I freakin' just got back from one!

She hurried into her home office, pulled out a suitcase and a duffle from her closet, and set those on her bed. She was trying to be organized, but she was feeling squeezed by the time frame.

Who can pack in ten minutes?

Next, she grabbed wigs, non-prescription eye glasses, two summer hats and a visor. She bolted into her bathroom, threw what she'd need into a large cosmetic bag. Then, she returned to her bedroom and threw in a few more items. After zipping her suitcase, she glanced around and spotted her book on the night table. That got tucked into the duffle. Down the hall she went. From the living room window, she peeked out the closed blinds.

A black sedan with tinted windows was parked out front. As instructed, she called Sin back.

"You ready?" he answered.

"Yes."

"Anton is out front. Stay on the phone with me so I can confirm it's him."

Frustration had her growling.

Her doorbell rang. She opened it. A tall, well-built man stood there in a black suit. He pulled off his sunglasses. "Hello, Ms. Skye. I'm Anton, Mr. Devlin's driver."

She handed him her phone.

"Hello?" Anton said. "Yes, sir. No, I wasn't followed." He handed back her phone.

"Hey," she said to Sin.

"Anton will take your bags to the car. Get in the back seat and don't call *anyone*. I'll see you when you get here." He hung up.

With bags in hand, she stepped outside. Anton took them from her, and she pulled the door closed. On went her sunglasses as she followed him to the waiting car.

He opened the door. She ducked down and peered inside.

She was alone. As soon as she slid in, he shut her door, stored her bags in the trunk, got behind the wheel, and drove out of her neighborhood.

The privacy screen was up, so she didn't have to make small talk. But she doubted he'd answer her questions anyway. While her fingers itched to make a call—or several—she folded her hands in her lap and stared out the window.

What other choice did she have?

She'd never stepped into the unknown like this. She had no idea where she was going or what to expect once she got there.

Hawk paced in ALPHA's conference room while Cooper went to find Tommy. A few moments later, he returned. All three sat at the table.

"Tommy, I'm sorry you had to experience that," Cooper began. "How are you doing?"

"I'm hanging in," Tommy replied.

"Tell us what happened," Cooper said.

"After we entered the home, Barry and I cleared the office together. He moved across the hall to the living room, I went into the dining room. When I moved into the kitchen, he wasn't there. I heard a pop from a gun and I rushed toward the sound. That's when I found Barry in the office."

"Did you see anyone?" Cooper asked.

"The front door was wide open and I saw a guy running."

"Can you describe him?" Cooper asked.

"No. I saw someone on the floor, thought it was Barry, so I was focused on him."

Hawk had fucked up. He shouldn't have paired Tommy with Barry. Tommy needed more supervision and it was Hawk's responsibility to ensure his training period went smoothly.

Cooper asked Tommy if he needed to talk to a therapist.

"I'll let you know," Tommy answered. "I'm pretty shaken up. I might need a coupla days. Can I take tomorrow off?"

"Yes," Cooper replied.

Tommy pushed out of his chair, regarded Hawk. "Sorry the mission didn't go as planned."

After he left, Cooper closed the door behind him, returned to the conference table.

"I'm sorry," Cooper said, "but I've gotta sideline you while we run an internal."

Hawk's stomach dropped. Cooper had to follow protocol. Didn't matter that Hawk had a perfect record. Barry was gone and it was his fault.

"Tommy probably shouldn't have done the mission," Hawk said.

"Why not?"

"He had his phone, even though I told everyone in the meeting, no phone, no ID, no jewelry. He had a few beers at lunch."

"What did you do?"

"I told him he couldn't do the job."

"But he did."

"Addison talked to him while I ran through my pre-flight checklist." Hawk raked his fingers through his hair.

"You're his mentor. Why wasn't he partnered with you?"

"Because Addison and I always work together. We've got a system."

"Alright," Cooper said. "Go home and try to relax. I'm gonna need a couple of days to sort this out."

"If there's anything I can do regarding Barry, let me know."

"I'll contact his family."

A heaviness followed Hawk all the way home. Had he changed up the partners, would someone else be dead? Had he worked with his cousin, would Addison be the one who hadn't made it out alive?

The thought of losing her made his heart hurt.

Anton drove Addison to Langley, pulled up to the security gate at the CIA. Now, Addison was completely confused. Sin ran Develin & Associates. He worked for ALPHA. He was on the BLACK OPS team. Why was he sending her to the CIA and what did *they* want?

"I'll transfer your bags," Anton said after he passed through the gate. He pulled up to the building, got out, and opened the back door.

She exited. "Where can I find them?"

"You'll have them when you leave." With a tight smile, he shut the door, but he didn't get into the vehicle. Instead, he escorted her to the front door.

"Good luck, Ms. Skye."

"Thank you for the ride, Anton."

In the lobby, she spotted Henry Bufford's assistant waiting on the other side of security. Once through, he came bustling over.

"Ms. Skye, come with me."

What was so urgent that she needed an armed escort and a chauffeured ride to the CIA on a Sunday?

They entered the elevator. He inserted a key, then pushed a button marked with a star. The doors closed and the elevator descended. Up until that moment, she didn't know there was a "down".

The doors split open to a quiet hallway devoid of employees. The walls were a bright white, the hall well-lit. She was whisked to a windowless room where three people sat at a conference table talking. They grew silent as their eyes met hers.

Sin sat at the head. Flanking him were Anita Robinson and Henry Bufford. Her mouth went dry.

"Hello, Addison." Sin slid his unblinking gaze to Henry's assistant. "Bring Ms. Skye a bottle of water."

"Water for anyone else?" the assistant asked.

Addison wasn't sure she wanted one, but at the moment, that seemed pretty damn irrelevant. She sat on the edge of the chair next to Henry. "What's going on?"

"Your asset, Melinda, is dead," Sin said, like he was reading a financial report.

Her chest constricted while the air got sucked out of her lungs. "No, no, no. That's not true."

"I'm sorry, Addison," Anita said. "She didn't show up for work yesterday or this morning. Her employees were concerned and one of them called the police for a welfare check. She was found in her apartment."

"Was it a burglary?" Addison silently prayed that Melinda's death was random. Wrong place, wrong time.

"No," Anita replied. "Gunshot wound. Her neighbors didn't hear or see anything. The lock was picked, but it appears nothing was taken."

The assistant returned with the bottle of water. With shaking fingers, she took a few sips. The chilled water hit her stomach and she felt like she was going to throw up. "Excuse me." She stood. The room went all wonky, so she dropped back down. "I need a minute." She didn't care that they were staring at her. She sat there, peering at the table, trying to calm her frenetic heartbeat and stop her shaking.

First, Ronald, now Melinda.

Anita placed her hand over Addison's. "Would you like an escort to the ladies' room?"

Addison swallowed hard, raised her chin, shook her head. "Melinda was a wonderful person, and she was my friend."

"When was the last time you saw her?" Sin asked.

"Thursday night at her coffee shop."

"Did you contact her by text or phone?" Henry asked.

No point in making them ask her for every little detail.

"I was concerned for her safety, so I stopped by her shop that morning and told her I'd be back at ten thirty. That evening, I took care to be sure I wasn't tailed, and I parked in the alley by the employee entrance. I told her about Ronald, offered to hire a guard for protection, and told her I'd pay for it. We chatted for a little while, then I drove back to my nightclub and worked there until it closed." Her shoulders dropped. "It's my fault she's dead."

Her heart was shredded.

Addison wanted to scream, she wanted to pound her fists on the table. She wanted to break down and sob. But her dad's mantra kept her from losing her shit.

"What happens when we let emotion take over?"

"We become vulnerable."

Stealing her spine, Addison said, "Someone must have followed me." Her throat tightened, tears pricked her eyes. "Melinda helped me find Haqazzii and I got her killed."

"We can't jump to that conclusion," Anita said. "But we need to ensure your safety going forward. We've contacted everyone from that mission. Some are still working for us. Others moved on to the public sector or retired. It's a very unsettling time for us."

"What do you mean, ensure my safety?"

"You'll need security," Sin said.

Was this a joke? She needed protection? She'd kill the mother fucker before he realized he'd even been made.

Anita rose. "Sin, you have this, yes?"

He nodded.

Ohgod, he's going to tell me I have to move in with my dad. While she loved her father, there was *no* way she could live with him.

"Please be careful, Addison," Henry said. "If this is related to Abdel Haqazzii, these deaths are three years in the making. We could be up against an entire terror cell."

Anita and Henry left, shutting the door behind them.

She shifted toward Sin. "What's your plan?"

"You've got camouflage paint on your jawline," he said with a sliver of a smile.

"I think that's the least of my problems."

"We've got a hurdle to get you over, that's all. I won't to let anything happen to you."

She hitched a brow. "I'm not scared."

That made him smile. "I'd be surprised if you were, but we still need to take precautions."

"Will I be living with my dad?"

"No, we can't risk putting him in jeopardy."

"Well, I'm not staying by myself at the black site. That place is fine during the day, when you and Dakota are there, but—"

"Not there."

"I'm plumb out of guesses. She folded her arms. "Your turn."

"An Operative will guard you."

"Don't you mean *babysit* me?" she quipped.

"You need someone who's going to have your back."

"Is this up for negotiation?"

"No."

"I want Hawk."

"You don't get to choose who we assign to you."

"Why the hell not?" she bit out. "I've got to be able to trust that person *completely*. If I can't stay at home, I need to be somewhere I feel safe. If you assign me some random guard, I'll be gone in minutes."

"Z would never let that happen."

She grunted. "This is ridiculous. Are you going to tell me I can't go to Stryker and Emerson's wedding or to the hospital when Livy and Jericho have their baby?"

"There will be so much fire power at that wedding, no one would make it out alive if they tried to hurt you. The only one who won't be armed will be the bride."

Addison smiled. "Don't count Emerson out. It's easy to hide a weapon under a wedding gown. So, where are we going?"

"Black site, for now."

"I'll go if Hawk will meet us there."

Sin chuckled. "You're as strong-willed as Evangeline."

"Then, you should be well versed in the art of compromise."

"It's no art, and I'm not sure how much *compromising* is going on when it comes to my wife."

That made her smile.

Sinclair extended his hand. "You have a deal, as long as you don't leave his side."

She shook it. "Make it happen." Then, she stood and left the conference room. As she made her way to the elevator, she realized Sin wasn't by her side. She pivoted.

He stood outside the conference room, texting on his phone. When finished, he said, "This way." And he took off in the opposite direction.

They left through a fire door, which put them underground in a parking garage beneath the building. Another surprise.

"How long has this been here?" she asked.

"A while."

Once at his black SUV, he opened the liftgate. Her suitcase and duffle were already there, waiting for her.

"Put on a wig. Do you have large sunglasses that cover more of your face?"

She opened the duffle, tied her hair into a ponytail that she clipped to her head. Next, she rummaged for her blonde wig and pulled it on. Using the window as a mirror, she fluffed the bangs, then found an oversized pair of black sunglasses. After slipping those into place, she closed up the bags.

"Is this okay?" she asked.

"It's good," he said. "If you go out, wear a disguise. Don't tell anyone what's going on."

"And what will I tell people who ask *why* I'm disguising myself?"

That elicited a brief upturn of his lips. "You were with the Agency for five years, and you've been with ALPHA for three. You'll come up with something."

She went to open the passenger door.

"No," Sin said. "Sit in the back."

"Ridiculous," she mumbled before climbing in the back.

He got behind the wheel and headed toward the black site. Ten minutes later, he pulled off the main road and passed the No Trespassing sign. The road ended, but he continued on the well-worn dirt lane. As he pulled up to the warehouse structure, then drove around back, she wondered how this new arrangement with Hawk would play out.

"What happens if Hawk won't partner with me?"

"You know he will," Sin replied. "He never says no to close friends or family." He stopped in front of the oversized hangar and the door began to roll up. "Ever wonder why?"

"No," she replied. "Do you?"

"I don't have to wonder. I *know* why."

18

ADDISON'S SHADOW

Hawk's guts were in knots and his chest hurt where the armor had stopped the bullets. But he'd never complain. He was alive. His teammate was not. And that was all on him.

As he drove out of ALPHA, he started running through the mission. What could he have done differently? How had things gone to shit?

I fucked up, big time.

He couldn't go home. The silence would be deafening. His mind would wander to dark places. He'd be on the phone with Prescott in seconds. There was nothing his brother could do to erase the past. He couldn't fix the present either. He'd have to manage through the emotional backslide until it passed. No other option.

He wouldn't burden his parents either. They had enough on their plates with his grandparents.

On his way home, his phone rang. It was Sin.

"Hey," he answered.

"How you doing?" Sin asked.

"My answer depends on how much you know," Hawk replied.

"Assume I know."

"Not good."

"Meet me at the black site," Sin said.

"I don't want to talk about it," Hawk pushed back.

"I've got an assignment for you."

"I've been sidelined."

"This overrides that," Sin said. "How far away are you?"

"Ten."

"Good." The line went dead.

How badly had Barry's death fucked with Tommy's psyche? What about the fugitive who got away? After a mission, he always checked to see how his team was doing. This time, he already knew they weren't okay.

Like years ago, he couldn't fix this either.

He drove to the black site, parked in the hangar, made his way inside. Sin was leaning against the wall outside the conference room.

"I'm sorry," Sin said.

"Not as sorry as I am," Hawk replied.

"Barry's death isn't your fault."

"My mission, my team. Six go in, five come out, so yeah, it's my fault." He glanced around. "Why am I here?"

"See for yourself." Sin opened the door.

Hawk stepped into the low-lit conference room. Addison was there, wearing a blonde wig. She jumped out of the chair and rushed over. The minute he wrapped her in his arms, the darkness lifted a little.

"Thank you for doing this," she whispered.

He broke away, stared at her. "What am I doing?"

"Let's sit," Sin said.

Once they had, Sin said, "Addison is in danger."

Hawk flicked his gaze to her. Sadness shone in her eyes, but she didn't look scared.

"The SEAL triggerman who took out Haqazzii is dead," Sin began.

Hawk acknowledged with a nod.

"Addison's primary asset—a woman, who'd relocated to the area—is also dead. She was murdered over the weekend."

"Oh, no," Hawk ground out.

"Addison isn't safe," Sin said.

"Gotcha," Hawk replied.

"She needs round-the-clock protection," Sin continued. "She's against it, but she's willing to be—"

"Babysat," she blurted.

Hawk bit back a smile.

"She's willing to work with me on this, if *you're* the Operative who'll partner with her."

Again, he slid his gaze to her. He wasn't expecting this. They'd be together all the time. She'd just friend-zoned him. He'd want her in his bed, in his arms. How the hell was he going to manage through this?

But, he'd tell her no, especially if she was in danger. Despite the wedge she'd put between them, Barry's death had brought them closer. They were both hurting, both reminded of the fragility of life.

She raised her eyebrows.

"Of course, I'll do it," he said.

"Thank you," she murmured.

"Good," Sin said. "Addison already asked about Stryker and Emerson's wedding and about going to the hospital when Liv goes into labor. There's no limitation to what she can do... as long as you're together." He stood. "Addison, your bags will be in Hawk's vehicle. Let me know if you need anything."

He left, the tapping of his dress shoes on the hard flooring faded away to silence.

Alone with Addison.

He didn't deserve to be happy, but here he was with the best gig he never imagined having. He shifted to her. She was waiting. He laid his hands, palms up, on the table. She stared at them. He waited. After a few seconds, she placed hers in his.

"I got you, but you gotta work with me," he said. "I know you're private and independent, but I can't have you sneaking out in the middle of the night. I'm having a hard-enough time with Barry's death." Pausing, he inhaled a deep breath. "Losing you would wreck me."

Her eyes went soft, her lips curved at the ends. "Losing you would kill me, too. Thank you for doing this. I thought you might not, until Sin reminded me that you never say no to your friends or family." She tilted her head. "Why is that?"

He broke eye contact. He wasn't about to tell her the real reason. Instead, he said, "No is never an option."

Addison was doing her best to keep it together, but she was gutted. Losing Ronald, then Brian, and now Melinda was more than she could handle. She didn't give a fuck about her dad's mantra. Sometimes a good cry was necessary.

"Let's get outta here," he said.

They made their way through the bland hallways and into the hangar. Having Hawk by her side was the right choice. There was no one else in ALPHA she trusted like him, no one else she'd rather be stuck with.

Before climbing in the back seat, she said, "I'm sorry."

As he drove out, she thought about Ronald, Becky, and their children. She thought about how gutted she'd been when her mom had left. The difference? Her mom *chose* to leave. The Jenning family didn't choose this. So much had changed since she was ten. Then, she couldn't distinguish between death and abandonment. All she knew was that her mom was gone and she wasn't coming back. Their anchor had been yanked up and they were getting tossed around on a violent sea.

Her thoughts shifted to Barry, and her heart broke again. A heartless, extremely dangerous criminal got to live another day, but this man was gone forever. Tears pricked her eyes.

As if sensing her pain, Hawk glanced at her in the rearview mirror. "I got you."

She cleared her throat. "Thank you."

Addison had *thought* she was doing the right thing by warning Melinda, but she'd led them straight to her. The pain sliced through her, the guilt was eating away at her. She wanted to right this terrible wrong, but the damage was done. A brave young woman had risked her life, then gotten a chance to start over in a foreign country. Mustering her courage, she left her homeland behind. She had no family. Beyond Addison, she had no friends. The months turned into years and Melinda had carved out a life she loved.

She would never get over losing Melinda.

Hawk drove into his upscale Alexandria neighborhood and pulled over. After waiting to confirm they hadn't been tailed, he drove home and parked in the garage. While he pulled her bags from the back, she eyed his new motorcycle.

"Computer, close the garage door," Hawk commanded.

"Welcome home, Nicholas," the computer said as the door folded down.

"What happened to El Diablo?" Addison asked.

"Sold it for the Low Rider."

"It's beautiful," she replied. "Have you taken it out yet?"

"A couple of times." He stood in front of the scanner leading into his home.

"You have a guest," said the computer.

Hawk stepped out of the way so Addison could get scanned. "Welcome back, Addison. You're cleared to enter."

Addison opened the door, stepped inside. He carried her bags from the basement level to the main floor.

"I want you to feel safe and comfortable here." He set down her bags. "If you need anything, tell me. Okay?"

"Thanks."

They paused to remove their boots and tug off their socks. Then, she pulled off the wig.

"Let's reprogram the security system," he said.

Within minutes, he'd scanned her retina and set her up for voice activation.

She appreciated that he was going out of his way to make her feel welcome, but she could see the grief in his eyes, the weight of the mission bearing down on him. She wanted to throw her arms around him and sob. She wanted to crawl in his lap and stay there for days.

Instead, she stood there, peering up at him. She couldn't miss the frustration rolling off him. His jaw muscles hadn't stopped ticking and his signature scowl was front and center.

He took her on a house tour. It felt stilted and forced, because she'd been there so many times. Maybe not upstairs, but she'd eaten burgers in his kitchen, chilled with a glass of wine on his balcony.

For the next few days, maybe a week, this would be her home, so she paid attention to things she glossed over or took for granted because she'd seen it before.

The stunning, three-level townhome was designed with spectacular views of the Potomac river. Lots of water-facing windows. The kitchen cupboards were white, some had glass fronts. The island was white marble, the backsplash shades of white and light gray subway tiles. No clutter anywhere, except for a large stack of unopened mail in his home office, also on the main level. Several framed photos completed his built-in book cases behind his massive desk.

The living and dining rooms were filled with white furniture, save for the dining room table, which was dark walnut. If she described the home, beyond the sheer elegance, she'd call it relaxed and comforting.

Like him.

When he brought her upstairs, she admired his ass. Hard and tight. *So perfect.* Her fingers tingled to touch him, but she was his assignment, not his overnight guest.

On the second floor, two medium-sized bedrooms shared a bath. These rooms were filled with more white furniture, white bed linens, and light-colored upholstered headboards. While the rooms were bright, they lacked splashes of color.

He led her into the next room, and she stifled a gasp. This room was in stark contrast to the rest of his home.

"My bedroom," he said.

The walls were black, the furniture black, the bed linens also black. The table lamps were covered in black shades. Even though the black curtains were open, it felt like she stepped into death. No other way to describe it. She was seeing a completely different side of Nicholas Hawk for the very first time.

The dark theme continued into his bathroom. Black marble counters and flooring, dark walls, a black window treatment.

Before exiting his bedroom, she eyed his bed. How many women had tumbled in for late-night *and* early-morning fun with him?

I had that chance, but I was too guarded and too scared to take it.

On their way downstairs, they passed the spare bedrooms. "Take either one," he said.

Her heart plummeted, but that was her fault. He'd never ask her to stay in his bedroom, not after what she'd said to him.

They returned to the first floor. "I went to the gym," he said. "It didn't help. I'll make us something to eat."

"I'm not hungry," she said.

"Yeah, neither am I."

"Sin said I've got paint on my chin."

Hawk stepped close, his penetrating gaze studying every inch of her face. He ran his long index finger across her jawline, and her skin tingled from his touch.

"Do you mind if I shower?" she asked.

"You don't have to ask," he replied.

He carried her bags upstairs and set them in the larger of the two spare rooms. Then, he left her alone with her thoughts. The guilt and anger hovered just below the surface, threatening to escape.

They'd get through the next day or two, then she'd tell him her plan. She would hunt down the people who killed her friends. And she would show no mercy.

She made her way to the adjoining bathroom, turned on the shower. While the water heated, she stripped down. As she was about to step in, she realized there was no soap, no shampoo, no conditioner.

She shut off the water, wrapped a towel around herself, collected her clothes, and made her way into his bedroom. This bathroom was massive with a glass-free, double-wide shower stall and waterfall faucet.

Again, her thoughts jumped to all the random women who'd showered there.

For fuck's sake, who cares?

On went the faucet. She dropped the towel and stepped in to the cavernous structure. Black tiles, dark flooring softened by the incandescent light of the chandelier. The water turned hot, the liquid drenching her. Her chest hurt from the hit, but she could endure the physical pain. It was the deaths that wrecked her.

And that's when the tears started flowing. Ugly, gut-wrenching sobs. She couldn't stop, couldn't get herself together to pick up the soap, or the bottle of shampoo. She just stood there balling her eyes out.

He was by her side, his eyes wide with concern. Fully clothed and barefoot, he pulled her into his arms and he held her against him.

"I'm right here, baby," he murmured, "and we're gonna be okay."

She clung to him and cried, releasing the anguish and the pain long held inside.

Her mom told her that people were good. That kindness prevailed. That sharing meant caring. But that had been fleeting because her mom had ghosted, proving that not *all* people were good *or* kind.

Then, her dad taught her to keep her chin up, to be on her guard, and to trust no one. He told her that evil existed, then handed her an opportunity to help rid the world of it, but that came with a cost.

Every death sucked the life out of her soul.

As her sobbing subsided, and she was able to catch her breath, she knew that Hawk was a balance of both worlds. He knew the evil, but he believed in the good.

She wiped her eyes, regarded his soaked face. She knew how she felt, had known for a while. She was falling in love with him and she was absolutely, flat-out terrified.

"I'm sorry I acted like a bitch and a brat at the club," she said running her fingers through his silky, wet hair. "I'm sorry I friend-zoned you right before our mission. I blame myself for telling you Tommy was capable of completing that mission."

He peered down at her, wiped the water droplets from her face. "You don't have to apologize. Did the cry help?"

She sighed. "I don't know." She was pressed so tightly against him, but she wanted more.

"We'll get through this," he said, his warm breath on her cheeks.

"How do you know that?"

"Because we'll do it together." He kissed her forehead,

then vanished around the wall of the shower. Her heart plummeted. He was doing the right thing, but she didn't want right. She wanted raw and wild and intense. But she couldn't tell him one thing, then flip-flop. He wasn't a yo-yo. He was her friend and, now, her protector and guardian. Day and night.

All night. Every night.

Despite feeling drained, she washed her hair and soaped up, then rinsed away the suds. Before turning off the water, she said, "Are you still in here?"

"Yeah, babe." He walked around the shower wall, this time wearing a black bathrobe. "Whatcha need?"

That was a loaded question. She was standing there naked.

"Can you check my chin for paint?"

This time, he didn't enter the shower, but regarded her from a safe distance. "You're good."

She turned off the water, made her way out. He held out a towel, then wrapped her in it. Then, he retrieved another for her hair.

"Bend over," he instructed.

After doing that, she said, "Whoa, that hurts."

"Taking a hit to the chest with Kevlar will save your life, but it won't stop the pain." He gently collected her wet hair in the towel and twisted the cotton fabric.

When she stood, she just stared at him. Like his generous massage, he was taking care of her in such a tender, loving way.

"Want something for the pain?" he asked.

"I'm gonna gut it out."

"My bad-ass Addison." He kissed her forehead. "Do you like my bathroom better than yours?" After disrobing, he walked into the shower.

Mygod, he's an Adonis.

A naked Hawk was a very, very sexy Hawk. She wanted to behave, but a stunningly beautiful man stood inches away. Her gaze dropped to his chest, eight-pack, his semi, those muscular thighs and sizable feet.

"Stop eye-fucking me," he said. "What's wrong with *your* bathroom?"

She jumped her gaze back to his eyes. "No soap, shampoo."

"It's in the closet." He pumped the wall dispenser, rubbed shampoo on his head.

She stood there, mesmerized by his every movement. When he opened his eyes, his gaze met hers. But she couldn't tell if he was surprised she was still standing there. He didn't give anything away, except that he was now sporting an impressive erection.

She wanted to blurt out, "I can help with that." Instead, she said, "Do you have a hair dryer?"

"Center drawer between the sinks."

She should have taken the dryer and left, but she didn't want to be alone. Not now, and certainly not when they could be together. She removed the towel wrapping her hair and started drying. He was done showering before she'd finished.

It had been years since she'd gotten ready beside a man. College, senior year. She had a boyfriend who would stay at her place sometimes, until she found out he was splitting his time between her and his *other* girlfriend. He wasn't invited back. But that was nothing compared to her post-college boyfriend. He'd been a real doozy.

Hawk finished toweling off, but rather than leave, he studied his whiskered face in the mirror. "Shave or no shave?"

If he was going to be kissing her, that three-day-old stubble might feel like a porcupine. But from a purely visual perspective, the dark whiskers looked sexy as hell.

"It stays," he answered himself, before leaving her alone in his bathroom.

With the towel still wrapped around her, she exited.

Hawk was pulling on shorts as she made her way into the

guest bedroom. After dressing in a shirt and shorts, she went downstairs.

He was in the kitchen ladling blueberry-dotted pancake batter onto a griddle. An egg carton and package of turkey bacon waited on the counter.

"We gotta eat something," he said, "then we need a plan. Two people are dead. You are *not* gonna become number three, but we can't hide here. We've got a club to manage and I've got a company to run. You can't work on your BLACK OPS project here. We're going in a bunch of different directions, but we gotta stick together."

She went in search of a frying pan. "How do you like your eggs?"

"Not raw."

His snarky comments always made her smile. But not today. Today, nothing was funny.

Despite their grief, he was pushing forward. She appreciated that about him. After finding the pan, she got busy. She had no appetite, but he was right. Food first, then a plan.

"Computer, jazz music," he said, and sound floated down from speakers built into the walls.

"Are you okay?" she asked.

"I'm never okay, but life goes on, right? You cried enough for both of us."

What does 'I'm never okay' mean?

As she fried up the bacon and eggs, she thought about Sin's words. *He never says no to close friends or family. Ever wonder why?*

She hadn't, until now. As she glanced around his spacious kitchen, she thought about how he never talked about his past. Did Hawk have secrets? What skeletons would she find by living under his roof?

19

HAWK'S MAJOR EFFIN' SECURITY BREACH

Hawk loved having Addison in his home. Always had. Except now, he wanted her in his bedroom, not staying in the room down the hall. Seeing her in his shower had jump-started his libido. But Hawk did not deserve to feel good, on any level. While Barry's loss had gutted him, his only concern now was protecting Addison.

With her plate in-hand, she made her way toward the French doors leading to the balcony.

"Whoa, woman, where are you going?" Hawk asked, stepping in front of her.

"To eat outside."

"We can't discuss our plan on the balcony. I've got neighbors."

They sat at his kitchen table. Having her there made it feel more like a home, something he hadn't had in a long time. As he handed her the maple syrup, he soaked up the view.

Looking at her was much better than staring at the river. Water was water, but Addison was a one-of-a-kind work of art. Timeless beauty peered back at him.

"You can't leave here without a disguise. And to keep the neighbors guessing, switch up the wigs."

"Are they used to seeing you with different women? I mean—sure, no problem."

"I don't bring women here."

"Ever?"

"No."

Why not?"

"I didn't want them to know where I live."

With a nod, she forked in pancakes. "Love the blueberries."

"Let's get clear on schedules," he said. "If you need to go to the black site, I'll take you and stay. I can work remotely. If I need to go to my company, you'll come with me. I'll tell everyone you're a consultant with Providence's shell, Luck Marketing. You can work in my office."

After a nod, she sipped the coffee. "When we go to the club, I'll put on a costume and a wig. No one will question that."

"Good."

His cell phone rang, but he ignored it.

"Aren't you going to get that?"

"No. You're my priority."

He loved the impact that had on her. Her expression softened, her pupils dilated.

"We'll go to Stryker and Emerson's wedding together," he said, before taking a bite of egg.

"I need to swing by my house," she explained. "I didn't bring anything for the wedding."

"It might be safer to buy something new," he said.

"I'm *in* the wedding," she said pointing to herself. "Hello? I'm a bridesmaid."

He finished his bacon. "Right."

"It's my dad's birthday this week and we always have dinner at Carole Jean's."

"I won't have eyes on you if I'm waiting outside." His phone binged with an incoming text.

She barked out a laugh. "Wait outside? You're my friend. We're partners. You're having dinner with us. I'll call Georgia and change the res to three." She left the table, returning with her phone. "I need to make a couple of calls." She dialed, put the call on speaker.

"Hello, dear, are you with Hawk?" her dad asked.

"Hi, Daddy. I am, and you're on speaker."

"Hey Z," Hawk said. "How's it hanging?"

Z laughed and Addison's eyes grew large.

"It's hanging lower than I'd like. You've got a very, very important job."

"She's not gonna leave my side."

"Addison," Z said, "Stay close to him."

"Dad, I'm a little insulted. I lived in the Middle East for two years tracking down a vicious terrorist. This is nothing compared to that. Anyway, I'm taking you to Carole Jean's for your birthday this week."

"We can reschedule," he said.

Hawk's phone binged with another text.

"I made the reservations months ago. I'm going to be in disguise, but I wanted to let you know Hawk will be joining us."

"Wonderful," Z replied. "I look forward to it."

Hawk could hear the smile in her dad's voice.

Addison hitched an eyebrow. Z was formal and standoffish with everyone, but never with him.

"See you Thursday." Z ended the call.

Addison gawked at him. He said nothing.

"Okay, spill it," she said. "My dad shows no emotion with anyone, ever. You guys are joking, joking with each other. He's looking forward to seeing you. What is up with that?"

Hawk could blow it off or he could open up about himself

and his past. As he stared into her eyes, he knew the direction he wanted to take.

"Z and I—"

His phone rang again. This time, Addison jumped out of her chair and retrieved it. "It's a Ken Stoolin." She held out the phone.

"It's work. It'll take a second."

He answered, "Nicholas Hawk."

"It's Ken Stoolin. We've got a problem."

"What's going on?"

"Sabrina and I had a party last night," Ken explained. "Things got a little crazy. No big deal. What we do in our home stays in our home, right?"

"Not sure where you're going with this, Ken."

"Some of our X-rated videos have been posted online."

Hawk grabbed his laptop from his office, returned to the kitchen table and put the call on speaker so he could login. "Hold on, I'm checking your account."

"Fucking nightmare," Ken mumbled.

Hawk clicked on the client's account. At first glance, everything appeared normal. "I'm looking at your account now."

"Look all you want. There are videos of guests doing some crazy-ass things with my wife. And there are videos of me in there as well. My private orgy is trending!"

Hawk jumped online and found the videos. *Dammit.* Whoever had posted the videos had written, "This is what happens if you trust Hawk Security to protect your home."

Fuck. Fuck.

"I have no idea how this happened," Hawk said.

"Well, that's not my problem," Ken said. "Send a team down here tomorrow to take out your piece-of-shit security system."

"Let me—"

"If it was me and the wife having some private fun, I wouldn't care as much, but I've had several patients call me concerned about what they're seeing. My personal life is no one's goddamn business."

The man had a point.

"I want a full refund." The line went dead.

The need for a cigarette had Hawk patting down his pockets. Then, he searched the kitchen junk drawer. He'd thrown out the last pack. "Dammit to fuck."

"What are you looking for?" she called from the table.

"A cigarette."

"Are you out?"

"I quit cold turkey, last week."

Her face lit up. "Finally, something good. I'm so proud of you."

"If you weren't here, I'd run to the corner store and grab a carton."

"Lucky for you, I *am* here."

He returned to the table, leaned down, and gave her a half hug. A sigh floated from her lips, while her sweet vanilla scent drew him in. He kissed the top of her head.

This is pathetic. They'd been intimate with each other, now he was back to the way things used to be. He hated it, fucking hated it.

She turned in his direction. Big blue eyes met his. So beautiful, so fearless, completely irresistible. The desire to kiss her pulled him closer. His phone rang. She broke eye contact, severing their connection.

It was his GM, Mags. "Yo," he answered.

"We have a problem."

"I know. We've been hacked. Hold on." Hawk de-activated all the security cameras in the Stoolin home. "I heard it from a customer. How did you find out?"

"Same."

After they shared client stories, she said, "Lemme check the system to see if more customers were breached."

Addison started clearing the table.

Hawk put the call on mute. "You don't have to do that."

"I got this." She stacked the dishes, returning with the coffee pot. "Refill?"

"I'm back," Mags said.

"Thanks," Hawk said to Addison before he unmuted the call.

"I'm running a report," Mags said.

His phone buzzed with another incoming call. "Let me call you back. I've got another client calling."

Hawk took that call. A long-term client wanted him to know their bedroom camera had been turned on a few days ago. They hadn't noticed, hadn't gotten an email alert either.

"We turned it off," said the wife.

"Then, we went into the system and found that it had recorded us," added the husband. "We only turn that camera on when we're headed out of town. We turned it off, but we thought you'd want to know there's a problem with the system."

Hawk's guts churned. He needed to address the situation head-on. "Are either of you on social media?"

"I have an account," said the wife, "but I don't post anymore."

Hawk grimaced. "Jump online and let me know if that video was posted."

"You're kidding, right?" asked the husband.

"Unfortunately, no," Hawk replied. "Looks like we had a company-wide breach. Someone hacked in, turned on certain accounts, and might be posting those videos."

"I'm back," said the wife. "I don't see anything, but we'll keep an eye out."

"Our first porno movie," the husband said, and the couple laughed.

"I'm not sure there was much to see," she added. "We were under the covers."

"I'm sorry," Hawk said. "We're working to resolve the issue. Turn off your camera. I'll credit you for the month."

"Thanks," the husband said. "We're a little concerned that our account information was also hacked."

"We're looking into that too," Hawk said. "He thanked them for the call, hung up, and called Mags back. "Whad'ya find out?"

"Looks like eight residential accounts got hacked," she said.

They'd already heard from two, so they split the remaining six clients, each calling three.

Two were furious with Hawk. One fired him, the other said he'd give him a chance to remedy the problem, but he wanted some kind of financial compensation.

As Hawk hung up, Mags called him back.

"I lost all three customers," she said. "One threatened to sue us."

"I lost one," he said. "I think I know who did this."

"I figured it was a black-hat hacker," Mags said. "Company breaches happen all the time."

"But they steal information like credit card numbers and email addresses. They don't turn on bedroom security cams, then post videos on social media."

"What a mess," Mags murmured. "Who do you think did this?"

"Wayne," Hawk replied. "I fired him last week for screwing Sabrina Stoolin during the install."

"Ohgod. How did you know?"

"I was there."

"Ew," Mags said. "Did we get his laptop back?"

"Check with HR. I gotta figure out how to stop this from happening again." Hawk hung up, the agitation whirring through him.

This would take hours, days even. He'd have to hire a company to—

"Hey, Emerson," Addison said. "Do you have a second?" She listened. "I'm okay. Did Barry have a family?" More listening. "Thanks for telling me. Hey, I've got a question. Hawk's company was hacked. Would Stryker be able to help or should we call his office tomorrow—he's right here." She held out her phone. "Stryker will help you."

"You're a lifesaver." He took the phone. "Yo, baby."

"Talk to me," Stryker said.

After Hawk explained, Stryker said, "I'll check it out and call you back once I know more. Give me access to view your accounts."

After hanging up, Hawk gave Stryker online access, then went looking for his houseguest. Addison was passed out on the sofa looking like an angel. The tight lines around her eyes were gone. He wanted to hold her, comfort her, protect her.

As he headed toward the kitchen table, she murmured, "Don't leave me."

She sat up, he eased down beside her. After laying her legs across his, she snuggled close. He put his arm around her. "I never nap, but I've been up since yesterday morning," she whispered. "I just need ten."

They'd never napped together. Did "just friends" nap? She smelled so good. He was caressing her shoulder. Her skin was soft, her breathing slow and steady. She felt sensational in his arms.

He never slept in the middle of the day, but he'd sit with her for a little while. She needed him, so he'd be there for her. That's what friends did for each other, right? As her breathing changed and she fell asleep, he stared out his windows at the river and the sky. It was a million-dollar view that paled in comparison to the woman in his arms.

As he held her close, he wondered how long he'd be able to tolerate this "just friends" bullshit. He wanted her in every way a man wants a woman. He had to tell her how he felt. But not now. Now, he needed her to feel safe in his home. One step at a time, only this time, there'd be no backsliding.

As he relaxed into the sofa cushion, he knew that protecting Addison was more than an assignment. It was his path to salvation.

Addison was laughing hysterically. Hawk was lying on the floor while three small children climbed on him. Addison leaned down and kissed him, then she kissed each of the little ones. In all her life, she'd never felt this level of contentment and unconditional love.

A banging sound interrupted her happiness. She jerked awake. She and Hawk were lying face to face on the sofa. Her backside was smooshed against the cushion while his body pressed into hers. For the first few seconds, the joy from her dream enveloped her in peace.

Knock-knock-knock.

He was sleeping so soundly, she hated to wake him. She lifted her head. A beautiful sunset filled the dusky sky, the rays of pink and purple streaming across the sky. Hawk was so close, she couldn't resist. She pressed her lips to his. The instant hit of electricity flashed through her. She wanted another, so she kissed him again. And again.

"Mmm" he said, his eyes fluttering open. "This is cozy."

His raspy voice had to be the sexiest thing she'd ever heard. "I awakened you from a deep sleep. You must be Sleeping Beauty."

"Thank you, Princess."

She shot him a little smile. "There's someone at your front door."

Knock! Knock! Knock!

"You in there, Nicky?"

"Ah, fuck, it's Tommy." He kissed her, letting his lips linger on hers, before pushing off the sofa.

And just like that, they were back to kissing.

She rose, went to the back windows to appreciate the sky. That sky on a canvas would be beautiful, but she would never be able to replicate Mother Nature's astounding perfection.

"Come on in," Hawk said.

"I've been worried about you," Tommy said. "Plus, I've kinda been messed up over Barry."

Addison turned, her gaze leap-frogging from Hawk to Tommy and back to Hawk. Two handsome men, but her heart only wanted one of them.

"Hey, Addison," Tommy said. "Are you bummed about Barry too?"

Hawk opened the fridge. "You want something to drink?"

"I'll take a beer," Tommy said.

Hawk pulled one out, handed it to his cousin. "Addison?"

"I'm good," she replied.

Addison felt like she should give them a few minutes alone, but she didn't want to go upstairs. That would lead to questions from Tommy. No one could know she was camping out there.

"I was gonna order a pizza," Tommy said. "You guys want some?"

Hawk eyed Addison.

"Am I interrupting something?" Tommy asked.

Addison poured herself a glass of water. "Do you need to talk to Hawk because he's your mentor?"

"You don't have to leave, if that's why you're asking." Tommy strolled into the living room, stared out the picture window. "Great view."

"How'd you know where I live?" Hawk asked.

Tommy chuckled. "I called your mom." He pulled his phone before sitting in the oversized, upholstered chair. "What kind of toppings?"

As Tommy placed the order, Addison eased down on the sofa.

Instead of sitting next to her, Hawk carried over a kitchen counter stool, sat on that.

"How are you guys doing?" Tommy asked.

"It's been rough," Hawk replied. "How are you holding up?"

"Same. Things got intense as an undercover cop, but I never had anyone die on me during an arrest. That was brutal."

As Tommy continued chatting, Addison watched him peel the label off the beer bottle, then fold the label over and over until it was a tiny square.

"Anyway," Tommy said, "I don't know anyone else at ALPHA as well as I know you." He shifted toward Addison. "And you, too. I can't talk to anyone outside of ALPHA about this, so you guys are kinda stuck with me. I'm freaking out a little."

"Why?" Addison asked.

"Barry's gone, but the guy who killed him isn't. I'm hoping he didn't get a good look at me."

Hawk did more listening than talking. At some point, Tommy switched topics from Barry to women. By the time the pizza was delivered, Addison concluded that he was super lonely.

Hawk poured himself a water, refilled Addison's glass. "You want another beer?" he asked Tommy.

"I'll take a water."

They relocated to the kitchen table.

"I was planning to visit Granddad and Grandmom today," Hawk said, "but I'll swing by during the week."

"You see 'em a lot?" Tommy asked.

"As much as I can. Now that Granddad's out of the hospital, he and Grandmom are staying with my folks."

"What's gonna happen with the farm?" Tommy bit into the slice of pizza.

Hawk pulled two slices onto his plate. "No idea."

"They should sell it. They'd make a killing."

Hawk's phone rang. It was Mags. "Sorry, I gotta take this." He answered. "What's the latest?"

As he listened, his brows slashed down and his muscles started ticking in his cheek. "Mother fucker," he bit out. "Yeah, okay. Thanks for the call." He hung up.

"Everything okay?" Addison asked.

"Mags thinks the guy I fired hacked into the system. The HR director forgot to get his laptop." Hawk pushed out of his chair, ran his hands through his hair. "That installer was nothing but a pain in my ass."

"You're getting slammed pretty good," Tommy said. "First Barry, now your company."

"He'll be okay," Addison replied.

"So, do you two usually hang out together?" Tommy asked her.

"Sure," Addison replied.

Tommy slid his gaze to Hawk, then back to Addison. "Nice. Hey, so Liliana at your club is cool. We've been talking. She's busy with grad school, plus she has another job, but I'm hoping we can chill together."

When the pizza was devoured, Tommy stood. "Thanks for letting me hang with you guys. So, Addison, how come I've never seen you at ALPHA?"

"No idea," she replied, keeping her answer vague on purpose.

As soon as Tommy left, Hawk said, "Computer, activate the security system. Lock all exterior doors."

"Security is on," said the computer. "Exterior doors locked. Goodnight, Nicholas. Sweet dreams."

Addison cleared the table.

Hawk intercepted her. "You don't have to clean up."

"It's no big deal," she said. "Your cousin is some talker. He doesn't stop."

"I thought he could handle the mission, but it was too intense for him."

"He's in ALPHA. They're *all* intense." She cleaned her glass, set it in the dish drainer. "I'm going to sleep. What are you going to do?"

He stepped close, tilted her chin toward his. "Not what I *want* to do."

"What *do* you want to do?"

"You know exactly what I want." Then, his gaze softened. "But I've got this shit storm at work, so I gotta figure out what's happening."

"Thanks for stepping up to keep me safe," she said. "Can I hug you?"

"Two hours ago, you kissed me. Last week, we were going at it pretty good. You think I'm gonna refuse a hug?"

She pushed onto her toes, wrapped her arms around him and hugged him. He folded her into him and held her like she was his. This was where she wanted to be.

Then, she kissed his cheek.

"I don't want to mess this up again," she whispered. "You mean a lot to me and I don't want to lose you."

She broke away, started to leave, but he pulled her back and peered into her eyes. "If we take a step forward, there's no going back." Then, he took her by the hand. "I'll make sure you get upstairs okay."

As they climbed the steps, she caressed his finger with her thumb.

Outside her bedroom, she asked, "If we kiss again, are we still just friends?"

He regarded her for the longest time, and she squirmed from his wicked-hot gaze. Confidence oozed from him. "Call it whatever you want, baby. You need to get fucked on a regular basis and I'm the only man for *that* job."

Her mouth dropped open. *Oh. My. God.*

With more swagger than any one man should have, he headed back downstairs.

A little dirty talk, paired with the fire in his eyes, was enough to tip the scales. Determined to move toward intimacy, she marched into her bedroom and got ready for bed. Wearing a T-shirt and undies, she crawled between the most decadent silk sheets. When sleep wouldn't come, she found her book, got back in and started reading.

But it was impossible to concentrate with him downstairs. After too many minutes of reading the same page over and over, she turned off the light and lay there. Another thirty passed.

She heard him on the phone, then she heard him cussing. When she heard him on the stairs, her heart beat faster. She wanted him to slide in next to her and love her all night long. That's what she fantasized about, but it would take a herculean effort to divorce herself from costumed role playing. For some, porn was a crutch. For her, sex was physical pleasure devoid of any emotional connection. She couldn't get hurt because the hookup was just that. Fun fucking.

Hawk walked past her bedroom, didn't even glance in.

He turned on his bedroom light, then he went into his bathroom. Then, his bedroom light went out and she was plunged into darkness. Her heart sank.

She lay there for as long as she could stand it, but sleep wouldn't come. Pushing out of bed, she left the bedroom and stood in the hallway. To the left was his bedroom, to the right the stairs.

She was frozen on the spot, unable to decide.

He turned on a bedroom lamp, then appeared in his doorway, dressed in a pair of shorts.

"Can't sleep?" he asked.

"No."

He held out his hand. "Come on. I'll sleep better knowing you're beside me. Where's your Glock?"

"In my bag."

"Bring it."

"You're scaring me."

That made him smile. Seeing his beautiful expression kicked up her pulse.

"I'm going to protect you, not shoot you."

She retrieved her weapon. He was waiting in his bedroom doorway, his hands gripping the doorframe over his head. His eyes blazed with desire, his gaze cemented on hers.

The walk down the short hallway felt like the longest road she'd ever traveled. One step at a time, she made her way to him while his semi morphed into a hefty erection, tenting his shorts to the max.

"Ignore the Little General," he said.

The playfulness in his voice made her smile, but that erection was no laughing matter. He was ready.

But she was not.

"Your General might be a lot of things, but he's definitely not little." She slipped her hand in his and that missing puzzle piece clicked into place.

He walked her to the far side of his bed, then kissed her forehead. "Go to sleep."

"Uh-huh." With him next to her, how was that gonna happen?

He walked around the bed, slid in.

She flicked on the small table lamp, then opened the drawer to place her gun inside. A small, framed picture was there, so she shut the drawer, set her gun on the table, and crawled in beside him.

And she breathed easy for the first time in a long, long time.

"Thank you," she whispered. "I'm so sad about Ronald and Melinda, and now Barry."

"Me, too, babe." He paused, then said, "Computer, turn off the bedside lamp."

"I'm going to find who did this," she whispered. "And I'm gonna rip their hearts out."

Beneath the blanket, he clasped her hand. She rolled toward him, but she didn't run her fingers across his sculpted chest or down his washboard abs. If she did, that would be it. She'd be on him. He'd be in her. It would be over in a flash.

If she was going to take the next step with him, she had to be sure she could handle it. She'd risked losing him once. She wouldn't risk losing him again.

20

TOMMY, TOMMY EVERYWHERE

Hawk lay awake for a long time. He hadn't brought a woman into his bed in forever. Taking this next step with Addison was a confirmation of his feelings. As he listened to her gentle breathing, he had no clue how he'd get over this hurdle. He'd walled off his heart for so long, feeling this way felt alien.

But... it also made him feel alive.

He never imagined he'd have to protect her. She was so independent, such a badass. But, here they were working together to ensure she stayed alive. Going forward, she was his priority.

She rolled toward him, mumbled something. Then, she lay her head on his chest, her arm across his body, and snuggled flush up against him. He was trapped by a beautiful woman in his own bed and he wasn't gonna touch her.

How fucked up is this?

His throbbing boner was starting to irritate him, but it would stand down. Not his first choice, but he needed to take things slowly. Very slowly. The only time she'd had an emotional outburst was when he invited her home to role play.

He inhaled her fragrant scent and held her close. Was this really happening? And was he capable of loving again?

THE EARLY MORNING light brightened his bedroom. He glanced over. No Addison. Pushing out of bed, he went in search of his houseguest and found her sitting in the lotus position on his balcony in an auburn wig and oversized sunglasses.

She looked so peaceful.

Rather than interrupt, he got dressed, then headed to the kitchen to make coffee. A few minutes later, she walked in.

"Good morning." Her sweet smile buoyed his spirits. "I slept sooooo good. You?"

"It was good. Different."

"Yeah, for me, too."

She stayed on the other side of his large marble counter. He wanted to kiss her good morning and tell her how adorable she looked. Instead, he said, "Do you meditate every day?"

"Most." She walked around the counter and peered up at him. "Do you want to do it with me tomorrow?"

He hitched a brow. "I'll do it with you."

Somehow, her straightforward question sounded both dirty and enticing.

Her phone rang. "It's Cooper." She answered, put the call on speaker. "Good morning."

"How's everyone doing?"

"We're okay."

"Can you swing by HQ this morning?" Cooper asked.

Addison looked at him.

So damn pretty. He'd never seen her sleepy face before. There was something vulnerable about seeing someone just after they'd awakened.

"What's going on?" Hawk asked, his gaze still cemented on hers.

"I need to talk to you guys," Cooper replied.

"Yeah, we kinda figured that part out," Hawk ground out. "I've got a problem at work, so we're headed over there."

"It's important," Cooper said. "After we talk, I'll make sure Addison gets to your office."

"Call me," Hawk replied. "I'll come get her."

After ending the call, she sidled close. "You're taking your bodyguard job very seriously."

"Hell, yeah," he murmured before glancing at her mouth.

The air grew turbulent, the energy whipped through him. She was close enough to see the dark specs of blue in her bright eyes. Close enough to kiss her. The pull was irresistible. He dipped down and pressed his lips to hers.

"Ohgod," she whispered. "You kissed me good morning. Thanks for the sleepover party."

He smiled. "I could have been a *lot* more accommodating."

"I thought about taking our—this... us—to the next level, while I was meditating."

"I thought meditation is about clearing your mind."

She shrugged. "I do that, but this morning I focused on how I feel about you."

"And how *do* you feel about me?"

"You're my closest guy friend. I adore you. I'm super attracted to you. I have severe intimacy problems. Kinda obvious since I hide behind costumes."

Whoa, she's finally putting herself out there.

"You'd asked me to come home with you and role play here," she continued. "I'd like to do that tonight. I'm sorry I can't be just me with you, but—"

"I'm in," he said.

She leaned up, dropped a soft kiss on his mouth. "Thank you." She took a few steps, turned. "How do you feel about me?"

"Like I'm ready to see where this goes."

"You didn't answer my question," she replied. "How do you feel about *me*?"

He sauntered over, pulled off her wig, and placed his hands on her face. He kissed her softly. Once, twice, three times. Then, he deepened the kiss and she welcomed him into her mouth. The passion between them was like throwing gas on a campfire. Out of control and violently dangerous. She jumped into his arms, thrust her hands into his hair and groaned.

He ached for her, ached to be inside her.

She slowed the kiss down and stared into his eyes. "Welp, the lust is there, but how do you feel about me?"

He smiled. "I invited you into my bed and I didn't lay a hand on you." He hitched a brow. "I'm willing to play this *your* way at your speed. I haven't cared—*really cared*—about a woman in a decade. I haven't gotten close to anyone in a long time because—"

Silence.

"Don't stop," she whispered.

"Because I haven't." He set her down. He was done talking. He wasn't a talker. He was a doer. He was protecting her. Wasn't that enough? He was willing to take this at her pace. Wasn't that enough too?

She stood tall and kissed him gently. "I won't hurt you."

He broke away, poured them coffee.

She went in search of something, opening his cupboards, then vanishing into his pantry, returning with two boxes of cereal. "Are you eating?"

"Sure." He eased onto a stool at the counter while she pulled out bowls, spoons, and milk. Then, she sat beside him, but she didn't say a word.

He appreciated that she was giving him space. When they finished eating, she grabbed the wig and vanished upstairs, taking his heart with her.

Addison was confident there was more to Nicholas Hawk than he'd ever let on... a lot more.

She'd always assumed he bedded women because he liked to bed women. Now, as she got ready for work, she wondered why he never got emotionally attached to any of them over the years.

After dressing in a navy-blue pantsuit with a white blouse, she pulled on the auburn wig, grabbed her Glock and her bag. With her heels in hand, she trotted down the stairs. He was standing on his balcony, in shades, staring out at the water.

When she stepped outside, he faced her. "Look how pretty you are."

She smiled. "You like the wig?"

"I like *your* hair, but you look great."

She ran her hand down his back. "You can tell me anything, okay?"

"I know, babe. Ready to head out?"

Despite her protests, she couldn't ride shotgun. She'd been relegated to the back seat.

As he backed out of his garage, she said, "This is ridiculous. It's like you're my chauffer."

"If you like the way I drive, you can always tip me *real* good."

She laughed.

Once on the main road, he said, "No one can know you might be a target for a terror plot, so we've gotta come up with a reason why I'm driving you around."

"We're such good friends. I don't think anyone will notice. You haven't brought up what's going on with your company."

"Talking about it only pisses me off."

"Gotcha. I'm here if you need an ear or a second opinion."

"I fired an employee and he's trying to fuck with me," Hawk

said. "I've gotta do some damage control and put my system on lockdown until I confirm it's him."

Hawk pulled into ALPHA HQ, drove around back, and parked. They went inside and found Cooper working at his small conference table in his office.

"Thanks for coming in," he said. "Addison, can I have a minute with Hawk?"

"Sure." Addison left, shutting the door behind her.

Hawk pulled out a chair and sat.

"I'm reinstating you," Cooper said.

Relief pounded through him. "That was fast."

"It was determined you did nothing wrong."

"Who cleared me?"

"A committee," Cooper replied.

Led by Z.

Hawk's phone rang and he silenced it. "We good?"

"The helo mission's a go."

This took the edge off the shitstorm happening at his company. Not only was he reinstated, he was going back on the front line.

"You'll need at least two more Operatives."

"Well, I won't be taking Tommy."

"Yeah, about that, I'm gonna reassign him a new mentor."

"Good call."

"Who do you want on this job?" Cooper asked.

"Addison and Prescott, if he's in town." Hawk pushed out of the chair. "You want me to grab her?"

"Not yet," Copper said. "First, you need to know who you're going after. It's Aziz Haqazzii, son of deceased terror leader, Abdel Haqazzii."

Hawk's pulse shot up, while the fury he kept in check jumped to the surface.

"So, you know," Hawk murmured.

"I read your file, so yeah, I know. I just need to know if you can take out Haqazzii's son."

Hatred and revenge slithered up Hawk's spine, curling itself around his already hardened heart. "With pleasure."

"I've got to talk to Addison, then I'll tell you both about the mission," Cooper explained.

Years of seething rage were squeezing Hawk's chest so tight, he couldn't fucking breathe. "I'll get her."

He stepped into the hall and spotted Addison talking to Danielle. Seeing her sent that familiar zing of attraction through him. Tommy moseyed around the corner and stopped to chat with them. A growl shot out of him as he made his way toward them.

"Hey, Nicky," Tommy said. "You doing okay, I mean, being sidelined and all?"

"I got reinstated," Hawk replied.

His cousin's mouth dropped open, then his face split into a smile. "That's great. Congrats."

"Cooper's assigning you a new mentor. I'm not here enough to work with you."

"Bummer," Tommy said.

Hawk shifted his attention to Addison. "You're up."

She headed down the hall as Cooper stepped out of his office. They spoke quietly, then she called to Hawk, "Come join us."

Hawk tossed his cousin and Danielle a nod before strolling down the hall. They entered Cooper's office and he shut the door.

After settling at the conference table, Cooper said, "Addison said that anything I say to her, I can say in front of you."

Hawk regarded her. "Alright."

"It's a helo mission," Cooper continued, "so Hawk's primary. He asked for you and Prescott."

"I'm in," Addison replied.

"Before you agree, you need to know that the mission is to take out terror leader Aziz Haqazzii."

Addison sat upright. "Is he related to Abdel Haqazzii?"

Cooper nodded. "His son."

"How do you know who he is?" Hawk asked her.

"Abdel Haqazzii was my target for over two years when I was with the CIA." Though her tone remained steady, her jaw muscles flexed in her cheek and she was tapping her fingernails on the table. "I'd moved to the Middle East to be team lead for an operation that centered on finding him. I was at the Marine base camp the night DEVGRU took him out."

Holy fuck.

Hawk just stared at her. He knew she'd been with the CIA, but she never talked about it. Knowing she couldn't discuss her cases, he never asked.

Addison stared into her lap. "A friend of mine from Langley joined me over there, in part, because I asked for her." There was a vulnerability in her voice that he'd never heard before. "She got ambushed after following up on a tip from an informant. A bomb went off and she got killed. It was my fault she died."

What the hell.

Silence.

"Addison, you know that's not true," Cooper said.

"I appreciate your saying that, but she trusted me. We were like sisters and, like Melinda, she's dead... because of me."

"I'm sorry, babe," Hawk said.

"Anything to do with Haqazzii and his family, I take personally," Addison said, her tone filled with determination. "I'm *all in* on this mission."

Cooper flashed a picture of Aziz Haqazzii on the screen. Late-thirties, pleasant looking with a thick, dark brown beard and mustache. Deep brown eyes, short, dark hair. No smile. In his arms, he clutched a machine gun.

Hawk jumped back ten years when his heart had been shattered, his soul had died. A calloused man had emerged from the wreckage of his broken life. He shifted on the chair, forcing himself to stay present to the mission. He couldn't eliminate the SOB if he didn't know the specs.

As if Addison sensed something was wrong, she regarded him. He could feel her eyes burning into him. Rather than meet her gaze, he stared at the screen. Better to shut her out and manage through this alone.

Cooper showed them an aerial photo of an unremarkable one-story building. "This is Haqazzii's compound outside Sharpsburg, Maryland. He and his team live and work here." Cooper tapped his keyboard and a photo of a trailer flashed on the screen. "The trailer is parked on the property. We don't know its purpose."

Hawk's phone buzzed with a text, but he didn't check his phone.

"What's their MO?" Addison asked.

"Explosives," Cooper replied. "Over the past two years, there've been eleven bombs detonated worldwide killing thousands. Based on intel from our CIs, and the types of devices used, we're confident Haqazzii and his team are behind the bombings."

Hawk and Addison nodded their acknowledgment.

"The mission is Saturday, two a.m.," Cooper explained.

"Why the short timeline?" Hawk asked.

"A month ago, they turned a White House staffer who travels with the President to Camp David. The employee was providing intel to Haqazzii about an upcoming international summit the President is hosting next week."

"When do guests arrive?" Hawk asked.

"Sunday afternoon," Cooper replied. "Haqazzii and his team are planning to smuggle bombs into Camp David, set to detonate during the summit."

"Got it." Hawk scraped his fingers down his whiskered cheeks.

"The CIA has strong reason to believe Haqazzii is responsible for Ronald's and Melinda's deaths in retaliation for killing his father," Cooper continued.

"Understood," Addison replied.

"If you accept this, you'll miss Stryker and Emerson's rehearsal dinner," Cooper said.

"As long as I don't miss their wedding, I'm good," Addison added.

Hawk's phone rang. "I gotta take this." He answered, listened, hung up, then shifted his attention to Addison. "We'll prep later." He pushed out of the chair. "I gotta take off."

When Addison didn't get up, Hawk said, "You ready?"

"I need to talk to her about something else," Cooper said. "I'll make sure we get her to you."

"Call me when you're ready for a pick-up," Hawk said to her.

He swung open the door to find Tommy standing there.

Tommy peered around Hawk. "Can I come in?"

Pushing past him, Hawk bolted down the hall.

"Come in," Cooper said.

"Oh, sorry," Tommy said. "I didn't know you were in a meeting. I can come back."

"What do you need?" Cooper asked.

"Hawk told me the bad news," Tommy began. "I'm bummed he's not my mentor, but I wanted to see if Addison could do it."

Cooper shifted his gaze to her. She sat there stone-faced. Hopefully, Cooper knew her well enough to pick up on her non-verbal cues.

"Addison's not here every day. I'll find someone for you. Give me a few days to circle back."

Tommy peered over at her, but she stayed silent.

"Is that it?" Cooper asked Tommy.

"Oh, yeah." Tommy still hadn't moved.

"Can you shut the door on your way out?" Cooper asked.

When Tommy left, Cooper asked Addison about Hawk's mental state.

"He blames himself for Barry's death," Addison replied.

"I know," Cooper replied. "He's not going to tell me if anything's wrong, but I wanted to make sure he's up for this mission."

"Why wouldn't he be?" Addison asked.

"You said it. He feels responsible for Barry's death. You've been with him, so I need confirmation that he's mentally ready. Haqazzii is ruthless. Each of you has to be at the top of your game."

"Hawk is up for this mission. And so am I."

Hawk strode into Hawk Security and stopped. There had to be thirty employees milling in the lobby.

"We heard what happened," one of them said.

"What are we supposed to tell our customers?" asked another.

"Boss man, we're getting slammed with calls," said one of his receptionists. "Customers are concerned their cameras were activated without their knowledge."

"We'll get through this," Hawk said to his staff before addressing his senior receptionist. "Send an email to the exec team, managers, and account managers. Meeting in the big conference room, forty-five minutes."

The receptionist nodded. "I'm on it."

"Where's Mags?" he asked.

No one had seen her.

Skipping the elevator, angry energy propelled him upstairs. On the top floor, he stopped at Mags's office. She wasn't there. He called her cell.

"Hello." She sounded like hell.

"You got a cold?" he asked as he made his way toward his office.

"No," she replied. "Are you in the office?"

"Yeah. Are you?"

"I was in the restroom." He turned to see her standing in the hallway. As he made his way toward her, he couldn't miss her bloodshot eyes.

"You need to see a doc?" he asked.

"Can we talk in my office real quick?"

Once there, she shut the door. "Tommy stopped by late last night and ended things." She wiped her eyes. "I really liked him. Anyway, I know we've got a huge problem with the breach, but I probably should have called out sick."

"I didn't realize you guys were a thing."

"We went out a couple of times, hung at my place as well. Clearly, I was more into him than he was into me." She blew her nose. "I need to shake this off and get to work."

"I'm sorry it didn't work out," he said. "Take a day if you need to get yourself together."

"Last week, he sent me a pic of us." She spun her monitor around and clicked on an email with a photo of her and Tommy. "I opened it this morning and kinda lost it."

As much as he relied on her, her head wasn't in the game. He needed to handle things, then put out the fires from the breach.

"After I lock down the system, I'm meeting with the exec team and account managers," he said.

"I'll sit in on your meeting, that way I'll be up to speed."

Hawk left her office, strode down the hall and into his. But he didn't shut the door. He needed to create the illusion that he had this, which, at the moment, he wasn't sure he did. He fired up his computer and got to work.

First, he deactivated Wayne's ID, which HR should have done days ago. Then, he scanned every account. Twenty minutes later, he had the full picture.

A total of eleven residential clients had been hacked. Ten had bedroom videos posted online. The eleventh client was Ken and Sabrina Stoolin. Their orgy-party videos had been uploaded to several online websites. The person who posted them called himself The Truth.

The clients were well-known, prominent professionals in the community. Stoolin was a plastic surgeon. Four were high-powered attorneys. Three were popular politicos. Two were university presidents, and the last one was a retired CEO of a Tech company. Five lived in Northern Virginia, four lived in suburban Maryland, and two lived in DC.

With each of the videos, The Truth posted a caption.

Hawk Security ISN'T Secure

As bad as it was, it could have been much worse. None of his business or government accounts had been breached. For that, he was grateful.

He locked his system down, limiting the number of people who could view all accounts to him, Mags, and his VP of Client Accounts. It was a temporary solution until he determined who had fucked with his business.

Time for his meeting. He left his office, walked down the hall, and sailed into the conference room. Everyone grew silent, all eyes on him.

He sat at the head. "Hey, team, how's everyone doing?"

"I'm a little freaked, boss man," one of his account

managers admitted. "A bunch of my clients have called, and I'm not sure what to tell them."

Hawk was seething, but they didn't need to see that. His demeanor affected their actions. If he stayed calm and in control, they'd mirror his behavior. Half of them looked rattled enough on their own, no need to fuel the fire. His gaze floated around the room as he inhaled a calming breath.

"Eleven residential accounts were hacked," he began. "The breach didn't extend to our government or commercial accounts, which is great. Call your clients and tell them the truth. Let them know the situation is being resolved. Assure them that their security is our top priority and that the system has been locked down. If you've got customers who want out, email me their contact info and I'll talk to them."

Several nodded.

"Questions?"

"Our government contacts are freaking out," said one of his directors. "Was the breach across all sectors?"

"Eleven residential accounts were hacked," Hawk reiterated. "Residential only."

"Right," said the same director. "You did just say that. Sorry."

"We'll get through this," Hawk said, "and it'll make us a stronger company for it."

A few nodded, one leaned back in his chair, two even cracked smiles.

"If you've got all the accounts on lockdown, how can I access them?" asked one of his managers.

"You can view them, but you won't be able to make any changes," Hawk explained. "It's a temporary annoyance to ensure our clients' data and videos stay secure."

Once everyone's questions had been answered, Hawk returned to his office to investigate his former employee, Wayne. The installer had worked for another home security company for a few years, then had a string of jobs that lasted less than a year each. He had no priors, wasn't married, and was juggling three girlfriends at the same time.

While Hawk could see how the guy would be miffed for getting fired, it seemed out of character that he'd retaliate so aggressively. But he had a Hawk Security laptop, so he could have accessed these accounts, turned on their cameras, and captured the footage.

Armed with this information, Hawk remote-wiped Wayne's laptop. His HR director should have taken the laptop when Wayne was let go, but the ball had been dropped. Then, he sent out a company-wide email so all his employees were told about the breach. He stayed high level, didn't mention Wayne, and reassured everyone that the situation was being remedied ASAP.

His desk phone rang with a call from reception. "Nicholas Hawk," he answered.

"Boss man, Addison Skye is here to see you."

As he trotted down the stairs, he checked his cell phone. She'd texted him twenty minutes ago. "On my way."

In the lobby, he spotted Addison at reception, still in her auburn wig and sporting red-rimmed, fake prescription glasses. Warmth blanketed his chest when their eyes locked across the room.

Her smile made his heart pound hard.

I'm falling in love with her.

"Hey," she said. "Reception looks great."

Earlier in the year, before relocating his customer service and system monitoring teams into the building, Hawk had hired an architect and interior designer to upgrade work spaces, break rooms, even the two-story lobby. Having everyone in the same building had made all the difference. His employees loved the changes. He loved the impact the renovations and the consolidated teams had on productivity and morale.

Two employees skirted by. "Hey, boss man."

"Hey, guys."

His Director of Residential Accounts veered over. "That meeting made all the difference. I calmed down, and that helped when I talked to my teams."

Hawk shot her a smile. "I got this, no worries."

When he turned back to Addison, she was smiling. "What?" he asked.

"You're king of the castle," she murmured.

He winked. "What can I say, baby?"

Stepping close, she stroked his arm, sending a whoosh of energy through him. "You're super sexy running the show. You have all the power."

"I always have all the power, babe," he said, glancing at her mouth.

Damn, I want to kiss her.

Her cheeks flushed with color. "I love that about you," she whispered, her gaze drilling into his while the air turned chaotic around them. "Are you handling the breach?"

"Hell, yeah," he replied. "Did Coop drop you off?"

Tommy loomed into view.

Ah, fuck. Fuck me.

"Hey, cousin, long time no see." Tommy chuckled. "I heard Addison was coming over here, so I let her tagalong." He stepped close. "I told Mags I wanted to be friends. I'm checking in, you know, see how she's doing."

Tommy broke away to yuck it up with one of the receptionists.

Hawk wanted to tell him to leave Mags the hell alone. His being there would only mess with her head. But he wasn't getting involved. Mags's personal life wasn't his business.

He slid his gaze to Addison.

"Someone's pissed," she whispered.

"That obvious?" he hissed. "Babe, I need you safe."

"I *am* safe."

"How do I know that if I have no fucking idea where you are?" There was no hiding his agitation.

She glared at him as his GM stormed into the lobby.

Mags lasered in on Tommy, narrowed her gaze, and marched over to him. "What do you want?" she barked.

"Can we talk?" Tommy asked.

Mags crossed her arms. "I'm busy."

"I wanted to check in with you," Tommy continued. "Make sure you're cool."

Tommy didn't seem to care that everyone in the lobby was listening to their private conversation.

"You *dump* me, then you have the nerve pop over the *next* freakin' day to check on me. How the hell do you think I am?" Mag's razor-sharp voice rose to a fever pitch.

"We're friends," Tommy said. "Let's grab lunch."

"I liked you and you told me you really, really, really liked me. What kind of bullshitter says that?" Mags's voice echoed through the quiet space.

"Whoa, no need to go ballistic," Tommy said backing away.

"I don't need friends like you. Get lost."

Tommy glanced at the receptionist. "See ya," he said before moseying out.

"Let's go to my office," Hawk wrapped his fingers around Addison's arm and guided her to the elevator.

Mags stood at the elevator bank, her cheeks flaming red. They all rode upstairs together.

Talk about fucking awkward.

"That was embarrassing and unprofessional," Mags said. "Sorry, boss man."

"Don't sweat it," he replied.

On the top floor, after Mags veered into her office, Hawk glanced over at Addison.

She did not return his gaze.

They entered his corner office and he shut the door.

"That's why I don't have a boyfriend," she said. "I can't handle that drama. Been there, done that. Never again."

Rather than sit behind his desk, he leaned on the arm of his sofa. "I don't want drama either, but I don't want you hanging with Tommy."

Her eyes grew large. "I'm not *hanging* with him and when did *you* get all possessive? Are you still hung up on that thing that happened months ago?"

"You insisted I protect you," he ground out. "Let me do my fucking job and *protect* you. I don't want you getting into someone else's car. I don't like *not* knowing where you are. You might not take this seriously, but I sure as hell am."

"He's in ALPHA," she murmured. "If we can't trust the Operatives, who can we trust?"

He exhaled an exasperated grunt. "This is different," he murmured. "You aren't an assignment. You're someone I care about... a lot."

She nudged his thighs apart and squeezed between his legs. "Cooper and Danielle were going to drive me over, but Tommy stopped by Cooper's office to see if I'd be his mentor. When he found out I was coming here, he offered to drive me so he could check on Mags."

"*What*? Back up. He asked you to be his mentor?"

"Cooper said no, so I didn't have to. It's no big deal."

"His fascination with you has become an obsession."

She barked out a laugh. "He told me he was dating Mags, now he's interested in Liliana, from our club. He's just dating around." She draped her arms over his shoulders. "I don't want to waste another second talking about him." She kissed him, then kissed his cheek before breaking away.

As far as Addison was concerned, it was a closed conversation, but the agitation clung to Hawk like the July humidity hovering outside. Tommy might be dating around, but he was flat-out obsessed with Addison.

Of that, Hawk was certain.

21

MIDNIGHT CONFESSIONS

That evening, Hawk was ready to play things Addison's way, then *his* way.

"I need to change," she said.

"What's our scene?"

"I'll interview to be your assistant."

"Didn't you want to be the boss?" he asked, purposefully not touching her. Though she was hard to resist, he'd wait until their scene before he got physical with her.

"I did, but now I'm thinking I'd rather work under you." She offered a sly smile.

"So, I'm a scumbag," Hawk said.

"Exactly, but it's gonna make for some dirty, dirty fun." She started up the stairs, then turned back. "I don't want to see you before we play."

"After my shower, I'll be in my office," he said. "When you're in the living room, text me."

"That's perfect." She hurried up the stairs.

Twenty minutes later, his phone buzzed with an incoming text. "Hello, sir. I'm here."

He couldn't help but smile. She loved her role playing and

he was gonna enjoy the hell out of her for the next few hours. He'd dressed in a black suit, light pink shirt, no underwear. He slipped his bare feet into his loafers, made his way to the living room.

He walked in, and his brain skidded to a halt. She was sitting on his sofa wearing a tight and very short black dress with a front-facing zipper and a plunging V-neck that afforded him a great shot of her pushed-up breasts. On her feet, four-inch sandals. His cock twitched.

He would never, ever make fun of her role playing again.

"Mr. Smith." He offered his hand.

She rose, shook it. "I'm Bambi." She batted his eyelashes at him. "Thanks for seeing me."

He strolled to his dining room table, pulled out a chair for her, then sat at the head. "Tell me about yourself."

As she mentioned a couple of things, he found himself mesmerized. She'd parted her hair on the side, pulled it over and clipped it, so that it trailed down her breast. She'd worn a lot of dark eye makeup, but no lipstick. Her hands were folded in her lap, her back arched, which gave him a fantastic view of her breasts. He loved how into this she was. Making her happy mattered to him. It mattered a lot.

"You don't have any executive assistant experience," he continued. "Do you type?"

"Absolutely," she replied.

He did a few more general back-and-forth questions before moving the play along. "Bambi, I've interviewed several qualified candidates. What would set you apart from them?"

"I have an exceptional work ethic. I'm a total team player."

He held her gaze before eyeing her breasts. "I work late a lot, so you'd need to stay here."

"No problem."

"I travel. You'd accompany me."

"I can do that."

"I'm looking for an assistant who can offer me more than a good attitude and excellent typing skills. What else would you be willing to do, to set yourself apart from the other candidates?"

"I, um, I don't know. What were you thinking?"

"Let's move to the sofa."

"I'm good here," she said narrowing her gaze at him.

"Bambi, I've had a very long and frustrating day," he continued. "My company, my multi-million-dollar company had a security breach that ate up most of my day." Pausing for effect, he raked his fingers across his whiskered chin. "I need to relax and unwind. Rather than tell me how hard you work, why don't you show me how you can help restore my calm."

She rose and stared down at him. "What are you asking?"

"Do you like to fuck, Bambi?"

A desperate, edgy moan ripped from her throat. "I'm not very experienced, Mr. Smith."

He stood, peered down at her. "I like to fuck… and I do it a lot. If you want to be considered for this job, I'm going to need you to show me what you can do for me, outside of taking a typing test."

"Oh, I don't think—"

"If our interview goes well, I'll pay you a hundred grand a year, plus a substantial bonus. All you have to do is accommodate my overactive libido." He placed his hand on the zipper of her dress. "I'd love to see those fantastic tits of yours."

Her breath came out in a whoosh. "You're a pig."

"A very, very horny one."

She stared into his eyes for so long, he wanted to ask her if he was going in the wrong direction. But he knew she'd redirect the role play if she didn't like it.

"You can see yourself out if—" he began.

"I'll do it," she groaned out.

"Do what?"

"Let you fuck me."

"Smart decision, Bambi," he murmured. "I can't wait to come inside your hot little snatch."

"Ohmygod," she bit out and grabbed the back of the chair for support.

He wrapped his fingers around her arm and guided her into the living room. "Let's get you naked so I can start the *real* interview."

He removed his suit jacket, sat on the arm of the sofa, pulled her close, and tugged down the zipper. Her eyes were almost black with lust, her jagged breathing roaring in his ear. He moved her long hair off her shoulder as the dress opened, revealing a black push-up bra and a black thong. He slid the dress off her shoulders, and it tumbled to the floor.

His cock turned hard, blood surging through his veins. She was exquisite and so damn sexy.

"This is very naughty, sir," she said. "I don't think we should be doing this."

"How badly do you want this job?"

She caressed her lower lip with her tongue and his junk got harder still. "I'm kinda desperate."

"Take off my pants," he commanded, "and suck my cock."

After he toed off his shoes, she removed his pants and eyed his jutting hard-on. "You're so big," she murmured.

"Kneel and taste me."

"I've... I've never swallowed."

"You'll suck and swallow if you *get* the job," he said. "Tonight's all about how good of a fuck you are."

She swayed and grabbed his arms.

"Breathe," he murmured before inhaling. She mimicked him for a few seconds, then shot him a little smile.

"I'm good," she whispered.

He popped out of his sleaze-bag character to kiss her forehead.

She wrapped her fingers around his shaft and stroked. Up and down, up and down, spreading the wetness over his head. Then, she moved him to the sofa, knelt in front of him, and licked the head and shaft.

Her gritty moans sent electricity charging through him while she feasted on him, licking and sucking his boner.

He loved watching her pleasure him. Loved how she feasted on his hardness, her lips glistening with his wetness. But their "interview" would be over too fast if she continued.

"Enough," he commanded.

She gazed up at him, her lips wet, her eyelids hooded.

"Time to fuck, Bambi."

Addison was on fire, her body aching for a release. Hawk was hot, talented, and had a dirty mouth. He was an alpha in every way imaginable, took control of the scene, and wasted no time getting to the good stuff.

She stood.

"Take off your bra and thong," he commanded.

"Mmm," she bleated as she unhooked the bra and tossed it onto the chair. Then, she wiggled out of the wet thong, but she didn't remove her stilettos. Now, naked, she stared down at him.

Her heart was galloping in her chest, she couldn't wait to take him inside her. For a man who'd never done any role playing, he was so damn good.

Hawk pushed off the sofa. With his gaze drilling into hers, he removed his shirt, then cupped her breasts and ran his thumbs around and over her nipples until they firmed. "Very nice."

He dug out a condom from his pants pocket and rolled it on. Then, he dipped down, took her plump nipple in his mouth, and sucked.

"Oh, yes," she whimpered. "No, I mean, you shouldn't be doing this to me."

He sucked and sucked while she arched her back, pushing her nipples into his warm, wet mouth.

When he finished, his penetrating gaze made her tremble with excitement.

"Bend over the side of the sofa so I can fuck you."

She loved the grittiness in his voice, the fire raging in his eyes. She couldn't wait for him to plunge inside her and fuck her so good. But she needed to make him work for it.

"But fucking each other is bad," she said.

"I've got several other candidates who begged me to fuck them."

She sauntered away from him. "I don't think this is a good idea. I should probably get going."

He motioned with his index finger. "You're very uptight. I know just what you need to relax. I fuck good, and I'll make you come so hard. You like to fuck, don't you?"

"I don't—"

"Get your ass over here."

A groan ripped from her throat.

"Maybe, for just a minute, then you have to pull out." She sashayed into position, bent over the sofa arm, spread her legs, and chugged down a shaky breath.

He stood behind her, smacked her ass, the sting making her yelp. "Yes, I love that," she bit out.

After placing his cock at her opening, he tunneled inside.

A low groan shot out of her, the pleasure stealing her mind while she gripped the sofa and held on.

"I'm gonna fuck you hard, baby," he ground out.

In and out he thrust while his throaty grunts and groans made her cry out from the sheer exhilaration. The build was intense, fast, and fucking phenomenal. Every cell was racing toward a release while the pleasure spiraled through her in every direction.

She was reaching the point of no return, but she didn't want to come so quickly.

"I don't want to come yet," she blurted.

He stilled, his hardness rooted inside her. "Am I talking to Addison or Bambi?"

Craning around, she smiled. "Sorry, I should have called out our safe word."

He withdrew, pulled her close, and kissed her. After a few seconds, he said, "Lie on the floor, Bambi. I want to watch you under me when I come."

And just like that, he was back in the scene.

She laid down on the throw rug. "You're so fucking sexy," he said as he planked over her. With his jutting cock in hand, he entered her. She wrapped her legs around his lower back.

"I love your tight pussy," he murmured. "Tight just for big daddy."

A raspy moan rolled out of her throat. With his gaze on hers, he fucked her. Hard and fast and so damn good.

Their rhythm was intense. She raised her arms over her head and rested them on the floor, and he clasped both wrists in one of his large hands.

"You're trapped," he ground out as he thrust again and again.

The orgasm began in the depths of her soul.

"Ohgod, I'm coming," she blurted as the glorious spasms of ecstasy exploded through her.

As she shook and convulsed beneath him, he said, "Here I go, baby."

He kissed her, hard, their tongues stroking, searching while he emptied himself inside her.

When they finished, he rolled her onto him and stared into

her eyes while he wrapped his arms around her, shielding her from the evils of the world.

I'm gonna fall so hard for him, I just know it.

"Did I get the job?" she murmured after a few moments of gentle kissing.

"You nailed the interview," he replied with a just-got-laid smile. "Welcome aboard."

The tender kissing continued until they separated. After she collected her clothes, he whisked her into his arms.

"What are you doing?" she asked.

"Taking you to bed," he replied.

With every step he climbed, her heart pounded faster. She studied his serene face. All the angst had been erased. She could get pretty damn used to that. When he set her down in the hall, her heart squeezed.

Despite her anxiety regarding their intimacy, she wanted to stay in his bed with him again.

"Get your toothbrush," he said. "You're coming with me."

Excitement had her walking with purpose into the hall bathroom. She collected her toothbrush and makeup remover, then returned to him.

He dropped a soft kiss on her bare shoulder. "Can you sleep naked or do you want clothes?"

She loved how attentive he was to her needs.

"Naked."

"Good." He grasped her hand, brought her into his bedroom. "Computer, lock the exterior doors and alarm the system."

"Completed," the computer replied.

"I forgot my weapon," Addison said.

"I'll get it."

"It's in my handbag in the living room."

He retreated downstairs while she went into his bathroom.

A moment later, he joined her. They brushed their teeth like it was no big deal, but Addison was freaking out. She didn't do sleepovers. She played at a private party. And she left. The end.

Most women would be thrilled to be there with Nicholas Hawk. Memberships at Lost Souls were up fifty percent in the short time he'd co-owned the club.

When she finished cleansing her face, she walked into the separate room with the toilet, and shut the door. While she peed, she tried calming her palpitating heart, but it was ka-chugging away in her chest. She opened the door. He was standing there.

"My turn." He didn't close the door.

Getting ready for bed together felt like they were a couple, a very comfortable couple.

She didn't couple. There was no coupling.

When he finished, they left the bathroom. As high as she'd been during their scene, she was freaking out about their spending the night together. If she stayed tonight, was that setting the tone for nights to come?

Her Glock was on the night table. She opened the drawer, pulled out the photo, and set her weapon inside.

"I like my Glock in the drawer."

"Go for it," he replied.

She picked up the photo. It was of a much younger Hawk with a pretty blonde. They were at a park, she was sitting on his lap laughing. "She's pretty."

"I can take that."

She handed him the framed picture and he tucked it in a dresser drawer. Once in bed, he rolled toward her, then supported his head on his hand. She, however, stared at the ceiling.

"You're not okay," he murmured, his minty breath warming her face. "Talk to me, baby."

"I'm good."

Stop lying to him.

"We *were* good, until I told you you were sleeping with me," he said. "It's just us. No role playing, no shop talk." He kissed her. "What's going on?"

She could be honest or she could blow him off. Her gaze met his. His piercing turquoise eyes were searching for answers as they roamed her face.

She rolled toward him. "I have intimacy issues."

"Okay." His encouraging smile helped her push forward.

"My mom, sister, and I were really close," she began. "I loved my dad, but he worked a lot, so Mom was it. She was such a fun mom. She was super positive, and she encouraged us to try new things. She was kind, but there were rules. We had to eat our vegetables. We had to keep our rooms neat." She smiled at the memory. "Or neat enough. She taught us that people were good and life was an adventure. When I was nine, she started changing. She'd get angry with us. She started going to meetings after dinner. Sometimes, we'd be alone until our dad —Z—came home. We did our homework or played. Anyway, when I was ten, she just didn't come home one day. We never saw her again. Years later, my dad told me the truth. She'd fallen in love with this crazy cult leader and she ran off to live in his compound."

"Jesus, that's intense," he said.

"Yeah, so when she left, we were in shock. It was rough in the beginning. My dad changed his schedule to be home for dinner, but we didn't know how to cook. We ate cereal until we figured it out. The last time I saw my mom, we had a huge fight. After she left, I remember crying and crying and promising myself I'd never fight with anyone like that ever again. I blamed myself for her leaving."

"Oh, baby." Hawk gently brushed the tendrils from her face.

"My dad stepped up. He started coming to our stuff, like sports or school plays. But, he was so different from our mom.

He taught us that the world wasn't a utopia. That there were bad people and we had to be careful. He took us for karate lessons. My sister quit, but I liked it, in part, because he'd stay during my lesson and cheer me on. He wanted me to study International relations, and Government and Politics, which I did. I liked it, but I also wanted to please him. I never wanted him to leave me, like my mom had. Looking back, the more I followed his guidance, the prouder he was. He got me my job in the CIA and he opened doors for me at ALPHA."

"Thank you for telling me."

"There's more," she murmured, "but we can go to sleep—"

"No, Addison, I want to know."

She sat up, turned toward him, and the sheets pooled at her waist. He pulled the linens over her shoulders and she wrapped them around herself to help stop the trembling.

"Thank you," she murmured.

After clasping her shaking hand, he caressed her skin with his thumb.

"I had a boyfriend in college," she continued. "We were sleeping together until I found out he had another girlfriend. More defensive walls went up. After college, I tried again with another guy." She shot him an adorable smile. "Hopeless romantic, I guess. He was into tying me up, which I didn't mind, but then, he wanted me to have sex with a woman while he watched. I refused. One weekend, we went to a party. As the night wore on, I realized he was MIA. I found him in bed with two guys." She held up her hands in mock surrender. "I came to the realization that if I didn't give my heart away, I couldn't get hurt. Right after that, I left for my overseas assignment and I didn't get involved with anyone. When I got back, a few friends introduced me to the cosplay scene and I loved it. About a year ago, I started hooking up if I wanted to go a little crazy."

He leaned forward, kissed her. "But this is different," he murmured. "You know that, right?"

"We can't happen. There's too much at stake. Too much to lose. We don't just work together, we're partners. We own a nightclub together. I adore your family. We're the best of friends. In the three years I've known you, you've never gotten romantically involved with a woman, never had a girlfriend. If I give you my heart, you'll break it. As sad as that would be, losing your friendship would wreck me."

Hawk could tell her she wasn't going to lose his friendship, kiss her goodnight, and say nothing more.

Or I can man up and tell her the damn truth.

His mouth went dry. He hated talking about this. Fucking hated it.

"This is different," he said. "I'm falling in love with you."

"Oh, no," she whispered.

Strangely, that made him chuckle. "Definitely not the reaction I'd hoped for."

"No, you can't."

"Why the hell not?"

"Because... because... just..." She swallowed, her face flushed. "Because it's not allowed."

He cracked a smile. "It's not my fault. If it's anyone's fault, it's yours for being so fucking irresistible."

"Until I'm not enough," she whispered. "Until someone better comes along."

His heart broke for her. She was more than enough. So much more.

He pushed out of bed, retrieved the photo he'd stored away, and sat back down. He stared at the picture of him and Josie. Felt like a lifetime ago.

"Who is she?" Addison murmured. "Someone special?"

He set the photo on the bed, captured her hands in his.

When his gaze met hers, the words got lodged in his throat, along with more emotion than he could handle. He hadn't talked about her in years. His chest ached, his head hurt.

But Addison needed to know his love for her was sincere. She needed to know what drove him every single day.

"Josie was my wife."

Her mouth dropped open. "You were married?"

"Yeah."

The silence hung while she picked up the photo and studied the picture. Then, she set it face up on the black comforter and sat close, draping her legs across his lap. "What happened?"

"She was killed."

"I'm so sorry," she whispered. "You don't have to talk about this."

He stared into her eyes, the compassion spurring him on. "After tonight, we'll know."

Her brows pinched together. "Know? Know what?"

"If we've got what it takes to last a lifetime."

"You're totally freaking me out." She sucked in a deep breath, scooted out of bed and returned in a bathrobe. "I can't do this. Seriously, this is too much."

He pushed out of bed, tugged on shorts, and pulled her into his arms. She was shaking so damn hard. He held her close, rubbed her back until the trembling subsided.

"It's late," he said. "We've had a rough few days. Let's sleep—"

"I just bared my soul to you. You told me you're falling in love with me. Sleep? I don't think so."

"Let's go downstairs."

Hand in hand, they returned to his living room. "You want coffee?" he asked.

"I need something stronger."

He pulled a bottle of whiskey and a bottle of red wine.

She sat at the kitchen counter, pointed to the whiskey. "A shot."

He poured one for her and double for himself. He was too keyed up. Talking about Josie, talking about what happened, set him on edge and broke his heart. He stood on the other side of the counter.

She tossed back the shot. "Whoa, that burns."

He tossed back his.

"Tell me about your wife."

"She was my first love, the first woman I'd been with. We were young, naïve. We met our freshman year of college and got married our junior year. Our families thought it was fast, but we were in love."

She nodded.

"Senior year, we found out we were pregnant." The memory made him smile. "I couldn't wait to be a dad and Josie was so excited."

"Wow," Addison whispered.

"Her parents and younger siblings lived in the Middle East. Her dad was an ambassador, so they lived in the diplomat's residence. Just before graduation, Josie was finishing her first trimester and she was anxious to see them and tell them our baby news. She was going to be a primary school teacher, so her schedule was split between working as a teacher's aide and taking a couple of classes. I'd double majored and had a full schedule. We'd planned to go over together, but she changed her mind and flew over a few days ahead of me. She wanted me to go with her, but I would've missed too many finals, so I told her I'd fly out after my last one."

He paused, the emotion constricting his throat. "The night she arrived, terrorists attacked the residence." The loss had him tearing up, and he lowered his head so Addison wouldn't see.

She slid out of the chair, walked around the kitchen counter, and hugged him. "I'm sorry."

He fought against the emotion, but the pain was still so raw all these years later.

"She was killed along with everyone else," he murmured. "I blame myself for not going with her."

Addison pulled back, her eyes wide with concern. "But you would have died, too."

"I know, but I have this fucked-up version that I could have saved them, or at least her and our unborn child." After a beat, he said, "I was gutted. I was in a dark place for a long time."

"How did you pull yourself out?"

"About six months after Josie died, I lost it. I don't remember what triggered it, but Prescott was there for me. We lived together for a while and I leaned on him pretty hard."

He raked his hand through his hair. Talking about Josie was more difficult that he thought it would be. "I was wrecked, broken, barely functioning. Prescott introduced me to a man named Philip Skye who set me on this track."

Her mouth dropped open. "No way."

"Your dad saved my life."

22

IN LOVE

Addison stared at him in disbelief. "Did you say my dad?" The fact that Hawk had been married and was going to be a father was shocking enough, but... her dad had helped him? How did that happen?

"I'm the one who suggested he go by an initial," Hawk said. "Using his real name put him at risk, plus he was concerned you and your sister were too vulnerable. We went through the alphabet, got to the end, and Z stuck."

"Uh-huh."

"You wanna sit?"

"Uh-huh." She heard him. She could see him. But she just stood there staring up at him.

He poured himself another shot, then ushered her into the living room. She eased onto the sofa. He sat beside her, leaned against the cushion.

"Your dad must've seen something in me," Hawk continued, "because he mentored my career. I worked for him at the FBI for two years while I continued flying. He was able to get me trained to fly military aircraft, he made sure I learned combat fighting. Looking back, it was like he was grooming me to be an assassin, then he introduced me to the man who used to run ALPHA before Dakota and Providence took over. An equally powerful man named Luther Warschak. While he never said anything, I think the two of them ran the government."

"Unbelievable." She picked up his shot glass and sipped the whiskey. "Are you and my dad close?"

"We talk a couple of times a week," Hawk replied. "I stop by his dungeon office on occasion, and we get together for dinner once or twice a month."

Her eyes widened. "I had no idea."

"Sometimes Prescott meets us for dinner," he replied.

After a beat, she asked, "Why don't you ever say no to your friends or family?"

"When Josie and our unborn baby were killed, I promised myself I'd make sure the people in my life know how much they mean to me. Life is short—too fucking short—so I show up for them, every single time."

"Why haven't you been in another relationship?"

"I walled myself off, emotionally." He shot her a little smile and her pulse kicked up. "Same thing you told yourself. If I don't fall in love, I won't get hurt."

"What happened?"

"I met you."

She was flying high and freaking out all at the same time. This was a dream come true and system overload. Hawk wasn't who she thought he was. He was emotionally broken, like her.

He pushed off the sofa, scooped her into his arms.

"You're not done with your whiskey," she said.

"I don't need the booze, Addison. I need you."

He carried her up the stairs and into his bedroom, helped her off with her robe, and slid the picture of him and his late wife into the dresser drawer. After taking off his shorts, he crawled in beside her.

When she snuggled close, his arms folded around her like a protective cocoon.

"I don't want to scare you away," he murmured before kissing the top of her head, "but you've gotta know how I feel."

He turned out the light. The darkness and the silence soothed her, but she couldn't quiet her mind.

"Do your friends know?" she whispered.

"Only Prescott. I don't talk about Josie. Cooper found out when he took over ALPHA and read my files."

"You never told me which terror cell was responsible."

"Abdel Haqazzii," he replied. "The one your team took out."

"Did his death bring you any peace?"

"None." He gently caressed her back. "Being with you is the closest I've felt to peace in a long, long time."

As she lay there in his arms, her thoughts drifted over their conversation. He'd shared things with her that he hadn't even told his closest friends in the world. His band of brothers. And he'd told her he was falling in love with her. For a man who'd had deep love and lost it, he was taking a huge risk.

And how did she respond? By telling him she was freaking out.

Way to go.

She slipped out of bed.

"Where are you going?" he asked.

"I'm escaping." She shot him a smile. "Not really. I'll be back in two minutes." She padded into the hall bathroom and inserted her diaphragm. If he was willing to take a risk, so could she.

When she got back into bed, he snuggled close. "You smell good," he murmured.

She kissed him, then she kissed him again. "Make love to me," she whispered. "Just me, no costumes, no role play."

He swept her into his arms. Even though his kiss was filled with so much tenderness, she started trembling again.

He stopped and whispered, "I got you. You can relax, baby. This is the good stuff. It doesn't get any better than us."

She pulled him close. "No condom. I put my diaphragm in, plus I'm on the pill. I don't even think your potent troops can make it past that."

In that moment, she let go of her fear and she loved him. Their kisses were tender and rough, soft and ravaging. He took his time, appreciating every inch of her body, and she his. They moved slowly, finding their way as new lovers do. But it was the possessive way he held her, the intense look of love in his eyes that made her feel safe and adored.

She was just Addison and he was just Hawk. No stories, no costumes, no leaving his bed when their lovemaking ended.

"Thank you for trusting me," he said as he held her in his arms. "Loving you is the smartest thing I've ever done."

Nicholas Hawk had wrecked her for any other man.

Hawk was a renewed man. He did not deserve to feel this good, yet he did. As he glanced across his office at Addison, he knew she was the reason. He'd never envisioned loving anyone again, but last night had given him hope.

That morning, they'd driven to Hawk Security. She, in a blonde wig, he hyper-aware of everyone in traffic. Being that it was impossible to know if they were being followed, he'd pulled over twice during their commute, just to make sure.

He had a team meeting in the executive conference room, where he introduced Addison as a consultant. After lunch, he worked in his office while she sat nearby at his conference table. Didn't matter how many interruptions he had, she stayed laser-focused on her research. The CIA suspected Aziz Haqazzii of murdering Ronald and Melinda, but Addison wanted confirmation. He was confident her efforts would pay off.

His phone rang.

"Hey, Granddad," he answered. "How are you feeling?"

"Much better, Nicky. I know you're busy at work, but Grandmom and I are getting the family together tonight for a quick meeting at the farmhouse. Can you make it?"

He flicked his gaze to Addison. "I've got plans."

"What time?"

"Eight."

Addison pushed away from the conference table. Rubbing the back of her neck, she walked over to the window.

"Can you swing by at seven?" Granddad asked.

"I'll have Addison with me."

"That's fine. See you then." Granddad hung up.

Hawk slid his gaze to Addison. She was staring out the window. He sidled close and massaged her shoulders. "How's it going?"

"That feels great." She sighed. "I'm not making any progress at all."

"Maybe you are, but it doesn't feel that way."

"What does that mean?"

"If you can't ID the terror group responsible for their deaths, maybe their deaths aren't connected."

She shook her head. "That's too coincidental. I'm just missing something."

He stopped rubbing her shoulders and leaned his ass against the window, facing her. "I've got to head to the farmhouse tonight before we meet your dad for dinner."

"That's fine. Just meet us at Carole Jean's."

"I'm not dropping you at the restaurant," he said. "You're coming with me to the farmhouse."

"What time?"

"Seven."

It was five-forty. "Let's get outta here," she said. "I need to get ready."

On the drive home, Stryker called. Hawk put him on speaker. "Yo, baby."

"I've got an update on your security breach," Stryker said. "Good news, it wasn't your former employee. Bad news... it wasn't him. Based on network logs, I'm thinking it's an inside job."

"Fuck," Hawk bit out. "I've got over three-hundred employees including my customer service team."

"I'm looking at other log files from other computers, but it's gonna take me a little longer. I'm sorry, brother."

"You're getting married," Hawk said. "Give it to one of your hackers."

"I'm not delegating this. I'll let you know as soon as I figure it out."

"I'm sorry Addison and I won't be there for the rehearsal dinner," Hawk said.

"Don't miss my wedding," Stryker said.

"Hell, no," Hawk said before ending the call.

He released a growl. If it wasn't Wayne, then who was it? Why would an employee want to destroy his business? That made no sense at all.

"I can see you thinking," Addison said. "You want to talk about it?"

"I feel like a sitting duck," he said. "I've already limited the number of employees who have access to all the accounts. I'm so damn pissed. If it's not the guy I just fired, then who the hell is it?"

She offered some suggestions, which he appreciated, but until Stryker figured out where the security breach had originated, he had to run his company like it was under siege.

They drove home, parked in the garage. On the way in, she said, "I'll be in the shower if you want to join me."

She dropped a chaste kiss on his mouth before hurrying upstairs to get ready.

Rather than do the smart thing and join her, he opened his laptop and reviewed his employee teams. After a search that went nowhere, he found Addison putting on makeup in the bathroom.

"I'm sorry I missed you, baby," he said.

She set down her mascara and stepped behind him to massage his shoulders. "I'm here if you want to talk about it."

"I would if I had any idea who's behind this." He let out a sigh. "Feels great."

When she finished, she dotted his back with tender kisses. "You gotta get ready."

Fifteen minutes later, he found her relaxing on his balcony.

"You look stunning." He stepped back to admire her. She'd worn a little black dress that was conservative and classy. No peep show for the girls, but short enough to admire her shapely thighs. He stepped close and inhaled.

"You are like oxygen to me," he murmured before kissing her. "Where's your wig?"

"I'm not wearing it at the farm," she explained, "but I've got it for the restaurant."

"Let's get you inside." They walked into his living room. After he closed and locked the French doors, she whistled.

"You look hot, hot, hot," she said.

He'd worn a charcoal suit, crisp, white shirt, and patterned tie.

"I wore a suit for you," he said.

She laughed. "You wore a suit because you can't get into Carole Jean's without a jacket."

As she climbed into the back seat of his SUV, he said, "I miss having my co-pilot beside me."

He got behind the wheel and she squeezed his shoulder. "As

soon as we take Haqazzii out, I'll be right there next to you. So, what's this meeting at the farmhouse about?"

"No idea."

They arrived to find a slew of cars parked out front. The kitchen was packed with family. Kerri and Lamer were back from their honeymoon and chatting with his parents. Prescott was there. As he made his way over, he spotted Tommy, his siblings, and their mom and dad. Grandmom and Granddad were talking to Hawk's uncle and his family.

Granddad held up his arm. "Let's move into the living room," he hollered over the chatter.

Once everyone had migrated to the next room, he and Grandmom stood at the front.

For as tall as Grandad was, Grandmom was tiny. Seeing them together reminded Hawk of him and Addison. When Addison wasn't wearing stilettos, he towered nine inches over her.

"Thanks for coming out on such short notice," Grandmom said. "Granddad and I are moving tomorrow, so we wanted to get everyone together one last time before we left."

A hushed silence fell over the group.

"Oh, wow," Kerri said. "That's kinda sad."

"Congratulations," Tommy called out. "I think it's great."

Granddad clasped Grandmom's hand. "Grandmom and I are moving to an independent living facility not too far from here, but closer to all of you. We're sad to be leaving, but after my fall, it's the smart thing to do."

"Granddad has climbed a ladder for the last time and I'm so happy about that." She smiled at the family. "Over the past few months, we talked to each of you about the farm. Everyone encouraged us to sell."

"No one wanted it," Granddad added. "No one, except Nicky. He told us he loved this place. That it was filled with memories of summers when he lived here with us. He learned to drive a tractor, milk cows, and work the land. He told us, and I quote, 'I'd keep the farm in our family before I'd sell it. It's a part of our legacy'."

"So," Grandmom said, "we're putting the farm in Nicky's control for as long as he wants it. When he's ready—"

"He can sell it," Granddad explained. "When he does, all of you will split the money equally."

"I love that!" Tommy's sister called out.

"That works for me," Kerri echoed.

"What the hell!" Tommy blurted. "That doesn't sound fair at all."

"We talked to you, Tommy," Granddad said. "You don't like the farm and you told us you didn't want it."

"Well, I didn't think you'd give it to Nicky."

"If Nicky doesn't want it, he can put it on the market tomorrow," Grandmom said. "We made our decision based on what all of you told us."

"Nicky, what do you think of our idea?" Grandmom asked.

Hawk swept his gaze around the room while his entire family waited for his response. He, too, assumed his grandparents would sell their farm.

"Don't you need the money to live on?" Hawk asked.

"Oh, no," Grandmom replied. "We've always lived below our means. We've got plenty in savings and investments."

Granddad put his arm around Grandmom. "When I married Grandmom sixty-three-years ago, I told her that she would always be the only thing that mattered to me. That held true, only now, we have all of you. The memories here are what made me a rich man." Tears filled his eyes. "It's hard to walk away from our home, but Grandmom threatened to leave me if we didn't." He wiped away a tear. "I can't live without her, but I can live without this old building. It's all of you who gave us our wonderful memories."

"Dad, that's beautiful," Hawk's mom said.

"I've baked some pies and too many cookies," Grandmom said with a smile. "Let's go onto the porch and have one more party."

As everyone made their way toward the back of the house, Hawk's parents intercepted him. "What do you think of their decision?" his mom asked.

"I wasn't expecting that," Hawk replied.

"They talked to an attorney months ago," his dad said. "They're so happy they don't have to sell it. I think that would have been too difficult for them. What are you going to do with the farm?"

"Nothing at the moment. Addison and I have plans, so we gotta take off." He glanced over, but no Addison. She'd been standing there a minute ago. He spotted her talking to Kerri and Lamar. After saying goodbye to his mom and dad, he headed toward her.

As if she could sense his gaze on her, she turned in his direction. Her loving smile told him everything he needed to know.

She's my forever.

Tommy elbowed through the small crowd and joined the group, beside Addison.

"Welcome back," Hawk said to Kerri and Lamar.

"I'm so happy you want to keep the farm," Kerri said. "I love this place so much."

"Me too, sis." Hawk shifted toward Addison. "You ready to go?"

"Congrats on stealing the prize." Tommy slapped Hawk's back.

Hawk shook his head. "This house needs a shit-ton of work." He slid his gaze to Addison. "We gotta stop at the henhouse on the way out."

Her smile sent a bolt of adrenaline through him. "That'll be fun."

"Dude, you were just handed a multi-million-dollar property," Tommy said.

"Every building, even the land, needs a *lot* of work," Hawk replied. "You get to enjoy the farm without the headaches."

"Seriously Nicky, call a developer. It gets sold and we walk away with a bunch of cash," Tommy said.

Hawk peered over at Addison. "Or I could make memories of my own here."

Addison caressed Hawk's back. Despite her fear of intimacy, she loved the direction things were going for them. Small steps that made her heart sing.

"We've got to leave," Hawk said.

"You two look sharp," Lamar said. "Where're you headed?"

"We're taking my dad to dinner," Addison replied. "It's his birthday."

"Nice," Tommy replied. "Maybe I'll see you at Lost Souls this week. I'm looking forward to chatting with Liliana." He shot them a grin. "She's dope."

On the way out, he and Addison stopped to say goodbye to his parents and grandparents. "We're outta here," Hawk said to them.

"There's my number one," Granddad exclaimed with a grin.

No silencing his grandfather on that one. "Thank you both for entrusting the farm to me."

"We're delighted you're keeping it." Grandmom put her arm around Addison. "Look how pretty you are in that dress."

"Thank you. It's my dad's birthday, and I always take him to dinner at his favorite restaurant. Hawk's joining us."

With a smile, his mom glanced from her to Hawk. "I'm happy to hear that."

"Dad, can you find a couple of farmhands?" Hawk asked. "And a home for the chickens?"

"Absolutely," his dad replied.

Hawk hugged his grandparents. "Love you guys. I'll swing by and check on you after you get settled in."

When they left the house, they stopped at the henhouse. Inside, he pulled her close and kissed her.

"Thanks for coming with me." Hawk kissed her again.

"Congratulations," Addison said. "Like you're not busy enough."

He chuckled. "I know, but I can't get rid of this place. It's too special." He wrapped his arm around her waist, pulled her close "This place has a ton of memories. You were the only girl I kissed in the henhouse."

She smiled. "Well, that alone is reason to keep it."

Twenty minutes later, they pulled up to the upscale restaurant. Addison, now sitting in the back, was wearing a light brown wig with bangs and oversized sunglasses.

The valet opened the driver's door. "Good evening, sir. Welcome to Carole Jean's."

Hawk handed him a folded bill before opening the back door for Addison. As she exited, a shawl in hand, the attendant rushed around.

"I'm so sorry, ma'am," he said. "I didn't realize you were sitting in the back."

"I'm hiding from the paparazzi," she whispered.

"Yes, ma'am."

Once inside, the maître d' escorted them to the small salon in the back of the restaurant, where dancing flames in the large, gas fireplace reflected off the copper walls.

"I'm happy to see the lady has a shawl," he said. "A returning customer, no?"

"I've been here several times," she said as she eased into the chair.

"We keep the room chilly because of the fire. It generates a lot of heat. Is there anything I can assist you with before I leave?"

Hawk handed him his phone. "Can you snap a pic of us?"

They were seated catty-corner at a four top. Hawk pulled his chair close, put his arm around her. The attendant snapped a few pictures, handed Hawk back his phone. "Enjoy your evening."

Addison glanced at the customers seated at the tables. "Someone could be watching me," she whispered.

He caressed her back. "Watching, staring, gawking. You're so beautiful." He swept his gaze across the room. "I won't let anything happen to you. Do you have your weapon?"

She tapped her small clutch on the table next to her.

He leaned over, pecked her cheek. "I got you."

Before they could open their menus, Jericho's sister, Georgia Savage, hurried over. "It's great to see you both. What's the occasion?"

"My dad's birthday," Addison replied.

"I have a lovely cognac that pairs well with our complimentary birthday dessert," Georgia said. "What can I bring you from the bar?"

Addison ordered a Coche-Dury Corton-Charlemagne Grand Cru Chardonnay. Hawk, a Bombay Sapphire dry martini with a twist. Georgia vanished to fill the order as the maître d' returned with her dad.

She and Hawk stood.

"Happy birthday, Daddy," she said as she hugged him. He held her an extra second, then kissed her cheek.

"Thank you, dear," her dad replied.

Hawk pulled him in for a hug. "Happy birthday, Philip."

Addison watched as the most important and influential man in her life smiled warmly at Hawk. "Good to see you, Nicholas."

Nicholas?

Hawk seated her before he sat back down.

The attendant scurried over with their drinks. "Welcome, sir. What can I get you?"

"Coffee, black," her dad replied.

The server left.

"How many bodyguards do you have tonight?" she murmured.

"None," he replied.

"How'd you manage that?" she asked.

"I'm not on official business."

"They don't know you're out, do they?" Hawk asked.

A sly smile filled Z's face. "I escaped the castle."

"Don't you mean the dungeon?" Hawk asked.

Both men laughed.

She couldn't remember the last time her father laughed out loud. It was like she'd been dropped into an alternate universe.

The attendant returned with a cup, saucer, and a carafe. After pouring the piping hot coffee, he ran through the dinner specials. Since no one had looked at the menu, he left.

They grew silent as they read through the options.

"If you order the—" she began.

"Beef Wellington," Hawk interjected.

She smiled. "I'll get the—"

"Lobster and salmon ravioli."

"Perfect."

They set down their menus to find her dad eyeing them. "That was interesting."

"We've been doing this for years," she said. "I can never decide, so we share."

The attendant returned. "Is everyone ready?"

After placing their orders, her dad asked Hawk about his family.

"My grandparents are moving out of their farmhouse," Hawk replied, "and they put me in charge."

"How'd the family take that?"

"I gotta go with relieved. If I don't sell, I'm gonna have to do a lot of renovations. The place needs a complete overhaul."

"How do you like the farmhouse, honey?" asked her dad.

"It's got a lot of charm," she replied. "But Hawk's right, it needs to be updated."

"What helicopters have you piloted lately?" he asked Hawk.

As Hawk ran through his list, Addison studied both men. Her dad genuinely liked Hawk. It was mind-blowing and heart-warming at the same time. He rarely liked anyone. He was a loner who worked with others to get the job done. He didn't do the social thing, he wasn't a talker, but as she watched them chatting, she knew.

The Hawk Effect.

Hawk made her dad feel comfortable. He was a natural-born leader, but unlike Jericho, he wasn't a bull in a china shop. He led with quiet strength instead of bravado.

"Played poker with the guys lately?" her dad asked.

"About a week ago." Hawk sipped his martini.

The server delivered a sample appetizer tray of seared scallops, tuna tartare, and wagyu meatballs. "Happy birthday, sir. This is from Ms. Georgia."

"Please thank her for me," her dad replied.

"Enjoy." The server left.

"How'd you do?" his dad asked.

"Made a few bucks," Hawk replied. "You should join us next month."

"Okay," her dad replied. "I will."

Hawk flashed a smile. "How many years did *that* take?"

Her dad chuckled. "Several."

As a woman passed the table, she gawked at Hawk. A few

seconds later, she returned. "I'm sorry to interrupt, but are you Hawk?"

"Who's asking?" he responded.

"I met you a while back at Jericho Road," the woman said. "I gave you my number, but you didn't call."

"That happens," he replied.

"I've been back there a few times, but I haven't seen you. Maybe I could get your number and we can have coffee... or something." Her cheeks pinked.

Addison leaned back. She'd seen this play out dozens of times over the years. Though she'd never cared before, she cared now.

"That's a hard no for me, babe," Hawk replied. "I'm off the market. This is my fiancée and her dad."

Fiancée? She regarded her dad. A ghost of a smile flitted across his face. *This is crazy.*

"Don't you see us sitting here?" her dad asked.

"I had to ask. Men like him don't come along often. Have a nice evening." She walked away.

Addison flicked her gaze to Hawk. "Your fiancée? Have you lost your mind?"

To her surprise, Hawk and her dad laughed.

"Why is that so unbelievable?" her dad asked. "Why couldn't you be his fiancée?"

"What is happening?" she whispered.

"If I'd said I was here with my *parents*, I can see how that would be a problem for you, but c'mon, woman," Hawk said.

That made Addison laugh.

The server delivered their entrées, checked in with them, and left.

After trying the ravioli, she placed one on Hawk's plate. "So, so good. You'll love it."

He sliced off a piece of Wellington and held out his fork.

Normally, she'd let him feed her, but she took the fork from him and ate the premiere beef.

"Good, huh?" Hawk said as she handed him back his utensil.

"How are things, Addison?" her dad asked.

"Good," she replied. "Frustrating."

"No Easter Bunny hunting."

They spoke in code whenever they were in public. That was her dad telling her not to hunt down the person or persons who'd killed Ronald and Melinda.

"Well, I'm not doing *nothing*."

"Why not?"

"Because I lost two very valuable Easter eggs," she replied.

"It's a risk we take every day," her dad said.

"Exactly," she replied.

When they finished, and their dinner plates had been cleared, Georgia returned with their complimentary snifters of Grand Marnier Révélation.

Addison raised her glass. "To my amazing dad. You've been my inspiration and my rock. I hope this is a happy year for you. I love you."

They clinked and sipped.

"Delicious," Addison said as she savored the top-shelf liqueur.

Hawk raised his glass. "I wouldn't be the man I am today if it weren't for you. Thank you, Philip, and happy birthday."

Her dad had tears in his eyes. "Thank you both. Celebrating with my two favorite people is very special." They toasted once more.

Addison's heart swelled with unexpected joy. This was a magical night. One she'd remember for the rest of her life.

It was the night she fell head over heels in love with Nicholas Hawk.

23

CHEATING DEATH

Hawk collected the check as soon as the attendant set it on the table.

"Oh, no," Addison said. "I always take my dad out for his birthday. Hand that over."

After setting his credit card in the billfold, he winked. "You can pay next year."

"I bought myself a birthday present this year," Z said.

"That's great, Dad. You never buy yourself anything. What did you get?"

"A new car, which cost me a small fortune."

"Maserati?" Hawk asked.

"A Bentley Flying Spur Mulliner with bullet-proof windows and body."

"Nice," Hawk replied. "Did you schedule the camera installation?"

"Not yet," Z replied.

"My installers are running about two months out," Hawk explained, "When you call, tell them you're family. My scheduler will confirm with me and we'll get the cameras mounted on your vehicle the next day."

"Thank you," Z replied. "I'll show it to you when we leave."

"Did you valet park?" Addison asked.

"I never do that," Z replied. "I have no idea who's getting behind the wheel." He slid his gaze to Hawk. "Tell me you didn't use valet."

"Don't go there," Hawk said, trying to keep his tone relaxed.

Z leaned forward. "Ever heard of an explosive attached to a goddamn timer?" He shook his head. "You need to be smarter than everyone else. *Always.*"

He glared at Z. "Do *not* speak to me like that, Philip. I've got cameras mounted all over those SUVs, including the underbelly *and* the interior."

Z hitched an eyebrow. "You're guarding my child."

A growl shot out of Hawk. "For fuck's sake, I'm well aware who I'm protecting," he hissed. "You, of all people, know how much Addison means to me. How much she's always meant."

He wanted to throw the table across the room. Did Z think he would let *anything* happen to her?

"You two need to take it down a few notches," Addison murmured. "Daddy, Hawk hasn't let me out of his sight. And, in case you've forgotten, I can take care of myself."

"Be smart, Nicholas," Z bit out.

"I told you, I got this," Hawk warned. "*Nothing* is going to happen to her."

The fun vibe of the evening had been sucked into a black hole. Z was pissed. Hawk was fuming. Hawk shifted his gaze to Addison.

Her eyes softened. Beyond her unassuming beauty, she oozed confidence. It was a constant for as long as he'd known her, which was what attracted him to her in the beginning. Back when all he could offer her was his friendship.

He lips curved upward and his agitation stood down a little.

"I'm sorry I spoke to you like that," Z said. "I'm not rational when it comes to Addison."

"You gotta trust me," Hawk replied.

"I do," Z said.

The tension lifted. Hawk paid for dinner, collected his credit card, and they took off. Outside, he handed his ticket to the valet who went to fetch Hawk's vehicle.

"Are you in the parking lot?" Addison asked.

"It's a nice night," Z replied, "so I parked at the end of the street."

"Feels good to breathe fresh air, doesn't it?" Hawk asked. "You gotta get out of that shit hole of an office."

Z chuckled "I do need to get out more."

"Poker, next month," Hawk said.

While they waited for the SUV, Hawk pulled up the videos from the vehicle. Other than valets parking cars nearby, no one got near it, and the valet didn't leave anything inside.

"This is how I've programmed the entire fleet," Hawk said. "I would have gotten an alert if anyone touched it, set something under it, or left something inside. It's clear."

"I admit, I'm paranoid when it comes to Addison, especially with everything going on," Z said.

The valet drove up. Hawk tipped him, then opened the rear door for Addison. Once she was inside, he shot her wink before shutting it. As he walked around, Z got into the front passenger seat.

Hawk drove out and headed down the quiet side street, lined with parked cars.

"I'm the last one on the right." Z pulled out his key fob. "It came with remote start." He pressed the button.

KABOOM!!!

Z's car exploded, the sound reverberating through them while shards of glass from the Bentley's windows sprayed in every direction.

Hawk slammed on the brakes. "Hold on." He threw the SUV in reverse, glanced over his shoulder, and hit the gas.

They flew backward. He slammed on the breaks again, drifted through a one-eighty, and floored it in the opposite direction.

As they sped past the restaurant, Hawk asked, "Addison, are you okay?"

"Fine," she replied. "Dad?"

"What the hell!" Z exclaimed. "I cannot fucking believe it."

"We're going to the black site," Hawk bit out. "Addison, call Cooper."

"No," Z blurted. "I'll call Sin."

Z made a call, put the phone to his ear. "I'm being taken to the safe house. Yes, the black site. My car was bombed." He listened. "Remote start. I was leaving Carole Jean's with Addison and Hawk." More listening. "I think Addison was the target. What do you mean *lockdown*? Are you out of your fucking mind!" Z hung up.

Silence.

"Well, that pisses me off," Z said.

"What did he say?" Hawk asked.

"I have to stay at the safe house, tonight," Z replied through gritted teeth. "Addison, I'm concerned that explosion was meant for you. I want you and Hawk to stay there with me."

"No," Addison said. "No way."

"Don't argue," Z pushed back. "We could have been killed."

Silence.

As soon as they turned off Route 7, Hawk pulled over. "I'm checking for tails."

When he felt confident they weren't being followed, Hawk continued to the black site.

Once the security cameras cleared them for entrance into the building, they stepped inside.

"Is Sin coming to check on you?" Addison asked as they made their way through the quiet building.

"God, I hope not," Z said. "If he shows up, he'll bring the

National Guard with him, then declare this a terrorist attack on home soil."

"He might not be wrong," Hawk replied.

"I'm leaving in the morning," Z explained. "Sin is flying me in his private jet to an undisclosed location for a few days." Z rolled his eyes. "I'm concerned you're the target, dear. Why don't you and Hawk come with me?"

"No, Daddy," Addison replied "I'm staying here. Hawk and I are doing a good job keeping me safe." Z opened his mouth, but Addison shook her head. "We've got this."

"We'll stay here tonight," Hawk said. "I'll work from home the rest of the week."

"Thank you," Z said. "I'm going to sleep. That'll teach me for driving something other than an ALPHA SUV."

They walked past the offices and conference room and over to the residential wing where Z stopped in front of an open bedroom door.

"Thank you both for a lovely birthday dinner. It was a special evening. I'm sorry I doubted you, Nicholas. I should have known better." Z entered and shut the door behind him.

Finally, alone with Addison.

He didn't want to be apart from her, but he needed to keep their relationship under wraps a little longer. If Z learned they were falling in love, he might replace Hawk with another Operative. The thought of anyone else guarding Addison made his hackles stand on end.

When he placed his hand on the small of her back, everything shifted. The gargantuan weight on his shoulders lifted, and he could breathe for the first time since the explosion.

They continued to the end of the hall and into the large family room filled with sofas, recliners, a bookcase loaded up with books and games, and three large-screen TVs.

She wrapped her arms around him, snapping him from his

thoughts. Her soft lips pressed against his. "Thank you for protecting both of us."

"I got you, baby," he replied. "Has anyone tried to assassinate Z before?"

"I don't know." She peered into his eyes. "What are you thinking?"

"This is the second car explosion. Did Z have anything to do with taking out Abdel Haqazzii?"

"I didn't know all the players." She trembled and he pulled her close, caressed her back. "If my dad had gotten in his car, he'd be dead. I can't even wrap my brain around that." She hugged him hard. "I don't want to be apart from you, tonight. Let's sit on the sofa."

He dropped a tender kiss on her lips.

He craved her, but the desire went far beyond lust. Holding her calmed him. She was here, she was okay. He'd do whatever necessary to keep her safe.

He pulled his Glock, set it on the end table. She removed her wig, raked her fingers through her hair. They sat side by side. He held her hand. She rested her head on his shoulder. While he doubted he'd get much sleep, at least he could assure her safety.

He turned out the table lamp, but the lit hallway bathed the room in a warm glow. Having her there, with him, was what he needed.

"What did you mean when you told my dad, 'You, of all people, know much Addison means to me. How much she's always meant'."

"I loved you before I was ready to be loved," Hawk replied. "Before I was ready to risk my heart and love again."

"Oh, wow." She peered into his eyes for the longest time before she kissed him. "Are you ready now?"

"I'm ready."

She climbed in his lap and hugged him. "I love you, Nicholas Hawk."

"I love you too, baby."

The following morning, after a restless night, they said their goodbyes to Z in the giant hanger where Sin's driver, Anton, waited by the sedan.

"I love you," Z said before hugging Addison.

He extended his hand to Hawk who pulled him in for a hug.

"Be vigilant, both of you." Z got into the back seat, Anton slid behind the wheel, and the oversized garage door rolled up.

"Let's get outta here," Hawk said.

They got in the SUV, she in the back, he behind the wheel. He waited for the hanger door to close before he headed toward home.

"I could use a cigarette," he uttered.

"Can't say I blame you," she replied.

That evening, Addison had no intention of staying holed up in Hawk's townhouse. The club was open, and she needed to get out, be around people, listen to music, and feel the fun vibe.

She dressed in a black shirt, black pants. After strapping on her ankle holster, she slipped her secondary weapon in there, pulled on her shoulder harness, secured her Glock. Then, she shrugged into her full-length black duster and returned to the hall bathroom where she fluffed the bangs of her shoulder-length blonde wig and tied on a simple black masquerade mask.

She was armed and she was ready.

With her combat boots in hand, she made her way to Hawk's bedroom. She found him in his walk-in closet pulling on black jeans. His tanned and muscular back caught her eye.

Despite everything going on, she paused to soak him up. He was easy—*too easy*—on the eyes.

"How do I look?" she asked as he slipped into a white shirt.

He turned, his gaze met hers, and that familiar zing of energy shot through her. He raked his eyes over her, slowly. "So damn hot."

If she could halt time, she'd would. Life was easy and perfect when it was just the two of them.

"You sure you don't want to stay in?" he asked. "I can think of a much better way to spend our evening. And I promise you, it's completely stress free."

She released a sigh. He was right. They could stay in, avoid the world. Instead, she shook her head. "I'm not scared. If someone is stalking me, I want them to know I won't hide. I feel like we have a better chance of catching them if we're out. Otherwise, I'm here forever. I'll never give anyone that much control."

He curled his fingers under her chin, tipped her face toward his, and pressed his lips to hers. "That's one of my favorite things about you. Total badass."

"Yes, I am."

He took a step back. "Button me up, boss."

With a whisper of a smile brightening her eyes, she fastened his shirt. On went his shoulder harness, after which he secured one weapon in the holster and tucked his primary Glock behind his waist. He draped a sport coat over his arm and slid into his black loafers.

"I'm way too dressed up for the club," he said. "But I'm not leaving my weapons in the office. What the hell good is that?"

She pulled open her duster revealing her shoulder holster. "Back up's on my ankle."

"The *real* Addison Skye," he said with a smile. "My sultry, beautiful, brilliant badass."

After she stood on her toes and kissed his cheek, they left his bedroom.

On the first floor, he asked, "Do you think the person or group has been coming to our club?"

"No way. Do you?"

"Doubtful, but while we're there, I'm gonna run a member search to see if anyone is on a terror watch list."

"Seriously?"

"Everyone there knows you're the owner. It's not hard to find you. I think we should take our names off our website and pull them from social media."

"I don't want it to look like I'm running scared."

He shot her a smile. "You're going to your club. You're not hiding, you're not running, and you're definitely not scared."

They walked into his garage. He opened the back door of the SUV. She fisted her hands on her hips. "This is ridiculous. I want to sit in the front seat."

"C'mon, baby," he murmured. "I'm going to the club for you. Sit in the back... for *me*."

On a huff, she got in. He drove them to Lost Souls, parked in the owner's spot out front.

"Hey, Hawk." Tony slid his gaze to Addison. "How's it goin'?"

"Hi, Tony," Addison said.

Tony stared at her. "I didn't recognize you, boss. Love the Matrix vibe. You changed your hair, and the masquerade mask is a new look."

"Things been quiet out here?" she asked.

"All good." He opened the front door and they sailed inside.

Addison sighed. The music, the chill vibe, the costumed people calmed her. These clubbers just wanted to have fun. They weren't there to hunt her down.

As expected, Liliana was mixing drinks and making small talk with the patrons, but she was working the entire bar alone.

Once in their office, Addison dropped her handbag on the sofa. "Are you running that report now?"

"Yeah, baby. It won't take long to set it up."

Addison sat behind the desk, logged in. "There should be two bartenders tonight." A few clicks and she had her answer. Someone was scheduled, but he wasn't there. "We're short one. I'm going to help Liliana."

"I don't want you going out there without me," he pushed back.

She rose, walked over, and palmed his backside. "God, I love your ass." Then, she shot him a smile. "I'm not leaving the club. I won't go upstairs without you. You will be five minutes behind me." She kissed him. "I got this."

She left, pulling the door closed.

As she made her way through the crowd, the stress fell away. Most nights, members said "hello", but tonight, she was invisible in her disguise. She liked being unrecognizable and blending in.

She walked behind the bar. Liliana made her way over. "Sorry, but you can't be back here. What can I get you?"

"It's me, Addison."

Liliana's eyes widened. "Well, you got me." Then, she smiled. "I would have walked right by you. Love the hair. Why the new color?"

"It's a wig," she replied. "I used to wear them all the time, but I got lazy. Time to change things up."

"What can I get you?" Liliana asked.

"We're short one, so I'll work back here with you."

A surge in patrons kept them busy pouring drinks. Not long after, Hawk made his way behind the bar. "Need help?"

"We've got this," Addison replied. "How 'bout you sign up new members?"

He glanced around. The room was filling up. "I'll be nearby." He held her gaze for an extra beat before grabbing a tablet.

She loved how things were changing between them. They were definitely moving toward being a couple. Despite knowing the truth about him, and his past, she questioned whether being with just one woman would satisfy him.

Shaking away the thought, she turned her attention to the waiting customers. A few recognized her, but most didn't. Flying under the radar worked for her.

As Addison was making a cocktail, Tommy pulled up to the bar. He caught Liliana's attention. She flashed him a big smile, then hurried over. She leaned across the bar and whispered something to him. He grinned, then whispered something back.

After she made him his drink, he hung at the bar.

The crowd came in waves. During a less hectic time, Addison was pouring a draft beer when Tommy caught her eye.

"How's it going?" he asked.

"Can't complain," she replied. "You?"

"Waiting for my girl. Are you new?"

She bit back a smile. She loved that he didn't recognize her. After serving the patron, she said, "It's Addison."

His gaze floated over her wig and face, her eyes still framed by the black mask. As he broke into a smile, his cheeks flushed with color. Despite the low lighting, she couldn't miss his reaction.

"Damn," he said. "How'd I miss that?"

Liliana sidled over. "Do you mind if I take a break?"

"Let me get Hawk to fill in for you," Addison replied.

"Hawk's here?" Tommy asked.

"Hang for a sec." Addison left the bar in search of him. He wasn't on the dance floor, he wasn't at the picture place. *Maybe he's in the office.*

As she made her way down the dimly-lit hallway, she spotted a couple making out near the back door. The guy—tall with short, dark hair and broad shoulders—was standing with his back to her. Her stomach dropped.

Ohgod, it's Hawk.

Her heart was breaking, but she should have known better.

The office door swung open, the bright light illuminating the hallway. Hawk breezed out. When he saw her, his face lit up, and her heart rejoiced.

"There's my baby."

She flicked her gaze to the couple, now heading in her direction. "I thought—"

"How's it going?" the man asked as the couple walked by.

Hawk tossed them a nod.

"What's wrong?" Hawk asked.

She wasn't a jealous person. She wasn't possessive either. "I'm sorry," she murmured.

His brows slashed down. "For what?"

She pulled him into their office and shut the door. "I saw that couple making out and I thought that guy was you."

His expression fell. "You thought I was making out with a stranger?" He stared at her. "C'mon, woman. Do you think I'd do that to you... to us?"

"For the past three years, I've watched you hit on women and sleep with a bunch of them. It never bothered me. I introduced you to friends knowing you'd probably hookup." Her shoulders fell. "I don't want to turn into one of those women... you know... jealous and paranoid."

"I never cheated on Josie. I would never disrespect her or our marriage." He leaned his ass on the desk. "I know it was a different time in my life. I was innocent and naïve. I'm not that boy. Now, I'm a broken man, but I feel hopeful... because of *you*. I love you, Addison." Pausing, he stared into her eyes. "This isn't a game to me. I'm not playing you. I'm not going to hurt you. I'm ready for whatever life throws at us. *Us, Addison.* I won't cheat on you. I'm not interested in another woman or *any* woman. You do it for me. Just you."

Then, a sadness blanketed his eyes. "I get where you're coming from. That whole Tommy thing got to me. And you know me, I never get jealous. It's been a super stressful month. Let's go out there and have fun, okay?"

She threw her arms around him and kissed him again and again. "Thank you for being my rock. I'm sorry I doubted you. I won't do that again."

He kissed her with so much passion, her knees trembled while he held her snug against him. "We got this, babe."

As they gazed into each other's eyes, she smiled. "You're right. We got this."

Before leaving their office, she asked, "Did you run the report?"

"It's running. I hung back to see if the program would catch something right away, but I got nothing. Maybe that's good news. Maybe you're safe here, like you said."

"Tommy is here, and Liliana asked if she could take a break," Addison said.

"I'll work the bar with you." He kissed her forehead. "We good?"

"Yeah." One more kiss and they returned to the bar.

"I'll be back in thirty," Liliana said with a sly smile.

She and Tommy headed into the fray.

Addison got busy waiting on a customer. Before moving to the next, she glanced over at Hawk. He stood there, frozen.

"What?" she asked.

Hawk pressed his mouth to her ear, and whispered, "They're going upstairs."

"So?"

"Why here?" Hawk asked.

"Why not?" Addison replied before waiting on someone else.

She wasn't surprised Tommy was attracted to Liliana. She was tall and pretty with dark hair and beautiful brown eyes. She worked hard, was juggling a second job, and went to school.

They seemed like a better match than Tommy and Mags, but since Addison couldn't navigate her own new relationship, she'd be the last one to judge someone else's.

24

KABOOM!

Hawk killed the headlights as he drove down Addison's street. It was after two in the morning and she needed to pick up her bridesmaid dress from her house. Since she'd been living at Hawks', she hadn't gotten any security alerts, but to ensure her safety, he parked at the end of the block.

They hurried down the sidewalk, she, still in her blonde wig and black mask, their Glocks at the ready. They entered her home, kept the lights off, and stayed silent. Hawk shone his phone's flashlight as they hurried into Addison's bedroom.

With her weapon drawn, she opened her closet. It was clear. She collected her bridesmaid dress, still in the garment bag, then placed a few things into an overnight bag. They were outta there in less than five minutes.

"I miss my house," she said from the back seat as he drove them home.

"I like that you're staying with me," he replied.

"I love your home, but I'm not settled, you know? Most of my things are at my house."

"I like that you're living with me," he repeated. "What do you think about that?"

Silence.

Deafening silence.

He'd said too much. Well, he wasn't about to take it back now. Truth was, he did love her company. He wanted to see her every day. Wanted to wake up next to her and go to sleep every night holding her close.

"You okay back there?" he asked.

From the back seat, she caressed his shoulder. "I'm with you for now. We've gotta get past the bodyguard phase of our love affair."

He could hear the smile in her voice. "If you move back home, and I'm not with you, you won't last one night," he said.

She laughed. "You are the cockiest man I have ever known."

"Thank you."

Another chuckle from the back seat. "Once we figure out who's trying to terrorize me, we can talk about everything else."

He could live with that... for now.

They returned to his townhouse, and she vanished upstairs with her items. He slipped off his sport coat and poured two brandies. With a snifter in hand, he turned out the living room lights, walked onto his balcony. The gentle summer breeze warmed his skin while he gazed at the sky, dotted with twinkling stars.

Leaning on the railing, he sipped the top-shelf liqueur, letting the smooth burn roll down his throat.

The report he'd run had been a bust. No member of Lost Souls could be found on any terror watch list. No surprise there, but he had to be thorough.

Addison appeared with her drink. She tapped her glass to his, sipped.

She'd ditched the mask and wig, pulled her hair into braided pigtails, changed into a short silk nightie with spaghetti straps.

He let out a soft whistle. "Very sexy, baby."

Her sultry smile was her only reply. After another sip, she stroked his back. He put his arm around her while they stared out at the black river.

"I'm going to read." She left him standing there as she sashayed inside.

Unable to resist, he followed. In the living room, she sipped the brandy, set down the glass, and picked up a book with a man's picture on the cover. With her shapely, bare legs resting on the ottoman, she patted the cushion next to hers, and smiled up at him. "Sit with me."

Rather than sit beside her, he eased down on the opposite side, swung his legs onto her lap. "Whatcha reading?"

"It's a romance by my favorite author." She held up the book.

He stared at the cover. "Who's Stoni Alexander?"

"She writes romantic suspense."

He snickered. "I'm surprised you're reading that. I thought you'd be into crime thrillers. Aren't romance books just a bunch of fluff?"

"No. I love her stories."

He eyed the book cover. "And what's with the guy?"

"He's a total hottie." Then, she glanced over at him. "He looks a little like you. You want me to read to you?"

He didn't, but he wasn't stupid. No way would he refuse her. "Sure, but don't get mad if I fall asleep."

Her smarmy expression made him chuckle. "Oh, you won't be sleeping when I'm done reading this to you."

She opened the book and read an excerpt out loud.

"Her insides burned for him. She couldn't think about anything but him. She was desperate to strip him naked and take him inside her. He was beautiful, more beautiful than any man should be. But he was evil. A brooding, wicked man who used his smile like a

weapon. She didn't want anything beyond his perfectly sculpted body. Just him and his raw animal magnetism.

When she dropped her robe, he stood there staring long and hard at her naked body. His hungry gaze dropped to her breasts, to her hairless pussy, her muscular thighs before returning his gaze back to her eyes.

"I can't wait to fuck you," he ground out. "You ready to scream my name again and again while I fuck you for my own pleasure?"

Heat traveled up her neck to her cheeks. She wanted to cover herself from his sinful gaze, but she wanted him to see what he was about to have.

Her. All night long.

She'd waited months for this, and she'd thought about him dozens of times, fantasizing how good it would feel to fuck the enemy.'"

"Jesus," Hawk growled. "I'm hard."

Addison glanced over at him, wagged her eyebrows, and continued reading him the bedtime story.

"But she had to play this cool, like this didn't mean a thing. As he stalked his way over, one slow step at a time, the lust in his eyes had turned them black with desire. His breathing was slow and controlled, but when he ran his thumb over her nipple, she could feel him tremble.

He stared down at her. "I'm going to fuck you."

"I'm going to fuck you back," she replied.

"I'm not romantic. I'm not going to send you flowers or have your name tattooed on my back. I'm going to fuck you hard and fast and deep. For me."

"When are you going to stop talking about it and do it?" she replied.

Pausing, Addison glanced over. His cock had tented his pants. "Why don't you strip down?" she suggested.

As he got naked, he knew. This was his person. Addison was not a replacement. She was his destiny. He would always love Josie. He would always miss the child he lost. He would always be broken, but he knew the value of loving a person with everything he had. Addison deserved his best. If she would have him, he would make her his priority for the rest of his life.

After moving closer on the sofa, he caressed her silky thigh.

She eyed his erection. "Not laughing at my novel, now, are you?"

"No, babe, I'm not."

"Do you want to hear how he fucks her?"

"Hell, yeah."

Addison continued reading out loud.

"He didn't want her in bed or on the sofa. He wanted her on the hard surface of the kitchen floor, where she would have to feel the power of his thrusts, again and again. She would have to endure the raw, feral fucking that would be over much too fast. But, he wasn't going to delay the inevitable.

They came together in a wild embrace. It felt more like two territorial animals fighting to the death than two people making love. She kissed him hard, scraped her fingernails down his shoulders. He thrust his tongue in her mouth, pinched her nipples—"

"Mount me," Hawk commanded, his voice rough with need.

With a sexy gleam in her eyes, she set down the book and straddled him. "I've got my diaphragm in." Then, she shot him the most adorable smile. "If it's just gonna be us, you can toss the condoms."

"Just us," he replied. "Always, just us."

He reached up, slid his hand around the back of her neck and pulled her onto him. Their mouths came together, their tongues thrashing against each other's. Her mewls and moans turned him harder, but when her juices seeped onto him, he couldn't go slowly.

"I need you," he said. "Like the guy in the book."

"Yes," she bleated.

He rose with her in his arms and laid on the floor. With shaft in hand, he placed himself at her opening, and tunneled inside. The explosion of pleasure had them both moaning while he thrust to her end.

"Fuck," he said between gritted teeth.

"Suck my nipples," she commanded.

He dipped down, pulled her nipple into his mouth and sucked.

"Oh, yeah, hard like that," she said, her raspy voice filled with a dark desire.

Then, she started moving beneath him and he broke from her nipple to fuck her. The harder she bucked, the harder he fucked. She raised her arms over her head.

"Trap me," she said.

He held her in place, she wrapped her legs around his lower back, and he fucked her again and again.

"Baby, I'm gonna come," he said. "I can't hold on."

"Stop," she said.

He stilled. "Ohgod, am I hurting you?"

A devilish grin spread across her face. "No. I don't want you to come yet. I like edging, so I want to do that to you."

They stared into each other's eyes. "Does the guy in the book tell her that he loves her?" Hawk asked.

Addison's eyes softened. "Eventually, but it's way too soon for that. These two hate each other, so this is a hate fuck. I love those."

He started moving inside her again, the build slower this time, but when she started growling, he increased his speed, the intensity of his thrusting had her writhing under him.

"Fuck, fuck, baby," she blurted. "Oh, hell, I'm gonna come." She cried out his name while she convulsed hard beneath him. "Fuck me hard."

He pumped her again and again while the pleasure skyrocketed him to the moon. Her raw kisses ravaging him, the assault just shy of painful.

Spreading her legs wider, she arched up. "Oh, yes, I'm gonna come again."

Her second orgasm triggered his, the explosion of euphoria ripping through him. Wave after wave of ecstasy flooded him. When he finished, he continued moving slowly until they fell still, wrapped in each other's arms.

"Holy fuck, what the hell just happened?" he murmured.

"You got Stoni Alexandered," she whispered.

"She's my new favorite author."

"Not gonna make fun of me anymore, are you?" she murmured.

"No, baby, I'm not. You can read me a bedtime story *anytime* you want."

She regarded him for a long moment. "I think I'd like that. I'd like that a lot."

Friday night at eight, Prescott met them in the conference room at ALPHA HQ, where they spent the next two hours prepping for the Haqazzii mission. As they worked through their plan, they studied the compound using the photos Cooper had uploaded to the ALPHA portal. They familiarized themselves with the faces of evil... and their long list of atrocities against humanity.

Addison felt no remorse for what she was about to do. She was stopping six vicious killers before they smuggled bombs into one of the most secure sites in the world and wreaked international havoc at the Presidential summit.

Per the guest list, several of the leaders were bringing their families with them. If Haqazzii and his team succeeded, their destruction would throw the US into chaos, affect the global markets, and spark cries for another Middle East war.

"Are we going by the book or off-script?" Addison asked as she shifted her attention from Hawk to Prescott.

Hawk had been studying the layout of the building while Prescott had been eyeballing the faces of the terror cell. Both men looked over at her.

"It's us," Hawk said.

"Exactly," Prescott agreed.

"That means off-script," Addison replied.

"I hate playing by the damn rules," Hawk murmured. "Especially when it comes to a known terror leader."

"Same," Prescott agreed.

"What about torture?" Addison asked.

They grew silent while mulling that question.

"Depends," Prescott replied, after a long moment.

"I agree," Hawk said.

"We won't know until we're there," Prescott said.

"Who's dealing with the trailer?" Hawk asked.

"I hate splitting us up," Addison said. "We're already outnumbered."

"But we've got the element of surprise," Prescott said. "That's gotta count for something."

"We'll hit the trailer first, then breach the compound," Hawk said.

Their conversation continued until they solidified their plan, were in complete agreement, and ran through best- and worst-case scenarios.

"We go in together," Hawk said.

"We come out together," Prescott said.

"And we waste every last one of those scumbags," Addison added.

They'd each come dressed in black. No jewelry. Wallets and cell phones were left on the conference room table. Moving as a pack, with Addison in the middle, they headed toward the equipment room.

Additional weapons were secured, Kevlar vests went on, comms were checked. Hawk pocketed a burner. After collecting their helmets equipped with night vision goggles, they made their way to the chopper, waiting on the far side of the large ALPHA parking lot.

It was ten past eleven. Hawk spent the next fifteen doing his pre-flight check. With that completed, they climbed into the smaller Bell helicopter. Addison rode shotgun, Prescott in the back.

Seatbelts buckled, headsets on, they were ready to do this.

Hawk cleared to fly by ATC, then lifted off the ground. "Let's go get those motherfuckers."

During the thirty-six-minute flight, they moved into mission mode. Addison focused on her breathing, recalled the faces of the terrorists they were hunting. The senior Haqazzii had done so much damage to humankind. His son was just as much of a menace. While this was a dangerous mission, she wasn't nervous. Her senses were hyperaware, and she knew the risks. She was working with two of the best Operatives ALPHA had in its arsenal, and she was confident they'd get the job done.

Hawk landed the bird a mile from the compound. Helmets on, goggles in place, they attached the silencers before making their way on foot.

The compound was surrounded by an eight-foot fence. Rather than climb over, they found the double-wide doors.

"Breach," Hawk murmured before shooting out the lock.

Prescott pulled open the door, stuck his head inside, then retreated. "It's quiet. There's a light on in the trailer."

"Guard dogs?" Addison murmured.

"Nothing... yet," Prescott replied.

They each pulled their second weapon, made their way to the trailer, took their positions around it.

"On two," Prescott said at the front door. "One..."

Hawk pulled open the door. Prescott rushed in, Hawk close on his heels.

POP-POP-POP-POP.

"Two men down," Prescott said.

"Bathroom clear," Hawk added. "Exiting."

Addison waited at the rear prepared for anyone who tried to escape out the back. She hurried around as they emerged.

"They were watching porn and relieving themselves," Prescott murmured.

Addison shuddered. *Gross.* "Did you recognize them from the photos?" she whispered.

"Yes," Hawk replied.

They made their way to the back door.

"Not locked." Hawk slowly turned the handle.

With their weapons at the ready, they entered the dark hallway. Per their plan, they stayed together, covering each other as they headed into the first room.

Kitchen. Cleared. Empty.

Next room. A spacious work room equipped with five long tables, the bomb-making ingredients laid out like an assembly line.

They split up.

"Clear," Addison whispered from the east end.

"Clear," Hawk said from the west end.

"Got one," Prescott murmured.

They hurried over to him. Addison eyed the man sleeping on the sofa. "It's Haqazzii's second in command."

POP-POP. Prescott shot him twice in the head.

Someone shouted in a foreign language. A door slammed.

"Here we go," Hawk whispered.

They continued through the building, clearing room after room. If their intel was correct, there were three men left to find, one being Haqazzii himself.

They turned the corner. Two men were armed and waiting.

BANG! BANG! BANG! BANG! BANG! BANG!

They opened fire, all three using both their weapons.

POP-POP-POP-POP-POP-POP-POP-POP-POP-POP-POP-POP-POP-POP.

Both terrorists dropped.

"Fuck," Prescott bit out.

"Were you hit?" Hawk asked.

"In the armor," his brother replied.

"Listen," Addison said. "Haqazii's leaving."

Addison sprinted toward the front of the building, both men catching up to her. Before rounding the corner, she placed her back against the wall. Breathing hard, she peeked around.

Haqazzii was pulling out an automatic assault rifle from a cabinet by the front exit. She stepped into the hallway, opened fire.

POP-POP-POP-POP-POP-POP.

Haqazzii ran down the hall, opened a door, and pulled it shut behind him.

"Confirm that leads to the basement," she whispered.

Hawk pulled up beside her. "Confirmed." He pulled a smoke grenade from his belt.

Prescott and Addison did the same. They ran to the door. Hawk opened it. They yanked the pins and threw the grenades down the stairs.

"There's an exit. I'm going outside to stop him." Hawk took off in a full-on run.

"I'll stay here," Prescott said.

"I'm going with Hawk." Addison ran after him, wishing he'd waited for her.

She saw him vanish outside and pushed harder to catch up. When she did, he was readying his shot at the cellar door.

She hurried over, breathing hard.

The door flew open, Haqazzii emerged wearing a gas mask and cradling his assault rifle. She and Hawk opened fire.

POP-POP-POP-POP-POP-POP-POP-POP-POP-POP-POP-POP-POP-POP.

Haqazzii dropped.

"On my way out," Prescott exclaimed. "He's got the place wired to blow."

"Oh, fuck," Hawk bit out.

She and Hawk sprinted toward the front gate. As they rounded the corner of the building, Prescott was thirty feet ahead of them.

KABOOM!

An explosion in the back of the building had them running full-out toward the compound exit. Addison started falling behind, both men able to run so much faster than her. Hawk stopped and grabbed her hand as she ran past, then continued running.

KABOOM!

"You want me to carry you?" Hawk blurted between breaths.

"I got this," she replied, pushing harder than she'd ever run.

KABOOM!

Prescott pulled the fence gate open as they raced through it.

KABOOM! KABOOM! KABOOM! KABOOM!

The building erupted in a series of explosions.

"Don't stop," Hawk said as sections of the building came flying over the fence, crashing around them.

They continued racing toward the open field. Addison's lungs burned, her thighs hurt, she couldn't catch her breath, as debris continued falling all around them. Beyond pushing as hard as they could, they were jumping and leaping over downed pieces of the building.

"Jesus," Prescott murmured, the comm catching his voice. "What the hell!"

"I gotta slow down," Addison gasped out.

Hawk and Prescott had been running full-tilt with her between them. Hawk scooped her up and continued pushing hard. "I got you."

Addison was sucking down so much air, she couldn't respond.

When they'd run beyond the flying shards of metal and shrapnel from the building, he and Prescott slowed to a stride. Gasping for air, they beelined toward the helo.

"I'm soaked," Prescott said.

"I hope you didn't piss yourself," Hawk replied, and they both laughed.

"How can you two joke around?" Addison asked. "We almost *died*."

"But we live another day, baby," Hawk said.

"Another day of murder and mayhem," Prescott murmured under his breath.

"When you'd get so damn fast?" Hawk asked his brother.

"I got a head start," Prescott replied.

"I can walk," Addison said, and Hawk put her down.

"I'm gonna be sore," Prescott said.

"You wanna see the team doc?"

"Hell, no," his brother replied. "Not the first time the armor's saved me. Won't be the last."

"Addison, you hit?" Hawk asked.

"Negative. You?"

"I'm clear," Hawk answered.

Though soaked in sweat, they couldn't remove their helmets. They were walking in a pitch-black field, the new moon cloaking them in darkness. Without their night goggles, they wouldn't be able to find the chopper.

Hawk pulled out his burner, called Cooper, and put the phone on speaker.

"The compound just exploded!" Cooper said. "Confirm you're okay."

"Confirmed," Hawk replied.

"How the hell do you know that, Coop?" Prescott asked.

"I'm at Langley. We have satellite surveillance. You cut that close. Too close."

"No shit," Hawk said. "All targets eliminated."

"Nice work," Cooper said. "Take tomorrow off."

"I run a company," Hawk replied. "I don't get days off."

"I'll take you up on that," Addison said to Cooper.

"That looked intense," Cooper said.

"Just another day at work," Hawk replied.

"Addison, the threat of danger has been eliminated," Cooper said. "You're no longer on lockdown."

Addison and Hawk exchanged glances.

"Thank you," Addison replied.

While relieved Addison was now safe, his heart sank. Hawk loved keeping her close and ensuring her safety. Their relationship had changed so much. She'd turned his house into a home, and seeing her every morning and every evening had been the best parts of his day.

"We're sending in the teams. Great job, everyone." Cooper hung up.

Back at the helicopter, Addison and Prescott removed their helmets, but Hawk still needed his goggles. They could relax, but he had to get them home safely.

After they climbed in, Hawk walked around the craft and patted the metal side. "Take us home, baby."

He jumped in and powered up. Before checking the instrument panel, he turned to his partner. "We did good."

"Yeah, we did," she replied.

He buckled up, secured his headset, and lifted off the ground.

While he should have felt like he'd avenged his late wife by eliminating Haqazzii's son, he derived no enjoyment from taking a life. Despite the evil he chased, he would have preferred that none existed in the first place.

As he pointed the chopper toward home, he glanced over at Addison. She met his gaze. Their relationship was different from any other he'd ever had. Friends, partners, now lovers. They relied on each other in harrowing, dangerous situations. He trusted her with his life and he'd take a bullet to save hers.

Is she the one? Sure as hell looks that way.

"Nice job tonight," she said.

"You too," he replied.

"Thanks for the assist."

"Anytime, babe."

In the darkness of the aircraft, they shared a loving smile.

This was it... and he was all in. The only question that remained... was she?

Stryker and Emerson's wedding was finally here, and Addison was beyond excited to hang with her friends... and have fun with her man. The upscale event was being held at a boutique five-star hotel in DC. The past two hours had been a whirlwind in the bridal suite while the stylists worked their magic on the wedding party.

Addison's hair had been swept into a stunning French twist with soft tendrils framing her face. As she glanced around the room at her cousin Liv, Evangeline, Providence, Slash, and

Danielle, she smiled. How could she not? Being here, with them, was exactly what she needed. A break from the mayhem.

And Sammy Luck, Dakota and Providence's daughter, was the most adorable flower girl she'd ever seen.

Emerson, in a beautiful white, satin, wedding gown, asked Sammy what she liked best about the evening.

Sammy grinned at her. "I'm *in* the wedding with my mom and Aunt E-leen." She ran her small hand over her dress. "This is so pretty."

"I'm so glad you're my flower girl, Sammy." Emerson kissed the top of her head.

The bridesmaids wore full-length, wine-colored dresses. While the dresses were all the same color and style, the necklines varied, based on each woman's taste. Addison had selected the strapless neckline with a velvet choker around her neck.

Everyone looked beautiful.

Once they were all ready, Emerson called them over. "Thank you for making today so special for me and Stryker. I love you all like family." She set a medium-sized box on a table, opened it, and pulled out several small, hinged, jewelry boxes. "This is just a little something from me. The gift receipt is included and my feelings are not hurt if you exchange it."

Emerson handed one to each of her bridesmaids, then knelt and gave Sammy one, too.

Her eyes lit up. "Thank you."

Addison opened the gift, revealing a pair of diamond stud earrings. "Oh, I love these," she exclaimed as she slid them into her pierced ears. "Thank you. These are perfect."

"I thought you'd like them," Emerson replied.

Emerson had bought Sammy a necklace with two charms. A pink flower charm and one with the initial S. Both dangled from a delicate silver chain.

Sammy's eyes grew large and she beamed at Emerson. "It's

the prettiest necklace *ever*." Small fingers carefully removed the necklace, then she asked her mom to help her put it on. After Providence clasped it around her daughter's neck, Sammy hugged Emerson.

"Okay, ladies," Emerson said, "it's time for me to marry the man with the hair."

The women laughed.

The wedding planner entered and put her hand over her heart. "Everyone looks stunning." Her gaze stilled on Emerson. "You're a beautiful bride. Are you ready to do this?"

"So ready," Emerson replied with a smile.

They made their way down to the first floor and over to the ballroom reserved for the ceremony. The groomsmen waited nearby. They looked incredibly hot dressed in black, their muscles stretching against the suit fabric. More than ever, they looked like the badass band of brothers that they were.

Addison scanned the group, her heart skipping a beat when she found Hawk.

The men turned, their attention fixed on the women.

"Wow." Hawk kissed Addison's cheek. "You look amazing. All I want to do is kiss you."

"Maybe later, if you're lucky." She stepped back to check him out. "Whew, sexy."

He slipped his hand into his pants pocket, struck a pose. "All for you, baby."

She laughed. "Yeah, uh-huh."

She loved being in the wedding, loved that she wasn't wearing a wig, wasn't looking over her shoulder. More than any of those, she loved the man by her side.

Hawk couldn't take his eyes off her. "I'm a lucky man," he murmured.

"Yes, you are."

"I hate that we can't tell anyone what's going on with us."

"There's something going on with us?" She peered into his eyes. "Really?"

He leaned close. "We're in love."

"You think?"

He kissed her cheek. "I know."

"Cocky *and* a know-it-all." She shot him a smile. "You're a handful."

The processional music began, the wedding planner opened the ballroom doors and sent them down the aisle, a couple at a time.

"Here we go," Hawk murmured.

It was like a who's who of ALPHA. Beyond the wedding party—Cooper and Danielle, Jericho and Liv, Sin and Evangeline, Dakota and Providence, and Prescott escorting Slash. Almost every Operative was in attendance.

As they made their way down the aisle, Hawk looked over at her. She returned his gaze and they shared a smile.

When they came to a stop, Hawk kissed her cheek, and whispered, "I love you," before they parted.

She adored him with her entire being.

The beautiful ceremony was a mix of formality and fun, but it was Stryker and Emerson's vows that brought some of the guests to tears.

"My Em," Stryker began. "You look absolutely radiant, beyond gorgeous. I can't believe you're mine. How did I get so lucky? You are *always* the best part of my day. No matter what we do, life is better when we're together. You're the love of my life and I promise you, in front of our family and friends, that I will continue to put you first. I love what we're building together, one day at a time. We'll make it through the challenges together and be grateful for the wins. I vow to love you with all my heart."

The clergy asked Emerson to speak her vows.

"Stryker, I hope we spend the rest of our lives sharing hair ties and scrunchies."

The audience started laughing.

"You are a beautiful man, inside and out, and I fall more in love with you every day. I love our adventures and the challenges we've endured together. My life is so much better because you're in it. I love you so much and I know that our marriage will only bring us closer. I'm so excited to start this part of our lives, and to call you my husband. Loving you in the easiest thing I do."

They exchanged rings, the clergy pronounced them husband and wife, and the crowd erupted in applause while the newlyweds shared a loving kiss. Wearing huge grins, Stryker and Emerson made their way down the aisle as husband and wife.

This is the beginning of their forever adventure.

Never before Hawk had Addison wanted to spend her life *that* entwined with another person. As the wedding party filed out, Hawk clasped her hand, brought it to his lips, and kissed her finger. She melted from his tender gesture.

"It's all about being with the right person," she murmured under her breath.

"Sure is, baby," Hawk replied.

"Did I just say that out loud?"

"No, I can read your mind."

She smiled. "Stryker and Emerson look so happy."

"That's 'cause they are."

They made their way into the ballroom next door for the reception and over to the waiting newlyweds to congratulate them.

"I want that," Addison whispered.

Draping his arm over her shoulder, Hawk whispered, "You can have it all."

"You think?"

"I *know*," he replied.

25

MISSING

The following afternoon, Hawk and Addison entered the hospital and hurried to the directory.

"Fourth floor," Addison said. "I'm so excited Liv's in labor."

They squeezed into a full elevator, exited on the Labor and Delivery floor. Addison pulled him out of the way of foot traffic. "Are you going to be okay around them?"

"Yeah, I will," he replied. "It reminds me of what I lost, but —" he dipped down and kissed her—"you give me hope."

Her eyes widened. "You mean about us, right? You're not talking about our having babies?"

"Do you want children?" he asked.

"Oh, wow, so we're having this conversation?"

He waited.

"Okay, now's good," she replied. "My parents' divorce messed me up pretty good."

The dream she'd had with him and the three young children popped into her thoughts.

Tell him.

"If I found my forever man, I'd love three... three children."

"I like that number," he replied.

"How 'bout you?" she asked.

"It's a fucked-up world, but I'd love to be a dad. Like you said, the most important thing is being with the right person. My parents had problems, but they handled everything together."

"Did they fight?"

"They disagreed, but they were pretty decent about it. I heard my dad raise his voice a few times." Hawk smiled. "When he did, my mom would tell him she wasn't hard of hearing *yet* and to take it down a few notches."

Addison laughed. "Your mom is so cool. So, are we good on that?"

He smiled. "We're good."

"You ready to be a godparent?"

"I'm ready for anything as long as it's with you."

"So romantic," she said before dropping a tender kiss on his lips.

They made their way to Liv's private room where she and Jericho were talking quietly. Liv was propped in bed while Jericho sat in the bedside chair, holding her hand.

Liv's face lit up. "You made it!"

"Godparents extraordinaire," Hawk replied. "We take our jobs very seriously."

Jericho laughed. "We're due for another contraction. Those are a ton of fun."

Liv chuckled. "Easy for you to say."

"I'll do it," Addison volunteered. "Jericho, you want a break?"

"A break!" Liv uttered.

Jericho kissed her. "I'll grab coffee. Be back in ten."

The men took off and Addison sat on the bed next to her cousin. "How is it, really?"

"It painful, but the breathing helps. When the contractions

end, it's fine. I think this is going to be like pushing out a watermelon."

"Ouch," Addison said, and they laughed.

Liv inhaled. "Here comes one. I need you to count out loud for me."

As they managed through the contractions, Addison wondered if she'd want to put herself through this.

"Can I have the cup of ice?" Liv asked.

Addison handed it to her. "Are you hungry. Can you eat?"

"Some experts say eating is fine while others say not to," Liv replied. "If I get hungry, I'll have something light to eat."

Addison grew quiet. She didn't want Liv using up more energy than she had to.

After a moment of silence, Liv asked, "How are you?"

"Good."

"What's going on with you and Hawk?"

Addison stared at her. "What do you—"

"You two were different last night at the wedding. I asked Jericho, but he didn't notice. I'm not sure anyone did, except me. You know I love people watching. You two seemed a *lot* closer."

"I can't say."

"Because Jericho will tell Cooper and Cooper's by the book?"

Despite biting back a smile, Addison said nothing.

"I'm about to push a very large baby out my vagina," Liv said. "You gotta give me something. What happened to sharing *all* our secrets with each other?"

"We've fallen in love. Isn't that crazy?"

Liv smiled. "Not to me. I think it's awesome. Jericho told me the guys have been waiting for this to happen." She clasped Addison's hand. "I couldn't be happier. You two are so good together. Ow, ow, here comes another."

Addison helped her as Jericho and Hawk walked back into the room.

Jericho was by her side, taking control, and supporting his wife through it. The second he walked in, her expression changed. Despite the pain, she looked happier and relieved. Addison slid her gaze to Hawk. If they had that kind of connection, she would be a very happy woman.

When the contraction subsided, Liv leaned against the pillows. "Come on out, sweet baby. Mama and Dadda can't wait to meet you."

"We should take off," Addison said. "We're headed to the farmhouse."

Liv held out her hand to Addison. "Don't leave me. I love having you here. We only called you guys. Our families don't know we're in labor."

"We want to keep things nice and chill," Jericho explained.

"Can you go to the farmhouse without me?" Addison asked.

"What's going on there?" Jericho asked.

"I'm taking inventory of everything that needs to be repaired or replaced," Hawk replied.

"I'd write the word 'everything' on my list and be done," Jericho said and Liv laughed.

"I'll be back," Hawk said. "Deep breaths, Liv."

"I'll walk you out," Addison said.

In the hallway, she kissed him goodbye. "I'll see you in a couple of hours."

"Miss me." He flashed a smile before taking off toward the elevators.

I am so in love with that man.

On his way out of the hospital, Hawk called Prescott.

"Hey," Prescott answered.

"Wanna help me out at the farmhouse?"

"Sorry, bro, I'm at the airport."

"Business or fun?"

Prescott chuckled. "Fun? What the hell is that? I'm doing recon work. What's going on at the farm?"

"Inventory. I need a master list for the contractor."

"You're on your own. I'll call you when I get back."

"Be safe." Hawk hung up, jumped in the SUV, and headed west.

Twenty minutes later, he parked out front, made his way inside the farmhouse. His grandparents had left most of their old, outdated furniture, wanting to start afresh in their new home. As he walked around the old house, the silence settled into his bones.

Am I holding on to the past or do I want to live here?

Addison drifted into his thoughts. Was she the one? Their romance was so new, but their relationship wasn't. He thought of having children with her. The familiar pang shot through him. He'd never gotten over losing his first child.

Stopping in the kitchen, he surveyed the room. The wallpaper had to go, the appliances needed to be replaced, along with the cupboards. Water dripped from the faucet. He tightened the handle, but the leak didn't stop. He pulled out his phone and started a list.

Jericho's right. I should do a complete overhaul of the entire house.

With everything going on, he didn't have the time to do the work himself, but if he had, he would have loved fixing up the old house.

His phone rang. It was Tommy.

"Yo, baby," Hawk answered. "What's the word?"

"I'm heading to the shooting range. You wanna meet me there?"

"I'm at the farmhouse."

"Sell, sell, sell!" Tommy said. "What are you doing out there?"

"I'm making a list of what needs to be fixed."

"You planning on spending the night, 'cause you're gonna be there a *long* time."

Hawk chuckled.

"I was talking to a friend of mine," Tommy said. "He thought we could get ten mil for the land, no problem."

"I know, babe, but I'm not ready to sell."

"Alrighty, I'll let you go."

After Tommy hung up, Hawk continued through the house, noting everything that needed to be repaired or replaced.

"This is a hella list," he said as he made his way upstairs.

The house had always been a home. With Granddad and Grandmom gone, it was an old, rundown building that needed a lot of work. When he finished surveying the house, he stepped onto the back porch to view the landscape. He could unload the property, the money would get divided up, and he could move on with his life.

I wouldn't need to do a damn thing but make a few phone calls.

He stood there admiring the fiery streaks of fuchsia and orange-yellow as the day bowed to dusk. It was after seven. He hadn't gotten a text from Addison, so he sent her one.

"Baby Savage?" he texted her.

He thought about fixing up the property and what he would do with all that land. Would Addison want to live there or was she more of a city girl? He'd never thought about a future—with anyone—but as he stared at the acres and acres of land, he couldn't imagine his life without her.

Years ago, her friendship had breathed life back into him. Falling in love with her would never have worked any other way. For the first time in a decade he was ready to commit himself to her, and to spend the rest of his life with her... if she would have him.

Emotion gripped his throat. He would always love Josie and their unborn child, but he was ready to move forward.

His buzzing phone snapped him back to the present.

Addison had replied to his text.

"Baby's not in any rush to come out," Addison replied. "Liv's not dilating much, so they might give her something, but because it's her first, they're waiting. Jericho has been inviting the baby to join us in the world. It's hilarious! How's by you?"

"My list of repairs and upgrades is long."

"I can't wait to hear. When are you coming back?"

"Checking the henhouse and barn. Be there in forty," he texted back.

She sent three heart emojis.

He replied with one.

Next stop, the henhouse. No squawking chickens and no eggs. His dad had taken care of finding new homes for the birds. He'd never seen the room bare and he didn't like it. Henrietta might have been an ornery chicken, but she'd always made him smile.

He exited the henhouse to see Tommy getting out of his car. Hawk whistled and Tommy turned in his direction, then jogged over.

"How was the shooting range?" Hawk asked.

"Hit or miss." Tommy chuckled at his pun. "I figured you could use some help."

"I'm pretty much done. Just gotta check the barn."

The cousins made their way down the hill and into the old building. Years ago, his grandparents had owned horses. Though the stalls were long empty, they still used the walk-in freezer to store vegetables from their garden. Hawk opened the heavy freezer door.

"Woo, it's cold in there," Tommy said as Hawk stepped inside.

Hawk eyed the insulated bags of frozen corn, carrots,

soybeans, and green beans. On the shelf lay a large roll of plastic sheeting.

As the freezer door was about to shut, he turned. The lever to open the door from the inside was missing.

"Ah, fuck." Hawk grabbed the two-by-four resting against the wall of the freezer and wedged it between the door and the frame to keep it from closing.

From the outside, Tommy pulled open the door. "What's wrong?"

"The lever is broken," Hawk explained as Tommy stepped inside. "Make sure this board stays here."

"What the hell?" Tommy blurted. "Why didn't they get that fixed?"

That made Hawk laugh. He extracted his phone from his jeans pocket and showed him the list of items that needed repairing, replacing, or tossing.

"That's a long list. Seems more trouble than it's worth."

Hawk raked his hand through his hair. "I'm gonna get an estimate on everything. My head's telling me one thing, my heart another."

"Are Granddad and Grandmom paying for these repairs?"

"No. I am."

"We'd walk away with millions, but it sounds like you don't need the money," Tommy said. "Hawk Security's made you rich. It's a bummer that someone leaked videos of your clients. That slowed you down, but it didn't kill your business. You bounced back, no problem."

Hawk regarded him. "How'd you know about that?"

"I hear things." Tommy paused. "Poor Barry gets killed on one of *your* missions and you get a slap on the wrist. Big whoop. And let's not forget that you're Granddad's number one. He doesn't even try to hide it. I'm a decorated police officer who goes undercover to shut down a drug-trafficking ring, but

Granddad barely says a word to me. No one even fucking knows you're in ALPHA!"

Where the hell is this coming from?

"And let's not forget the best part. I meet a woman. She's gorgeous, totally chill, and loves to let loose at cosplay parties. While I'm in this shithole motel in Philly dealing with a bunch of low-life drug dealers, I think about her all the time. She's what gets me though that. When I get back, I run into her. Imagine how fucking thrilled I was. The woman of my dreams in the flesh. Then, I find out she's your buddy. Who has a buddy like that? Thanks to you, she's not interested in me."

"Hey, I'm sorry," Hawk said. "But Addison wasn't interested in you. That had nothing to do with me."

Tommy released a low growl. "Me, zero. You, every-fucking-thing."

Pausing, Hawk eyed his cousin. "You been drinking?" He rubbed his arms to warm his skin.

"I had some beers."

"C'mon, let's go talk." Hawk walked toward the freezer door.

Jolts of electricity pounded through him. He hit the floor, the searing pain incapacitating him.

Tommy pulled Hawk's phone from his pocket, then yanked out the Taser's barbed probes. At the door he turned back. "I killed Barry, hoping they'd kick your ass outta ALPHA. I leaked the videos from your company so your clients would bail and your company would fail. No matter what I did, you're fucking untouchable. This time, I'm gonna win, Nicky. I'm gonna sell this fucking farm *and* get the girl."

Tommy grabbed the board and rushed out, slamming the door behind him.

Hawk lay on the floor, unable to move. If he didn't get out, he'd freeze to death in a matter of minutes.

Addison smiled down at the tiny infant in her arms. "He's so beautiful. I can't stop staring at him." She peered over at Liv and Jericho. Liv was resting in bed while Jericho sat beside her beaming.

"What's his name?" Addison asked.

Liv and Jericho exchanged loving glances. "Liam Bryan Savage," Liv replied.

"Hello, Liam," Addison whispered. "I'm your godmother and I'm going to protect you and teach you and have so much fun with you."

Tears pricked her eyes.

She stood and placed Liam in Liv's waiting arms. Then, Addison pulled out her phone. "Let's get the first family photo."

Jericho leaned close, and Addison snapped a few, then texted them to Liv and Jericho. "I'm not going to tell Hawk. He'll be surprised when he gets here."

"Shouldn't he be back by now?" Jericho asked.

Addison shot Hawk a text. "Are you on your way?"

If he was driving, his phone might have blocked the text, so she called him, but it rolled to voicemail.

"Hmm, that's weird," she said.

"What?" Liv asked, her gaze still cemented on her newborn.

"The call went right to voicemail," Addison said. "Hawk never turns his phone off."

"Do you think he's outta juice?" Jericho asked.

"Doubtful." Addison didn't like that he was at the farm by himself. He could have fallen off the roof.

"Jericho, you're not leaving anytime soon, are you?" she asked.

"Whatcha need?"

"Your car," she replied. "I want to head over to the farmhouse and check on him."

Jericho handed her his keys. "It's the Escalade." Then, he told her where he'd parked.

"Congratulations, I'm so happy for you guys. I'll be back soon."

Fifteen minutes later, Addison pulled down the dark road leading to the farmhouse, then up the driveway. Hawk's ALPHA SUV was parked out front, but no lights shone from inside the home. Anxiety slithered down her spine.

Please be okay.

She pulled her Glock from her handbag, turned on her phone's flashlight, and ventured out. She ran around the perimeter of the house praying he wasn't lying injured on the ground. To her relief, he wasn't there, so she hurried up the farmhouse steps. The door was unlocked, she went inside. Urgency had her flipping on the foyer lights.

"Hawk!" she hollered.

No response. She ran through the first floor calling out to him, then up the stairs to check the bedrooms. He wasn't there either. Venturing into the basement sent a chill through her, but she flipped on the lights and hurried down the old steps. After running through it, and not finding him, she raced back upstairs.

Ohmygod, the tracker.

She pulled up the ALPHA app on her phone and signed in. Then, she typed in his name. The tracker wheel spun. Seconds later, it delivered a result.

He's in the barn.

Outside she ran, her heart now pounding hard and fast in her chest. He's probably fine, she told herself as she tore past the henhouse.

Relief and dread coursed through her as she rushed inside. The stalls were clean and empty. She hurried to the walk-in freezer and pulled open the door.

"Ohmygod!"

Hawk lay in a fetal position on the floor, wrapped in plastic and shaking. She hurried to him.

"The door," he chattered. "Broken."

She shoved open the door just before it closed, grabbed a stool next to one of the stalls, and propped it open. "I got you," she said.

Using all of her strength, she dragged a very frigid Hawk into the barn.

She removed the plastic. He was like a block of ice. Pushing out the fear, she focused on him. The August air was warm, but she needed to get him into the shower so she could slowly elevate his body temperature.

"I need to get you into the house, but I don't think I can carry you."

"Help me up," he said through chattering teeth.

Supporting him, she guided him toward the house. It was slow going up the porch steps, but he made it into the living room.

"I'm going to get blankets. Can you lie down?" She helped him to the floor, then flew up the stairs, flung open the hall closet, and grabbed two. Then, she ran into a bedroom and pulled two more from the bed. Dragging them behind her, she raced back down the stairs.

She laid out one blanket, helped him to move onto it, then removed his frozen clothing. After stripping off her own clothes, she lay on top of him to warm him with her body before pulling the remaining three blankets over them, making sure to wrap his head. Within minutes, she was sweating, but his shivering had subsided.

Several more moments passed while she hugged him, her body heat helping to elevate his while their breathing fell into sync. She needed to check his fingers and toes, then get him into the shower. She had so many questions, but she stayed quiet, grateful she'd gotten there in time. She lifted her face and peered at his.

His eyes fluttered open and he smiled. "If you wanted me

naked, you coulda just asked."

Her heart rejoiced. They'd deal with everything else in time... and together.

"Can you stand in a shower?" she murmured.

"Yeah," he replied.

She helped him up, then wrapped two blankets around his shoulders. After grabbing their clothes, she steadied him as they made their way up the upstairs and into the hall bathroom. Once the water had heated, she turned it back to cool and asked him to test it.

He shoved his hand under the shower. "Feels warm."

He got in and the water pounded him while she studied every inch of him. His fingers were flush with color, but his toes were purple and she worried that he might lose his pinkies.

While he stood there warming up, she got dressed.

"Wiggle your fingers," she said.

He did.

"Toes," she said.

He tried, but they were too stiff to move. Over the next several minutes, she continued to raise the heat level, as he could tolerate it.

"I feel better," he said.

"You ready to come out?"

He wiped the water from his face. "Yeah, baby, I am."

She inhaled her first calming breath since seeing him on the freezer floor. He turned off the water and stepped out. After wrapping him in two large bath towels, she found a hairdryer that had to be thirty years old.

"Look, an antique," she said.

His smile was the most beautiful thing she had ever seen. Filled with gratitude, and overcome with emotion, tears filled her eyes. Had she stayed at the hospital, he would have died.

Unable to stop the relief, tears slid down her cheeks. He

folded her in his arms and held her, close. "I'm okay, baby. You got to me in time and you knew what to do."

He placed his hands on her cheeks, dipped down and dropped a soft kiss on her lips. "Thank you for saving me."

She choked back a sob. "Is the freezer door broken from the inside?"

"Yeah."

"Oh, no, you got locked in."

"No, I didn't," he ground out. "Tommy tased me, locked me in there, and left me to die."

26

MARRY ME

Anger coursed through Hawk, but he needed to think this through. Then, exact his revenge, swiftly and thoroughly.

Addison just stared at him. "Your cousin did this to you?"

"Let's get outta here."

They killed the lights in the farmhouse. As they made their way to the barn, he clasped her hand. Touching her was a gift he'd never, ever take for granted.

"Do you think he'll come back here to..." Addison's voice trailed off.

"Make sure I'm dead?" Hawk bit out. "If he does, he's gonna freak-the-fuck out when he doesn't find my frozen body."

"I hate him so much," she whispered.

After Hawk unplugged the freezer, he turned out the barn lights. On their way toward their vehicles, he asked, "Did Liv have the baby?"

"Yeah."

"Are they okay?"

"Mama and baby are good. Can you tell me what happened?"

"It's a beautiful night," he said. "Come sit with me."

With his arm around her, he walked passed the SUVs and eased down on a porch step. "How are you doing?" he asked.

She sat next to him, caressed his back. He stared up at the star-filled sky, appreciating the chirping crickets, his love by his side. He was grateful to be alive.

"I'm okay now," she replied. "Not gonna lie, I was pretty scared when I saw you wrapped in plastic in the freezer."

"He saw me as an obstacle to having you."

"God, no," she murmured. "You were right. He *is* obsessed with me. I'm sorry I ever hooked up with him—"

"Don't go there, babe. This is *all* on him. All of it." He dropped a tender kiss on her lips. "He admitted to killing Barry, hoping I'd get kicked out of ALPHA."

"*What*? That's so messed up."

"He's the one who hacked into my client accounts, activated their cameras, and posted the videos."

"But why?"

"He wanted my business to fail."

After Hawk brought her up to speed, he said, "we've gotta arrest him, but we need backup. I'll call Cooper on the way to the hospital."

Addison pulled out her phone, logged in to ALPHA's secure site. "Tommy's at a bar in Arlington." She kissed his cheek. "How are you feeling?"

"Besides furious?"

She stroked his thigh. "Physically."

"I'm good. One of my toes is numb and another is pins and needles, but they'll come back." He'd been caressing her back, running his fingers through her long hair. "I love you."

Their eyes met. Her smile made his heart pound faster in his chest.

"I love you," she replied.

"I'm gonna miss you."

She stiffened. "What does that mean?"

He kissed her. "I love seeing you every day. Love that we live together."

She sighed. "I thought you were ending things."

"How'd you jump to that?"

"You told me you were gonna miss me."

"You don't need my protection, so I figured you'd move back home."

"What do *you* want?"

"You, babe. Every single day." He captured her face in his hands and kissed her. "How 'bout you?"

"Just you," she replied.

In the dark, they shared another kiss. "Move in with me," he murmured. "Or I'll move in with you. Either works, as long as we're together."

Her smile made his heart soar. "I would love that."

Addison's phone rang. "It's Jericho." She put the call on speaker. "Hey, how's everyone doing?" she asked.

"We're good," Jericho replied. "You've been gone a while."

"Yo, bro," Hawk said.

"Hey, what's goin' on?"

"I'll tell you when I see you," Hawk said. "Be there in twenty."

Hawk waited while Addison climbed into Jericho's vehicle before sliding behind the wheel of his SUV. Despite the temperate weather, he turned on the heat.

As he followed Addison to the hospital, he called Cooper.

After giving him the short version, Cooper said, "I'm gonna kill him."

"Aren't you gonna arrest him?"

"After I kill him," Cooper bit out.

"Addison found him through the app. He's at a bar near his house. Keep an eye on him for me," Hawk said. "After we drop Jericho's SUV at the hospital, we'll sync up."

"How are you feeling?" Cooper asked.

"Furious. He fucking killed Barry."

"How's Addison holding up?" Cooper asked.

"She's my rock."

"You ready to document your relationship with HR?" Cooper asked.

"That obvious?" Hawk replied.

"Only to everyone in the wedding party," Cooper replied, and the men laughed. "Seriously, I'm glad you're okay. You're always there for everyone, all the damn time. The thought of you in that freezer makes my blood run cold."

Hawk chuffed out a laugh. "Good one. I needed that."

"Tommy won't get away with this."

"The son of a bitch took my phone and turned it off, because he knows about the ALPHA tracker app."

"But he doesn't know about the chip in our necks," Cooper replied.

"No, he doesn't," Hawk replied. "I can't wait to see his expression when his dead cousin arrests his ass."

The call ended as Addison rolled into the hospital parking lot. She parked Jericho's Escalade, got in Hawk's SUV.

"I called Jericho and brought him up to speed," Addison said.

Hawk pulled up to the hospital entrance as Jericho strode outside. Both he and Addison got out.

Jericho pulled Hawk in for a hand-clasp. "You want me to kill him? Because I will. Just say the word."

"We got this," Hawk replied.

"You need me to come with?" Jericho asked.

"Liv just had your child," Hawk replied. "Stay with her."

"*She's* the one who told me to go," Jericho said. "Addison, you saved my boy."

She ran her hand down Hawk's back. "Best thing I've ever done."

"She's amazing," Hawk said before regarding Jericho. "Well, Papa, whad'ya have?"

Jericho beamed. "A son. Liam Bryan Savage."

Hawk hugged him. "Congratulations. I can't wait to meet my godson."

Addison handed Jericho his keys. "I parked right over there." She pointed. "Tell Livy I'll be back tomorrow to see her."

"*We'll* be back tomorrow," Hawk added.

"If it were up to me, I'd take him out." Jericho growled.

"Me, too," Addison ground out.

Her phone rang. "It's Cooper." She answered, put the call on speaker. "I'm here with Hawk and Jericho."

"He's on the move," Cooper said. "Who needs a weapon?"

"I do," Hawk replied.

"I've got mine," Addison said.

"We're gone," Hawk said to Jericho.

Jericho pulled him in for another hug. "Love you, bro."

"Love you, too," Hawk replied.

Jericho hugged Addison. "Thank you," he murmured.

Hawk and Addison jumped into the SUV and drove out of the parking lot.

"Where're we headed?" Hawk asked Cooper.

"He just pulled into a garden apartment complex in Arlington. I gotta check this address." Cooper went silent. After a minute, he said, "he's at home."

Ten minutes later they arrived, and parked next to Cooper. He and Addison exited the SUV.

"I brought backup," Cooper said after he and Danelle joined them.

Danielle held out two Kevlar vests. After Hawk and Addison put them on, Danielle handed Hawk a Glock.

"He lives on the ground floor, so I'm going around back," Danielle said.

"I'll go with you," Addison added.

Danielle handed comms to Hawk and Addison, and they slipped them into their ears. In silence, they strode toward the building.

"If he runs, we'll stop him," Addison said as she and Danielle made their way around the back of the building. When the women were in place, Hawk and Cooper walked down the short flight of stairs to Tommy's apartment.

Hawk waited in the shadows while Cooper approached the front door.

BAM! BAM! BAM!

"Tommy, it's Cooper Grant. Open up."

Hawk's fingers curled into fists, the fury rushing to the surface.

No response.

Cooper tried the handle. Locked. He raised his weapon to shoot out the lock when the door opened.

"Oh, whoa. Cooper," Tommy said.

Cooper pushed into the apartment, grabbed Tommy by his shirt, and shoved him face-first against the wall. "You're under the arrest for the murder of Barry Kase and the attempted murder of Nicholas Hawk."

Hawk moseyed in.

Cooper secured his wrists with a zip tie, then patted him down. When finished, he spun him around.

Tommy glared at Cooper, then his gaze jumped to Hawk. He gasped, his eyes grew large. "Oh, heyyyyyy, Nicky."

Hawk got up in Tommy's face. "You piece of shit. You're gonna rot in prison."

Hawk spotted his phone on the sofa, snatched it up, and turned it on.

"We're bringing him out," Cooper said to Addison and Danielle.

As they brought Tommy into the hall and up the stairs, curious neighbors peeked out their front doors. Outside, they led Tommy to Cooper's vehicle as Addison and Danielle strode over.

When Tommy saw Addison, he said, "You deserve better than him. I would have worshipped you."

"Shut the fuck up," Addison growled.

Danielle opened the back door of the SUV. "Hold him so I can zip tie his ankles."

As she knelt, a motorcycle whizzed over, stopped twenty feet away. The driver pulled a weapon—*POP! POP! POP!* —and sped away.

Tommy dropped. Cooper pulled him off Danielle and shoved him into the SUV. Addison aimed her weapon, but the bike was already flying down the street.

"Tommy's hit," Cooper said. "Team, talk to me."

"I'm okay." Hawk rushed over to Addison. "Are you hurt?"

"Not hit," Addison replied.

"Not hit," Danielle echoed.

"Coop?" Hawk asked.

"Negative," Cooper replied.

"We're going after that bike," Hawk said.

"No," Cooper said. "You could be ambushed."

Tommy had been once twice in the head, once in the chest, but Hawk still checked his carotid. "No pulse. Looks like Tommy had some enemies of his own."

"Anyone get the license plate?" Addison asked.

No one had.

"The biker was in all black with a tinted visor," Cooper said. "Do we have anything to go on?"

No one did.

"We'll take his body to the funeral home ALPHA uses," Cooper said. "I'm sorry, Hawk. Despite the hell he put you through, he was family."

"When you call his mom and dad—" Hawk paused. "They don't need to know the truth."

"I'll tell them he got shot in the line of duty." Cooper squeezed Hawk's shoulder. "You're a good man, Nicholas Hawk."

"I'm not doing it for him," Hawk replied. "I'm doing it for my family."

THE FOLLOWING MORNING, Hawk told Addison he had a meeting with Stryker. He hated lying to her, but she'd know the truth soon enough. After driving her home, he went inside and checked her house.

"Why are you clearing my home?" she asked. "The threat is gone."

He wrapped her in his arms and kissed her. "Well, I wasn't gonna just drop you off. You haven't been home in weeks. Haqazzii could have left a bomb here."

She shivered. "He's history."

"I'll be back in an hour or two," he said.

"I'll be busy packing." She kissed him.

"Why don't we hire a moving company?"

"I don't need one. I'm not keeping my furniture," she said. "Just my clothing and paintings."

One more panty-melting kiss before she walked him out front.

"Miss me," he said.

"You miss me," she replied with a wink.

He hopped into his sports car, slid on his shades, and left. It had been weeks since he'd driven the Mercedes and he appreciated the breeze in his hair, the sun on his face. It was a great day to be alive.

Once out of Addison's neighborhood, he made the call.

"Good morning, Nicholas," Z answered. "How're we doing?"

What Z meant was how is Addison doing.

"Addison's safe," Hawk replied.

"I'm asking about you," Z said. "I heard what happened."

"I'm okay. Hard to believe my cousin tried to kill me."

"Family dynamics are complicated."

"I need to talk to you. Should I drop by your office?"

"Swing by and pick me up. We'll have breakfast at Rudy's." The line went dead.

Twenty minutes later, he and Z were sitting in a booth at the greasy spoon.

"Always good to see you guys." Rudy filled their mugs with coffee. "The usual?"

They both nodded.

Rudy's was DC's best-kept secret. Delicious food served fast. Locals breezed by the hole-in-the-wall. Tourists didn't know the restaurant existed. The eatery was nestled in a neighborhood near the Capitol, so it was always filled with congresspersons and senators. On occasion, even the President stopped by for a burger.

"Any idea who took out Tommy?" Z murmured.

Rudy delivered their small orange juices and left.

"No," Hawk replied. "Cooper's got a team looking into it."

The conversation continued until their breakfasts were delivered and Rudy topped off their mugs. "We good?"

"Looks great, Rudy," Hawk replied.

"Best breakfast in DC," Z said.

"Thank you, thank you." Rudy left, and the men dug in.

"I've fallen in love with Addison," Hawk said.

Z grinned. "Finally."

Hawk chuckled. "How did everyone see what we couldn't?"

"It's that saying... can't see the forest for the trees." Z forked egg into his mouth.

"If you say so," Hawk replied. "She's at home packing. She's moving in with me."

Z arched an eyebrow.

"I'm asking her to marry me. Your blessing would be nice." Hawk dug into his hash browns.

That made Z chuckle. "You have it. You want the fatherly lecture?"

"Oh, sure, put me through the paces, 'cause I haven't been through enough."

Z chuffed out a laugh. "I'll be damn proud to call you my son-in-law. Does she know you're proposing?"

"Not a clue. If she says yes, we're going ring shopping today."

"I'm very cynical when it comes to relationships lasting, but that's because my own marriage ended so badly." Z set down the mug. "I think you two have what it takes to go the distance."

"So do I, Philip. I'm going to put her first, have her back, and be the loving husband she deserves."

"I know you will, but as her dad, I appreciate you saying that."

When the men finished, they stood. Z tossed cash on the table before extending his hand. "I hope she says yes."

"Any reason you think she won't?"

Z glanced over Hawk's shoulder. "One of the President's senior advisors just walked in. He's a talker. Let's duck out the back." Z pushed open the back door of the restaurant.

They made their way towards Hawk's car. "Addison was wrecked when her mom left. While she's extremely brave, she's very timid when it comes to romantic relationships. But you won't know until you ask her, right?"

When Hawk had arrived at Rudy's, he had all the confidence in the world. As he drove Z back to DOJ, he wondered if Addison was ready to make a lifelong commitment.

He was ready—more than ready—to commit himself to her for the rest of his life. After dropping Z off, he headed toward her place.

The only way I'll know is if I ask her.

His phone rang with a call from his mom.

Here we go.

"Hey, Mom."

"Nicky, I have the worst news," his mom said. "Tommy was killed."

"I'm sorry to hear that."

"It was work related. I don't know anything more."

"Thanks for telling me. How are you holding up?"

"I'm very sad, but I know his work was dangerous. Dad and I are so relieved you work in an office. So much safer."

"Yeah, me, too." He paused. "I've got good news to share."

"Oh, I'd love that."

"Addison's moving in with me."

"That's wonderful! I'm happy for you, honey."

Stryker was calling, so he ended the call with his mom and answered. "What's happening?"

"I found the point of entry for the security breach at your company," Stryker said.

"Had to be Tommy."

"Yeah. He got in through Margaret Larson's email," Stryker explained. "Mags is your GM, right?"

"Yeah," Hawk replied. "How'd he do it?"

"He sent her a photo of the two of them," Stryker said. "Embedded in the pic was an executable microprogram that created a VPN connection between the two machines. From there, he gained access to your clients, found the ones he wanted to target, turned on their cameras, and posted the videos. He'd cloaked his IP address, but I traced it back to the photo. He wanted to be you, bro."

"Looks that way, but he went too far," Hawk said. "Thanks for getting back to me. How's married life?"

"You know, I didn't think it would be different—"

"But it is," Hawk said, finishing his sentence.

"Yeah, it is. I'm happy. Hey, Em, you like being married?" He grew quiet, then laughed.

"What did she say?" Hawk asked.

"She told me she's happy now, but you should check back in a few hours."

On a laugh, Hawk hung up.

He rode the rest of the way in silence, his thoughts on Addison. Would she say yes? Would she want to spend her life with him, but *not* marry him? Asking Addison to marry him was a big step, but he was ready to take it.

He pulled down her street, parked out front. She walked outside, pulling two large suitcases. He hopped out.

"Hey!" she called out.

"Hey, baby." He lifted the heavy bag, set it in her SUV, then pulled her into his arms.

She peered into his eyes, then ran her fingertip between his eyebrows. "That worry line should be gone. What's wrong?"

He forced a smile. "All good." His gaze floated over her face.

She smiled up at him. "I've got more bags."

He loaded the second suitcase, then followed her inside. Once they'd filled her vehicle, they caravanned back to his townhouse.

After they brought everything into the living room, she hitched her hands to her hips and stared at the bags, duffels, and suitcases. "I'll do this later. Let's go play. I hardly ever call out at work."

They hopped in his sports car and drove out of his neighborhood.

"Where should we go?" she asked.

"I got this," he replied.

Addison turned up the tunes and started singing along. He joined her and they finished out the song.

"I love singing with you," she said. "I love that sometimes you're in tune, sometimes you aren't. There are times when we hit the harmonies just right. It's never the same and it always makes me happy."

At the stop light, he leaned over and kissed her. "I hope that's how our life is. Never the same, and it always makes you happy."

She smiled. "I love that you're so romantic."

He drove to the farmhouse. As he was parking, she said, "Somehow, all roads lead us here. I had a feeling this is where we'd end up."

"Why's that?" he asked.

She shrugged. "No idea."

He led her inside and up the stairs, then into one of the back bedrooms. He opened the window, stepped onto the flat roof of the back porch. He turned back, extended his hand.

She clasped it, climbed out. They walked to the middle and sat, staring out at the acres and acres of property.

"This is a fantastic view," she said.

"When I'd spend summers here, this was my bedroom," Hawk explained. "I'd climb out here at night, lay on the roof and stare up at the universe. When I was a teen, I smoked weed out here." Hawk smiled at the memory. "One time, Granddad joined me, took one hit, then told me to never, ever smoke it again."

They shared a laugh.

"Did you?" she asked.

"No."

"Why not?"

"Drugs aren't my thing, plus I respected him so much, I didn't want to disappoint him."

She ran the back of her fingers down his whiskered cheek.

"This place always felt like home to me, though I loved the house I grew up in," Hawk continued. "I haven't been on the roof in years. Feels right to be here with you."

She leaned her head on his shoulder. "Thank you for sharing this with me."

"Do you think I should sell or renovate the house and cultivate the land?"

"Would you live here?" she asked.

He turned toward her. "Hard to give up my townhouse. I love having a view of the river."

"You can have both," she replied.

He captured her hands in his, stroked her soft skin. "What would *you* want?"

She broke away and stared out at the property. "For you to be happy."

His heart kicked up speed. He had to tell her how he felt, what he wanted.

This is it.

"I remember the first time I saw you," he began. "You'd just started with ALPHA and we passed each other in the hallway. I turned around and followed you into the break room to welcome you to the team."

Turning to face him, she smiled. "I remember meeting you."

"For me, the attraction was instant. Your smile got tattooed on my brain." He tapped his head.

"I remember you had *great* eye contact."

"That's 'cause I couldn't stop looking at you." He chuckled. "When we started working together, I knew you were special. Once we started hanging out, I realized that our relationship was different from anything I'd ever had. The only reason I didn't screw this up is because we stayed friends. I'm angry, disappointed, and sad over what happened with Tommy. But everything changed for me when he told me he'd been with you."

"Oh, wow," she whispered.

"I've never been jealous in my life, but knowing that made me crazy."

"You had my heart," she whispered. "He was a stranger at some party."

"It was the kick in the ass I needed to stop being afraid to love again." He lifted her hand to his lips, kissed her soft skin. It's always been you, Addison."

She smiled. "I loved that you kissed me in the henhouse."

He captured her face in his hands and kissed her, their tongues softly stroking each other. When the kiss ended, he peered into her eyes.

"I will always put you first," he continued. "Being with you is what matters most. I love that we're Operatives, that we're partners, but I want it all with you."

"Children?" she murmured.

"I didn't want any, because of what I'd lost. That level of emotional pain wrecked me, and I wasn't even a dad yet."

"You were a dad the minute you found out you were having a baby," she replied.

He nodded. After a pause, he said, "I would love to have children with you, babe."

She stared into her lap, then turned toward the property. Not wanting to rush her, he stayed quiet while the August sun beat down on them.

After a long moment, she said, "I want to be a mom, but I would need to know, in my heart, that my relationship with my partner or spouse was unbreakable." She gazed into his eyes. "I think that's an unreasonable expectation for anyone, especially in a world where things are always changing. Someone better could come along. Younger, prettier, smarter, or just different."

"Addison, are you concerned I'd leave you, like your mom left your family?"

Her chest tightened. "Yeah."

"Do you trust me on a mission?"

"With my life."

"Do you know that you're my best friend?"

She smiled. "I'm your best *female* friend. You've got your band of brothers and that bond *is* unbreakable."

"I would rather have a lifetime with you and *no* children, than a life with someone else and children."

She stared at him for the longest time. "My heart is so full right now."

"I love you. That won't change. I know myself. I know my heart. As long as we're together, I'm a happy man."

Her loving smile made his heart soar.

"There's just more thing," he said.

"What's that?"

"Marry me, Addison."

Her mouth fell open. "*What?*"

Without question, Addison adored him. Flat-out loved Hawk with her entire being. But marry him?

"When I thought I was going to die in that freezer, I made myself a promise," he said. "If I got out alive, I was going to put myself out there with you."

"Okay," she murmured.

"You're my missing puzzle piece... and I'm yours. Baby, this is our happily ever after. All you gotta do is say yes."

Saying yes terrified her, but...saying no? That would be the biggest mistake of her life. As she gazed into his eyes, an inner peace came over her, and her heart overflowed with love.

"Yes, I'll marry you. I can't imagine our lives with anyone but each other."

Their kisses were tender, filled with passion and unwavering love. She melted at the way he peered into her eyes, how he caressed the back of her neck, the smile that spread across his beautiful face.

"I'm excited and terrified," she whispered.

"We got this," he replied. "One step at a time."

"Whew, so we're not running to the courthouse this afternoon?"

"Hell, no," he replied. "But I am putting a rock on your finger."

She shot him a smile. "That sounds fun."

"There's one more thing I want to run by you."

"Please, no," she murmured. "I'm not sure I can take any more."

He laughed, then pointed to the property. "I want to buy out my family and own this outright with you."

"Wow, well you're definitely a man of action, but we don't need to do all of this in a day."

Hawk stood, extended his hands. "How 'bout we swing by the hospital and visit our godson, then go check out some engagement rings?"

She placed her hands in his and he pulled her to her feet. "Love it," she replied.

They crawled back inside, he shut the window.

"We're engaged!" she exclaimed. "That's crazy."

"Sounds *perfect* to me."

As they made their way downstairs, he said, "I asked your dad for his blessing."

She stopped on the last step. Eye-to-eye, she draped her arms over his shoulders. "You planned to ask me?"

"Hell, yeah. This is the most important decision of our lives. I met your dad this morning at Rudy's. I'm sorry I lied about meeting with Stryker, but I couldn't tell you without inviting you... and I couldn't do that."

She kissed him. "You're forgiven. Was he surprised?"

"Maybe, but he's happy for us. He thinks we have what it takes for the long haul."

Addison smiled. "Me too."

They swung by the hospital. Livy was resting in bed. Jericho was holding Liam and whispering to him.

"What are you doing here?" Livy asked.

"I gotta meet my godson," Hawk replied.

"How are you back on your feet after what happened yesterday?" Livy asked.

"Life's too short to waste one second," Hawk said as he took the infant from Jericho.

"Hi, Liam. I'm Nicky, your godfather. How you doing, little guy?" Hawk smiled down at him. "He's beautiful. How are you feeling?"

"I feel great," Jericho replied, and they laughed.

"Idiot," Hawk said. "Liv, how are you?"

"Doing good. I'm ready to get Liam home. How are you?"

Hawk slid his gaze to Addison. "We're doing great, don'tcha think, babe?"

"We got engaged," Addison blurted.

Jericho grinned. "Now we're talkin'!"

"Congratulations!" Livy exclaimed. "That's so exciting."

"Got a ring?" Jericho asked.

"Not yet." Addison grinned. "That's next."

Jericho pulled out his phone. "I got you." He made a call. "Nico, Jericho Savage. A close friend of mine got engaged." Jericho listened. "Appreciate that. Hawk and Addison." Jericho hung up. "Go to Nico's in Chevy Chase. He'll take care of you."

After spending another hour with their godson, they took off for the jewelry store.

Nico welcomed them in, raved about Jericho.

"We love him too," Addison agreed.

Nico ushered them to the engagement ring case. "We can use these as our starting point to create a custom ring. I'll give you some time to look everything over."

"These are beautiful," she said, "but I don't want an engagement ring." She moseyed over to the eternity band case. "I'd like an eternity band."

Hawk joined her. "It's different. I like these."

"Me, too," she replied.

Nico pulled out several, and they sat at the fitting desk while she tried them on.

"I can also design a ring for you," Nico explained. "Will you both be wearing a wedding band?"

"Yes," they answered in unison.

"I can create an engagement band that compliments your wedding band," Nico said. "Or are you moving the engagement ring to a different finger?"

Addison studied the rings. "I'll move the engagement to my right hand."

After trying on several, she selected a platinum band with brilliant round diamonds, interspersed between platinum Xs.

"That looks beautiful on you, babe," Hawk said.

"Classic and stunning," Nico said. "Let's measure your finger."

Once they'd ordered the engagement band, Hawk suggested they check out all the jewelry. Several minutes later, Addison found a pair of drop heart earrings in silver that she liked. With a promise from Nico that the engagement band would be ready in a few weeks, they left the store.

On the way back to Hawk's, Addison's phone rang.

"I want to shut out the world for one day," she said. "Just one day. Is that too much to ask?"

"Don't answer it," he replied.

She pulled out her phone. "It's Liliana from the club. I gotta take this." She answered. "Hi, Liliana."

"Hey, Addison, I'm sorry to bother you, but I have news."

27

NO TIME TO DIE

"What's going on?" Addison asked.

"I got offered a job that's related to my graduate studies," Liliana explained. "Unfortunately, I have to resign from the club."

"Congratulations," Addison said. "You must be excited."

"Absolutely," Liliana replied. "You were so great to work for. I have a little something for you. I know it's super short notice, but are you free for happy hour today?"

"Hang on a sec." Addison muted the phone. "Liliana's quitting the club. She wants to get together for a drink."

"Go," Hawk said.

She kissed him, then unmuted the phone. "I can make it."

"Perfect. My condo building does this great cocktail party on the rooftop. It's to die for. How's five thirty?"

It was just after four.

"That'll work," Addison replied.

"I'll text you the address and meet you in the lobby. Can't wait."

Addison hung up. "We need a GM to handle the day-to-day at the club."

Hawk drove down his street. "I'll put the word out about that. Let's invite your dad to dinner this week."

"I love that." She dialed his number, put the call on speaker.

"Hello, dear," answered her dad. "How's your day going?"

"Daddy, Hawk and I want you to come for dinner one night this week. What's your schedule like?"

"How's tomorrow?" her dad asked.

Hawk nodded.

"That's great. See you then." She hung up.

Hawk pulled into the garage. After cutting the engine, he wrapped his hand around her thigh. "After you get back from happy hour, we'll have the evening to ourselves." He hitched a brow. "What should we do?"

"Celebrate," she replied. "All night long."

AT FIVE-FORTY, ADDISON walked into the upscale lobby of Liliana's high-rise condo building, near the Navy Yard in Southeast DC.

Liliana was dressed in a white maxidress, her dark hair pulled into a pretty updo. Smiling broadly, she hurried over and hugged Addison. "Thanks for coming. Let's head upstairs to our table."

Hawk parked in ALPHA's lot, grabbed his laptop bag, and walked to the retina scanner on the back door. He wanted to share his good news with Cooper and report his relationship with Addison to HR. The light turned green and he breezed inside. He wound his way through the building 'til he got to his boss's office.

Cooper was working at his desk. His brother, Prescott, was at the conference table, head down, focused on a cell phone.

"Hey, when'd you get back?" Hawk asked his brother.

"Just now." Prescott pulled him in for a hug.

Hawk laughed. "Why are we hugging it out?"

"Cooper told me that Tommy tried to kill you," Prescott said.

"Prescott lost it," Cooper added. "If Tommy wasn't already dead, Prescott would have wasted him."

"My big brother loves me," Hawk said before eyeing the cell phone. "Whatcha doin' with that burner?"

"I need your software," Prescott said.

"We found it at Tommy's," Cooper replied.

Hawk pulled out a cable, connected the phone to his laptop, sat down, and got to work. After he started his program, he eyed the guys.

"I got engaged," Hawk stated, matter-of-factly.

Both men stared at him.

Cooper chuckled. "No, you didn't. He's messing with us."

Prescott broke into a grin. "No, he's not. Congratulations, Nicky!"

"Addison and I got close," Hawk said. "When I thought I was gonna die in that freezer, I didn't want to live another moment without her."

"It's always been you two," Prescott said. "But you weren't ready."

"I'm super happy for you," Cooper said extending his hand.

"Life is good," Hawk said.

Prescott smiled. "I'm happy to hear you say that, Nicky."

"Me, too, brother."

Ding!

Hawk's software program had unlocked the burner. He unplugged it from the cable and handed it to Prescott.

"I'm gonna head to HR to let them know about Addison and me," Hawk said.

Prescott attention was fixed on Tommy's burner. "Whoa, this is messed up." He handed the phone to Hawk.

Hawk read through the text thread on Tommy's phone. "What the fucking fuck."

"Read them to me," Cooper said.

Hawk read out loud.

"*Eliminate Hawk.*"

"*Just take him out already.*"

"*Kill the motherfucker.*"

"Jesus," Cooper bit out.

"This one says, '*Once he's gone, Addison is yours. What are you waiting for?*'"

"He had an accomplice," Cooper said, "but why would he turn on Tommy?"

"Tommy only sent one text," Hawk said.

"Read it to us," Cooper urged.

"It says, '*I did it. I killed him.*' And Tommy's accomplice responded with, '*Nice work.*'"

Hawk's blood turned to ice, while dread made his stomach drop.

Tommy was gone, but his accomplice wasn't.

At the moment, he was safe... but was Addison?

Addison and Liliana rode the elevator to the penthouse level.

"Tell me about your new job," Addison said.

"It's my dream job," Liliana said. "I'm going to be working with my family."

The doors slid open and Liliana led the way toward the flight of stairs to the rooftop. Through the door they went and up the stairs.

At the top of the steps, Addison shoved open another door and stepped outside. She expected to see a finished balcony with several tables, a bar, and a few wait staff. Instead, the rooftop was unfinished. In the center of the expansive space stood a small, round table with two chairs.

"What the hell is this?" Addison blurted.

"A one-way party for two." The harshness in Liliana's voice made Addison spin toward her. On instinct, Addison went for her weapon, but she'd left it at Hawk's.

Dread filled her soul.

Cooper's phone rang. "Cooper Grant." As he listened, his eyebrows pinched together, and he strode to his laptop. A few clicks later, he said, "Got it."

Cooper hung up, slid his gaze to Hawk and Prescott. "That was CIA Associate Director, Anita Robinson. Months ago, they got word that Aziz Haqazzii—the terrorist you just took out—had an accomplice who'd gotten into the country undetected, despite being on the No-Fly List. They followed up, but the lead went nowhere... until today. Anita just sent over a picture."

Hawk walked around Cooper's desk and eyed the picture of a woman dressed in military fatigues, a machine gun cradled in her arms.

Adrenaline pounded through him. "Fuck, no."

Everything went into slow motion.

"Cooper, I'm firing up the chopper. Call whoever the fuck you need to and make sure there aren't F-18s on my ass when I enter the No-Fly Zone. Prescott, you're with me. Weapon-up."

"Where are you going?" Cooper asked.

"To take that terrorist out."

"You know who she is?" Cooper asked.

"That's the bartender at our nightclub, and Addison is with her now."

"Ah, fuck." Cooper snatched up his phone.

"Where are they?" Prescott asked.

"On a rooftop in DC." Hawk bolted from the office, his legs eating up the floor.

"This is never gonna work," Prescott said after he caught up.

"I'm not gonna lose her. Not now. Not ever."

Addison glanced around. She was on the roof of a fifteen-story building. Her only escape route—the heavy, metal door—was blocked by Liliana. But it was the thick, winter vest Liliana had shrugged into that made Addison's mouth go bone dry.

"What's with the vest?" Addison asked, trying to sound casual.

Liliana strode toward her, a crazed look in her eyes. She went to grab Addison, who blocked her arm, spun around, and kicked her.

Liliana jumped out of the way, grabbed Addison's leg and rushed forward, sending Addison crashing down. Flat on her back and in pain, she stared up at Liliana.

Liliana pointed a gun at her. "Where's your phone?"

Go fuck yourself. Addison refused to answer.

"Get. Up." Her sinister tone caught Addison's ear.

Addison pushed off the cement rooftop.

"Hands behind your head," Liliana ordered.

Addison did as commanded. When Liliana patted her down, Addison grabbed her arm, twisted, and snatched the weapon.

"Face down on the ground," Addison bit out. "Now!"

Liliana threw back her head and laughed. "No bullets, bitch." She pulled open the vest, revealing explosives duct taped to the inside. "I don't need a gun. We're about to blow sky high."

Ohgod, no. Addison's pulse kicked up as her mind raced with possible escape routes.

"Now, give me your goddamn phone!" Liliana slapped Addison across her face.

The sharp sting made her eyes water, but she refused to make a sound. As she handed over her phone, she held her finger over the emergency button.

"No," barked Liliana as she grabbed the phone from her and turned it off.

Addison bolted to the fire door, grabbed the handle, and yanked, almost wrenching her arm from the socket. It was locked.

Liliana moseyed over, a menacing smile etched on her face. "Nope, not an exit. Only one way down and that'll be in a thousand little pieces. Boo-hoo."

Addison was running out of options to save herself.

"Let's sit," Liliana said. "I know so much about you, but you know nothing about me."

Addison glanced back at the door before making her way toward the table. The longer Liliana talked, the better Addison's chance of survival. She sat on the edge of the chair, her thoughts focused on finding a way out.

Liliana stood behind the chair across from her and glowered. Then, she spun the chair around and sat.

After a long pause, she said, "Family means everything to me, so you can imagine how much I hate you."

"I don't know your family."

"My real name is Haqazzii," Liliana said. "You and your CIA team killed my father, Abdel Haqazzii."

Addison stared at her in disbelief.

This is bad. Really bad.

"I watched in horror as that military monster from America murdered him in cold blood. Revenge became my way of life. I learned how to build bombs, then a new identity was created for me, as a student. In America, I was reunited with my brother, Aziz." Her face split into a menacing grin. "That was a joyous day."

Pausing, Liliana stared out at the horizon before flicking her gaze back to Addison.

"If Ronald Jenning hadn't gone public, I would never have found him." She hitched an eyebrow. "Finding you took me three long years. Then, you led me right to that snitch, Habibi, and her stupid coffee shop."

"Abdel Haqazzii was a terrorist, responsible for thousands of deaths," Addison bit out.

"A lie," Liliana said. "He was a respected businessman."

She's drunk so much Kool-Aid, she's drowning in it.

"But that wasn't enough. I wanted you to suffer like I did. My dad was gone. I wanted yours gone too." Liliana's shoulders slumped. "But I failed."

"Ohgod," Addison whispered. "The car bomb."

"I did my homework on you, honey," Liliana said. "The mental mind games started from the minute we met. I told you my name is Liliana Moore. Hey, that's your mom's name. The mom who abandoned you. What a crazy coincidence. Liliana Moore, Liliana Moore. Say it with me."

Addison glared at her.

"Everything I told you was a lie. My birthday isn't in August. I'm not a GW grad student, and I don't have an older sister who's an artist. All lies to give you a false sense of security. You thought we had so much in common. You trusted me, but I hated you and I hated working at your stupid club. I hated pretending that we were friends."

Liliana fell silent.

Addison eyed her phone on the roof. *If I can knock her out, I can call for help.*

"I shot out the cameras at your home," Liliana said. "I tried to kill your little boyfriend when you were playing cops and robbers at that shooting range. Lucky for you, I'm a terrible shot."

Addison seethed with hatred. For months, she'd been Liliana's target and she hadn't suspected a damn thing.

"What about Tommy?" Addison asked. "Was that real?"

"Nothing about me is real," Liliana hissed. "Tommy was obsessed with you and so jealous of Hawk that I actually pitied him. He was a mess, but that's what made him so easy to manipulate. I encouraged him to kill Hawk. As soon as he did, I killed Tommy. He'd served his purpose."

"Hawk's not dead," Addison said.

Liliana narrowed her gaze. "Tommy couldn't even get that right."

Addison eyed the vest. *Can I get that off her?*

She couldn't throw it off the roof. The bombs would explode, potentially injuring or killing dozens. If she could heave it to the other side of the roof, would she be far enough way to save herself if it detonated?

"My brother, Aziz, was hours away from completing one of the most successful missions of our lives," Liliana said, snapping Addison from her thoughts.

"He was going to assassinate world leaders, something our father would have been so proud of. But he blew himself and his base station up. Today, I will be reunited with him and our father, and we will rejoice in our triumph that you are dead."

She thought of Hawk. *We could have had the best life together.*

Addison's heart was broken. She didn't want to die like this, but she wasn't going to beg. And she would not cry. She, too, had been trained. Survivor training, imprisonment training. She would leave this life with dignity and grace.

Her dad's familiar words comforted her.

"What happens when we let emotion take over?"

"We become vulnerable."

She would rather die than show Liliana any fear.

In order to pull off this mission, Hawk needed the Venom, the larger, Marine helicopter with the open cargo area.

As he finished his scaled-down pre-flight check, he patted the side of the large bird. "Do right by us, baby."

He hopped inside, fired it up, then glanced back at his brother.

"Strap in," he said to Prescott through the headset.

Prescott's phone rang. He answered, listened, and hung up.

"You've got to let ATC know you're flying into the No-Fly Zone," Prescott explained. "Cooper called them, but they need to hear from you."

"Copy," Hawk replied. "Here we go, babe."

He lifted the helo off the ground.

"Tower, this is Bravo King Whiskey Alpha Alpha," Hawk said. "Alpha Alpha requests permission to land on rooftop, 1100 First Street, Southeast DC."

"Alpha Alpha, that's in the NFZ—"

"I'm flying there whether you clear me or not," Hawk replied, keeping his tone relaxed and even-keeled on purpose.

"You're in violation—"

"This should have been cleared," Hawk replied.

As he flew east, Hawk yanked out his phone and dialed.

Z answered. "Did you pop the question?"

"Addison is being held by a terrorist," Hawk said. "I'm flying into DCs NFZ. If F-18s are deployed, then it needs to be for a fucking escort back to ALPHA."

"Where is she?" Z asked.

He gave Z the address. "I can do this, and so can Addison. I just need to get to her without interference. Make it happen." He hung up and pulled his headset back into place.

"If you violate the no-fly zone, military aircraft will be deployed," said the air traffic controller.

Ignoring that, he refocused his full attention on his destination and increased his speed.

Two minutes later, the controller said, "Alpha Alpha, you're clear to land at 1100 First Street, Southeast DC."

"Alpha Alpha cleared to land," Hawk replied.

Thank you, Philip.

Five minutes later, he arrived in DC and had pinpointed Addison's location. Prescott slid open the side door of the aircraft and was peering out with binos.

"What do you see?" Hawk asked.

"Still looking," Prescott replied. A few seconds later, he said, "Got her. She's facing the west. What's your plan? Are you landing on the roof?"

"No, it can't support the weight of the bird. Drop the rope ladder out and make sure it's secured to the craft."

"That's insane, Nicky."

"Just fucking do it," Hawk barked. "Then, waste that terrorist."

Addison had spotted the helo in the distance and hope welled up inside her. Liliana was pacing on the other side of the table, back and forth while she ranted about her magnificent family. Addison had stopped listening, her thoughts fully engaged on listening for the aircraft.

Please be him. Please come for me.

Addison's gaze swept the roof. It wasn't big enough for the helo to land on, plus the building might not be able to withstand its weight. Addison closed her eyes, started doing her rhythmic breathing. A four-count inhale, hold for four, release slowly. Pause. Repeat.

"Are you fucking sleeping?" Liliana screamed.

Nice and easy.

Addison opened her eyes, her gaze sweeping the horizon. The sound had grown louder, but she didn't have a visual on the craft.

Then, like the Phoenix rising from the ashes, the giant bird rose up from the side of the building. Addison's heart leapt, but she kept her breathing in check. Hawk was in the cockpit, the side door open, Prescott strapped in, a long gun in his grip.

Then, she saw the rope ladder and her hope fell flat... as flat as she'd be if she jumped off that building and landed with a splat on the hard pavement below.

Ohgod, no, Hawk. I can't.

Liliana spun around and marched toward the craft, waving her arms, like she was being attacked by a swarm of killer bees. "Motherfuckers! Get the hell away from us."

Liliana opened the jacket, revealing the sticks of C-4, taped to her vest.

Addison waved Hawk away. "Go," she screamed, even though he couldn't hear her. She continued waving him off, but he wouldn't fly away.

Liliana pulled out a hand-held detonator. "You can't win!"

BANG! BANG! BANG! BANG!

Liliana dropped, the detonator falling from her hand. Addison ran over to confirm she was dead. That's when she saw the timer attached to the explosives, counting down, with fifteen seconds left.

It's now or never.

She eyed the dangling rope ladder.

Do it! You can do it!

Mustering all her courage, Addison started running. She had one chance. She homed in one of the rungs, ran to the edge and jumped. She crashed into the ladder, grabbed a rung, but the ladder started swinging from the force of her impact.

Hawk pulled away from the building with her trailing behind, like a kite's tail blowing in the wind. She started climbing, squeezing the rungs with all her strength. She could barely catch her breath, the chopper blades whipping the air in a million different directions.

One rung at a time she climbed toward her future with the man of her dreams.

Prescott reached out, but she was too scared to let go, so she climbed another step. He grabbed her with both hands and yanked her into the craft. She landed with a thud, and Prescott whipped the door shut.

"Go!" he yelled.

KABOOM!!!!!!!!

The helicopter wobbled from the concussion, then started to rotate sideways.

"Hold on," Hawk said through the headset. He gunned the craft and the bird rose. Glass from building windows rained down on the streets below.

While strapping herself in, Addison watched as the building grew smaller and smaller, her terrifying brush with death fading into the distance.

Prescott handed her a headset and she slipped it on.

Her heart was thumping hard and fast in her chest, adrenaline charging through her. She struggled to catch her breath and closed her eyes to focus on calming down.

Moments passed. Her heart rate slowed enough for her to take a full breath. Then, the reality of what she'd just done crashed down on her, and she started shaking. She hugged herself while continuing her slow, rhythmic breathing.

"What the fuck just happened?" Prescott murmured.

Despite her emotional trauma, she laughed.

"That was me throwing my woman a life line," Hawk replied. "And she was brave enough to take it."

Prescott clutched Addison's shaking hand. "I got you."

"Addison," Hawk said. "Talk to me, babe."

"I'm here," she replied, "and I'm okay."

More moments passed while the adrenaline rush subsided, and she started calming down.

"Thanks for the lift, boys," she said when she'd stopped trembling.

"Anytime, babe," Hawk said.

She could hear the smile in his voice. He'd believed so completely in her that he'd expected her to do the impossible... and succeed.

She would never have taken that leap if anyone else had been piloting the craft. She was running toward her future with Hawk, something she now knew she couldn't live without.

As they touched down at ALPHA, she couldn't wait to start her new life with him. Couldn't wait to be his wife, to forge their own unbreakable bond. Her destiny had always been him... just like his had been with her.

They just had to jump over a lot of life-altering hurdles to get there.

28

HAPPY BIRTHDAY

On their drive home, Hawk called Z, put the call on speaker.

"I think I had my first heart attack when I found out you jumped off that building," Z answered.

"I'm okay, Daddy," Addison said. "It was all Hawk. He saved me."

"I think you *both* saved you," Z said. "Are you okay?"

"It hasn't sunk in yet," she replied. "But, yes, I'm okay."

"If you need to see a mental health specialist for any PTSD—"

"I have Livy," she replied.

"If you're up for it, I'll be by tomorrow for dinner," Z said.

"I'd love that, Dad."

"Nicholas?" Z asked.

"I'm still here."

"Thank you. Get some rest." The line went dead.

"Rest?" Addison asked. "I'm going to spend the entire night loving my man."

"You gotta take it easy, honey. You've been through a —"

"What I need is you," Addison said. "You, you, and more you, and definitely the rest of the week off."

Hawk smiled. "Not gonna argue with that, babe."

They got home, fell into bed, and loved each other with their entire souls. In that moment, he'd never connected with anyone like he did with her. He'd been terrified he was going to lose her, yet completely confident he could help save her. Ultimately, she had to make the jump... and complete it successfully.

In the aftermath, as they cuddled close, she stared into his eyes. "If I hadn't already agreed to marry you, I would definitely be doing that now. In fact, I think we should get married this year. The sooner the better."

He smiled. "I would love that. What changed your mind?"

"Staring death in the face. I jumped because of you." She ran her soft fingertips over his tanned shoulder and down his muscular chest. "If I didn't try, I was going to die. If I tried and failed, at least I'd have tried. You'd risked your life, and Prescott's life, to bring me home. I had to go for it." She cuddled closer. "I'm going to play this down, especially with my dad, but it was the scariest thing I've ever done. When I grabbed the ladder and you took off, I thought for sure I was going to—"

He stopped her with a loving kiss. "I'm so sorry you had to go through that, but now you know you can do *anything*. My beautiful, badass fiancée."

"No stress for a couple of days. No missions, no terrorists, and definitely no BLACK OPS talks."

"I'll let Cooper know we're taking the week off," he said.

"That's perfect. Right now, I'd like to do something fun." With a gleam in her eyes, she collected his penis in her hand and gently stroked his shaft.

"That feels great," Hawk murmured, "but I should be giving you a massage."

"You didn't give up on me," she whispered.

"Never." With a smile, he kissed her. "I will always have your back, no matter what life throws at us."

"I love you." She kissed him, letting her tongue swirl with his. He groaned into her mouth as a coo escaped hers.

And then, she ended the kiss. "Who wants a blowjob?"

"It's one of my absolute *favorite* things."

"You know," she said, as she vanished beneath the blanket, "I'm not very good at baking."

He chuckled. "And that's important because?"

"I could spend time doing this or learn how to bake." She took him into her mouth, gently licking and sucking.

"No baking, Addison. Ever."

He closed his eyes, relishing the talented way she worked his cock, the pleasure flooding his senses and quieting his mind.

He was gonna play the rescue down, too, because losing her would have killed him.

As the euphoria spread through him, he let go... and he let Addison love him like only she could.

THE FOLLOWING EVENING, Hawk, Addison, and Z were enjoying a bottle of champagne on their balcony as the sun dropped into the horizon. The day had been filled with nothing but Addison.

No work. No discussion of work. No crises. No emergencies.

It had been a perfect day. A run in the morning, then they swung by Jericho and Liv's to see baby Liam. Lunch in Jericho's booth at The Road, back home for some good afternoon loving, then a romantic stroll along the river in Hawk's neighborhood. They deserved that after what they'd been through.

"We have news," Hawk said to Z.

"We got engaged," Addison added.

Z stared at them for a beat, then a grin brightened his face.

"Congratulations. That's wonderful. I'm very happy... for both of you."

"We went ring shopping," Addison said.

"How'd you fit that in?" Z asked.

"Who knows?" Addison's sarcasm made Z chuckle. "My ring will be ready in a few weeks."

Hawk topped their flutes, then excused himself. In his home office, he opened the credenza, and pulled out his gift. Back on the balcony, he set it in front of Addison, then eased back down in the chair.

"Happy birthday, babe," he said.

She smiled. "I completely forgot."

"We've had a lot going on," Hawk said.

"My baby is thirty." Z pulled an envelope from the inside breast pocket of his suit jacket. "From me."

She pulled out the card from her dad and read it out loud.

"Dear Addison, happy birthday. Enjoy two relaxing weeks at my condo. All expenses paid. All my love, Dad.
P.S. This gift is for Nicholas, too."

Hawk laughed. "Thanks for making that clear."

"You have a condo?" Addison asked.

"In Bali."

Her eyes grew large. "Is that where you go when you leave the country?"

"Sometimes."

She kissed his cheek. "Thank you, Daddy. This is so generous of you." She turned toward Hawk. "When do you want to go?"

"We could go as early as Friday, if we got it approved, or we could wait—"

"No waiting. I'm so there." She smiled. "I love this present. Thank you, Dad."

After a beat, she picked up the gift box, unwrapped it, and extracted two small jewelry boxes.

"Two?" she asked.

"I couldn't decide," Hawk replied. "I thought they'd both look great on you."

Inside the first box was a pair of sterling silver drop heart earrings with diamond studs.

"You remembered," she said as she gently pulled one out of the box, slid it into her ear. "These are from Nico's."

"Of course, I remembered," Hawk replied.

Then, she pulled her hair away and modeled it for them. "How do I look?" she asked.

"Beautiful," Hawk replied. "And you look great in those earrings, too."

"Very pretty, dear," said Z.

Next, she opened the second box and gasped. "You did not." She turned the box around to display a pair of diamond earrings that matched her engagement band. "That's a lot of diamonds."

"If it's too much of the same, Nico said we can swap them for whatever you'd like," Hawk said.

She kissed him. "They're stunning." After pulling one out, she slipped it into her other pierced ear and modeled that one.

"Very fancy," Z said.

"I didn't want a traditional engagement ring," Addison explained to him, "so I chose an eternity band. This is what the ring looks like."

"It's beautiful," Z replied.

"Happy birthday, babe," Hawk said.

"Thank you, my love." Addison dropped a light kiss on Hawk's lips.

"Have you set a date?" Z asked.

"Not yet," she replied.

"I'd marry you in Bali," Hawk replied.

"Absolutely not," Z said. "I *must* be at the wedding."

"I'll have it here, just to get you out of that cave of an office you work in," Hawk said, and Addison laughed.

"I'm thinking maybe the farmhouse," Addison said. "Something small. Family and close friends."

"I'm surprised you want to get married there," Hawk replied.

"I loved Kerri and Jamal's wedding. You were the one who thought it was too hot."

Hawk chuffed out a laugh. "It *was* too hot."

"I have some fatherly advice, if you're interested."

"Absolutely," Addison said.

"The saying 'never go to sleep angry' is bullshit," Z said. "Go to sleep angry and have fantastic make-up sex."

Hawk burst out laughing.

"Daddy!"

Her dad chuckled. "Be good to each other and always have each other's backs. Never keep secrets, and choose to be *together* every chance you get. Everything else can wait." He raised his champagne glass. "If I'd picked anyone for you, Addison, it would have been Nicholas. You deserve the absolute best... and he's that man."

Z slid his gaze to Hawk. "I trust that you will do right by my daughter. She is the most precious person in my life... and I hope she becomes that to you."

"She already is, Philip," Hawk said. "And she always will be." He extended his hand and Z shook it. "I will spend the rest of my life showing her how much I adore her. You have my word."

They ate dinner on the balcony, then moved their party inside for cake and coffee.

After he and Z sang happy birthday to her, Addison blew

out the candles, then smiled at them. "My wish did come true. I have the best dad and the best fiancé. Thank you both for making my thirtieth birthday so special."

When the party ended, they walked Z outside and waved goodbye as he backed his ALPHA SUV out of the driveway and drove away. Back in the kitchen, Addison started cleaning up, but Hawk pulled her into his arms.

"Your dad said everything else can wait." He brushed his lips against hers. "Happy birthday to the love of my life."

Pushing on her toes, she kissed him. "Thank you for the party, the earrings, the cake, and for going out of your way to make my birthday very special."

"I'm sorry the cake wasn't homemade, but I don't bake either." He shot her a smile. "But there is something I *will* do that you'll enjoy a lot more."

A moan escaped her throat. "What would that be?"

He broke away to pull a hidden present from the credenza in the dining room.

Inside the wrapped gift box were two police officer costumes. One for him and one for her. "Oooieee, I love these!"

"As the birthday girl, how do you want to play this? Am I the arresting cop or are you?"

"Hmm." She gave him the once-over. "You arrest me."

"For what?"

She palmed his ass. "I'm a high-end escort and you raided the bachelor party I was working."

"Baby, I love your wild imagination." Pulling her close, he wrapped her in his arms. "I love you, Addison."

"I love you, too, Nicholas."

"Every day for the rest of our lives," he murmured before brushing his lips to hers.

"Every single day," she replied with a smile.

EPILOGUE

One month later, end of September

Hawk leaned on the balcony of their Alexandria townhome, staring out at the sparkling river, while Addison finished getting ready.

Their Bali getaway had been picture-perfect. They'd soaked up the sun, explored the beautiful island, and gotten pampered at the resort. Not surprising, he'd fallen more in love with her, and he couldn't wait to make their engagement official.

Addison joined him on the balcony. "Hey, babe."

He turned and was hit by a familiar shot of adrenaline. Her beauty never got old. Truth was, he could skip the work event and hang with her at home. That's how much he loved being around her.

"You look gorgeous." He dropped a doting kiss on her soft lips, made darker by the deep red lipstick.

She'd worn a black cocktail dress that hugged her curves, and pulled her hair into a ponytail. "I wore the dangling heart earrings."

His gaze floated over her face. "You make the earrings look even better."

On a laugh, she stepped back to check him out. "Love you all dressed up. Gonna love it more when I strip those clothes off you."

He'd worn a sport jacket, black shirt, and black pants.

She turned toward the water. "I'm trying to hang on to the calm we found on vacation, but reality is starting to kick back in."

He caressed her back. "Work?"

She nodded.

"Talk to me, baby."

"I'm good."

"Our vacation was incredible, but life with you is even better," he said. "Being with you makes me happy. Are you happy?"

"You'll do." Then, a sweet smile lit up her face. "Very, very happy. I love you, love the life we're building together."

They drove to Carole Jean's and breezed inside. The main dining room was filling up with the first seating of the evening, but he and Addison were headed to a party in the salon. Hand-in-hand, they followed the maître d' through the popular Tysons restaurant.

The employee opened the door to the private dining room. "Enjoy your evening."

With a nod, Hawk waited for Addison to walk in before he entered. Once inside, he swept his gaze around the room until he found his target sitting at a table with Jericho and Liv, her back to everyone. Addison had absolutely no idea what he'd planned for her. He bit back a smile as Stryker made his way over.

"Hey, you two," Stryker said. "Still on your vacation high?"

"Yeah, baby," Hawk replied.

"Reality is sneaking back in," Addison said.

Everyone was sipping cocktails and talking in small groups. An attendant appeared with a tray of flutes.

"Babe, champagne?" Hawk asked.

"Thank you." She took the glass from him as Emerson joined them.

"You still look so relaxed," Emerson said. "I told Stryker I'm booking our honeymoon. We're always so busy, but we're going."

"Did you take my recommendation?" Addison asked.

"Bali, baby!" Stryker said, and they all clinked glasses.

"The resort is amazing," Hawk said. "You won't want to come back."

Servers, dressed in crisp black uniforms, let the group know it was time to be seated for dinner. Stryker and Emerson led the way to their four-top.

After everyone had gotten comfortable in their chairs, Hawk whispered, "You ready to do this, babe?"

"Absolutely." Addison pushed out of her chair as Hawk stood.

"Hey, team," Hawk called out, "can I get your attention?"

Most quieted, but a few on the other side of the salon continued chatting.

"Yo, team," Jericho boomed. "Hawk and Addison have somethin' to say."

A stillness fell over the room.

"Thanks, babe," Hawk said to Jericho.

Pausing, Hawk swept his gaze over the familiar faces of ALPHA employees. This career path wasn't an easy one. Missions were intense and dangerous. Work hours were irregular. There was no honor in being an assassin. It was a job that he, and everyone else in that room, had signed up for, regardless of the risks.

Most missions ended well. They were well trained and highly skilled. On occasion, things went sideways. For the first time in his career, one of his missions had gone horribly wrong. And he had to do something to balance the scales.

"Addison and I want to take a moment and remember teammate Barry Kase," Hawk began. "Losing one of our own is rough, but the toll on the family is much worse. Addison and I have started a scholarship in Barry's honor for families in our organization who experience the devastating loss of a loved one. We're want to ensure Barry's memory lives on."

Hawk paused while the group applauded.

"Any amount is appreciated," Addison said. "Hawk and I donated fifty thousand to make sure the Kase family is taken care of this year."

The group broke into hoots and hollers, but Hawk held up his hand. "Barry should never have died. This is the least we can do for his family."

"Thanks for considering our request," Addison said.

"There is one more thing," Hawk said.

On those words, Cooper, Stryker, and Jericho pulled out their phones.

Hawk had waited a long time for this moment... and a long time to find his forever love.

After pulling a small box from his sport coat, he dropped to one knee. "I adore you, Addison.

"Oh, Nicholas," she whispered.

"You are 'it' for me. I love working with you, love that we're partners. Being with you is my favorite thing. Doesn't matter what we're doing. It's always better when we're together." He opened the ring box, displaying the radiant diamond engagement band that sparkled in the glow of the fireplace. "Marry me."

She beamed at him. "You know, I will, Nicholas Hawk. I love you to the depths of my soul." Leaning down, she kissed him.

He stood and they shared a tender kiss, then he pulled her close and held her flush against him. This was it... and he was ready. Without a doubt, she was his forever. He felt complete... and at peace for the first time in a long, long time.

Holding up her hand, Addison said, "It's official. I'm stuck with him."

The group laughed as he and Addison sat back down.

"Thanks for recording that," Hawk said to Stryker.

"I took a bunch of photos," Emerson offered," and I'm texting them over." After doing that, she said, "Okay, let's see the ring."

Addison displayed her engagement band.

"It's gorgeous," Emerson said. "An eternity band."

"Congratulations," Stryker said. "This was a long time coming."

As the servers delivered the dinner salads, and the chatter resumed, Stryker said, "Em and I will match your donation."

"Thank you," Addison said. "That's so generous."

"Thank you, both," Hawk said. "We appreciate that."

Between courses, Cooper and Danielle swung by. "Thanks for setting up the fund. Danielle and I will also pledge fifty grand."

Hawk pushed out of his chair and pulled Cooper in for a bro-hug. "That means a lot."

"Show me the good stuff," Danielle said to Addison.

"Not here, babe," Cooper replied, and they cracked up laughing.

As Danielle was admiring Addison's ring, Jericho sauntered over.

"Put me and Livy down for fifty, too."

Hawk pulled his close friend in for a hug. "Thank you, brother."

"Try not to shoulder Barry's loss," Jericho said.

"I'm trying," Hawk replied.

Several more Operatives stopped by throughout dinner to

let him and Addison know they were interested in donating money.

After coffee had been served, Addison asked, "Who's that sitting with Livy and Jericho? I thought this was a work event, but I don't recognize the woman with them."

"Addison hasn't talked to her yet?" Emerson asked Hawk.

"She's holding baby Liam," Addison added. "Is that their nanny?"

"Let's go find out," Hawk replied.

Together, they made their way to Liv and Jericho's table.

The stranger smiled up at them. "Good to see you, Nicholas."

"You, too," Hawk replied. "Thanks for being here."

Jericho pushed out of his seat. "Sit. We'll hang with Stryker and Emerson."

"He's so beautiful," the woman said as she handed the infant to Liv.

"Babe, this is Stoni Alexander," Hawk said.

Addison whipped her gaze to the woman. She was slender with long brown hair, streaked with blonde highlights.

"You did not," Addison said to Hawk before gaping at Stoni. "It's a pleasure to meet you, Ms. Alexander. I'm a huge, huge fan."

"Stoni, please," she said with a smile. "Why don't you join me?"

Before sitting, Addison flicked her gaze to Hawk. "What's going on?"

"Surprise, baby. It's your favorite author." Hawk kissed Addison's cheek, then shifted his attention to Stoni. "Addison's got me hooked on your books."

"They're fun to read together," Stoni replied. "Do you have a favorite?"

"Whichever one is my bedtime story." With a wink, he headed into the crowd.

Addison eased into the chair across from Stoni.

"I'm a friend of your dad's," Stoni began. "That's how I know most everyone here."

"I'm a huge fan of your books," Addison said. "I've read all of them once, and some of them twice."

Stoni smiled. "Thank you. I'm so happy to hear you enjoy them."

"They're so realistic. Wait... did you say you know my dad?"

"We used to work together at the Bureau, years before he moved himself to the basement."

Addison shook her head. "Have you seen his office? That place creeps me out."

"It's perfect for him. He never liked being in the middle of everything."

"How are you even here? No one knows about our work."

"Where do you think my story ideas come from?"

"Isn't that a security risk?"

Stoni tucked her hair behind her ear. "I write fiction. No one thinks my stories are true."

"Does my dad know?"

Stoni smiled. "He's the one feeding me the information. We'd lost touch, but several years ago, my husband met him while playing golf. The two struck up a friendship, then we had Z over for dinner. He was so surprised to see me, and I was just as shocked that Z was my friend Philip Skye. We had a big laugh over it. Anyway, I know you and Nicholas have been through a lot these past few months. It's going to make the best story."

"No way."

Stoni nodded. "I've met a lot of Operatives over the years, but you're definitely the bravest." She leaned over. "Leaping off a building? That took so much courage. Writing your love story will be a lot of fun."

Addison felt like she was in a dream. She was talking to Stoni Alexander about ALPHA missions.

Sin and Evangeline moseyed over.

"Congratulations on your engagement," Evangeline said to Addison. "Sin and I have been hoping you and Hawk would figure out you're perfect together."

Addison beamed. "Thank you. Do you know—"

"We know Stoni," Sin replied before regarding Stoni. "Anton's waiting outside, whenever you're ready."

After acknowledging Sin with a nod, Stoni addressed Addison. "I'm so glad we got the chance to meet."

"Me, too," Addison replied.

"My husband, Johnny, and I are taking Sin's jet to Florida in the morning and we've got a million things to do before we leave."

"What's in Florida?"

"Sin's condo," Stoni replied. "Whenever I finish writing a novel, Sin lets us use his vacation home for a week, so I can chill and let my imagination refuel." She slid a check across the table. "For the Kase Foundation."

"You don't—"

"I insist." Stoni rose.

Addison stood and Stoni hugged her goodbye. "I hope you take the BLACK OPS position."

Addison smiled. "I can't wait to read my own love story."

"I can't wait to write it." Flanked by Sin and Evangeline, Stoni made her way through the salon, pausing to say goodbye to Cooper and Danielle, Stryker and Emerson, Jericho, Livy, and a kiss on the forehead for Liam. A hug for Hawk before she left.

Grinning, Addison made her way over to him. "I cannot

believe you did that for me. That was crazy. I just met my favorite author... and she knows my dad."

"Like I promised you on the farmhouse rooftop, I will always put you first," Hawk replied. "When I found out that Z knew her, I set it up. She's pretty cool."

"She's going to write our love story," Addison murmured.

Hawk clasped her hands, stared into her eyes. "And we're gonna live it, baby, one day at a time."

"Every day for the rest of our lives," she replied with a smile.

Early April, the following year

Addison and her friend, Becky Jenning, stepped onto the back porch of the farmhouse as Hawk rode past on a closed-cab tractor. Becky's children sat beside him, big smiles filling their young faces.

"Seeing them this happy is the best gift," Becky said. "Thank you so much for this weekend."

Addison set the tray of glasses and pitcher of lemonade on the table, then sat facing the back of the spacious property. "We love having you all here."

Two months ago, the Jennings had moved back to the area and found a home in their old neighborhood. Hawk and Addison had gotten together with them before, but this was their first weekend visit at the farmhouse. They'd taken the family to a few kid-centric activities, but Becky's children liked riding in the tractor best. Addison had wanted to wait to see how Becky was doing before she broached the subject of Ronald's death.

"I'm glad you've moved back," Addison said. "You're family to me."

"I consider you family as well." Becky joined her on the sofa. "I wanted to stay in the house Ronald and I bought, but our families live here. It's important the kids spend time with both sets of grandparents, so it just made sense to move back."

Pausing, the women sipped the cold, sweet drink.

"I promised you answers to help you with closure," Addison said. "I have them."

Becky set down the glass, her gaze sliding from the tractor to Addison.

"I can't get into details," Addison began, "and you can never share this with anyone, not even your children."

"I miss Ronald every day. The kids miss their dad. It's a void that's just there. Anything you share with me is more than anyone else has told me."

"The daughter of Abdel Haqazzii, the terrorist Ronald took out, spent the last three years hunting all of us down," Addison began.

"Ohmygod. Was she arrested?"

"No, she's dead."

"What more can you tell me?" Becky asked. "Did she murder anyone else?

"She killed one of my former assets, then she tried to kill my dad and me as well."

Becky gasped. "That must've been scary for you."

"It was, but it comes with my job."

"Thank you for confiding in me."

Hawk drove the tractor past the house and he and the kids waved at them. Becky's smile sent relief coursing through her.

"The asset—her name was Melinda—had started a new life, here, in the states. Just like you and Ronald helped me when I came back, I helped Melinda." After a pause, Addison murmured, "I blame myself for her death."

"Why?"

Addison shook her head. "I can't get into those details. Hawk and I wanted to find a way to honor both Ronald and Melinda, so we're building a facility on the property that will serve as a home for SEAL team families who lose someone in the line of duty, and have nowhere to live as a result... and for refugees, like Melinda, who served our country in exchange for freedom from theirs. We're breaking ground next week on a hundred-bed facility that will be right over there." Addison pointed due west. "Hawk's grandparents have so much land, there will be plenty of options for the rest of the property. We just want to start with one building."

"That'll be life changing for so many people."

"We hope so." Addison sipped the lemonade. "My career doesn't afford me time to run it, so Hawk and I want to offer that job to you."

Becky's eyes widened. "Seriously?"

"You'd be the managing director, but your children come first. We don't want you to have to hire day care for after school, so there are some details to work out, but the job is yours if you'd like it." Addison clasped Becky's hand, gave it a little squeeze. "Give it some thought, you don't—"

"I'd love to." Becky threw her arms around Addison. "Moving back here has kept me busy, then making sure the kids were settled in school took up my time. I've started looking for a job, but haven't found the right fit. Working with you will be perfect."

The tractor stilled and the sweet sound of children's laughter caught their ears.

A moment later, Hawk and the kids came traipsing up the stairs. They walked onto the porch and eyed the pitcher of lemonade.

Addison poured three glasses. As the kids chugged theirs, Hawk kissed Addison's forehead. "Did you have a good talk?" he asked.

"Becky's on board," Addison replied.

Hawk extended his hand. "Congratulations."

"What are you talking about?" Becky's daughter, Dana, asked.

"I just got offered a job," Becky exclaimed.

"Yay," said Dana, while Becky's son held up his little hand. With a smile, Becky high-fived him.

"How was the tractor ride?" Addison asked the kids.

"Sooooo much fun," Aaron answered.

"Fun and bumpy," Dana added.

Addison and Becky laughed.

After they finished up their lemonade, Becky said they had to head out.

"Are you sure you can't stay for dinner?" Addison asked. "I'd love you to meet the family."

Becky smiled. "We've been here for three days. Aren't you ready to get rid of us?"

"Of course not," Addison replied.

"My folks are having us over tonight," Becky said.

"I don't want to leave," said Aaron.

"It's Grandpa's birthday, so we're having a party for him, and that means cake and ice cream."

Aaron's face split into an adorable smile. "I love cake."

Hawk loved having the kids for the weekend. They were sweet children who were managing through life without their dad. If he could help bring a smile to their faces, he was all in.

They headed through the house, stopped to collect their bags from the foyer. He and Addison walked them outside. He loaded their car while they said their goodbyes.

"Kids, what do we say?" Becky prodded.

"Thank you for having us," said Dana. "I had the best time."

"What was your favorite thing to do?" Addison asked.

"The campfire, the sleepover in the family room, and the airplane museum," the little girl replied.

"How 'bout you, sport?" Hawk asked Aaron

"Tractor rides and petting farm." He giggled. "The goat was funny." He flung his arms around Hawk's legs. "Thank youuuuuuuu!"

Hawk picked him up and gave him a hug. "We'll have you back again, okay?"

The kids scrambled into their car seats and Becky buckled them in, then hugged Addison and Hawk before getting behind the wheel.

"Thanks for making us feel like family *and* for the job offer," Becky said.

"You *are* family," Addison said before Becky drove away.

Hawk draped his arms around Addison, pausing to stare into her eyes. "Hello, baby." He kissed her. "I haven't seen much of you this weekend."

She peered up at him. "I'm happy we had them over. I talked to Becky about Ronald."

"Did it help?"

"Hard to say." Addison slipped her arm around him. "She liked hearing about the center and she's excited to be our managing director."

He draped his arm over her shoulder, and they moseyed up the repaved driveway toward their new cobblestone walkway.

The past six months had been nonstop renovations at the farmhouse. While he and Addison had considered demolishing the building, they'd opted to keep the structure and expand the back of the house, which included the family room, kitchen, and screened porch. Wallpaper had been replaced with fresh coats of paint, furnishings had been swapped out for an updated interior, and the outdated kitchen and bathrooms had been gutted for a stylish, sophisticated look.

Addison called it country chic.

Now, the home felt like theirs, and they spent most weekends there.

"We've got two hours before the fam shows up," Addison said.

"And then, more mayhem," Hawk added.

One more kiss before they made their way up the rebuilt stairs to the front door. Just as Addison turned the door handle, the roar of a motorcycle caught their ears.

Prescott parked in the driveway, removed his helmet, and strode toward them.

"*Perfect* timing." Hawk's biting tone made Addison laugh.

Prescott glanced from him to Addison, back to him. "Are you being serious or sarcastic?"

"We're always happy to see you," Addison said. "It's just that the party doesn't start for a couple of hours."

Prescott raked a hand through his hair. "What party?"

"We sent a group text," Addison pulled her phone from the back pocket of her jeans, then flipped it around so Prescott could see. "You're included."

Prescott exhaled a frustrated grunt. "I missed it."

"The family's coming over," Hawk said.

"My dad too," Addison added.

Prescott took a step back. "I'll come back."

Hawk studied his brother. Worry lines between his eyebrows were etched deep. Normally, he was chill, but his jawline muscles were ticking in his cheek.

"Whoa, baby," Hawk said.

"Don't leave," Addison added.

"I've been dealing with something," Prescott replied.

"Come on in," Addison said. "You want a lemonade?"

"I'm gonna need something stronger than that," Prescott replied as the three made their way into the house.

In the kitchen, Hawk broke out the liquor. After Prescott tossed back a shot of Widow Jane bourbon, he asked for a second.

With their drinks in hand, they got comfortable on the back

porch. He and Addison side by side on the sofa while Prescott leaned against the chair rail.

"What's going on?" Hawk asked.

"I have a sister," his brother replied.

"Right, Kerri," Hawk said.

"I have a sister on my *dad's* side." Prescott paused to sip the bourbon. "Before my dad met and married Mom, he had a relationship with someone else. She got pregnant, never told him, and had the child. That child is now my thirty-five-year-old sister."

"Jesus," Hawk murmured.

"Have you met her?" Addison asked.

"Yeah," Prescott replied. "She contacted me a few months ago and we video chatted. I didn't believe her, but DNA doesn't lie. She never knew our dad, and I don't remember him."

"Do Mom and Dad know?" Hawk asked.

"No, you guys are hearing about it first." Prescott sat on the edge of the lounge chair and scraped his hand through his hair. "She and her late husband have a son. He's two."

"What happened to her husband?" Addison asked.

"I didn't ask."

"Does she want money?" Hawk asked.

"She hasn't mentioned it. She told me she has no family, outside of her child... and now me. Her mom got cancer and died a few years ago. I invited her and her son to visit."

Addison smiled. "We'd love to meet her."

"She's flying in this afternoon," Prescott replied.

"Do you think meeting everyone at the same time would be too much?" Addison asked.

Prescott shrugged. "How the hell would I know? I just met the woman."

"How long is she staying?" Hawk asked.

"A few days." Prescott tossed back the whiskey. "I don't

know what to make of it. I ran a background check. Nothing sketchy. She's a successful financial advisor."

"Maybe she's telling the truth," Addison said. "She's just trying to connect with her only living relative, besides her son."

"You want us to be there when you meet her?" Hawk asked.

"You've got the party," Prescott replied as he pushed out of the chair. "I feel better telling you guys."

"We'll meet her over the next couple of days," Addison said. "She and her little boy should come here for dinner."

"Thanks," Prescott said before heading toward the kitchen.

Hawk pushed off the sofa. "I'll walk him out."

Prescott set his glass in the sink, glanced around the room. "Place looks great, Nicky."

Hawk walked him out front. "Is your sister staying with you?"

"No, at an Airbnb," Prescott replied. "She said she was going through some boxes from her mom. Thought I'd want to see what she found."

"How 'bout we meet them tomorrow after work?" Hawk suggested.

"Lemme see how things go. Thanks for listening." Prescott mounted his bike, pulled on his helmet. "Tell Mom and Dad I'm sorry I couldn't make it. Have fun." He started the bike, rolled down the driveway and onto the street.

Hawk returned to the porch to find Addison on her feet, staring out at the property.

"I've made a decision regarding BLACK OPS," she said, her attention fixed on the backyard.

"Tell me what I want to hear."

She peered into his eyes. "I'm doing it."

He picked her up, twirled her around. Her sweet laughter made his heart soar. While the missions would be super dangerous, he was confident she could handle them.

"You'll be kick-ass, babe."

"I've been thinking about it for a while now, but it was something Stoni Alexander said that helped me decide. She told me I was the bravest ALPHA she'd ever met."

"I agree," he replied.

"Thank you, my love. I'm calling Dakota." She made the call, put it on speaker.

"Hey, Addison," Dakota answered. "What's going on?"

"I accept your work offer. I'm all in."

"That's great. We'll talk more next week. Thanks for the call."

After she hung up, Hawk wrapped her in his arms and kissed her. "Congratulations. How does it feel?"

"Awesome." After a beat, she said, "But I don't think Prescott is."

"Neither do I. I'll call him later." He dropped a kiss on her forehead. "How long do we have before the fam starts showing up?"

Leaning up, she kissed him. "A little while." She turned toward the spacious property. "I love it here."

"Is this your happy place?"

She shot him a smile. "No, you are."

"I feel the same way about you."

As they peered into each other's eyes, they shared a loving smile.

"We're getting married in less than a month," Addison murmured. "Married, Nicholas. Together forever."

"I can't wait."

"Do you miss me?" she asked.

"Like crazy, but abstaining has been the right thing to do."

She rolled her eyes, playfully. "I guess."

Again, he kissed her. "I want our honeymoon to be something we'll never forget."

"Then, we should probably postpone the trip and spend those ten days in bed."

Hawk chuckled. "The wait will be worth it. Trust me. I waited three long years for you."

"And now you have me."

"Forever, my sweet baby."

"Forever," she replied with a smile.

Another Happily Ever After by Stoni Alexander

A Note from Stoni

Thanks so much for reading WRECKED! I hope my novel was a fun, exciting escape for you! Writing is my passion, so I'm grateful you've chosen to read my book. Hearing from readers always brighten my day, so drop me a note and say hello!

While I love all my heroes and heroines, I have my favorites. I gotta say, Nicholas Hawk has given me a serious book-boyfriend hangover. He's fearless, crazy loyal, super chill, very confident, a total alpha, and super easy on the eyes.

I invite you to join my Inner Circle to find out when my next book is releasing or if I'm having a Kindle e-book sale. Once you sign up, you'll receive METRO MAN, a short story about a man, a woman, and a steamy subway ride. Go to Stoni-Alexander.com.

All my books are available exclusively on Amazon, and you can read them free with a Kindle Unlimited subscription.

Thank you for spending time in Hawk and Addison's world. Walking away from these two is hard, but it's time to shift my focus to Hawk's ruggedly handsome brother, Prescott Armstrong.

Be well. Be happy.
Cheers to Romance,

Stoni Alexander

Coming Fall 2023

THE VIGILANTES, Book Five - Romantic Suspense

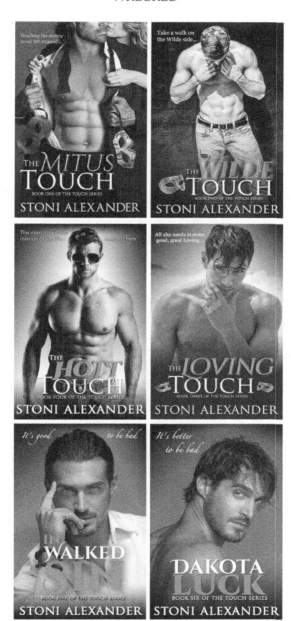

THE TOUCH SERIES - Romantic Suspense

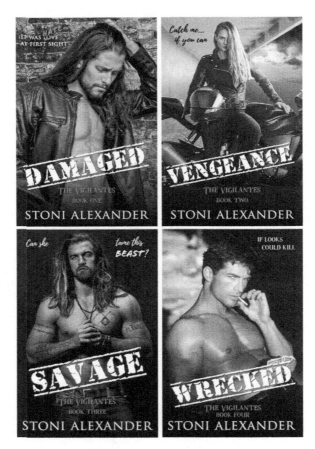

THE VIGILANTES - Romantic Suspense

LOOKING FOR A SEXY STANDALONE?

 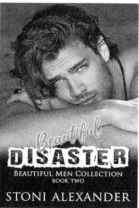

BEAUTIFUL MEN COLLECTION - Contemporary Romance

Buy them on Amazon or Read FREE with Kindle Unlimited!

ABOUT THE AUTHOR

Stoni Alexander writes sexy romantic suspense and contemporary romance about tortured alpha males and independent, strong-willed females. Her passion is creating love stories where the hero and heroine help each other through a crisis so that, in the end, they're equal partners in more ways than love alone. The heat level is high, the romance is forever, and the suspense keeps readers guessing until the very end.

Visit Stoni's website:
StoniAlexander.com

Sign up for Stoni's newsletter on her website and she'll gift you a free steamy short story, only available to her Inner Circle.

Here's where you can follow Stoni online. She looks forward to connecting with you!

- amazon.com/author/stonialexander
- bookbub.com/authors/stoni-alexander
- facebook.com/StoniBooks
- goodreads.com/stonialexander
- instagram.com/stonialexander

Made in the USA
Monee, IL
05 March 2023

29232534R00267